Ale pushed the door shut and looked over the world.

Wings flapped like giant sails.

Fire tore a line of pain across the top of his right shoulder. The slug whistled past. Ale drew breath for a scream. Behind him, claws scraped stone. An alien voice rasped into a screech, and then a chitter.

Terror paralyzed him. Desperate, he fought it. If he did not move, he would die.

KEVIN O'DONNELL, JR.

BERKLEY BOOKS, NEW YORK

ORA:CLE

A Berkley Book / published by arrangement with
the author

PRINTING HISTORY
Berkley edition / August 1984

ISBN: 0-425-07260-6

Acknowledgments

During the too many years **ORA:CLE** took to write, too many people read parts of it for me even to remember, much less mention, each of them individually. Let me thank them collectively and generically: if sections of this seem so familiar that you could swear you critiqued them, you probably did, and I'm grateful.

I do remember those who read all of it, in all its various manifestations, from its beginning in early 1980 to its end in late 1983. Mary Kittredge, Mark J. McGarry, Joel Rosenberg—how can I thank you enough?

For the folks at the 21st Milford (at Telluride) Writers' Conference, who insisted this idea needed more room than the 26 pages I'd allotted it...you were right.

My very special thanks to Howard Morhaim, for his masterful agenting, to Susan Allison, for her superb editing, and to Kim, for herself.

To Tze Yee Yuan Tchang:

Mother-in-law par excellence.

For her faith, her humor, and her cooking,

I dedicate this book with love.

TOP TEN NEWS STORIES OF THE HOUR

Monday, 15 June 2188; 1100 EDT
New England Region

RANK HEADLINE	price	LEAD SENTENCE
#1 MUSLIM-REPUBLICANS TO THE RESCUE AGAIN	.20	Fresh from last week's triumphant evacuation of greater Peking, the Muslim-Republican Directorate of Public Safety and the Social-Tech Directorate of Public Transportation have again joined forces, this time to move some seventeen million Floridians out of the reach of Hurricane Dora, predicted to be the most devastating in history.
#2 * * * * * * 10,000 HOMELESS IN NYC FIRE	.20	#2 * * * * * * A fire of undetermined origin swept down a Manhattan street early this morning, killing six, injuring two hundred seven, and releasing seventeen tons of CO_2 into the atmosphere.
#3 * * * * * * "CANNIBAL KILLER" FINALLY CAUGHT IN RIO HIGH-RISE	.15	#3 * * * * * * The hatchet-wielding terror of Rio de Janeiro's largest public housing complex was apprehended yesterday, after eluding inept Marx/Com cops for six weeks, a spokesrep for the MC Directorate of Public Security announced this morning.

RANK HEADLINE	price	LEAD SENTENCE

#4 * * * * * * *

COURTESY TITLES TO GO? HEARINGS SET ON THREE-CHARACTER SUBSTITUTES .10

#4 * * * * * * *

In yet another attempt to enforce total computer compatibility, the Coalition's Directorate of Public Statistics today proposed adding three occupation-keyed characters to the fifteen character ID/dress; if adopted as the fourth ID/dress expansion in the last century, the new code would lead off the ID/dress, replacing all traditional courtesy titles.

#5 * * * * * * *

DACS DOWN JETLINER: 485 FEARED DEAD .20

#5 * * * * * * *

ST/DeepTrans Flight 1963, carrying four hundred eighty-five passengers and crewmembers, crashed to Earth outside Osaka at 0943 (EDST) this morning; witnesses claim to have seen a Dac mothership launch missiles at it instants before the crash.

#6 * * * * * * *

BEEF PRICE HIKES DUE TO MV/DEEPAG ACTIONS COWPOKE SAYS .10

#6 * * * * * * *

The President of the Argentine Cattleraisers' Association charged that recent rises in the price of beef are tied directly to production ceilings imposed by the Marian-Vegetarian Directorate of Public Agriculture that controls most of the best grazing land in Argentina.

#7 * * * * * * *

MARKET DROPS IN EUROPE .10

#7 * * * * * * *

The stock market is down over forty points on European exchanges this morning, as investors rush to unload shares in PFG, the large building contractor rocked by allegations of bribery.

#8 * * * * * *	**#8** * * * * * *
TWELVE MORE DIE IN LONDON POISONING .10	Spokesreps for the Green-Rad Directorate of Public Health have confirmed that twelve more residents of a London high-rise have succumbed to trimethylcolchicinic acid released into the high-rise's water supply by GR DPUtilities, bringing the total known dead since Wednesday to three hundred forty-eight.
#9 * * * * * *	**#9** * * * * * *
SHORT-SIGHTED MARX/COM CUTS STRANGLING BASIC RESEARCH .10	The chair of the University of Moscow's Plasma Physics Department complained today that funding cuts contemplated by the Marx/Com Directorate of Public Education will force the closure of her department.
#10 * * * * * *	**#10** * * * * * *
SIXTH DAC SHIP ENTERS SYSTEM; HEADED FOR L5 SLOT .10	An MIT/ToDai robot observatory in high-altitude Pluto orbit reported today that a Dac starship on a trajectory for L5 has penetrated the solar system; it will be the sixth Dac starship to park there since the Unilateral Cease Fire, and the second in the last year.

This update has been provided as a public service by all data management corporations participating in NEWSBANK/MR, a news data base organized and supervised by the Muslim/Republican Directorate of Public Information.

To read any of the above news stories in full, simply highlight the title and press ACCEPT. The article will be transmatted to your unit's memory. Your bank balance will be debited by the sum in the column headed "price."

To see the headlines of the day's other news stories, simply scroll your screen up.

Thank you, and do be careful.

Watering-can heavy in his hand, Ale Elatey Aefay Aitches'see
Enefefsix stopped to check the DacWatch alarm light. In theory, he could skip the precaution and survive. If the tell-tale
burned red, unlatching the terrace door should trigger a ninety-
decibel buzzer. And the light on the warning system reddened
whenever the apartment computer which controlled it told it
anything but "no extra-terrestrials within fifteen kilometers."
The DacWatch—with a price tag larger than Ale's monthly
paycheck—even had an Uninterruptable Power Source that
turned on a scarlet strobe when the ap-comp crashed. According
to its money-back guarantee, it offered near-perfect protection.
In theory.

In practice—Barely aware of what he was doing, Ale Elatey
stroked the metal disc under the skin behind his right temple.
—trusting anything electronic is a gamble. That was experience
speaking, not superstition: Twice his implant had glitched; twice
bright static had sparkled so white, so loud in his brain that he
had gone into seizure, biting his tongue, soiling himself. He
dreaded the future shocks which would come, less terminally
than death, less regularly than taxes, but no less certainly than
either. Yet to be a Seeley—to have the respect he had hungered
for since childhood—he had to take that one risk, at least.

So he took as few others as he could.

The tell-tale was green, but he always double-checked. Better his cherished bonsai go a few minutes drier than never be
watered again. He pressed the re-set button. The light winked
cherry; the device hummed. A query flashed to three million
computers scattered over south-central Connecticut.

Ale Elatey saw the world as one huge circuit, integrated
with such sophistication and intricacy that the human nervous
system looked simple in comparison. The last person who
claimed to understand it had died a century earlier; those re-

sponsible for maintaining it lagged years behind those enlarging, enhancing, and expanding it. A million points of interrelationship offered a million and one opportunities for error.

When the world-circuit worked, of course, it made magic seem clumsy—but as hovee news had reported that morning, Thursday's power surge in Boston had glitched a Chicago mainframe that packaged aerosol anti-perspirants. Held in a warm hand for ninety seconds and then squeezed, the affected cans exploded.

Money-back guarantees, Ale figured, mean very little to the dead.

And Ale wanted to live. In a world of Three Horsemen—excess carbon dioxide, unstable technology, and hostile aliens—survival demanded care.

Water dripped onto his left shoe, soaking through the canvas and reminding him that care extended to more mundane things, too—like re-caulking a leaky watering-can. He shook his head, exasperated by his own forgetfulness. He had meant to touch up the seam last week.

Still waiting, he ran a critical gaze along the forty potted spider plants mounted on the living room's left wall. Dozens of brown leaves twisted in the tangle of green and white. It would take an hour or so to trim them clean. Probably time to fertilize, too. Maybe even to change the grow-lights. He made a mental note of that.

The hovee beeped. He and his wife let it run all day, mostly as background light and music, but had cued the ap-comp to switch it to broadcasts on any of a dozen pre-selected topics. At the moment, it swirled purple spirals; an announcer read: "—oxide levels; sunny and continued warm—"

Its survey of area monitors done, the DacWatch clicked, and flashed Ale an emerald invitation: No aliens flew within fifteen kilometers of Haven Manor.

The doorbell rang.

Not again. He looked through the glass wall to his right, into his wife's office, hoping that she was free. Emdy dealt with neighbors better than he did. Besides, he wanted to water his bonsai while it was safe. But she sat behind her desk, elbows planted, bending forward. Silken blonde hair obscuring her profile, she concentrated on the hook-nosed face in her pholo sphere. He could not disturb her.

With a sigh, he set down the can, and wiped his hands on

his blue shorts. *This is the sixth time today someone's come round. Neighborliness is nice, but are we the only ones with work to do? Wish we could put up a "do-not-disturb" sign without insulting the whole complex....*

A five-meter-long planter divided the parquet-floored vestibule from the dining area. As he approached, its six diffenbachia reproved him with bowed stalks and wilting leaves. "Video."

The screen above the doorframe flickered, then said, "Broken."

"Damn. Oh, well... open up."

Locks clicked. The slab of metal swayed ajar.

An old black man with a silver goatee stepped inside. "Good morning, Ale, have you a minute?" He was panting slightly in the CO_2-heavy air.

"To tell the truth, Mr. B'jay Awu—"

B'jay Awu thrust a clipboard at him. "I shan't leave till I've got your signature."

He took it warily. Once before he had signed something B'jay Awu had handed him; for months thereafter, advertising pitches from a dozen oddball outfits had clogged his ap-comp's memory. He suspected the old man of selling his co-signers' names. "What is this, exactly?"

"A petition. More precisely, a petition to the Consumers and Citizens United Party Directorate of Public Safety, demanding either that it force the owner of this ramshackle building to upgrade the wiring, or that it prohibit hundred-kilogram mass-transceivers on the premises. Implicit in the petition is the threat that Haven Manor will elect another party to ensure our safety if the CCU continues to ignore our justifiable complaints."

"Well—" He tried to pick his words with care, so as not to hurt the other's feelings. B'jay Awu thought highly of his own schemes, even if few agreed with him. "Ah, the CCU/DeepSafe's reputation for responsiveness isn't very—"

"It is necessary, as you know full well. The wiring is simply too weak to support a hundred-key massie. Are you aware that Mr. Efwy Soo went thirty-two hours without electricity last week? Yesterday, a momentary glitch in elevator one fractured Mr. Eugee Teton's leg in three places. The cinema in the shopping mall downstairs is air-conditioned to seven degrees Celsius. The—"

"I understand." One either cut B'jay off abruptly, or listened to him recite incident after incident until he sputtered into silence, like an emergency generator running out of methane. And that could take hours. "Our electrical system *is* lousy." *Talk about understatement,* he thought. Haven Manor's circuits switched on and off individually, arhythmically, like the blinking lights on a Christmas tree. "If it's the massies' fault..." He shook his head. "I'll sign." He did. "And best of luck to you." Patting B'jay on the shoulder, he ushered him out.

The light on the terrace door still glowed green. He nodded, but squinted into the June sun anyway. Not even a cloud in the sky. Blinking away bright after-images, he grabbed the can and slid the door open. The wind off the harbor, crisp but humid, almost metallic from the noon-hot New Haven day, whuffed into his face and tousled his hair. To walk into it from the air-conditioned living room felt like falling into the Amazon.

Clearly a two-trip morning, thanks to that wind. One can of water would drench only eight of his eleven bonsai, and the others could not wait till Tuesday. Dwarfed plants in small pots dried out quickly, especially in hot breezes on a thirty-eighth floor balcony. High CO_2 levels parched them that much faster.

He stepped onto the flagstones, hoping that the birds had let the yew keep its three red berries. Odd that Mrs. M'ti Emtenne, his next door neighbor, was still inside. She rarely missed a chance to sunbathe. He pushed the door shut and looked over the crown of the cherry—

Wings flapped like giant sails.

Fire tore a line of pain across the top of his right shoulder. The slug whistled past—buried itself in the earthenware pot of a sixty-two-year-old azalea—and exploded.

Ale drew breath for a scream. The air was so thick, it was like inhaling soup.

Behind him, claws scraped stone. An alien voice rasped into a screech, and then a chitter.

Terror paralyzed him. Desperate, he fought it. If he did not move, he would die.

—2—

For an eerie moment he saw himself from outside his body, as though he watched from the next balcony. Short, brown-haired, he stood frozen in horror, left hand raised high enough to show the potting soil under his fingernails. The tight red T-shirt clung to his narrow shoulders and slipped up over the pudgy inch around his waist that Emdy Ofivo liked to tweak. Across the front of the shirt, white letters spelled out HAR-VARD UNIVERSITY. The Dac's next bullet would emerge between the "E" and the "R"—unless it burst in his chest, first.

He moved. Whirling to his right, he swung the watering-can like a tennis racket, wristing it up and into an overhead backhand shot. He had plenty of time because time had slowed. A sub broke water in New Haven harbor. The wrought-iron railing cast a short, slanted shadow. The Dac mothership drifted three klicks overhead. His lungs were already laboring.

To his right, great bat-wings fluttered as the Dac tried to balance itself. The five-centimeter claws of its knobbly eagle's feet skidded slightly on the flagstones. Its carrot-colored beak snapped in frustration, flashing razor-sharp teeth and a pred-ator's hook to the upper jaw. Its huge head bounced on its child-sized torso. Its hand—with a thumb, three fingers, and retractable claws—wavered as it tried to aim the gun that gleamed like silver.

Ale had spun nearly a hundred and eighty degrees. Thinking, *But the damn alarm was guaranteed!* he hurled the watering-can.

Red, of dented cheap tin, silicon-caulked at the lower seams of the long curved spout, it turned end over end. Water sloshed and splashed. The can wobbled in flight.

The Dac had finally found its balance, and was lining up its second shot.

Ale ran straight at it, a step or two behind the can, sucking air in monstrous gulps.

Two kilos of water and tin smacked the Dac in the middle of its thin, scaled chest. It dropped the gun and sat down hard. Its speckled orange beak snapped twice. It gave a strangled hiss.

Three more strides would put Ale on top of it.

It scrambled for the handgun.

Ale planted his left foot, snapped his right foot forward—

Bronze eyes blinking, it raised pencil-thin arms—

His sneakered foot slammed sideways into its pipestem throat.

Its neck snapped. It pissed as it died. The green puddle spread out from its corpse. It stank—and it smoked in the sunlight.

Gasping, Ale stood over the dead alien. *I killed it*. His heart pounded in his ears. *It didn't get me*. Adrenalin overdrive shut off. *I don't believe it*. The world spun; time resumed its normal gait. *Unreal*. The aftermath left him shaky, dizzy, almost ready to vomit over the edge of the terrace onto the unsuspecting trees thirty-eight stories below. Not that the trees would mind. They could stand anything but wood-hunting streeters and compacted soil.

His legs began to give way. Sinking to his haunches, he sagged back against the wrought-iron railing. Hugging himself, shivering, he searched the sky for other Dacs. *Damn that alarm! Why didn't it work?*

Only once before had he killed anything larger than a roach, and that, some twenty years ago, a rat. Probably poisoned, it had swayed out from behind the refrigerator and staggered toward him. He had killed that with a kick, too, a sudden reflexive out-lashing that booted the thing across the room and into the wall, which it slapped with an audible crunch. He had screamed, and sobbed, and shaken until his father came and, with a look of disgust, flipped the furry, still body into the trash shaft. Ten minutes later, Ale's shoes plummeted down that same shaft.

As the ones he was wearing probably would.

I don't believe it. I'm alive.

The wind off the harbor smelled very, very good.

Watering-can's shot to hell, though. He trembled.

I'd better call the cops. An empty gesture, that: The Marian-Vegetarian Directorate of Public Security, which covered Haven Manor, would only note that there was, indeed, a dead Dac on his terrace—but one had to observe the formalities and the protocols. And fill out the forms. Envisioning, suddenly, the number of forms he would have to fill out, he groaned. *If I were really and truly as smart as I am supposed to be, I would just nudge that thing over the edge and keep my mouth shut*. . . . But even as he thought it, he knew he could not. One reported incidents like that. Those were the rules.

He rose, and took a step toward the sliding glass door. A shard from the shattered pot crunched underfoot; his knees almost buckled again. Stopping, still panting, he went back to the corpse. He had forgotten something.

Its gun.

He wanted it. He was not sure why. A trophy, perhaps. Or an artifact that might provide insights into a culture that would cross space, steal the sky, and kill every unsheltered human in sight—yet would not communicate. Or perhaps the gun would defend him if the dead Dac's friends came to avenge it. Assuming Dacs had friends.

Vengeance they practiced. Thirty-two hundred residents of a condominium in Guilford had died in proof of that.

Squatting, he touched his left hand to a clean flagstone for balance, and picked up the gun. Cold, metallic, it weighed half a kilo. His fingers could not wrap comfortably around the butt. But he could squeeze the trigger. Oh, yes, he could do that—if they came for him.

Still shaking, he stood. He scanned the skies. Nothing moved in them except the kilometer-long mothership three klicks over the city. He slipped the gun into his pants pocket, crossed the terrace, and scooped up branches from the dead azalea before he went inside. He would root the casualties when he got the chance.

As he locked the door, another wave of dizziness shivered through him. He leaned against the glass, pressing his forehead to it. The sun warmed him. The trembles slowed. For the first time since the instant of attack, he felt he could speak without his voice cracking. But his foot needed scrubbing.

Taking a deep breath, he turned. Then made a face. Emdy was still on the pholo and, from the numerals that danced across her computer screen, it had to be a business call. Long-distance, no less: Ale could recognize Arabic, even if he could not speak it.

He wanted desperately to talk to her—to cling to her, face buried in her cornsilk hair while he told the horror of the moment when the world lurches sideways and death snatches at you through the crack—but she was negotiating a contract, and an interruption could cost millions.

With a sigh, he went to the kitchen. After storing the alien gun in a cupboard, he slipped the branches into a blue ceramic vase, and filled it with water. It seemed an insane thing to be doing, but it did occupy his hands and his mind. And gradually it calmed him. Plants always did. Their needs were so simple, yet so strict, that attempting to provide for them gave a different perspective on his own troubles.

Besides, azaleas wilt quickly; once wilted, they will not root. And he refused to let his favorite plant, one nearly twice his age, die without issue. That would be wrong.

There. He carried the vase into the living room, and positioned it on a shelf by the middle window.

Time to call the police.

And then the DacWatch Service Department.

Sinking into the nearest sofa, he silenced the burbling blue hovee with: "Hovee-off." Funny. His shoulder barely hurt. It smelled like burnt pork chops, but only stung a little. Shock? Or maybe the super-heated bullet had cauterized the nerves into numbness. Or maybe . . . but guessing was futile. If he really wanted to know, he could find out. From a world-renowned expert, at that.

He shut his eyes and rubbed them. Phosphenes flashed inside, drawing his vision along a tunnel of blackness spattered with orange. The inward focusing eased him toward interface.

He always visualized a mountain, honey-combed with tunnels and caverns full of sweet, heady air. He had his own entrance through the phosphenes: one narrow passage that, after a while, debouched into a lightless chamber a kilometer wide and high. To avoid tumbling into the blackness, he had to know just when to stop, but the air in the mountain so sharpened his senses that he could feel the edge from twenty meters off. So there he sat, legs dangling, while twenty thousand other spelunkers hummed and buzzed in the distance. He knew some of them quite well, but greeted none. That could wait. He sat, breathing exhilaration, until a massive voice as coldly mechanical as an android troll's boomed in his ear.

#You are early, Mr. Ale Elatey. The voice of the switchboard program called The Oracle seemed to originate a few centimeters above and before his right ear: about where the surgeons had implanted the microchip three years earlier, when ORA:CLE, Inc. had hired him as a Computer-Linked Expert.

Emergency. Please patch me through to the local MV/DeepSec.

#We thought something was wrong.# Tiny clicks and snickers sounded behind its voice as it opened a line.

The air shimmered blue; a bored voice said, MARIAN-VEGETARIAN DIRECTORATE OF PUBLIC SECURITY, CONNECTICUT BRANCH, EMERGENCY PROGRAM.

Ale thanked The Oracle, then turned to the dispatcher. Quickly, he gave his Identity/Address and the facts of the case. *And I'd really appreciate it if somebody could come over and pick up this corpse.* He withdrew.

The Oracle said, #Congratulations, Mr. Ale Elatey. We have ordered medical assistance for you.#

What made you think something was wrong?

#Our Medical Monitors reported abnormal pulse and respiration rates.# It paused while its Conversational Program located the most appropriate subroutine. Ale wished it would not do that. The brief interruptions always sounded like hesitations, as though it were thinking of how best to say what it wanted next to say. Although, come to think of it, that was — in a non-anthropomorphic way—exactly what it was doing. . . . #Had they not dropped as quickly as they did, we would have had to summon an ambulance for you.#

They almost dropped quicker and farther.

#We heard. We are pleased you survived. Scholars of East Asia, 1500–2000 AD, are an endangered species; we would not gladly lose one of our best.#

Only one *of the best?* He regretted the banter instantly, but it was too late.

#For the rating period January 1 to—#

Cancel. I'll be back later.

#Very good, sir.#

Yawning, he pulled away from interface by opening his eyes. In her office, directly opposite him, Emdy Ofivo slapped her desktop. She looked tired, frayed by stress. "Damn!" She came out to see him. "The circuit just died, right in the middle—he's never going to believe I didn't do it." She ran her fingers through her shoulder-length blonde hair. "Moroccans! They spend half the time making sexist slurs about female incompetence—and if you want their phosphate, you have to pretend it doesn't bother you—but just one little comment out of you, and they get all hot under the hood. I swear, if I lose this contract, I'm going to sue the pholo company." She narrowed her eyes. "You're really pale. What's wrong?"

He opened his mouth. Five minutes earlier, that would have been enough to unpen a frightened herd of words, butting and bleating and trampling each other in their stampede for the exit. Now his adrenalin levels had dropped, stripping away the freedom from self-consciousness the hormone had conferred. Now the depth of his fear, and the extent of his collapse afterward, embarrassed him.

Time would dim that memory, he supposed, and he would come to view the scene as a heroic, even a noble defiance of fate—but for the moment, he felt a perfect fool. He shut his mouth.

"Ale?"

"Sorry, I . . ." His shoulder twinged sharply; then the pain subsided to a prickly tingling. "I was, ah, just attacked, and . . ."

Puzzlement crinkled her oval face. "Attacked? But—my god, your shoulder, you've been burned!" She reached him in two quick strides. "Ale, what happened?"

"I went outside—" He shifted on the sofa to ease the growing discomfort. "—and a Dac jumped me." Though not his usual style, he could not resist adding, "So I killed it."

"You killed a Dac?" She shook her head. Brief disbelief widened her eyes. A white ring rimmed her china-blue irises. "Out there? How did you—" As training suppressed instinct, she caught a deep breath. Still a distraught spouse, she became the seasoned executive. "First, how badly are you hurt?"

"Not badly at all. I should—"

"Let me look." Her long fingers parted the shirt at the burn. She hissed. "That smells awful. You're not in any danger, but it'll scar without treatment. I'll call a black bag."

"The Oracle's sending one."

"Good, good." Competence and concern shared control of her face. Gently she sat on the next cushion. "Poor Ale, it must have been horrible. How—"

The doorbell chimed twice, a mellow high-low.

"That'll be the police." He started to rise, but allowed her to bar his way with spread-fingered hand. "Pretty quick, though, even for a building cop. Maybe it's just a blue."

"I'll get it." She patted his knee. "But it's not a blue, not at the hall door."

"Huh? Yeah." He had to be in shock. Blues landed on terraces. Roofs. Front doorsteps, if people still had them. Never inside a building. His head flopped against the pillowed sofaback. His shoulder throbbed, now; its stink was beginning to disgust him. He thought about going to the bathroom to wash it, but could not find the energy. He decided just to lie motionless and hope the queasiness would drain away.

Door hinges squeaked; voices mumbled. Emdy's heels clicked on the parquet of the vestibule, were echoed by another, broader pair, then muffled out on the olive green carpet. "Over here," she was saying. "Ale?"

He lifted his head and blinked. Following Emdy came a short, pear-shaped man with beige skin; his straight blond hair looked stiff as straw. He wore a lightweight green suit and held a brown leather wallet.

"Hi," said Ale. "That was quick."

The stranger flipped open the wallet. Metal flashed briefly, then disappeared as he snapped it shut and returned it to his jacket pocket. "Yuai Bethresicks." He accented the "Beh." "District Commander, Coalition, Intelligence. I was upstairs when the call came, thank God. We might not have a lot of time here, so where's the rifle?" As he spoke, he crossed to the ap-comp and slipped his ID/dress card into an empty slot.

If he had said "gun"; or if he had asked about Ale's wounds; or if warmth rather than impatience had infused his voice, then Ale would probably have told him about the alien weapon. Instead he said, "What rifle?"

"The one you bipped the Dac with. Hurry, man! They'll be here any minute, and they'll want that rifle."

"I don't have a rifle—and who are 'they,' anyway?" Hearing the snap in his voice, he warned himself to be polite. Coalition people made very bad enemies. "Look, Commander, I'm sorry, but my shoulder's killing me, and I'm sort of shook up. What are you talking about?"

"If you didn't use a rifle, how'd you bring down a Dac?"

"Bring down? I didn't bring it down, it did that itself."

The Commander grabbed a chair from the dinner table, spun it around, and plopped into it. He gave off a scent of lemon and thyme; a popular cologne, but easy to overdo. Checking that his lapel mike was still in place, he said, "Did you use any sort of projectile weapon to kill the Dac?"

"No, that's what I'm telling you!" Wincing, he turned his head. Emdy looked nervous. "Please, call the hospital, see where the black bag is. It should have gotten here by now."

Yuai Bethresicks said, "All right, take it from load. What happened?"

"I went outside—"

"You mean onto your terrace?"

"I don't mean onto the street!" Again he made a face. "Sorry—"

Yuai held up a hand. "No, it's okay. Go on."

"Well, it must have been landing, because just as I turned to close the door, it shot me."

"And missed."

"Missed, hell!" He pointed to his shoulder. "Does that look like a miss to you?"

"It missed your back, is what I meant. They usually aim so

the bullet explodes in the chest cavity. That way it doesn't damage the nose." The Coalition man shook his head. "Bastards. Go on."

"All right, in that sense, it missed. The Dac made a noise, I don't know, like a cross between a crow and a snake— frustrated-sounding, you know? I turned around and threw my watering-can. I know that sounds stupid, but it worked. The can hit it right here—" He thumped his own breastbone. "—the Dac fell over, and I broke its neck."

The Commander leaned forward, licking his lips. "How?"

"I kicked it."

"And you didn't use a gun?"

"I told you—"

"Just checking." He sighed. "You heard about Guilford Glens?"

"My aunt lived there." He would like someday to see in person, rather than on hovee, the gravestone which her condominium had become. Dac guns had melted the high-rise into a mound of dirty-grey cinderblock, baking thirty-two hundred people inside like raisins in a cake.

"Yeah, well, I caught that case, too. I can't prove it's cause and effect, but right before it got slagged, some guy stuck a shotgun out a window and bipped a cruising Dac. Now, there've been, uh, eleven Dacs that have had their wings clipped in North America since '82—"

"Only eleven?" That surprised Ale. It seemed too few for six years of hatred, six years of opportunity.

"Since the Cease Fire, yeah. Before then . . ." He shrugged. "Don't store this, but I don't believe the official counts. We never got a million of them. Hell, they didn't start cruising unarmored until we declared the Unilateral Cease Fire and ran the weapons sweeps." He scratched his head. His hair rustled dryly. "Where was I?"

"Cause and effect, and eleven dead Dacs since '82."

"Right, right." He leaned back and patted his belly. "Now, of those eleven, four were killed by gunfire. Three of the buildings got slagged. The fourth, though, the guy who did it surrendered himself and his zip-gun to the Dacs, and they left the building alone."

Ale shuddered. *Greater love hath no man, and all, but still. . . .* He could not imagine *letting* those talonlike hands fasten onto you. His stomach twisted. "What happened to him?"

"Never saw him again." Yuai waved a hand. "Of the other

seven, you got three knives; nothing happened. One ceremonial spear; nothing happened. One golf club; nothing. One bow-and-arrow; no surrender; slagged."

Ale had been counting. "And the seventh?"

"That's you. And what I figure is, since you didn't use any sort of projectile weapon, I probably won't have to evacuate six thousand Haven Manor residents in the next six minutes. Assuming I could find some place for all of them to go. That's what I figure. But I won't take bets." He yawned, and stretched. The ceiling light went out. "Wha—?"

"Happens all the time," said Ale wearily. "Glitched circuitry. It'll recover in a minute." He snapped his fingers; a table lamp came on. His shoulder ached. To Emdy he said, "You know, B'jay Awu thinks it's the massies; he says they draw too much power."

Emdy Ofivo shook her head. "I heard that a month ago, so I checked it out. According to my machine, if the real wiring is even close to the blueprints, the massies shouldn't be a problem." She pointed at the agent. "*That's* what you ought to be investigating—builders who blackmail you into taking their service contracts by making sure nobody else can make it work right."

"Hey, I'm Coa/Intel; we handle Dacs, anarchist bombers, neo-Napoleons, and nothing else." He laced his fingers behind his head. "But this is an apartment, not a condo-com, right? So it's your landlord's problem. If *he* wants to make a formal complaint—"

"She doesn't," said Emdy.

"Well, then." He looked around the room, squinting a bit. The light winked back on.

The Commander turned half-about and took the black marble ashtray from the dinner table. "Smoke won't hurt your plants, will it?"

"Tobacco?" asked Ale.

"Dope."

"I'd rather you didn't."

Yuai narrowed his eyes. "You a Templer, or what?"

Ale sighed. Why did the popular mind equate abstention from intoxicants with religious fanaticism? Had they never heard of allergies? Or was it an instinct coded in the genes, a reflex run by a binary chromosome that broke the world into Us and Them, and hinted that They were more than a little peculiar? "I'm a Seeley."

"Hell, I knew that. It's in your ID/dress file."

"It's not supposed to be." It perturbed him: ORA:CLE guaranteed anonymity to its employees, and the word inside said it kept that promise no matter what. Then he frowned. "Wait a minute. I've seen my ID/dress file, and that's *not* in it."

"You really expect to see what I see?" He grinned, and in that flash of square, polished teeth shone the easy arrogance of the unelected official. "When you call your file, what do you get, two, three pages?" At Ale's nod, he went on. "I got seven. That's cause I'm a six, and you're a zero. If I was a nine, I'd probably find a whole bubble."

I should have remembered that. . . . He lifted his head suddenly. Yuai just might be able to tell him what he had wanted to learn for over three years. "What's my code name?"

"Wasn't there." He gave a small laugh. "Considering ORA:CLE's reputation, it probably wouldn't be on the bubble a nine'd pull, either."

"Just a thought."

"But getting back. If you're not a Templer, then why no dope?"

"It sponges up the interface. Any kind of drug does. Even an extra cup of coffee." *Or just plain nerves,* he thought, remembering his first day on the job, when he had not been able to make contact at all. "I don't take anything for four hours before I go to work."

"You mean if you breathe in what I breathe out, you won't get through?"

"Not easily or clearly."

The Commander blinked, squirmed, then tried to sit still. "What about tobacco, then? Would that be okay?"

It pleased Ale that he could discomfit someone who had just been as smugly superior as Yuai—and it pleased him more that the other was a Coalition man, most of whom found amusement in making ordinary citizens nervous—but he knew better than to push it too far. "Sure."

"Thanks." He took out a cigarette and lit it. "Officially, I'm done here. MV Deep/Sec can handle the details—but Ale Elatey, before I go, I've got to tell you, going outside without looking for Dacs is the dumbest—"

"The door's got a DacWatch."

Surprised, Yuai inhaled wrong. He coughed. Then: "Hooked into your apartment-computer?"

"Of course!"

"And your ID/dress card's slotted into the ap-comp, too?"

"Do I really look that disorganized?" He gestured to the terrace wall, where the machine sat on a shelf between two windows. Eight small slots perforated the ap-comp's front panel; from three of them protruded the edges of his, Emdy's, and Yuai's Identity/Address cards. "It was right there where it always is."

"Well, then, why didn't you check the tell—"

"What I'm trying to get through to you is that I *did* check it, and it gave me the green. Something has to be wrong with it."

From the window, Emdy called, "Here comes the black bag."

"High time. Let it in."

Stubbing out his cigarette, Yuai grunted to his feet and walked to the terrace door. "This tell-tale given you problems before?"

"Never," Emdy said.

"Well—holy shit!"

"Ale!"

The sharpness of their alarm jolted him. Pushing out of the sofa, he reached them just as four Dacs alit on the terrace railing.

—3—

Though the media had tagged them "pterodactyls" when they first dropped out of the sky, six and a half years earlier, they looked nothing like flying reptiles. Their large, earless heads sat awkwardly on scrawny torsos. From webbed chest harnesses hung tools, communications devices—and weapons. Thick legs ended in lumpy clawed feet; their leatherlike wings, furling now, spread a full seven meters. Their beaks, orange with black speckles, hooked on top; razor-sharp teeth studded the lower jaw. Their four-fingered hands held guns—and aimed them at the three stunned people behind the sliding glass doors.

The black bag touched down on the flagstones and began to accordion up its propeller. After a brief glance, all seven ignored it.

"Don't move," said Yuai. "They're here for the body.

Uh . . . did you mutilate it or anything?"

"Uh-uh." He shivered, but tried not to show it. It seemed important to stand straight before the aliens who had seized outdoor Earth. He wished he had not put the gun away, though—just in case.

Two of them hopped off the railing and waddled to the corpse. Gesturing, they chittered; the sound came faintly through the thick thermal glass. They scanned the corpse's front, rolled it onto its stomach, lifted and spread its death-crumpled wings—then spoke to the two that still perched.

The one on the right, the only crested one of the four, clipped its gun to its harness. From another hook it removed a grey plastic box sporting two buttons and a dial. Eyeing the humans, it raised the box to its beak.

A *radio,* Ale figured, just as the one on the left beckoned at him with its gun.

"Get out there," said the Commander.

He went cold all over. "Are you crazy?"

"You want them to slag the building?"

Emdy gave a quick, sharp gasp. He winced. His heart hammered in his chest. Yet he had no choice. He might have to die, but he could not take his wife with him. He touched the door latch. "Wh-what are they going to do to me?" The telltale flashed bright red.

"Probably won't hurt you—but I was never on the scene before. Go on, man. Don't offend them."

"One of them tries to kill me and you're afraid *I'll* offend *them?*"

"You're alive, and that one isn't, and if they want—"

"Yeah, I heard you the first time." Outside, the black bag rolled to the door, extending a tentacle that curled into a tight knot. It rapped on the glass. "Emdy—" He looked into her deep blue eyes. With a careful finger he tucked a strand of loose blonde hair behind her ear. "As I go through, back away, slowly. Keep going till you're in the hall."

"No." She intercepted his hand, and squeezed it. "If anything hap—"

The black bag knocked again, more forcefully.

The crested Dac motioned with its radio.

"Open up!" said the black bag. The glass thinned its voice to a whisper. "Doctor! Is this the house that called for medical assistance?"

Ale swallowed hard. He tugged on the latch. The DacWatch buzzed at ninety decibels, drowning out his thoughts. Which was just as well. If he could hear what he was thinking, he would never step outside.

He slid the door to the side. The wind whipped his hair. The black bag scuttled past, saying, "Is this the residence of Ale Elatey? Please take me to him at once. I've been sent to assist him."

Emdy said, "He just went out. Wait a minute."

Facing the aliens, he reached behind his back and closed the door. He gritted his teeth. When the DacWatch fell silent, his pulse roared in his ears. He was terrified: this would be like playing blind-man's-buff on a parapet. "What do you want?"

The crested Dac pointed to the two beside the corpse. They had completed their examination, and stared at Ale through bronze eyes shiny and unblinking. Palms up, three fingers curled, each made a too-human gesture of beckoning.

Heart racing, nausea rising, he approached. An azalea twig snapped beneath his boots. At the edge of his vision, behind the sun-pierced glass wall, Yuai moved. Ale wondered why, at a time like this, the man would bend over to frown at the tell-tale.

Two meters ahead, the Dac on the right slid a knife from a jeweled sheath.

Ale's terror peaked. He froze, backed away—and almost impaled himself on the barrel of an alien gun. The sharp pain in his right kidney eased only when he moved forward again.

The implant in his skull went: *BEEPEEPEEP*

Oh God, all this and you too?

Despite Ale's tension, a connection opened from The Oracle. #Mr. Ale Elatey: Your vital signs are spiking to worrisome heights.# Thick curtains of poor interface muffled The Oracle's voice; the cavern image smeared out of focus around the edges. #What is wrong?#

He took a deep breath. *Since you're on line, tape what's happening for future analysis.*

#What is happening?#

I don't know, dammit! I think I'm about to be executed.

The tips of his boots almost trod on the alien's tail, wrinkled and dulling in death. The Oracle kept quiet. The knife-wielder raised its other hand, the empty one.

He stopped, hoping he had understood. When the gun did

not jab him again, he relaxed—slightly.

The one with the knife nodded. It pressed the edge of the blade against the corpse's face. And sliced its beak off. The stump came away all sheeny coppery with alien blood.

Then the Dac stood, took a bouncing step as pompously as a pigeon, and offered the beak to Ale.

"Hey, now, wait a minute, I'm—"

The gun poked him once. Twice—

Fingers trembling, he reached out his hand.

The Dac laid the warm, wet thing on his palm. Sunlight glinted off oozing cartilage.

He clamped his jaws shut against the churning in his stomach.

With a screech and a cackle the four Dacs leaped on their fallen comrade, each binding one of its short, stubby limbs with a length of shimmery cord. Great wings spread. Flapping, they buffeted Ale with their scaley edges.

They leaped into the air, corpse slung between them. Slowly they beat their way to the sky, spiraling along the updrafts, rising to the silver discus that hung motionless three thousand meters above New Haven.

Ale looked at the lump of speckled-orange horn. Drained of blood, it was nearly translucent. He moved his hand. A moist, severed tongue slid across his fingers.

"Oh, my God!" Clutching his throat, he dropped the thing— spun—and vomited over the railing. The trees below, the unreachable trees, withstood the assault in dignity.

#A most unusual custom,# said The Oracle.

Leave me alone!

#I assume you had killed the dead one?#

Dammit, I—

#They take the noses of those they kill. It is, apparently, some sort of trophy. Conjecture: They are making certain that you have received your trophy.#

Behind him, the glass door slid open. Small gears whirred as the black bag said, "Mr. Ale Elatey! Would you please let me examine you? I have other patients to visit after I leave here."

With a shudder, he complied. But not before lifting his face to the high blue sky. The Dacs had already climbed to a thousand meters, and all but disappeared. Only the great flexing vees of their wings remained visible. Their wings, and their burden.

Back inside, when he had locked the door, Yuai said, "Mr. Ale Elatey? Do you have any idea why someone—some human, I mean—tried to murder you?"

TOP TEN NEWS STORIES OF THE HOUR

Monday, 15 June 2188, 1200 EDT
New England Region

RANK HEADLINE	price	LEAD SENTENCE
#1 485 DIE IN JAPAN AIR CRASH	.20	Teams in search of surivors are scrabbling, so far fruitlessly, through the wreckage of ST/Deep Trans Flight 1963 from Osaka to Tokyo; ST/Deep Trans continues to deny responsibility, and to blame the crash on Dac missiles.
#2 * * * * * * EVAC TEAMS REACH IMPERILED FLORIDA	.20	#2 * * * * * * In anticipation of Hurricane Dora, expected to hit South Florida on Thursday, 4000 helicopters and 3500 wide-bodied jets began the evacuation of the region's residents at 0900 EDT this morning.
#3 * * * * * * NYC KILLER FIRE DELIBERATE, COPS SAY	.20	#3 * * * * * * Investigators from the CD/Directorate of Public Security revealed at an 1135 EDT news conference that the fire which swept Eighth Avenue at dawn this morning, killing six, was ignited by a flaming mattress thrown into the forest.
#4 * * * * * * "CANNIBAL KILLER" SENTENCED TO	.20	#4 * * * * * * Rio de Janeiro's "cannibal killer," a hatchet-waving

**FIRING SQUAD IN
RIO**

teenager apprehended late
Sunday evening in the
boiler room of the housing
complex he had terrorized
for six weeks, was tried,
convicted of irremediable
socio-psychopathy, and
executed at 1050 (EDT) this
morning.

#5   *   *   *   *   *   *   *

**BOLD MARX/COM
REPS OPPOSE
COALITION DRIVE
FOR NEW ID/DRESS
CODE**

.10

#5   *   *   *   *   *   *

Citing the Coa/DP Statistics
attempt to add three
occupation-denoting
characters to the front of
the ID/dress code as "elitist
attempts to reimpose class
distinctions," Marxist-
Communist representatives
to the Coalition this
morning voted unanimously
to reject the proposal.

#6   *   *   *   *   *   *   *

**COWPOKE FULL OF
IT, MV/DEEP AG
SAYS**

.10

#6   *   *   *   *   *   *

Spokesreps for the Marian-
Vegetarian Directorate of
Public Agriculture, angrily
refuting charges leveled by
the President of the
Argentinian Cattleraisers'
Association, said that recent
increases in beef prices were
due solely to "breeders'
greed," and that MV/
DeepAg-imposed production
ceilings played no part in
the hikes.

#7   *   *   *   *   *   *   *

**SCIENTIST, SPOUSE
IN SUICIDE PACT**

.10

#7   *   *   *   *   *   *

Uhuru-Episcopal Directorate
of Public Security spokesreps
have confirmed reports that
Nobel-prize winning
physicist BFA90 AJOMVR
WMSS and his wife, HGK60
ANSWJC WM99, were found
dead beneath the terrace of
their Nairobi apartment last

night, apparent partners in
a suicide pact.

#8 * * * * * * *

SAH TO WED .20
GRANDFATHER OF
SEVENTEEN

#8 * * * * * * *

A spokesrep for Sah, the
most popular singer to come
out of Southeast Asia in
forty years, announced
today the singer's
engagement to DFF20
AVHSLX RZPV, a thrice-
divorced sixty-five-year-old
whose oldest granddaughter
is three years older than his
fiancée.

#9 * * * * * * *

AID EMSISO TO RUN .15
ON CCU TICKET

#9 * * * * * * *

Ho-soap star Aid Emsiso
(ADM60 AYIPCX NAAA)
announced this morning
that he would be leaving the
popular show DOOMED
CHILDREN "as soon as they
can write me out," in order
to enter the political arena.

#10 * * * * * * *

DAC SHIP NUMBER .10
SIX DUE IN TEN
DAYS

#10 * * * * * * *

The MIT/ToDai robot probe
that first spotted the sixth
Dac ship to intrude on the
system in the last six years
has reported that the craft
is decelerating at nearly
twenty meters per second,
and should reach L5 on the
afternoon of the twenty-fifth.

This update has been provided as a public service by all data management corporations participating in NEWSBANK/MC, a news data
base organized and supervised by the Marxist/Communist Directorate
of Public Information.

To read any of the above news stories in full, simply highlight the
title and press ACCEPT. The article will be transmitted to your unit's
memory. Your bank balance will be debited by the sum in the column
headed "price."

To see the headlines of the day's other news stories, simply scroll
your screen up.

Thank you, and do be careful.

II

He recoiled. "You're saying that someone did?"

"Yes. I—"

"Will you *please* let me examine my patient in peace and quiet?" Cobralike, the black bag's tentacle swayed up to tap Ale's left shoulder. It smelled ever-so-faintly of lubricating oil. "Mr. Ale Elatey, really, I have a number of appointments today, and the more time I spend here, the less likely it is that I will be able to complete my rounds before—"

"Hold on a minute, will you?" He looked from Yuai to Emdy, whose blue eyes had widened in surprise, then back to the Coalition man. "Nobody'd want to kill me. What makes you think someone tried?"

"Because your DacWatch works perfectly."

Ale shook his head. "No, it—"

"I tested it." He let that sink in before continuing. "Then, while you were out there—" He pointed to the terrace with another of his ID/dress cards. Blue instead of white, it had his name, picture, and rows of micromagdots. "I queried downtown. That mothership showed up about dawn. Which means if you got green, it's because somebody tampered with either the main feed off DacWatch, or your unit's line to the feed. So I queried your machine—and a dozen others in this building, picked at random—about the voltage coming in off DacWatch. You're about fifteen percent lower than anybody else. So. Somewhere between this room and the main feed, somebody tapped into your line—overrode the warning signal—and sent you the all-clear. I'm not asking you *who*—don't expect you to know—but I am asking, why? I mean, what about you would make someone want you bipped? Are you doing anything—"

"I'll bet it's the Chinese," said Emdy.

"Don't be silly." At the expression on her face, he wished he had phrased it differently. "Uh—"

"Ale." She enunciated each word with care and precision. "I am many things, but I am rarely silly. I resent—"

"I'm sorry, I didn't mean it that way."

Her eyebrows arched, as if to say, "How else could you have meant it?" but she inclined her head a centimeter. "Apology accepted. If not the Chinese, though, who could it be?"

Head swiveling like a tennis judge's, Yuai raised a hand. They ignored him.

Ale said, "But how could they do it? And why—"

"You haven't dropped it yet, have you?"

The Coalition man interrupted. "Whoah! What's this all about Chinese?"

Ale sighed. "I'm doing a translation of the poems and letters of Tan Wang Ch'i, and—"

"Who?" The Commander touched his lapel mike again.

"Tan Wang Ch'i."

"I thought all Asian ID/dresses had 'F' for a second character."

"It only seems that way, 'cause so many have black hair and brown eyes. But Tan lived before ID/dresses. You've never heard of him; he's nobody famous. He was born in 1840 and died in 1927—historically significant dates for his country, but not because of him. He was an infant at one end and a senile old man at the other. But in between he did a little bit of almost everything, traveled all over China, and wrote lots and lots of letters."

"Mr. Ale Elatey!" The black bag tugged at his sleeve.

"Oh, all right. Come on, all three of you. We can do this in the kitchen, can't we?"

"Perfectly acceptable. Access to hot water is useful. Do you have a table large enough to lie on?"

Emdy made a face. "The whole room's not large enough to lie down in."

"Now, now, it's not that small." To the device he said, "I thought I'd sit on a stool." Walking past the dining area and turning left, he snapped his fingers. The overhead panel fluoresced into brilliance; the trim on the stove and refrigerator sparkled. "Unless that would raise me up too high?"

"Not if you don't mind my standing on a second stool." It stopped in the doorway, spun thirty degrees to its right and then to its left, and tilted back on its wheels to scan the ceiling.

"Adequate. Four square meters of floor space, which is rather larger than Ms. Emdy Ofivo had led me to believe. Hardly sterile, but we don't require that for this, do we?"

"I sure to God hope not." Ale pulled two stools from the bar counter and sat on one. "Where were we, Commander?"

The black bag said, "Would someone please lift me up?"

Yuai took hold of its handle. "Unh! What do you weigh, anyway?"

"Seventeen point nine kilos. A man of your stature should be able to lift me easily."

"I don't spend much time in our condo-com's gym." He squatted, used both hands, and lifted with his legs. Setting the bag on the second stool, he let out his breath with a whoosh. Then he stepped to the sink and rinsed his fingers; he dried them on a terrycloth hand-towel he took from his jacket pocket. "Now, about this guy Tan—"

"Remove your shirt, please." It extruded a stethoscope.

Ale tried to get the shirt off, but his shoulder hurt when he moved his arm. "Emdy, can you—"

"Sure." Her heels tapped on the floor's ivory tiles; her hands worked with gentle, competent care. She slipped the garment down his arms, then tousled his hair. "There you go." She left the room to look on from the far side of the bar counter.

"Thanks." He turned to Yuai, but another metal tentacle pushed his jaw back to the right. "Hey!"

"You'll feel better if you don't watch."

Coolness swabbed his skin; mint-scent broke free. "Commander, if you could stand over on my other side?"

The intelligence man moved heavily. "You were saying?"

"Basically, that's who Tan was. He was an incredible observer—understand, now, he was incompetent as a *doer:* I mean, he got on the wrong side of two, no, three, revolutions, launched one business failure after another, insisted that Portugal would be the dominant Western country in East Asia . . . like I said, incompetent as a doer. But as an observer he was first class. He had a reporter's eye, a scholar's attention to detail, and his prose wasn't bad, either. Fascinating family, too. His great-great grandson was K. T. Thomas Tan, the guy who worked out the theory on how to force even the smallest of stars to go supernova."

Yuai leaned against a counter and drummed his fingernails on the cupboard door beneath. For the first time Ale noticed the man's nails: thick, yellowish, and square cut, they looked more like toenails. "All right, fine, but what does this have to do with—"

"I'm coming to that." Out of the corner of his eye he caught a glint of light on scalpel. The black bag was right—not watching *would* feel better. Swallowing hard, he twisted his head even farther to the left. "See, I started collecting Tan's work— his private letters, articles he wrote for newspapers and magazines, even his poems."

"It must be worth a fortune." Yuai eyed Emdy as though remembering the old catchphrase: *cui bono?*

Ale snorted. "It's not worth a penny—it's all facsimile. I just wanted it so I could translate it. But anyway. I scouted up everything I could on my own, then put ads in the major Bulletin Boards, in the Wanted to Buy section? And I got a lot of material."

Emdy bent across the bar. "Plus some death threats."

Yuai raised his eyebrows. "Did you report them?"

"They weren't *death* threats—just anonymous letters with vague promises of divine retribution and all." The bag's needle zipped through his flesh; he squirmed. "See—"

"Ale, they said they'd kill you!"

"Emdy—" He sighed. The argument was so old, and they had run through it so many times, that each had the other's lines memorized. It was like waltzing. So he spoke to the Coalition man, instead. "Look, the notes were signed by a radical Chinese group that wants to restore the Ch'ing Dynasty, of all things."

Yuai made a noise that suggested he took as little interest in politics as possible. "They a local party that got voted out, or what?"

"They ruled China from 1642 to 1911—and they weren't even Chinese. They were Manchu. Invaders. For a while they had a pretty good government, but then—"

"You can put your shirt back on, Mr. Ale Elatey." Whirring, clicking, the black bag retracted tentacles and replaced instruments. "I'll drop in to see you in a week. And now, if someone will help me down and let me out onto the terrace, I'll be off."

Ale looked at Yuai, who groaned, but moved across the kitchen. While the blond man struggled with the bag, Ale asked, "Uh—is it okay if I take a shower?"

The Commander said, "Can you at least wait till I'm done?"

"I was asking the medic."

"Of course it is all right. I sealed the stitches with Falskin; by the time it dries up and flakes off, the wound should have healed completely. Good day, sir."

"I'll let it out," said Emdy. "Come on."

Yuai rinsed his fingers again. Drying them on the square of white terrycloth, he asked over his shoulder, "So their government went bad, huh?"

"Yeah. Corruption. Inefficiency. And a bunch of Westerners knocking on the doors. They couldn't handle it. They lost a couple of wars, and eventually got overthrown by Sun Yat-sen and his people."

Yuai shook his head. "So why would anybody want to restore them?"

Ale shrugged, and was pleased to discover that the motion did not hurt—whoever had been tele-factoring the black bag knew its job. "I really ought to charge you for the answer to that."

"The Seeley Code of Ethics, huh?" But he smiled.

"The way I figure it, even though the founders of the Ch'ing Dynasty were foreigners, the Dynasty itself was, in concept, outlook, and world view, the last authentically Chinese government ever. It was definitely the last pure Confucian government. All the governments since then have been based on one Western ideology or another, in whole or in part."

The other cocked his head. A strand of coarse yellow hair slipped down across his forehead. "I could maybe buy that. Lots of people looking back these days—like those Peruvians with their Inca colony on the Moon?—but what I don't get is, I don't get why they threatened you."

"Because for the first sixty-some years of his life, Tan Wang Ch'i hated the Ch'ing. The letters he wrote—the articles and poems, too—focused on the inadequacies of the Manchu Dynasty. He wrote about greedy landlords and starving children and corrupt magistrates who did everything but pass out rate cards. Tan never did figure if he was a revolutionary or a reformer, but he did everything in his power to defame the Ch'ing. If I translate his stuff and store it in the Public Data Banks, it'll embarrass anyone who claims the Ch'ing *should* be restored. And they don't want that."

Yuai scratched the tip of his nose. "You still got the threats?"

"Yeah." He boosted himself off the stool. A wave of dizziness spun his head around, but he blinked a few times and it receded.

"Wobbly?"

"Yeah."

"Shock. It'll wear off pretty quick. Where we going?"

"My study." He led the way out of the kitchen, to the right, to the right again into the corridor past Emdy's office and the master bedroom, where he turned right a third time, then left into his study. Snapping on a light, he gestured nonchalantly to his near left. "My pride and joy."

The light fell on three dozen strap-leaved bromeliads, seventeen of them in bloom, growing from pockets in the rough-textured cork wall. Water trickled down the cork, moistening their roots, then disappeared into the recycling system at the bottom. The flowers' fragrance filled the room.

Yuai stopped. "Whoof!"

Ale liked eliciting that reaction. "Have a seat." Smiling, he moved to the recliner in the left rear corner. He felt comfortable, there by his desk: an oblong of plywood bolted to the wall at three corners, and suspended from the ceiling at the fourth. A computer terminal with an oversize color screen rested in the middle; beside it hunkered a xeroprinter. Ale slipped into his chair and pushed it back.

Yuai had to settle for unfolding one of the chairs stacked against the wall. "That's a long way to go for a cup of coffee. Why don't you unlock that door between the kitchen and here?"

"That's the massie chamber." With a flick of his thumb, Ale summoned the screen to life. "I walk through it, but not too many visitors enjoy it." Another button brought up the index, crisp black letters on parchment-white background. He stared at it. "I can't remember what I stored them under . . . no listing for threats. . . . Oh, wait a minute. It's under AA."

Yuai cleared his throat. "Alcoholics Anonymous?"

"Assholes, anonymous." His fingers roamed the slick plastic keys; an instant later, the first of the threats appeared.

"It's in *Chinese*." Yuai sounded cheated.

"You expected Swahili?" He jabbed another button. "This'll bring up the translation." The Chinese shrank into the left half of the screen; English appeared on the right.

"Yeah? Your machine translates for you?"

"This? No. It'll give me a rough approximation of the original—sometimes. If it can read the original. Printing it can handle pretty well, but this"—he gestured to the sleek, fluid lines on display—"is 'grass writing' and it's a little too much for my software. I hear they have a good program in Peking, one that'll translate all but the most illegible grass writing into modern simplified, and I'm saving up to buy it. Be a while yet. Last I heard, it cost like $20,000."

Yuai leaned over Ale's shoulder to peer at the screen. "'He who shakes the harmony of heaven and earth will find himself shaken in turn, as if dashed from the highest peak.' That is vague. I can see why you're not too upset."

Before Ale could reply, Emdy entered. "Try getting one a day for three weeks, and then see how cheerful you are."

"Come on, Emdy." She was so cautious. Always preparing for things that *might* happen. After a while the contingency planning got constricting. "If the expert doesn't think it's anything to worry about—"

"I didn't say that, exactly." Yuai gave a rueful smile. "When crazies send you weird letters, you have to worry a little—it's just that you have to keep things in proportion. And remember, I'm Coalition—I worry about Dacs, not politics."

"Oh, thanks."

Emdy said, "See?" Before she could say more, the pholo rang; she left to answer it.

"Look, could I have a hard copy of the originals? And the translations, too, of course?"

"I thought you just hinted that this isn't your jurisdiction."

"The threats aren't. But a jimmied DacWatch is."

"You're the boss. I'll zip them to your machine, what's the—"

"Paper, please. I'm sort of old-fashioned."

"Sounds funny from somebody named Yuai. The 'U' *does* still denote a former female, doesn't it?"

Yuai's beige skin flushed even darker. "All right, in *some* ways I'm old-fashioned. I'd really rather have hard copy, though."

He swiveled in his chair, hit three keys, and the machine began to whir. A tongue of paper stuck out of the xeroprinter. The machine clicked in a way that managed to sound reproving; a moment later, a red light flashed.

"Dammit." Using his good arm, Ale levered himself up. "Paper jammed again."

"I'll get it. My kids have the same model, and until I rebuilt it, they used to spend half their time tugging paper through the rollers." He delved into his pocket for a manicure set which in turn yielded a miniature screwdriver. After unfastening the front of the xeroprinter, he tapped the black rubber roller. "What it is, they built these with sub-standard parts—you did buy it on special?"

"Yeah, like sixty percent off."

"Well, this is why. No warranty, either, right?"

"Right. Or service agreement. If I have to have a repair cart over, it costs like $525.00 an hour."

"Uh-huh." He chewed delicately on his lower lip while he freed the sheet of paper. The machine's innards had wadded it into a ball. "Well, what you do is, you order a new one of these parts from a printing supply store. Cost you, oh, I don't know, a hundred and a half? Something like that. It screws in and out at either end. Take the old one out, pop the new one in. No more jammed paper; no more repair carts. Or at least—" He grunted as he screwed the faceplate back on. "—at least not so many repair carts."

"Thanks. I'll give it a try."

"You can start your printer up again."

He touched the button. The machine clicked into action.

In the meantime, Yuai had smoothed out the one crumpled sheet of paper. "You got twenty-one of these?"

"All told."

"And the last one came—"

"I don't know, eight weeks ago? Maybe longer, I can't be sure."

"Well—" The printer beeped as it finished. Yuai took the papers from the tray, shuffled through them, and said, "I'll look into these—but you know, I really don't think a bunch of reactionary Chinese gimmicked your DacWatch."

"That makes two of us."

"I guess that's about it." He tucked the papers under his arm. "You get any more of these, let me know." He stuck out his hand. "Nice meeting you; wish the circumstances had been better."

"Yeah." Yuai's grip was firm and warm—the kind that always made Ale worry that he might be risking a squeezing contest. This time, his fingers emerged uncrunched. "The door's this way."

Yuai waved him off. "I can find it." He made a snorting

laugh. "They run a special course at the Academy, 'Finding Your Way Out of Strange Apartments.' First semester covers with the lights on; second, with 'em off. Take care of yourself."

—2—

The Chinese characters on the screen drew Ale, and he sank into his chair ready to spend the usual two hours with Tan Wang Ch'i. This was his greatest pleasure: groping his way into the thoughts and the feelings of a nineteenth century Chinese writer, and understanding them as though they were his own.

Too, there was in him a wistfulness, a nostalgia for the time before the CO_2 crisis, when the outdoors were not out of bounds, for the days when one could sink a spade into rich black loam, plant a seed, and let it grow to harvest it without a permit. . . . Tan Wang Ch'i had walked from Canton to Peking— and back. Ale had never walked farther than to the nearest elevator.

The next letter on the schedule excited him. Ten thousand words long, Tan had sent it to Yuan Shih K'ai concerning the behavior of Yuan's troops in Korea—behavior that would, eventually, break the Korean satellite off the Chinese Empire and toss it into orbit around Japan. Fifty years would pass before the Koreans found any independence at all. And all because they, like the Chinese, had refused to confront the reality that the modernization of the West and of Japan had changed the way the world worked. The Koreans had tried to cling to tradition, to a Sino-centric world order that had once protected them but no longer functioned—and it had cost them dearly.

Already remembering how the colloquialism in the seventeenth line had frustrated his every attempt to translate it, Ale called up the letter—then snapped his fingers in exasperation. The bonsai! He had never finished—hell, he had not even started to water them.

And throwing the watering-can at the Dac had dented it beyond repair.

With a sigh, he wiped Tan's letter from the screen, replaced it with the pholo directory, and found the number of Montgomery Sears. Switching on the pholo, he punched in the number. The equipment hummed. The laser housings crackled as they warmed. A sphere of white light formed in the center of the room, a meter from where he sat; it jiggled as the pholo rang.

On the fourth ring, the salesrep appeared in the sphere. "Good afternoon, and thank you for calling Montgomery Sears. How may I help you?"

"I'd like a watering-can, please. Four-liter capacity."

The salesrep smiled. He was a pleasant-faced man, with silver hair that fluffed out from his skull like a dandelion's puffball. "Would you happen to know if that would be in Gardening Supplies? Or Home Furnishings?"

Ale laughed. "Common sense would suggest Gardening Supplies, but given Murphy's Law—"

"We'll check Home Furnishings, first." He glanced down at something out of pholo range, presumably the screen of his desktop computer. His bushy silver eyebrows lifted. "Murphy's Law wins again. It is Home Furnishings. Let me just call it up so you can get a look at it—"

The sphere reverted to white, then darkened with a new image. A bronze watering-can hung in mid-air. It had a swan neck, a stout handle, and a small rosette pierced by hundreds of holes. "This is our Green Thumb model," said the salesrep, "and it retails for $79.99, plus tax. It has a warranty, of course: ninety-days-defective-workmanship-no-abuse. Shall I—"

"Can you unscrew the rosette?"

"Uh. . . ." The can slowly revolved, displaying intricate side-panel etchings that twined up and around its spout. Keys clicked. Ale assumed the salesrep was retrieving promotional infor-mation. "Oh, yes, here we go. Yes, you can remove the rosette. In fact, you are advised to remove it at least once every sixty days and apply silicon to the threading, so as to resist corrosion. Shall I—"

"You're sure it's four-liter? Looks more like three to me."

"Well, this is the Green Thumb, Model 4-L? Yes, yes . . . definitely."

"And you said $79.99 plus tax?"

"Yes. Which will come to—" Buttons snickered. "Let's see, that's $6.80 sales tax and $10.40 VAT brings it to $97.19."

"All right," he said, thinking *Got to answer two extra ques-tions to pay for it, but it is good-looking.* . . . "Send it over."

"Let me just double-check here." The salesrep dropped his gaze to his desktop screen again. "You are ALL80 AFAHSC NFF6? Of 38-Q Haven Manor?"

"One and the same."

"Very good, sir. We'll transmat this to you right away."

"How long will it be? My plants are drying out right now—I don't want to wait till next Tuesday."

"Let me just ascertain the availability—" He looked down again. He nodded, then raised his gaze to stare, apparently, straight into Ale's eyes. "The warehouse says it has it in stock, and it will be able to transmat it within eleven minutes. At this time of day, Central Transshipping runs on a five-second lag. Can your plants wait that long?"

He smiled. "Yes. I think they can hang on for another eleven minutes."

"Excellent, Mr. Ale Elatey. Your account will be debited at the moment of transmission; refunds must be claimed within forty-eight hours, except in cases of defective workmanship. Thank you, sir, and have a safe afternoon."

The sphere winked white. Ale switched off the pholo. The lasers hummed on the edge of audibility, then fell over into silence. He stretched out in the recliner, comforted by its softness, by its hollows that, over the years, had migrated into a perfect mold of his backside. Almost meditatively, he wondered how the new can would fit his hand. Probably not as well as the old one had. New things always feel strange, awkward. *It's all a matter of getting used to it. I've grown accustomed to your spout. . . .* He nearly got up, then, to prowl the terrace and see if any of his bonsai had begun to wilt, so that he would know which ones to tend to first . . . but he yawned, and settled back, instead. The plants had looked okay; they could last a few minutes longer. And he was tired. The adrenalin generated by the attack had burned away, leaving him lethargic and more than a little depressed.

Why would anyone want to kill him? It made absolutely no sense. He had no personal enemies. And when he worked for ORA:CLE as a "Computer-Linked Expert"—a Seeley—he worked under a code name that even he did not know. In the unlikely event that one of his answers had so provoked someone that homicide seemed preferable to a refund, the disgruntled customer would have had no way to track him down. Not through ORA:CLE, at least. A basic tenet of the service was that it would not jeopardize its experts' anonymity.

But who would want him dead? The neo-Boxers? Not a chance. They were centered twelve thousand miles away, and in an era of government-run transportation, with all its attendant priority rankings and red-tape delays, radical groups found it hard physically to operate more than a few meters from home. Besides, the neo-Boxers would scorn that sort of sabotage— it was too high-tech for their tastes, which ran to more time-honored methods of assassination like poison and sleeve-sheathed daggers.

The door in the north corner of his study snapped shut, sucked inward by its electromagnets. Montgomery Sears was transmatting the can. He sat up, half-convinced that if they sent it that quickly, they had probably sent the wrong model. Things usually worked out that way.

The warning light inset between the door's upper panels flashed ruby-red for one long pulse, then faded. A muted chime rang high and clear. It was just loud enough to be heard throughout the apartment, and even onto the terrace if the sliding glass doors were open, but not loud enough to cut through the thin walls and disturb the neighbors on either side. Not that it would bother old Mrs. M'ti Emtenne: she was hard of hearing, and kept her own reception alarm at full volume. Every time she got a delivery, Ale felt compelled to check his receiver—just in case.

A turn of the doorknob cut off the electromagnets. The interior light came on. On the floor lay a box whose label read, "Green Thumb, Model 4-L."

"What do you know, they got it right after all." He picked it up, then opened the door opposite to step through the massie into the kitchen. There, on the formica counter between the sink and the stove, he unpacked the box.

Ah, it was lovely. It gleamed softly in the fluorescent light; at an experimental tug, its handle wiggled not at all. Better yet, the seam where the spout met the reservoir looked sound, very sound.

Filling it, he wiped off a stray drop of water, and hefted it to test whether the handle would cut into his palm. Then he held it at eye level and examined every centimeter of the seams for the glisten of seeping water.

"All right!"

"What's all right?" called Emdy from her office.

"My new watering-can just got here; it looks perfect."

"Oh . . . well, that's . . ." The pholo rang; he suspected she appreciated the interruption. "Hello?" she said. "Oh." And switched into Arabic.

Satisfied that the can would hold its water, that it would not burst just as he crossed the living room (that had happened, once, one week after the carpet had been laid; Emdy had been so angry that she had accused him of malice aforethought, because they had bought the olive-green rug instead of the orange shag he had preferred), Ale took the alien gun from the kitchen cupboard, then headed for the terrace. The DacWatch glowed green—but he refused to take chances.

The doorbell rang. Groaning, he set down the can and retraced his steps. "Video." The small screen on the inside of the door showed a fuzzy picture of a woman. *How nice—it seems to have fixed itself.* "Open." The three heavy-duty bolts released simultaneously.

After making certain that his pocket concealed the alien gun, he pulled the door inwards. "Can I help you?"

"L'ai Aichtueni." She held out her hand. "I just got off shift."

Shaking her hand, he tried not to stare, but failed. She was an albino: translucent skin, pink eyes, and silky white hair a good half-meter long. She wore it tied above her right ear; the mane fell over her bare right shoulder and tumbled down her side. "I'm pleased to meet you."

"*Dr.* L'ai Aichtueni." Her eyes glittered; impatience edged her voice.

He swallowed hard. Her dilated pupils and odd expression made him suspect the influence of drugs. He *hated* dealing with squashheads. They were too damn touchy. "I'm sorry, I—"

"I was telling the black bag that took care of you."

"Oh! Well, uh, thank you, you did a superb job." *All things considered....*

She cocked her head to one side. "I know what you're thinking, and you're right, I am flat. But I was not, then. I refuse to work squashed. I pop the very instant my shift ends, but never even a microsecond before. One does have one's ethics, you know."

"Ah...."

"Anyway. As I live only three flights up, I thought I'd come down to see you in the flesh, as it were." Swaying slightly, she stepped inside.

"A house call?" He gave way before her, but she kept coming on.

"One could call it that—I rarely get such interesting patients." She wore a floral perfume that washed across him in waves. "How is the wound?"

"Just fine."

"Wonderful, wonderful." She looked around with jerky birdlike twitches of her head. "Hah! As I suspected, the color controls on my monitor have slipped out of phase. I shall have to have that fixed."

If only he could ask her to leave—but one did not do that. Not without committing a grievous *faux pas*. Privacy was so precious that when strangers came calling in person, one had to assume they had important reasons for disrupting one's privacy. But he wished Emdy were there. She handled this sort of thing so much better than he did. "Well. Ah. . . ."

Cool amusement filled her gaze. "Let me be honest with you—I'm a recruiter for the Social-Tech Party and we're searching for candidates from Haven Manor."

"Uh, listen, Doctor—"

"L'ai. 'Water,' to my close associates." She ran her tongue along her lips. "And I do hope we will be . . . associates."

"Uh. L'ai—"

"Water."

"I'm not interested in politics."

She smiled. "That trait alone will make you an excellent candidate."

"Yes, but—"

"Hush. Listen." She reached for his elbow, to guide him to the sofa.

"Hands off!" said Emdy. She had risen from her desk chair and was approaching them.

"It's hardly *that*, Ms. Emdy Ofivo," said L'ai calmly, "but I do see that I'm interrupting both of you. Ale, we'll speak of this some other time. Good day." She nodded, turned, and walked out, pulling the door shut as she left.

"Lock," said Emdy with a snap equal to the bolts'. "Who is she?"

"She's the one who was running the black bag that came—a squashhead, though. Says she lives upstairs, came down to, uh—" He waggled his eyebrows. "—recruit me."

"Uh-huh. Cute, Ale. Real cute." Narrowing her eyes, she tapped her right foot on the floor. "How long have you known her?"

He held up his hand. "Hey. I just met her ten seconds ago, when the bell rang. Honest." He frowned. "You know, what confuses me is why the Social-Tech Party would let a drug user recruit for them."

"You're still in the Ch'ing Dynasty. Half the population's on squash—and the rest drink. What did you say her name was?"

"Dr. L'ai Aichtueni, nicknamed Water. Why?"

She snorted. "An ex-male—that explains the clumsiness. Doctor or not, addict or not, she's in politics, and that means major trouble. Don't get tangled up with her."

"I don't plan to." He meant it. And not solely because of the drugs. The politics of the Tokugawa Shogunate fascinated him; contemporary politics, even on the individual building level, baffled him. When one party provided police protection, and another refuse removal, and a third consumer services . . . uh-uh. Not for him.

"Well, she's planning something completely different, so you watch it." She turned, stopped, and pivoted about again. "Oh. Something—two somethings I just thought of. First, we got word from MR/Deep Preparedness; we're taking in a refugee tomorrow or the day after."

"Those Florida hurricanes?"

"Yes, they're due late next week, so this guy shouldn't be here too long, unless his place is flattened, which let us hope it isn't, because I really hate having strangers underfoot."

"I know what you mean." Their last refugee, eighteen months previously, had commandeered Ale's study and run up a pholo bill that had taken them three months to get properly re-debited. "What's the other thing?"

"Before you go to work tonight—"

"Now what?"

"You'll have time for your plants," she said with mock exasperation.

"And for Tan Wang Ch'i?"

She made a face. "Depends how quick you are. But it struck me that you should write up a first-person account of your run-in with the Dac—get your version into a databank first, and you might be able to afford three or four replacements for the bonsai you lost."

"You just hit me in my weak spot."

She smiled broadly.

"And you knew it, too, didn't you?" He slipped an arm around her waist and pulled her toward him. "You really think it's worth it?"

She wiggled her hips and laughed at his surprise. "That wisteria you bought—what did the plant itself cost?"

He frowned, trying to remember. . . . "Uh, a hundred-fifty, maybe two hundred with tax."

"And the shipping charges?"

He winced. Living things did not survive matter transmission: they required manual delivery. "Another five hundred."

"Now, you don't *have* to replace the azalea—"

"What? And leave its pedestal bare?"

She tickled him under the chin. "If you want a new one—"

"I do."

She nodded. "Then it's your choice: Don't write the article, buy a plastic plant, and have them masstrans it; or do write it, buy a live one, and have it delivered."

"All right, all right, I'll write it. . . ." He hugged her, relishing her warmth, her firmness against his body. "But the last piece I wrote netted what, eighty-three cents?"

"Approximately, uh-huh. But you didn't advertise it, none of the Readers mentioned it in their RecLists, and besides that, it was history."

"But it was good!"

"Of course it was good—but Ale, how many people care about—I mean, really get interested in—the Meiji Restoration?"

Stiffly, he said, "I get three or four questions a day about it."

She poked a finger into his midriff. "To make money off the Data Banks, you need three or four thousand a day. . . . You're getting flabby again."

"Hey, come on!" He grabbed her hands to keep her from pinching the roll of excess around his waist. She was always giving him grief about that. "I'll write the thing, but will you handle the business end? I don't know anything about it, and—"

"Do I get my standard commission?"

"You really are mercenary!"

She shrugged. "On the other hand, I'm worth it."

"All right. Let me go water my plants, then I'll write the damn thing."

"Okay. I'll be in my office when you're done."

As she returned to her desk, he again picked up the watering-can. The DacWatch still read green. He re-set it—waited for it to insist that the area was safe—then squatted to peer up into the hazy afternoon sky. Or as much of it as he could see, given that their upstairs neighbor's terrace roofed his field of vision. But it looked clear, and Mrs. M'ti Emtenne was sunning herself, so he went outside. With a small gulp. And a surreptitious touch of the alien metal in his pocket.

—3—

The ten surviving plants were as dry as he had expected, but none had started to wilt. After a wilt, bonsai dropped leaves as though autumn had come. Even this drying-out would probably precipitate a mild shedding.

He hurried along the row, pouring gently, careful not to disturb the shallow-rooted ground covers growing in most of the pots. A green speck on the trunk of the ginkgo caught his eye; instinctively, he reached for the bud, intending to rub it off before it grew into a branch that could spoil the shape of the tree. Then he stopped, imagining how the tree would look with that bud permitted—encouraged, even—to develop, *say, out to here, and then wire it so it comes just a little around, pinch it, of course, keep the top third, no, half, bushy as all get-out.* . . . He withdrew his finger, already pleased with the tree's new form, already anticipating its maturity.

Down the line he went, tilting the can whose rosette broke the flow into a hundred tiny droplet streams that fell like soft, warm rain on the baby's breath and the moss and the gnarled, knobby knees of the roots. While he waited for the water to run out the holes in the pot-bottoms and patter on the flagstones, he inspected twigs and branches and leaves, here picking off a gypsy moth caterpillar, there frowning at the curled brown edge of a wisteria leaf. A couple of mealy bugs had invaded the upright yew, but not enough to cause any alarm. Yet.

His DacWatch beeped in unison with Mrs. M'ti Emtenne's. She called, "Dacs, Ale!" and vanished indoors in a rustle of terrycloth.

He spun around, looking for—there, way out in the harbor, half a kilometer high, a pair of Dacs played tag above the water. Nonetheless. He hurried back along the terrace, slipped inside, and slapped the door shut, locking it with a reflexive flick of his fingers. One close call a day was more than enough for him.

Pausing, he stared at the DacWatch irresolutely, wondering why it had worked this time and not last. Then he shook his head. Investigating it was beyond him. He just hoped Yuai would let him know what had happened.

Dropping off the watering-can on the counter between the kitchen and the dining room, passing through the matter-transceiver (because it made him feel daring; it always had. It was perfectly safe—sensors in the floor, walls, and ceiling blocked reception until the cabinet had been evacuated—but still. He liked that tang of excitement), he made his way to his recliner.

He pushed it back, took the computer's keyboard off the bookshelf, and switched the screen on. He adjusted the angle of the CRT so he could reach it without craning his neck. His fingers roamed over the keys; characters, words, sentences appeared on the screen. It surprised him how easy it was to tell his story—until he realized that he was comparing it to the preparation of a scholarly document. *That's right,* he thought, while he backspaced to change "big" to "large," because he had already used "big" four times on that page, *I don't have to footnote this thing. Sure goes quicker when you don't have to window into memory every third line. . . .*

In less than an hour he had told it all, even to the point of reliving the nausea that had seized him when the alien's head had smacked backwards into the flagstones. He ran a quick program to check spelling and grammar, and made ready to send it to Emdy's terminal.

Then he stopped. Chewing his lip, he reread the paragraphs about the others who had killed Dacs, and their fates. He was not sure, but it seemed likely—given the habits of the Coalition—that Yuai Bethresicks would want to clear the article before Ale and Emdy deposited it. One never knew what those people would construe as a threat to the Coalition's eventual eradication of the Dacs, and it was always wiser to check first.

He punched the local number of the Coalition into his pholo, and waited for the sphere of light to coalesce into a receptionist.

It took a while. Eighteen rings, in fact.

"Yes?" He had a waxed head and a surgically bobbed nose. Triple jowls quivered under his throat. His voice sounded as bored as it could be.

"I'd like to speak to Commander Yuai Bethresicks, please."

"And the rest of that ID/dress?"

"I don't know, I'm sorry."

With a sniff, the receptionist consulted his keyboard. His thin black eyebrows twitched once. Then he looked up. "Sorry."

Ale frowned. "He's not available?"

"I haven't the faintest notion about his availability, Mr.—?"

"Ale Elatey. I don't understand what you mean."

"Really?" The receptionist pursed his lips. "Then let me put it more simply: No one by that name works here."

The recliner thudded into the upright position as Ale leaned forward. "What? But—"

The bright sphere burst like a soap bubble. A wisp of smoke curled from the laser housing.

TOP TEN NEWS STORIES OF THE HOUR

Monday, 15 June 2188, 1400 EDT
New England Region

RANK HEADLINE	price	LEAD SENTENCE
#1 MIAMI EVAC WELL AHEAD OF SCHEDULE	.20	The evacuation of Greater Miami in anticipation of Hurricane Dora commenced at 0900 (EDT) this morning; by 1330, special ST/DPTrans and MR/DPS crews had flown over two and one-half million residents of the area to safety.
#2 * * * * * * COALITION TO PROBE BEEF PRICES	.15	#2 * * * * * * At the joint request of the Argentinian Cattleraisers' Association and the Marian/ Vegetarian Directorate of Public Agriculture, an investigative team with powers of arbitration has been appointed by the Coalition to look into the recent surge in beef prices.
#3 * * * * * * DOW DOWN TEN	.10	#3 * * * * * * Unsettled trading conditions on European markets are being blamed for the five-point drop suffered by the Dow Jones Industrial Average over the last two hours.
#4 * * * * * * JETLINER DELIBERATELY	.15	#4 * * * * * * Coalition aviation experts, after examining the flight

RANK	HEADLINE	price	LEAD SENTENCE
	LURED OUT OF BOUNDS		recorder of ST/DPTrans Flight 1963, have determined that unidentified signals lured the Tokyo-bound jetliner out of the safepath minutes after departing Osaka International Airport.

#5 * * * * * * *

SCIENTIST FAKED EVIDENCE .10

#5 * * * * * * *

Coalition investigators called in by the Uhuru-Episcopal DP/Security in Nairobi announced at a 1300 (EDT) news conference that Nobel Prize Winner BFA90 AJOMVR WMSS had altered the results of the experiments for which he received the prestigious science award.

#6 * * * * * * *

SAH PLANS BASH OF CENTURY .10

#6 * * * * * * *

A Hanoi spokesrep for Sah said this morning that over eleven hundred invitations to the pop singer's wedding have already been mailed; Cable Arts, Inc. will pipe the festivities worldwide.

#7 * * * * * * *

"MOMMY JUST SNAPPED," SAYS FIVE-YEAR-OLD .10

#7 * * * * * * *

The five-year-old girl who alone survived a Pittsburgh woman's homicidal rampage could offer MR/DPSec investigators no motive for her mother's behavior; the child is quoted as stating, "She just snapped."

#8 * * * * * * *

CCU TABS AID EMSISO FOR AD/NE/ CCU/DPI .10

#8 * * * * * * *

Saying, "His name on our ticket should increase CCU circulation by one hundred and fifty percent," an obviously elated spokesrep for the Citizens &

RANK HEADLINE price LEAD SENTENCE

Consumers United Party announced this morning that popular ho-soap star Aid Emsiso (ADM60 AYIPCX NAAA) will be its party's candidate for Associate Director, New England Region, CCU/DP Information.

#9 * * * * * * *

DACS DUE IN TIME .10
FOR TEA

#9 * * * * * * *

A spokesrep for the MIT/ToDai research project that first discovered the latest Dac starship to penetrate the solar system announced today that updated calculations predict an ETA of 1800 (EDT) on 25 June 2188.

#10 * * * * * * *

LAB INTROS AID TO .10
TELESENSORS

#10 * * * * * * *

Upjohn/Squibb labs has gained final ST/DPDrugs approval for "TeleBetter," a capsule claimed to increase both interface sensitivity and powers of concentration in telesensors; the ST/DPD action will allow the drug to reach the market immediately.

This update has been provided as a public service by all data management corporations participating in NEWSBANK/ST, a news data base organized and supervised by the Social Technology Directorate of Public Information.

To read any of the above news stories in full, simply highlight the title and press ACCEPT. The article will be transmitted to your unit's memory. Your bank balance will be debited by the sum in the column headed "price."

To see the headlines of the day's other news stories, simply scroll your screen up.

Thank you, and do be careful.

III

"Oh, no." This was not Ale's day for appliances. Bouncing to his feet, he slid the keyboard onto its shelf. In the ceiling, a panel retracted. He took a deep breath. The door to the matter transceiver thunked shut. He ran for the corridor. That door was swinging—

Its edge nicked his left shoulder as he burst through.

BEEPEEPEEP

"Dammit!"

A mechanically courteous voice said, #Five minutes to start of shift, Mr. Ale Elatey.#

I'll be there.

#Very good, sir.#

Rubbing his shoulder, he walked along the corridor to Emdy's open office door. Even from there he could hear the hiss of the fire extinguishers. *At least I got out in time.*

Emdy looked up from her screen. "All done?"

"Yeah, I think so. You'll have to read it before you send it out, but *I* think it's pretty good." He winked at her. "Of course, I usually do. . . . A couple things, though. That damn pholo just shorted out again—"

"Is *that* what that strangled squawk was all about?" She leaned back in her chair and laughed.

"It was not a strangled squawk. An exclamation of heartfelt dismay, maybe, but a strangled squawk? Never. Anyway, I've got to get to work. Can you call the company?" At her nod, he went on. "The other thing is, the guy who answered the pholo at the Coalition office here claims Yuai Bethresicks doesn't work there. Now, I don't know if that's a bureaucratic screwup or if the guy who came was an impostor—"

"He wasn't. I put his ID/dress card through the reader before I let him in. He was genuine."

"Then somebody screwed up. But the point is, if this is the

kind of thing that draws the Coalition's attention, I was thinking it might be better to clear the article with them before we bank it. You know? Just to save ourselves some hassle."

She shook her head so vehemently that her blonde hair fanned out like a skater's skirt. "You know them—they'll sit on it till two hundred uncleared articles have shown up about it, and we wouldn't make back our storage costs. Forget it. Something like this, the worst they'll do to us afterwards is say we should have submitted it to them for clearance. Don't worry about it."

"Okay." He shrugged. "Call it up and do your thing." He cocked his head and listened. The extinguishers had stopped sputtering. "I've got to get to work."

"Remember to air the room out."

"Right. And, thanks." He blew her a kiss, and went back down the dog-leg corridor to his study. The knob turned easily: the fire alarm had judged the room safe for entry. It was chilly, though, and the air was so full of carbon dioxide that he panted while crossing the room. *Good for the plants, but I wish I had a window in here.* . . . He pulled back the door to the massie, leaned into its cubicle to open the one to the kitchen, then hit the switch for the exhaust fan. A dry gentle breeze tickled his ankles when the fan overhead came on. He nodded, and went to his recliner.

Pushing it all the way back, he closed his eyes. He wriggled around till his hips settled in the appropriate hollows. With a slow gentle rub of his eyeballs, he passed into his mountain.

Hi, he said, once he reached the ledge.

#Good afternoon, Mr. Ale Elatey. Nothing for you yet, I'm afraid.#

I can wait. Seeleys got used to idling away the hours until a question came their way. Opinions, Research, Advice: Computer-Linked Experts—ORA:CLE, Inc.—charged dearly for the services of its CLE's; probably less than one percent of the world's ten billion people could afford to call on them. And even they were not about to spend upwards of a hundred dollars every time something piqued their curiosity.

Emdy's voice murmured around the corner, barely penetrating his quasi-trance. She spoke in English, though; he presumed she was calling the pholo company's repair service.

He hoped Yuai would get back to them soon. If somebody meant Ale harm, he wanted to know who and why as soon as possible.

The Oracle cut in with its perfect diction: #What was the most significant cause for the failure of nineteenth century, Ch'ing Dynasty China to adopt a modernization program as successful as that of Japan's?#

The monitor tweeted; he slapped the arm of his recliner in disgust.

REPLY PROHIBITED, said the Coalition's computer.

"Asshole." He said it to the apartment, not the interface. The Coalition did not condone on-line vulgarity, either.

The Oracle stayed silent. Ale would have to deal with the computer himself.

I appeal that ruling. Having invoked the evasion formula five or six times a week for the last year—since the Coalition had placed its ORA:CLE/Monitor program on line—he could recite it by heart: *The answer will be based substantially upon data available to the general public, and in no way offers any aid, comfort, or information to the enemy.*

PROCEED, THEN.

Normally, he had to research, extract, compile, and analyze to find an answer—which was why he received at least fifty per query—but for the late Ch'ing, he had merely to . . . well, what it *felt* like was that he shifted his stance until the mountain dissolved into a city-sized library, through the stacks of which he ran at the speed of light in search of the right book, a portion of which he read aloud. What he *did* do was access the Ivy League Remote Data Base for his Ph.D. thesis, a few paragraphs of which he read, slowly, carefully, and with just a trace of sub-vocalization so ORA:CLE's transceiver would pick him up clearly.

In Confucian political science, Tien—*the guiding principles of the universe, loosely translated as "Heaven"—bestowed upon an Emperor a mandate to rule; without it, no one had true authority. Possession of the mandate was "proven" by widespread prosperity; natural disasters and politico/military setbacks suggested that it had been withdrawn. As the nineteenth century brought China a succession of natural catastrophes, internal rebellions, and external humiliations, the Chinese came to believe that the Ch'ing Dynasty had lost favor with the universe. Once perceived as illegitimate, the Dynasty could not convince the people to supplant old ways with new. Therefore, modernization programs failed, repeatedly, until Mao inherited the Mandate of Heaven in 1949.*

In Japan, however, by usurping power and ruling for cen-

turies, the Shogunate had preserved the legitimacy of the Im-
perial House while gradually forfeiting its own. When the Meiji
Emperor swept the Shogun aside and reasserted Imperial au-
thority, he was perceived as the rightful ruler, and received
all the popular approval he needed.

He dismissed the thesis. As he switched back to The Oracle's
channel, bright static burst in his mind. *What the hell was that?*
he wondered, then fell silent to await the client's evaluation of
the answer.

"This way." Emdy's heels clicked on the kitchen tiles; behind her rumbled motor-driven wheels.

He parted his eyelids. Into his field of vision moved a blurry
gleam: the pholo company repair cart. While part of him stayed
tuned to The Oracle, he closed his eyes so he could listen to
Emdy.

"He said the light went out, then the whatchamacallit up
there started to smoke. It got hot enough to trigger the fire
extinguishers."

"That's the third unit in this building today that's happened
to. . . . You guys didn't buy a service contract from whoever
built this place, did you?"

"No. I bring it up with the landlady every time I see her,
but she doesn't want to pay."

"I got the same kind of landlord. Only my building, the
wiring's fine, it's the water you got to watch out for." Tools
rattled. "Once in a while we get a nice dose of industrial waste
the sensors don't pick up. The builder says, we buy a service
contract from him, everything works the way it's supposed to;
we don't, it's our tough luck. Had a guy die six months ago,
some kind of weird chemical in his coffee. I buy bottled,
myself." Gears whirred. "Hey, listen, lady, I'm telling another
unit across town—got a couple guys out today with the hic-
cups—and I'd like to put this one on automatic."

"Fine by me," said Emdy.

"Well, yeah, but the thing is, your man there? If he wakes
up and finds me here—I mean, what's he on, anyway? Or is
he just simpled out?"

"He's a Seeley."

"Oh. . . ." It sounded embarrassed. "Ho-kay. Sorry about
that. But there was this squashhead, you know? Came out of
the john, found my cart in his bedroom. The cart was on auto.
Well, I don't know what he thought it was, but by the time
my board flashed the malfunc light, he'd rolled the cart upside

down and torn its wheels off. When the blue got there, the cart was scrap, just sweep it up for the resike. Boy, 'd I get pinked for that one. Anyway, lemme get going on this—"

#The client reports satisfaction,# said The Oracle.

Why didn't you just route it to the data base? That's all I did.

The program had the appropriate response ready: #The client addressed the question to you personally, Mr. Ale Elatey.#

In his throat he made a sound with equal parts of a cough, a snort, and a laugh.

The Oracle's Conversation Program paused for judicious subroutine selection. Ale really wished it would not do that.

#Very well, then—to your code name—which is gaining a reputation for insight and accuracy. You should have realized that when your rates went up.#

Am I good enough to know my own code name yet?

#Of course not.# Its mechanical tone mimicked asperity. #"Truth is palatable to power—"#

Yeah, I know, "—only when the truthful remain unknown." But ancient Asian history, for Chrissakes? The Coalition seems to be cutting in on every other question these days.

#Once every four point seven times.#

He made no reply; the switchboard stayed silent. It would not speak until another query on "East Asia: 1500–2000 AD" closed a circuit. Even then it would debit the questioner's bank account before relaying the inquiry.

His eyes were still closed. The darkness hung like a blackout curtain while the repair cart, now on automatic, hummed and clanked and clattered.

He wanted to watch it—it fascinated him that machines could conduct complex repairs without human guidance—but the current returned to let the voice roll out: #Given that the Mao Interregnum attempted to eradicate Confucian political philosophy, is the concept of *Tien* in any way applicable to its toppling in the late twentieth century?#

Yes.

The program waited for amplification. After a few moments' silence it said, #The client deserves a more complete answer than that.#

Oh, all right. He paused to array his thoughts. *Put briefly, the Interregnum was respected for its vigor, but was, ultimately, judged in terms of* Tien: *the wars lost to Russia, Viet Nam, and Hong Kong cast its legitimacy in doubt; the nation's poverty relative to the capitalist economies of Japan, Korea, Taiwan, and Hong Kong made it seem less in harmony with the universe than they; and then, in 1996, a catastrophic earthquake leveled Peking. This was seen as especially symbolic given the emphasis that Mao and his successors had placed on the then-fledgling art/science of earthquake prediction. When the bureaucracy, crippled by the loss of its top people, doubled taxes in the unaffected provinces, yet could not save ten million people from dying of famine in the Peking-Tientsin metropolitan area, uprisings began, spread, and brought down the government. The Mandate had passed irrevocably.*

#The client reports satisfaction, Mr. Ale Elatety.#

Fine. Anything else?

#Not yet. Will you stay on line?#

For a while, yeah. He wanted to crawl backwards out of that vast interior chamber, so he could lay the keyboard on his lap again and return once more to the dry wit and keen eye of Tan Wang Ch'i, but he could hardly afford to knock off work after only two questions. *Let's see if anybody else calls in.*

#Very good, sir.#

The voice died away. For a moment he sat, alone and pensive on the dark ledge, then changed position. The mountain dissolved. He stood—hung, rather—in the midst of nothing.

Uncomfortable, he sketched a setting: yellow sun, blue sky, brown earth beneath his feet stretching flat and featureless to a curving horizon. . . . Much better. He sank into a tailor's cross-legged stance, moved his hands through the air, and created a wide, shallow pot. He lifted it to the light. The air grew warm; he summoned a breeze. The pot's bottom lacked a drainage hole. He jabbed at its center; where his finger touched, baked clay vanished. "All right," he murmured. "Some pea gravel—" it rattled into the pot to a depth of two centimeters "—and some potting soil." When he snapped his fingers, the soil filled the pot with its rich black fluffiness. "And now, I think—yeah, okay . . . another azalea."

It sprouted at once, spreading its seed leaves like a butterfly extending new wings to dry. A moment later, true leaves appeared—

"Speed it up."

—and another a dozen a bud a burst of flame six branches thirty leaves—

"Whoah."

Growth stopped.

Squinting at the young bush, he inscribed a circle in the air with his forefinger. The pot revolved as though on a turntable. Three-quarters of the way around, it stopped when he held up his hand.

This was definitely the front. Or would be, when the azalea had reached fuller growth. But that branch there, the one angling back and to the right—no, it had to come out.

Staring at it, he snapped his fingers. The branch disappeared.

"Nice. . . ." But there was something else—

#Mr. Ale Elatey.#

"Damn." *Coming*. "Store this."

click

Back on the ledge, peering into a darkness alive with the whispers and buzzes of all the other Seeleys on call, he said, *What is it?*

#Query: What similarities do you see between mid-Ch'ing China and the present day?#

It struck him as odd that the Coalition's ORA:CLE/Monitor Program did not intervene. He gave a silent shrug. *Defining "mid-Ching" as 1750 to 1839—i.e., after the Manchu royalty became Sinicized, but before the first Opium War—a number of surface similarities become apparent immediately. Among them are a long period of relative peace, both internally and externally; a massive growth in population; technical and scientific stagnation—*

CORRECTION REQUIRED.

He groaned. *To offer an opinion*, he quoted, *is within the scope of my expertise, and therefore no correction is required.*

The monitor program mulled that over for a moment. CORRECTION UNNECESSARY: QUALIFICATION MANDATORY. CIRCUIT BROKEN UNTIL QUALIFICATION FORTHCOMING.

The monitor program was beginning greatly to aggravate him. And that was bad. Hormonal disturbances like those churned up by anger shook his equilibrium, and made interface more difficult. He took three deep breaths, but light was infiltrating the cavern—

Emdy said, "What are you doing?" and then, after a moment, in an annoyed grumble: "I forgot; you're on auto."

Interface almost failed right then. After four more deep breaths, he said, *What sort of qualification is required?*

TWO-FOLD. (A) THAT STATEMENT RE: STAGNA-

TION, TECHNICAL & SCIENTIFIC, IS SOLELY PER-
SONAL OPINION. (B) THAT CERTIFICATE OF
EXPERTISE IN MODERN WORLD HISTORY HAS NOT
BEEN BESTOWED.

In the background rose a hum. He fought to keep it from
his awareness, to keep it from disrupting further his tenuous
hold on interface—

Sheet metal clanged. Concentrating, he—

"Ale!"

His forehead hurt, but he—

"Ale!"

A hand slapped his cheek.

He snapped aware. His wife stood before him, hand out for
another swing. "Emdy! What the hell—" He stopped abruptly.
Smoke tainted the air. A scorch mark ran along the wall to his
left. It ended in a hole burned right through the particleboard.
And his forehead ached. "What happened?"

"Your pholo almost killed you."

TOP TEN NEWS STORIES OF THE HOUR

15 June 2188, 1500 EDT
New England Region

RANK HEADLINE	price	LEAD SENTENCE
#1 LM2 PREXY MURDERED ON MOON	.25	BHK30 BHXNDP JUH2, long-time President of Lunar Mining and Manufacturing, Inc., died moments ago at ground-breaking ceremonies for LM2's new factory, as three assassins, in full view of hovee cameras, held witnesses at bay and sliced his air suit open.
#2 * * * * * * COMPUTER CRASH COSTLY	.20	#2 * * * * * * Twelve lives, $40,000,000, and an elephant were lost at 1134 (EDT) this morning as a result of the crash of a Mao-Com supervised computer net centered around Wichita, Kansas.
#3 * * * * * * FEARS RISING IN MIAMI AS EVAC PLODS FORWARD	.15	#3 * * * * * * Evacuation crews working to remove the population of South Florida from the reach of Hurricane Dora have flown only twenty percent of the region's population to safety, embarrassed Social Tech officials admitted this morning.
#4 * * * * * * DOW ENDS DAY UP	.10	#4 * * * * * * At the close of today's

trading, the Dow Jones Industrial Average finished up 0.56, on a volume of one hundred ninety-eight million shares.

#5 * * * * * * *

DI FEH FATOOH ALL THERE, SAYS SAH .10

#5 * * * * * * *

At a hastily called 1230 (EDT) news conference, a spokesrep for Sah denied persistent rumors that the pop singer's intended is a permanent resident of the Da Nang Hostel for the Incurably Senile.

#6 * * * * * * *

TOKYO-OSAKA SAFEPATH UNSAFE AT ANY ALTITUDE .10

#6 * * * * * * *

Coalition investigators revealed earlier this afternoon that the radio beacons defining the safepath between Tokyo and Osaka had been tampered with, presumably by streeters retaliating for last month's sweep.

#7 * * * * * * *

AID EMSISO NEW AD/NE DEEP INFO .10

#7 * * * * * * *

Ho-soap star Aid Emsiso won big on his first foray into electoral politics today, not only outpolling the other candidate for the CCU post by a large majority, but also increasing CCU enrollment in the New England region by thirty-eight percent.

#8 * * * * * * *

NEW DRUG REAPS MILLIONS FOR DRUG FIRM .10

#8 * * * * * * *

In a news release geared at quelling stockholder dissatisfaction with upper management, Upjohn/ Squibb Labs reported that sales of its new product "TeleBetter" are running at a pace of $18,000,000 a day.

RANK HEADLINE	price	LEAD SENTENCE
#9 * * * * *		#9 * * * * * *
COALITION 'SCOPE CONFIRMS LATEST ARRIVAL	.10	In a brief 1430 (EDT) announcement, a spokesrep for the Coalition's Directorate of Public Research confirmed the MIT/ToDai sighting of a sixth Dac vessel, and agreed with their estimate as to its arrival time.
#10 * * * * * *		#10 * * * * * *
NEW HAVEN MAN KILLS DAC	.10	ALL80 AFAHSC NFF6, a New Haven resident and terrace gardener, killed a Dac that attacked him while he was watering his bonsai, Ale reported in a recent copyrighted article; informed sources say he is a Seeley specializing in East Asian History.

IV

—1—

Next door, old Mrs. M'ti Emtenne screamed. Her wail—high, wheezy, and hoarse—blared loud enough to scrape most vocal cords raw. "Arthur! Oh my God my Arthur Arthur my God! Police! Poh-leeeeeeece!"

Emdy paled. "I didn't know, I . . ." At her feet, the repair cart stood immobile. "Lord, if I've hurt her—"

"Her angelfish." He winced, and wished he had not, for it hurt to tighten the skin across his forehead. "If I remember right, Arthur's tank was on the bookcase on the other side of this wall—just about where the hole is. Oh, God." He sagged back in his recliner. "What do you mean, my pholo tried to kill me?"

"When I came in, to tell you that I'd banked your article, the cart was having trouble putting the cover back on the laser housing. Maybe something was in the wrong position. So it plugged the thing in, I guess to get the motor loose, and all of a sudden the housing swung to point at you. I didn't think anything of it—until it hummed and the laser tube pulsed and it hit you above and between the eyes. That's when I smacked it. It swiveled around and burned right through the wall before I got the plug out." She trembled, though her voice stayed steady. "Ale, what's going on today? If I hadn't come in—"

"Yeah." He said it softly, drawing it into an exhalation that was more a grateful breath than a word. "Jesus." He tried a laugh, but it came out weak and shaky. "What a follow-up that would make, huh? 'Man Escapes Dac Only to Fall to Pholo.' I don't believe—how could it *happen?*"

"It can't be accidental, not twice in one day." She nudged the cart with her foot. "This must have done something—"

"Sure, but why would it—"

#Mr. Ale Elatey? Is everything all right?#

Hold on a minute. "Listen, I have a client waiting for the rest of an answer—"

Exasperation flashed across her face. "Ale, I think somebody's trying to kill you—"

"C'mon, Doc, who'd want—"

Three solid thumps rattled the front door; a deep strong voice shouted, "Police! Open up!"

Emdy raised her hands in surrender. "You go put some salve on your forehead, I'll deal—"

From the terrace came a brief siren blast—a blue had landed.

Emdy said, "I'll bet she called Coalition DeePeeDefense, too."

"Probably." He pushed himself out of his chair. "If not person-to-person to Director Ohe Ainainine herself." A ripple of dizziness ran through him; he blinked, bowed his head, and touched the desktop for support.

"Ale, are you all right?"

"It's just been a godawful day, that's all. . . ." He straightened up with an effort. "I'll be okay in a minute. Why don't you handle them; I've *got* to answer this damn question."

"Will do." She passed through the matter transceiver room to get to the front door. He went the other way, the few steps down the hall to the bath.

Flicking on the light, looking in the mirror, he groaned. A brick-red line ran from a blister two centimeters above the bridge of his nose to his left temple. He smoothed salve onto it. The pain brought tears to his eyes.

#Mr. Ale Elatey?#

Just a minute, okay? We had another glitch here. . . .

#The client is impatient.#

The client can— But no, it was only his third query of the day, and three queries a day barely covered his half of the household expenses. *Please tell the client I'll be right with it.*

#Yes, sir.#

Back in his recliner, eyes closed and lungs pumping with a forced regularity, he slipped back into full interface. *Where was I?*

#You were about to provide the requisite qualifications.#

Oh, yeah. Ah . . . my statement concerning the technical and scientific stagnation of modern-day culture is, of course, solely my personal opinion, and should not be taken as the official viewpoint of either ORA:CLE, Inc., or the Coalition Direc-

torate of Public Education. Further, I am not now, nor have I ever been, a certified expert in modern world history. He waited.

Forty-five seconds later, the ORA:CLE/Monitor said, SATISFACTORY. CIRCUIT RE-ESTABLISHED. PROCEED.

Other readily apparent similarities—

#The client has disconnected.#

Oh, damn.

#Partial payment has been made.#

Well, that was better than nothing. But still. . . . He pushed the chair a notch farther back. The sting on his face was beginning to subside.

"It could have fried me! Look what it did to poor Arthur!"

He tried to shut out Mrs. M'ti Emtenne's voice. It was so damn high-pitched, though—and she was such an excitable old lady—that he would probably be slipping in and out of interface till the argument was over.

At least the Haven Manor cop stayed quiet and reasonable: "Lady, it's not her fault the thing went down. She said she's sorry, right? Right. You just have to stay calm. These things happen all the time. You know that, you've lived here fifteen years."

But Mrs. M'ti Emtenne remained as hysterical as a siren. "It could have been me!"

Concentrate. He shifted his narrow shoulders. He wished again that he could set up shop beneath a mossy-trunked maple. To hear the leaves, and feel the cool soil. . . . *Dream on.*

It was one of the few things for which he envied Tan Wang Ch'i: the muddle-headed, superstitious, goat-bearded old journalist had had the right to go outdoors any time he pleased.

Ale Elatey had never gone outdoors. As part of its drive to absorb excess carbon dioxide, the Coalition had not issued a ground-level permit in twenty years. Not even a five-minute snapshot pass. The smallest of weeds was too precious to bruise.

And the streeters were out there waiting.

Footsteps sounded in the kitchen. The cop said, "The guy in there's your husband?"

Mrs. M'ti Emtenne cut in. "Look at the legs on that loafer! Don't you think he could have moved so I would have—"

"He's a Seeley," said Emdy patiently, "and he was in interface, and if you want my opinion somebody tampered with—"

"I don't know what that has to do with my poor Arthur. He—"

"Lady, the point is, the machine broke. Mr. Ale Elatey there didn't do nothing. And he didn't get off so easy, either—see where he got burned? It's not his fault, so let's just let him get back to—" The door closed.

Ale relaxed. He had heard too many squabbles about defective appliances, ranging from immersion heaters on up to matter transceivers, and he hated the bickering. The aftermath never varied anyway. Once everybody calmed down, the cop would file a report. The pholo company would fix the thing. In three weeks the CCU/Directorate of Public Safety would shoot his computer a megabit questionnaire on the pholo and its maintenance record.

The door opened again. "—whole wall," Emdy was saying. "So when the pholo company comes to fix it—which I presume they will, since it was their equipment—I'll make sure they come next door and repair yours, too."

"I thought I'd have a heart attack!"

Ale cracked one eyelid a fraction. As he had thought: Mrs. M'ti Emtenne wore short-shorts. She had the ugliest legs . . . and absolutely nothing to do with her life but sunbathe, stroll the halls, and collect pension credits. Plus insist, in private, that her neighbors call her Madeleine.

"The way that laser flashed through the wall—"

"Well, I am sorry about that, but I've told you already, if I hadn't shoved it away, it would have killed my husband. Which I think was somebody's intention all along. I really didn't point it at you on purpose."

The cop said something in a low, quiet voice that The Oracle drowned out with its perfect diction: #Why should anyone waste its life studying the history of a culture that is not only dead, but has also had minimal influence on contemporary society?#

Over the years, a number of questions had come Ale's way, but this was the first insult. He was tired, twice-burned, and more than a little nervous. For a moment he reacted badly—interface wavered. Then he calmed himself enough to say, *The query contains three mistaken assumptions. First, the concept of "waste" is relative. If one devotes his life to studying East Asian history, one discovers that one has developed a marketable skill. People will pay for knowledge. An expert willing to accept the ORA:CLE implant can become a CLE; most Seeleys earn better than a living wage. Perhaps not as much as a blickstrobe champ, but rather more than the average telefactor.*

Second, East Asian culture is hardly dead. Altered, evolved, mutated, Westernized, yes—but it is the foundation on which modern Asian culture has arisen. Just as we Americans would be struck dumb if deprived of the Latinate words derived from the "dead" Roman culture, so would modern Asians react if denied the use of the Han Chinese that forms the basis of most of their languages.

Third, concerning its influence on modern-day culture—

#Please hold.#

Hold? A lot of things were happening for the first time today.

#It appears the client's parent has just discovered the client at the family's computer, and is loathe to allow an eleven-year-old to run our bill any higher.#

They shouldn't have given the kid the password. But he had to smile. Sooner or later every child demands that its teacher justify the time and effort it puts into its work—at five, Ale had insisted that his Read 'n' Write Program *prove* the undesirability of illiteracy—but the kid should have known better than to ask ORA:CLE, with its hundred dollar minimum ... unless it wanted a *truly* expert opinion....

#The client is satisfied.#

The client's parent, you mean.

#The client is always the bill-payer, sir.#

Ah.... Having nothing more to say, he called back the file in which he had stored the bonsai azalea. It solidified before his eyes; its petals glowed softly, cleanly green, as though fresh from a gentle rain. He motioned a branch into cautious growth—

"Ms. Emdy Ofivo! Yo! Hey, Ms. Emdy!" Gears whirred softly.

He cracked an eyelid. The repair cart's turret was swiveling from side to side. Hinges creaked as Emdy stepped through the matter transceiver into Ale's study. "Yes?"

"I'm back. What's the problem?"

"What's the problem? I just this minute finished telling—"

"My supervisor, I know, I know, that's why I'm here, but see, all they pass on is 'Malfunction, Emergency Repair Required,' and they don't tell me soggy doughnut holes about the malfunction itself, probably they figure they pay me to find out for myself what's wrong. So what's the problem?"

Ale closed his eyes and stored the bonsai. Listening off the side of his mind for The Oracle, he eavesdropped on Emdy and the repair cart.

"The problem is, you just tried to ki—"

"Wait. Let's get one thing clear, lady. *I* was on the other side of town; the cart here was on automatic. So whatever happened, the *cart* did it."

"Can you prove that?"

"You better believe it."

"Okay, fine. We'll play it your way. I walked in and you— *it* was trying to get the cover back on—" Her voice sank to a murmur as she recounted the incident.

"That's impossible!"

"Tell it to the hole in the wall."

"Yeah. . . . Something's real wrong here, you shouldn't be able to get that much power out of—" Something ratcheted up; a motor hummed briefly. "Well pink me off! An industrial laser tube! What the hell is it doing in here?" Glass clinked. "It's the only one that size in my bag, too. . . . Lemme quick replay—goddammit! I can't pull the files on this job, they're supposed to be recorded on my console but they went downtown instead. Have to get 'em from there. No wonder you're feeling paranoid, though. . . . Well, let's put in one the right size—" Metal holders, hissed on glass. "—check the wiring, yeah, looks fine, so we snap the cover shut and test 'er out."

"Not so fast."

"Now what's wrong?"

"Make sure it's pointing at something that can't be damaged. Or killed."

"Lady, the laser that's in there now—the one you *watched* me screw in—lady, that couldn't burn its way through a cobweb. Don't worry, huh?"

"But I *will* worry until it's working perfectly safely, and I think I have excellent reasons for it. Point it at that blank wall there."

"You're the boss."

"Thank you."

Something hummed. "You see? Nothing to worry about."

#Your shift has ended, Mr. Ale Elatey.#

Already?

#Yes.#

What did I make today?

#One hundred eighteen dollars and seventy-five cents, before withholding; sixty-seven dollars and thirty-three cents have been credited to your account.#

Gee, thanks. . . . It was not enough. His share of the basic living expenses alone came to seventy-two a day. *You need anybody on standby?*

#No.# But then, as if to soften its mechanical bluntness, it said, #Were we to call you anyway, would you return for a brief answer or two?#

You know it. Any time of day or night. As long as the money's right.

#Very well, then. Good night, Mr. Ale Elatey.#

Good ni— But it had already withdrawn from interface, leaving him alone on the dark ledge in the imaginary cavern. He turned around and came out into the light.

—2—

From the sounds floating down the dog-leg corridor, Emdy was talking to the Moroccans again.

Ale's pholo rang. He eyed it skeptically—then shrugged. He had heard Emdy and the repair cart operator okay the system. . . . Still in his chair, he answered it.

The sphere of light formed immediately in the center of the room. An older woman peered out of it at him; she had bushy eyebrows and a lantern jaw. "Nasty burn there, Ale."

He kept his sigh silent. "Hello, Mother."

"It's nice to know my only son is still alive—as he damn well better be, at least until he manages to provide me with a grandson. It's not so nice to find out—from that cigar-chewing old man down the hall, no less—that my only son almost became my late son."

"Almost doesn't count, Mother."

"You should have called and told me you were all right."

"By then it was all over, and I've been busy."

"If you had time to write an article for the Data Banks, you had time to call." She scowled. "At the very least, you could have sent me a complimentary copy of your article, instead of making me hunt through the Index so I could order my own copy."

"Mother—" He spoke through clenched teeth. "—first, you

can call up any article by the author's name; you don't need to—"

"Don't tell me how to run computers; I've been running them since thirty years before you were born. If I want to Index line by line, that's my prerogative, and you know it." She squinted out of the bubble at him. "I thought the burn was on your shoulder—was that poetic license, or what?"

"No, this—" He pointed to his forehead. "—was something else. A little trouble with the pholo." He shrugged. No sense getting her excited about it; she would only—

"You're still in that wretched building, aren't you?" At his nod, she slapped something before her, something out of camera range. A card table, by the sound of it. "I knew something like that would happen. If I've told you once, I've told you a thousand times, never—"

"—live anywhere that hasn't got a service contract with the builder. I know that. But you know what that does to the rent. It adds a thousand a month, right there. And frankly, for us, right now, that would be cutting it too thin. Later on, sure."

"Hah!" She glowered at him. "So how's your shoulder?"

"Just fine. The black bag did a good job; I hardly feel it."

"That's good." Out of camera, a light flashed, suffusing her left cheek in amber. "Ale, I have to go, the tournament's about to start."

"Okay. It's been—"

"It was a good article, Ale. You should make a lot of money off it."

"I hope so."

"And when you do, don't you *dare* spend it on more plants! You move into a better building right away, and then get to work on my grandson." She winked at him. "Not that it would be work, not with Emdy. I'll talk to you later."

The sphere dwindled and disappeared.

Ale shook his head, then got up and went to Emdy's office. She was tapping keys on her terminal, idly changing the parameters of a long equation.

"Hi."

She looked up, a smile crossing her face. "Done for the day?"

"Looks that way. And my pholo works—my mother just called."

She made a face, then sighed. "I'm sorry. Just that sometimes—"

"I know what you mean; it's okay." He decided not to tell her that his mother was tightening the grandchild screws again. "I heard some of what you and the cart were saying, but not all of it. Do they have any idea what happened?"

"At this point, no. Just guesses. Supposedly the whole thing's on bubble downtown, and the cart operator said he'd get back to us, but you know repair reps. . . . The only thing that's definite is that when the cart was on auto, it put in a bolt-cutter instead of a pholo laser."

"Uh-huh. So why did it focus on me?"

"A restraining band snapped."

"Come on."

She spread her hands. "All I know is what they told me, which is nôt to say I believe it. I don't. Not after what the Commander said. But they were very apologetic."

"How nice." He intended it to sound dry. "They going to repair the wall?"

"They advised us to route the bill to their Accounting Office." Her perfect teeth flashed in an impish smile. "I also argued them into paying for something to cover the burns until the repairs are made. They didn't like that at all, but then I started talking about trauma and mental anguish and very good lawyers."

He was surprised: she had seemed so calm throughout that he had not realized how much it had affected her. It made him feel guilty that he had thought only of himself and of his own close call. Walking over, he put his arms around her. "I'm sorry. I should have known you'd be shook up, too."

"Don't be silly." She rubbed against him, then wriggled free. "I told them it was *your* anguish . . . which," she said reflectively, "wasn't all that convincing, with you lost in contemplative bliss, but I said that that was just shock, and that you'd be shaking real good by the time the trial began." She winked at him. "They said I should buy a painting or something, if it'd calm your nerves."

"If they're going to buy me off," he said, "I'd rather have a nice old mugho pine, properly bonsai'd."

"Wouldn't have covered the scars, not sitting on the terrace. So . . ." She sank back into her chair, put her feet on her desktop, and beamed. "Remember that Japanese scroll you saw in the gallery catalog? I can never remember the guy's name, but—"

"Tomioka Tessai?" he said sharply.

"That's the one. It'll be transmatted tomorrow."

"My God, Doc, that's a hundred thousand dollar painting!"

"The pholo company's paying, remember?" She grinned like a child at a circus. "I thought that would cover the laser burn very nicely."

"You're incredible!" Torn between glee and disbelief, he clapped his hands once, loudly. "An original Tessai just to hide a hole in the wall? The pholo company will scream!"

"Let 'em," she said, her gaze sobering. "I almost lost you because of their stupidity—maybe they'll learn from the experience."

"Tomorrow, huh?" Eager, now, he paced the width of her office. "My God, a Tessai!" Closing his eyes, he visualized the scroll, with its swoops of ink stroking life into the background white. "Oh I can't wait! A Tessai. . . ."

"One other thing. After this refugee leaves, can we move? With your raise, and the article, and the profits off this phosphate deal—"

He stopped and spun. "Did that come through?"

"Ah-yup." Her smile split her cheeks. "We just finalized everything ten minutes ago. You are looking at a high-class wheeler and dealer, Ale Elatey."

"I've known that for a long time." Crossing to her desk, he pulled her to her feet and lifted her off the floor with a bone-rattling hug. "Congratulations! That's fantastic!"

"Isn't it just, though." She nibbled on his ear lobe. "Put me down before I chew this off completely and spoil my appetite."

He did. "So you want to move?"

"Yes. Most definitely."

He looked around the five-room apartment. "The thirty-eighth floor isn't low enough for you any more, huh? I heard about an opening on the sixteenth, we can ride down and inspect it."

"No." Her dark blue eyes looked out the windows to the building across the way. "We need more space, at least one more bedroom—and I'd like someplace with a real good service contract."

"I don't know. I mean, the expense—"

"We can afford it." She tapped the screen of her computer. "I ran off an analysis just before you came in. You want to see it?"

"No." He held up his hands. "I trust you; you do numbers better than I do."

"Well, then?"

"I suppose. . . ." He frowned. "Who do we have for DP Transportation, Social-Tech?"

"Uh—" She queried her computer. "Yeah, ST."

"Could be worse . . . still, even they take six months to process private applications, which makes the whole thing depressing to begin with. . . ." He remembered the nightmare the first six months of their marriage had been, sleeping on the living room couch at her parents' place while they waited for the bureaucracy to act. They had come close to a divorce right then. "I suppose so, though—as long as it's got a southern balcony, all right? I won't take a northern balcony, no way. Okay?"

"You and your damn plants." She made a theatrical, heaven-imploring gesture meant to show she was teasing him.

"And you'll do the applications?"

"My pleasure."

"Okay, let me get dinner started." The pholo in his study rang.

"*I'll* start dinner; you get the machine."

Turning into the hall, he checked his watch: 1945 EDT. "I don't know who it could be this late—"

"Maybe it's Yuai Bethresicks, finally getting back to you."

"I didn't leave a message."

"With CoaIntel, you don't need to. Beans or peas?"

"Beans." He slipped into the recliner and flicked on the pholo.

An albino head took shape in the sphere of light: L'ai Aichtueni. Her pink eyes had the flat unfocused stare of squash. "Hello, Ale."

He stifled a groan. "Evening, Doctor."

She frowned. "That's 'Water' to my friends."

"Uh, yeah, that's right. Sorry. What can I do for you?"

"There's an opening in the Social Tech Directorate of Connecticut Public Education; I'd like to get your name on the ticket—"

"No," he said quickly.

"Ale, you'd be perfect! You're a scholar, temporarily well-known, and I'll bet you'd boost our enrollment by ten percent."

The door from the matter transceiver into the study opened, and Emdy appeared behind the holographic caller. She drew a finger across her throat.

Apparently L'ai saw Ale's gaze shift. "Did your wife just come in?"

He nodded. "It's dinner time."

"Oh, I am sorry. I always eat early because it leaves my evenings free for ah, other things. . . . So what do you say? Will you—"

"Water, I really have to go, I'm starving. Been nice talking to you." With a final smile and nod, he hit the disconnect button. The ball of light imploded. "Sheesh! How can someone get so thoroughly on your nerves after such a short acquaintance?"

"I warned you about her. My folks are on the other line; they want to talk to you, too."

"Living room?" He got to his feet. "Or your office?"

"Living room. I'll hold dinner for a couple more minutes."

"Thanks." He headed for the doorway to the hall—and just as he reached it, the pholo behind him buzzed. "Dammit!"

"It's the price of fame, Ale. I'll get this one; you say hi to my parents."

By the time he had finished assuring Emdy's mother and father that he was in excellent shape, both physically and mentally, a call had come in on Emdy's office line. He fielded it on his way back to the study—and found himself talking to the computer that interpreted for a burly South American who wanted to know if he would speak, via satellite transmission, to a class of xenobiologists at the University of Buenos Aires. Then to the study, where a London teenager wanted him to confirm the teenager's belief that Dacs were really robots. Back to the living room and a red-nosed businessman who offered him fifty thousand dollars for the beak of the Dac. "Fifty thousand? It's all yours!" But when he went to the terrace—ignoring the pholos ringing in the study and Emdy's office—the beak was gone. The businessman accused him of trying to drive up the price, called him three terse obscene names, and hung up. Back to the study—

Emdy stopped him in the corridor. "Ale, I'm putting a screen on the lines—is there anybody you would definitely want to talk to tonight?"

"Not that I can think of," he said after a moment. "Just Yuai Bethresicks, I guess. And family, of course."

"Consider it done."

By the time he finished the last two calls—one from a

religious fanatic who accused him of murdering an angel of the Lord; the other from a Canadian who thought Ale really should lengthen the article into a book—Emdy had raised the screens and the pholos stopped ringing.

"And I also pulled a quick royalty statement," she said, as they sat at last to a dinner that the oven had kept warm, if not moist and tender. "You've sold ninety thousand copies of that article already."

"At a dime apiece?"

"A nickel—the banks take a nickel for transmission charges and all."

"But still, that's, uh..." His calculator was in the study. He dipped a finger in the water glass and sketched the numbers on the shiny formica of the tabletop. "Forty-five hundred, that's not bad."

"You forgot that sixty-three percent goes for taxes." She smiled in quiet amusement as he wrinkled his face. To figure five percent of ninety with a wet finger and a smooth surface is easy; thirty-seven per cent of forty-five is not.... "I already worked it out—it's sixteen hundred sixty-five dollars. Give or take a couple of cents, because it's not exactly sixty-three percent."

"But still..." He rolled the numbers over in his head. Sixteen hundred and sixty-five. One thousand, six hundred, sixty-five. One. Six. Six. Five. For two hours work! "You know, Doc?"

"What?"

"I think I see how I'll be able to afford that new bonsai, now...."

She chuckled. "And the article hasn't hit its circulation peak yet, either."

"It hasn't?"

She looked at the wall clock. "I put that into the bank at what, two o'clock? Two-thirty? The circ peak on a news item like this comes about, I can't remember exactly, but about eleven and a half hours after the item's banked."

"Then it cuts off, huh?"

"No, Ale." With a sigh, she rose from her seat, came over to him, and leaned over his shoulder. Sticking her finger in his water glass—

"Hey!" He tugged the lock of blonde hair that hung before him. "That's my water you're contaminating there."

"You did it."

"That's different."

"Hush. Look." She drew a bell curve on the tabletop. "See up here? That's banking time plus eleven and a half hours. That's when you get your maximum orders per minute. Then the opm taper off for the next eleven and a half hours until you're almost back to zero opm. Although it'll never hit absolute zero; you'll still be getting orders six months from now. Just not very many. All right?"

"I guess." Looking at the squiggle, he wondered how much money it represented. Clearly, it would be much more than he had already earned. A pleasing thought, that. They could use the money—to pay the mover, to buy new furniture (surely their next apartment would have more rooms), perhaps even to buy *two* bonsai. . . .

And yet it was a discouraging thought, as well. Here, after devoting so much of his life to becoming an expert on East Asia, two hours writing the story of his good fortune proved more profitable than three weeks practicing his profession.

Emdy touched his wrist lightly. "What's the matter?"

He looked into her deep blue eyes, and gave a small shrug. "Just thinking, I ought to do this more often."

She laughed. "There's lots of people who spend years trying to do it once."

"Yeah?"

"Millions. And the ones who get rich are the ones who are lucky enough to be nearby when something dramatic—something important—something heartwarming happens. And that's not easy to arrange, you know? To have real news occur right off your balcony. . . . This is a piece of good luck, Ale, but don't expect lightning to strike twice. Okay?"

"I won't." Standing, he picked up his plate and silverware, and carried them over to the sink.

She moved to the counter. "Coffee?"

"Yea—no. I'm jumpy enough; I don't need anything else that might keep me awake."

She poured tea for herself and carried it out into the living room. "Ale, don't you have the windows on auto?"

"Yeah." Drying his water glass, he stepped to the doorway. Through the large glass windows the lights of New Haven sparkled. Moonlight spattered the terrace. "Well, I thought I did."

"Why haven't they polarized yet?"

"These circuit glitches are driving me crazy. . . . Hit the button."

She did. The view faded as the window panes turned black, shimmered a moment, and silvered. "That did it."

"It usually does." He began to stack the dinner dishes in the drainer. "We're going to have to get a new photocell, I think—that's the fourth or fifth time this week that it's screwed up. This morning the room was black."

"Can you fix it, or do we have to call a cart?"

"All you do is screw it in." He yawned as he walked into the living room. "Hey, Doc, this has been a real long day—I think I'm going to call it a night."

"Would you like some company?"

"As long as the company remembers that the anesthetic is beginning to wear off. And that the forehead of the accompanied is quite tender to the touch."

She snapped her fingers twice; the table lamp went off. "The accompanied—" She got up from the sofa and walked toward him. "The accompanied should know that his forehead is about the last thing the company plans to touch." She grinned.

So did he.

—3—

He awoke to a sound that was mostly roar with a touch of high whine; the windows shivered in frames too tight for rattles. "Time," he called. On the ceiling, cool-green numerals half a meter tall glowed 0659.

Almost time to get up anyway. In sixteen minutes the alarm clock would spill soft music, the windows would slowly clear to admit the bright June morning, and Emdy Ofivo, burying her face in the pillows, would mumble that she had changed her mind, he should re-set the windows and come back to get her in an hour.

So he would re-set them, and tip-toe gladly out of the room. He liked his first hour alone. He could sip coffee, skim the headlines, and map out what he wanted to do later. By the time he returned to the bedroom to tickle her awake, he would be well into a normal day.

He lay on his back. Overhead the clock began to fade into invisibility, there to wait until summoned again. He slipped his hands behind his head, under the pillow, and yawned.

Let's see, get up, start the percolator, showershavebrush-myteeth (yawn) *what the hell is that out there, sounds like helis bringing in a building.*

He sat up abruptly, the sheets falling into his lap. Emdy stirred, grumbled in her sleep, and tugged the sheets back up over her bare shoulder. "Sorry," he whispered.

Eyes wide and morning alertness surging into him, he slipped out of bed and re-set the machinery. Then he paused, debating whether or not to awaken Emdy now, discounting her protests in advance. They had a refugee coming—those helis had to be carrying the people from Florida—and she would probably want to be up, dressed, and on the outside of a mug of tea before a stranger moved into her house.

Ah, but she would, in any event, stay in bed until he had finished in the bathroom, so he would wait till then to rouse her. He moved quietly into the hallway, and closed the door behind himself.

Dark silence lay to his right as he stepped out of the bedroom: the photocell had failed again. With a muffled curse, he walked the three meters to the perimeter of the living room and snapped his fingers. The lamp on the end table nearest him lit up. He crossed to the apartment's control center and depolarized the windows.

Brightness entered, but no direct sun, not yet, not at this time of day and year. Still, it was enough to make him blink. He turned his head for a moment, giving his eyes time to adjust, then looked out and up.

On its way to the sky, his gaze swept over the bonsai. Instinctively he noted that the Japanese maple had lost a leaf or two overnight. The rest stood gnarled and proud.

But inspection could wait. A stream of helis chopped its way out of the southeast, presumably from the New York airports. They flew well below the three-thousand-meter mark at which the Dacs would open fire. He squatted to widen his field of vision and counted the huge black shapes quickly before they passed overhead. Twenty-six, no seven, and more roaring up from New York. *They must be moving all of South Florida up here,* he thought. *Bet every household in Connecticut gets a refugee today.*

Even though the helis were whirring north, he hurried to the bathroom. Given the fleet of vehicles ST/Deep Trans had at its command, one of them would soon begin to disgorge its four hundred passengers on the roof of Ale's building.

Showering, he studied his shoulder. Still tender to the touch, and pink around the seams of the Falskin, it flexed easily, and looked well on its way toward complete recovery.

As did his forehead, when he faced the mirror to shave. He applied more salve—wincing slightly—then stopped, open-mouthed. After a moment he began to grin.

My Tessai's coming today! It's coming today!

As the stinging eased into perfumed numbness, something else occurred to him. He laughed, clapped his hands, and would have whooped had he not remembered, just in time, that Emdy was still asleep.

And I'll bet I've got enough royalties now to buy a super good bonsai!

He could not wait for his morning coffee. Or for his clothes, even. Towel wrapped loosely around his waist and held in place by a clenched left fist, he dashed down the corridor to his study, leaving on the carpet dark moist prints that the fabric slowly absorbed.

He sat in his chair, snatched the keyboard, and flicked the machine on. Calling up the royalties program, he typed in "Dac Attack" and ran it. The screen winked. Numbers danced. The program formatted a royalty statement for his inspection. He read it slowly.

And whistled softly.

In the preceding sixteen hours, one million, one hundred fifty-nine thousand, eight hundred eighty people had ordered copies of "Dac Attack."

After all deductions, his share came to $21,457.78 ± $1.23.

He did not understand that ± $1.23, but the rest of the statement came through clear as a bell: he was rich.

Well, not rich, not exactly—but my God, I've never had so much money in my account in my life! Twenty-one thousand! I don't believe it. There has to be a catch. Something glitched up somewhere and—

The doorbell rang.

"Dammit!" He shut off the machine. The damp bath towel-sarong slipped as he got up. Suddenly self-conscious, he hurried to the bedroom for a robe.

By the time he got back to the living room, the front door stood open. As did the the coat closet immediately to its right, the closet hidden from the rest of the room by the meter-tall planter from which grew diffenbachia, dracaena, and schefflera. But something moved behind the foliage.

Ale froze. Was this the DacWatch tamperer, back to finish the job? For a moment he did not know what to do. Call for help? But the built-in liquor cabinet offered a solution.

Cautiously, he opened its small doors—holding his breath because he *knew* a hinge would creak—and withdrew an empty cut-glass decanter. He hefted it. It would probably shatter, but not before stunning the intruder.

Or killing it.

Weapon high, he moved.

TOP TEN NEWS STORIES OF THE HOUR

16 June 2188; 0800 EDT
New England Region

RANK HEADLINE	price	LEAD SENTENCE
#1 KANSAS COMPUTER CRASH HITS CHICAGO	.20	As desperate Mao-Com technicians battled to shunt processing operations to other networks, the computer crash that began last night in Wichita disrupted Chicago air traffic early this morning.
#2 * * * * * * MYSTERY BLAST ROCKS GIBRALTAR	.15	#2 * * * * * * An explosion of unknown origins shook this island between the Atlantic and the Mediterranean Oceans at 0637 (EDT) this morning; authorities claim to have neither explanations nor suspicions.
#3 * * * * * * BOY SNAPS, SLAYS EIGHT	.10	#3 * * * * * * A twelve-year-old Parisian schoolboy, angry at being ejected from his high-rise's sauna, locked the sauna door and turned the thermostat up to one hundred degrees Celsius, said a spokesrep for the Paris MR/DP Security this morning.
#4 * * * * * * NO SUSPECTS IN LM2 MURDER	.10	#4 * * * * * * As expected, Luna ST/DP Security forces report no progress in tracking down

the murderers of BHK30 BHXNDP JUH2, popular long-time President of Lunar Mining & Manufacturing, Inc.

#5 * * * * * *

DAC KILLER BEST SELLER

.10

#5 * * * * * *

ALL80 AFAHSC NFF6, the New Haven man who yesterday escaped death at the claws of a Dac, has risen to the best-seller charts with his first-person account of his good fortune.

#6 * * * * * *

AID EMSISICKS SAVES BIG BUCKS IN DPI REVAMP

.10

#6 * * * * * *

Aid Emsisicks, hastily promoted from Aid Emsiso, announced this morning a reorganization of the CCU's Directorate of Public Information that, Emsisicks claims, will save its voters half a billion annually in regulatory expenses.

#7 * * * * * *

STREETERS FACE WRATH OF TOKYO

.10

#7 * * * * * *

Outraged by charges that a jetliner was shot down because street people tampered with safepath beacons, an *ad hoc* umbrella group of Tokyo parties launched an unauthorized sweep of suburban hideouts late last night, Tokyo time.

#8 * * * * * *

NEW DAC NO CHANGE, SAYS PROBE

.10

#8 * * * * * *

Further reports from the MIT/ToDai robot observatory near Pluto say the latest addition to the Dac armada at L5 is virtually identical to the five already parked there.

RANK	HEADLINE	price	LEAD SENTENCE

#9 * * * * * * *

NEW PARTY FORMS IN ST. LOUIS   .10

#9 * * * * * * *

Citing long years of neglect and discrimination, Mississippi rafters established The American Boat Party at their annual convention in St. Louis last night; the party's ostensible goal is to ensure that as much cargo as possible is carried via water, and that boats be provided with the latest in anti-Dac technology.

#10 * * * * * *

SOCIOLOGIST SAYS TOP TEN IS NEW LOW   .10

#10 * * * * * *

In a report to be read at the Eighty-third International Conference of Sociologists, Dr. MDU90 BKBUTE J1PM accuses major newsbanks of "pandering to the sensationalistic appetites of the multitudes by providing the news that they *want* to see, rather than the news they *should* see."

This update has been provided as a public service by all data management corporations participating in NEWSBANK/MV, a news data base organized and supervised by the Marian-Vegetarian Directorate of Public Information.

To read any of the above news stories in full, simply highlight the title and press ACCEPT. The article will be transmitted to your unit's memory. Your bank balance will be debited by the sum in the column headed "price."

To see the headlines of the day's other news stories, simply scroll your screen up.

Thank you, and do be careful.

V

The foliage parted. A wrinkled, coppery-skinned face popped through—"Hi! Wait a minute."—then disappeared. Boot heels grated on the parquet floor. An old, small man with long black braids emerged, right hand outstretched. "You must be Al Elaeto. I'm Wef DiNaini, your refugee." Fatigue rasped his medium-high voice. "Let myself in; hope you don't mind."

Nonplussed, Ale set the decanter down and automatically shook the proffered hand. Hard and thin, it gripped firmly and withdrew at once. "How the hell did you get in?"

Wef shrugged. "Your locks're all computer-driven." His brown eyes, washed with yellow and webbed with red, scanned the living room until they found the main terminal on the far wall. "What you got there is okay, though I'd have figured an Eighty would do better by himself. Took about a minute and a half, that's all. But don't you worry, Al—"

"Ale. Ale Elatey."

"Ah. Okay. Like I was saying, Al, before I leave I'll have your machine set so it'll take a Ninety-nine an hour and a half to coax the codes out of it. Least I can do. Where do you want these coats?" He gestured to the floor, where hall coats still on their hangers covered the glossy squares.

"What'd you do that for?" He strode forward, pushing past Wef but feeling foolish, given the scrawny hairy bareness of his legs, and the knobbiness of his knees. He knew all too well that even in tailored clothing he did not cut an impressive figure. In a bathrobe. . . . He lifted a stack of coats and brushed them gently. "I mean, it's bad enough your breaking in—"

"Hey, I just talked to your lock, that's all."

He raised the coats. "But why—"

"Well, I had to make room."

"For what? You've only got this one little bag—" He nudged

the leather suitcase with his foot; a stench of mildew wafted up. "—and even if you hung everything in it on its own hanger, you still wouldn't fill even half the closet."

"It's not for that." Wef dropped his gaze and gave a squirming shrug. "It's for me. To sleep in."

Ale blinked, and shook his head. "To sleep in?"

The old man's cheeks darkened. "I'm an agoraphobe. I can't sleep except in places where I can touch the walls—all four at once, I mean."

It was early morning and he had not yet drunk his first cup of coffee; his thoughts ran slow and sluggish. He draped the coats over his shoulder. "You're planning to sleep in this closet?"

"Unless you've got a smaller one. One I could really curl up in."

"I, uh—"

"Ale?" called Emdy. "What's going on out there?"

"My wife," he told Wef. "Excuse me." He walked toward the hall to the bedroom. "Morning, Doc. Our refugee's arrived." He rounded the corner.

"What?" Flashing a sleek bare curve of rump, she slammed the door.

"Uh-huh," he said to himself, then went back to their guest. "Ah . . . could I offer you a cup of coffee or something?"

"Naw, I ate on the plane." Wef picked up the remaining coats by their hangers. "Where did you say you wanted these?"

"Here, I'll take them. Why don't you, ah—" The plastic hooks of the loaded hangers bit into his right hand. "Ah, make yourself comfortable. I'll get you some blankets and—we've got an extra mattress, off the foldaway bed over there—" He gestured into the living room. "—but I don't know if it'll fit in the closet, I mean, I think—"

"It's okay. I brought a sleeping bag. Sheets and blankets are too roomy." He nodded to the terminal. "You going to be using the machine?"

"Not just yet, I—"

"Good." He turned his back on Ale and crossed directly to the computer. Sitting before it, poising his hands above its keyboard like a pianist commencing a concert, he gave a small sigh and an even smaller shake of the head. Clearly, he still did not believe an Eighty could be content with such primitive equipment. Then his fingers blurred. Keys clicked. The screen came alive.

Maybe I'm still asleep. He decided to stash the flock of

coats in the bedroom closet. *I have to be. Even the Texan last summer wasn't this weird.* He pushed open the bedroom door.

Emdy was just zipping her blouse. Surprise rippled across her face. "Ale, what—"

Forcing the overcrowded closet to swallow the coats, he explained.

"That's crazy."

"You're right. But it's what he wants."

"Where is he now?"

"At the terminal in the living room." He stripped off the robe and began to get dressed.

"You said he's a Ninety?"

"Yeah, why?"

"For one thing, it means he won't run up our computer bill." Hand on the doorknob, she paused. "I also have a lead on some real nice antiques, but I'll need a custom-made provenance-check program, and maybe..."

He shrugged as he pulled on his shirt. "Maybe. It can't hurt to ask."

"Exactly what I was thinking. You are done in the john, aren't you?"

"It's all yours. Oh, hey!" In the confusion he had completely forgotten. "My article! The net's up to twenty-one thousand four hundred fifty-seven."

Her eyes lit up; a smile splashed across her face. "That's— that's fantastic! Oh, Ale, that's just—" She reached him with three quick strides and hugged him hard. "Ale, you're incredible. I am so proud of you. Twenty-one thou and the run's not done yet. It's definitely time to start househunting."

"You sure we can af—"

"Positive." Stepping back, she winked. "That's my department, remember? Trust me. Not only can we afford it, we'll have money left over once we've bought it."

"Yeah, I know. Just I get nervous."

"Don't." She patted him on the cheek. "Let me go brush my teeth."

He followed her out; when she turned left, he turned right. More comfortable and confident with his clothes on, he called, "Hey, Wef—sure I can't interest you in a cup of coffee?"

The old man spun the chair around. "I'd rather have a beer, if you've got one."

"Uh..." *At eight in the morning?* "There should be some, let me see." Opening the refrigerator, he pawed through fluffy bags of bean sprouts. Two cans of beer sat at the back of the bottom shelf. A sticky amber substance flecked with black crudded the tops of both. Something on a higher shelf had obviously dripped—and weeks earlier, at that. Scowling, he rinsed a can clean at the sink. Then he found a mug and carried both out to the refugee. "Here you go."

Wef frowned at the familiar blue and white can. "You've got rotten taste in beer, Al."

"It's Ale."

"The hell it is. Says right here, 'Premium Draft Beer,'"

He winced. "I meant my *name*, Wef. Ale. Ale Elatey."

"Oh." He popped the can and poured so that it developed almost no head. "Sorry about that. Down in Florida we always call it Al. Old habits, you know? Hard to break. But you still have rotten taste in beer. I'll order some better stuff later on." Looking up, he crossed glances with Ale. "Don't you worry about me running up your tab, either. I'll put it on mine." He took a cautious pull at the beer. "God that's awful."

"Good morning," said Emdy, coming up behind Ale. "You must be Wef DiNaini."

The old man pushed himself to his feet. "And you're Emdy." His hand reached out to envelop hers. "I knew from the name I'd be staying with a blue-eyed blonde, but damn me if I knew you'd be this pretty. I think I just might enjoy myself here."

She grinned at him. "I can see already we're going to have to do something about this shyness problem of yours, Mr. Wef DiNaini."

"Oh, call me Wef, Emdy. No need to be formal when we're going to be real good friends." He stroked the back of her hand. "I mean real good friends."

"Down, Wef." She slipped her hand out of his grasp. "What will you have for breakfast?"

"Ate at the airport. And on the plane 'fore that. And at the airport before that." He patted his paunch. "To tell the truth, I've had enough to last me till Tuesday. Assuming we get some good beer into the house."

"We'll take care of it. Ale? What do you want?"

"The usual."

"Coming right up." She pivoted and headed for the kitchen.

Wef dropped back into the seat and reached for the beer mug. "You know, you should have told me you were a celebrity, Al. I mean, Ale."

"Huh?"

"That article—nice job you did. Glad it's sold so well for you. How is old Yuai?"

Ale was off-balance. The royalty programs were supposed to be sealed to everyone but the Coalition Directorate of Income Verification and the authors themselves; that this old man had somehow broken those codes, too, was exasperating. But when he followed up the revelation with a reference to . . . "You know Yuai Bethresicks?"

"Yuai? Sure, we're old buddies. He put me away, let's see, what was it, seven years ago? Eight? Caught me with my fingers in the current, did three years for it."

"So he *is* a Coalition agent?"

"Last I looked he was, yeah."

"I can't get a number for him out of the local office; they say he doesn't work for them." Emdy bore a covered plate to the dining room; he drifted over, talking as he went. "I don't know what to think."

"Just don't think that crap they fed you is the truth." Wef followed a meter behind Ale, sniffing every step or two. "Emdy honey, that smells real good there—what is it?"

"Coffee, mushroom omelettes, and sausage. Want some?"

Wef slid into the nearest chair and lifted the cover of the plate. "I don't see any coffee in here."

"Funny, Wef," she said. "And yes, there is enough for you, if you've changed your mind."

"Well . . . maybe just a little of this omelette." His left hand shot out to snatch Ale's plate; scooping up the serving spoon, he flicked three sausages and an omelette onto it. "It does smell awful good." Without waiting for the other two, he started eating.

Ale puffed his cheeks and blew air in bemusement. Grumbling to himself, he went to the kitchen for another plate and set of silverware.

Emdy joined him. In a low voice, she said, "He's getting on your nerves, isn't he?"

"I wish you'd quit encouraging him."

"But I'm not!"

"Sure seems like it." He grabbed an extra napkin and headed back to the table.

Wef had already cleaned his plate. Tilting his chair onto its rear legs, he fished in his shirt pocket for a fat brown cigar, and lit it. "Real good breakfast, honey." He rolled a thick grey smoke ring across the table.

She had speared a piece of sausage on her fork, and now held it in front of herself. "If you honestly think so," she said, "then you might let us taste it before you fumigate the room."

Extending the cigar to arm's length, he studied its glowing tip. "The smell bugs you?"

"The smell *nauseates* me."

"Oh." He let the chair thump forward and stubbed the cigar out on his plate. He seemed to shrink in upon himself, as though Emdy's jab had deflated him. "Sorry."

She nodded, looked at her loaded fork, and set it down. "Cigarettes are okay. So's dope, if Ale's not working for the next six hours or so. But cigars—" She made a face. "Those you can smoke on the terrace."

"But there's Dacs out there!"

"We have a DacWatch."

"Hah!" Swiveling sideways in his chair, he nudged Ale in the ribs. "Didn't do you much good, did it?"

The elbow made Ale swallow wrong. He coughed. "Your friend Yuai said somebody'd tampered with it."

"That bothers me about Yuai. Somebody's doing something strange. I think I'm going to check up on it—is there a public computer in the building?"

"Down in the library, sure. Second floor. I think they have, what, six?"

"Eight," said Emdy.

"But you can use ours—I mean, you don't use up all your free time, do you?"

Wef grinned. "Most months I do, not that I ever pay for the overage. But that's not why I asked. Probably shouldn't tell you this, but the kind of inquiry I'm going to make, you wouldn't want to have traced back to your machine."

Emdy frowned. "Why not?"

"Because, honey, it's my guess that my old buddy is in deep shit with the Coalition. It's my further guess that, for whatever reason, it was Yuai who slipped me in here." A thoughtful scowl passed over his face. "I wonder, does he figure you all need protection?" He shook his head. "Whatever, I'm going to find it out. Got to be a way to turn a quick buck on it. But believe you me, you would not want them to know— or even suspect—that you know what's happening. Which is why"—he pushed his chair back and rose—"if you'll excuse me, I'm headed for those public computers downstairs."

Ale swallowed another mouthful of omelette. "Why?" It

came out hoarse and dry. "I mean, why would Yuai Bethresicks be in trouble? All he did was interview me. It doesn't make sense."

"I don't know what he did, but CoaData should have had him banked. If he'd quit, or been fired, they'd have given you his home number. If a Dac got him while he was leaving, or he had a heart attack, or anything like that, they wouldn't have been in any hurry to wipe his name from the banks. Fact, what they'd have done is, list him as 'deceased, refer all professional calls to such-and-such a number, all personal calls to so-and-so.' And as for why'd he be in trouble? He's always been a little too curious for his own good. He probably found something he shouldn't ought to have. And when I find out what it is, I'm willing to bet there'll be money underneath it." He wiped his mouth on the back of his hand. "I'll be a while, so don't hold lunch." He replaced his chair at the table and walked out the front door.

Ale sipped at his coffee. It had cooled almost to the temperature he liked. Another few minutes. Setting it down, he looked at Emdy. "Is he paranoid, or what?"

"Just cautious.... The Coalition really doesn't like anybody investigating them. This Australian I know brokered some titanium for the Coalition. He asked what they were using it for; they wouldn't tell him. So he tried to find out on his own— he wanted to be ready with a low bid when they'd used up that consignment?—and ran into a booby trap on the Net that wiped all of his files, then pretty much melted his computer. A real secretive bunch."

Ah, the coffee had reached perfection. He smiled in satisfaction. "Well, I'll tell you, I'm beginning to wonder if there are ever any normal people in imminent disaster areas."

"Just the luck of the draw, Ale." She patted her lips with the napkin. "But that cigar!" She pushed her half-full plate away. "I don't know how people can stand to smoke them."

Ale gathered the dishes and the silverware, and carried them to the kitchen. "What time's the Tessai due?" Faucet on, he reached for the sponge.

"Another half-hour or so—they said around ten this morning. Anxious?"

"Who, me?" He laughed. "Not so anybody'd notice—from the next building."

"I have some calls to make. What time do you go on?"

"Ah . . . two-thirty. Unless they get flooded with queries this morning."

"Uh-huh."

"Well, it has happened before."

"Once." Heading for her office, she took her coffee cup with her.

"Hey, don't leave wet spoons on the table."

"You're going to wipe it off anyway, aren't you?"

"Yeah, but still." He hated housework—especially when thoughtlessness made it more difficult than it had to be. "Before you go—"

She stopped in the doorway.

"I'd planned to espalier a pear tree along the terrace wall here, but since we're moving, I don't know. Would a landlord call that an improvement? I mean the kind you get paid for."

"That depends. How many years before you get any fruit off it?"

"Hard to say. It's a dwarf; they bear quick. None this year, of course. Maybe a couple next year—good harvest the year after that, though."

She scrunched her eyes closed while she thought. "Do it. If they won't pay us what it cost plus, say, fifteen percent, we'll take it with us."

"Okay, great." He filled his watering-can and headed for the terrace. At the door he stopped. He still did not trust the DacWatch, but . . . but what else was there to depend on? It was too early, and too cloudy, for Mrs. M'ti Emtenne to be sunning. No one moved on the balconies across the way. He had to trust the DacWatch. Re-setting it, he waited for the green, crouched to scan the clouds with his own eyes . . . then opened the door. Holding his breath.

The sky stayed empty. He edged onto the flagstones, looked around as carefully as he could, then shrugged. *Nerves. Makes you jumpy, to get attacked . . . probably be months before I stop looking over my shoulder.* The wind caught his hair; he had to tuck it behind his ears. When his fingers brushed the welt on his forehead, he shuddered. *All's well that ends well, I suppose, but still . . .*

As he began to water the trough of tomatoes, The Oracle buzzed him.

Yes?

#Sorry to distrub you so early, Mr. Ale Elatey. Have you

a bubble, tape, or hard-copy of your Ph.D. thesis?#

Of course not. He frowned. *But why? It's on file—*

#We had occasion to refer to it, whereupon the Ivy League Remote Data Base confessed that yesterday it experienced a minor explosion in the bubble arrays—sewer gas, it said— and your thesis was destroyed#

Doesn't anything work right any more? He sighed. *There's another copy—*

#Michigan?#

Yes.

#Also gone—some two years ago, the records show— they'd planned to dupe the ILRDB bubble, but had not scheduled it till next January. Will you consent to hypnosis to recall the thesis?#

Aw, dammit! You mean to say that the only copy of my thesis anywhere is in my subconscious? He could not believe it. *Surely somewhere—*

#That seems to be the situation.#

Dammit, dammit, dammit. . . . He hated hypnosis. The drugs rendered one the zombie of the interrogator—a hollow-eyed, empty-voiced robot waiting for instructions. To reconstruct his thesis would take weeks, if not months. He shuddered. *If I have to, I have to—but this time, I'm going to want a hard-copy.*

#Understandably.#

I'll tell you, my luck lately has been either super good—

#Your article? Congratulations on the reception it has enjoyed.#

Thanks. For a moment he groped for the thread of thought The Oracle's interruption had snapped. *Oh, yeah. It's either incredibly good luck, or purely rotten luck. Hey. While you're here: What are the odds of having a heavy-duty industrial laser installed in a home pholo?*

No perceptible time elapsed. #One in one hundred fifty billion.#

Has it ever happened before?

#Never.#

The freakishness of the accident made his escape seem even more narrow, as though he had sidestepped a meteor. Even eighteen hours after the incident, it shook him. He turned to rest his elbows on the balcony railing. The wrought iron, he noted absently, needed painting again. *Oh my God . . . one in one hundred fifty billion . . . and my thesis, five years of re-*

search, pfft! I can't believe they lost it. Idiots. Stupid, bumbling. . . . One in a hundred fifty billion. . . . He kicked the railing. And jerked his foot back in alarm as a bit of loose cement bounced over the edge.

It plummeted to the breeze-ruffled canopy of the scrub forest growing in what had once been a street. Though stunted and light-starved, the greenery still provoked bittersweet joy. More than mere visual delight, it sopped up the atmosphere's excess carbon dioxide, just like the environmental experts had predicted. Along with a billion of its cousins around the world, Chapel Street was keeping the planet from suffocating in its own wastes.

He wished he could walk on that street.

From the kitchen came a *ding* as the matter transceiver accepted a package. Emdy called, "That must be your scroll. I'm on the john; you better get it yourself."

"You know I will!" *The Tessai's here—at least something's going right.* He spun—and knocked over the potted pear tree he had planned to espalier. "Damn." He bent down. With quick, sure hands he scooped up the spilled soil, shoveled it back into the thick plastic pot, and then pushed the container against the cinderblock wall between the terrace door and the first window.

The wall shook. Puzzled, he began to straighten—

The glass doors blew out in a shower of sparkles.

Behind the glitter roared a *WHOOMPH!* Dust gushed onto the balcony.

And Emdy Ofivo screamed.

TOP TEN NEWS STORIES OF THE HOUR

16 June 2188; 1000 EDT
New England Region

RANK HEADLINE	price	LEAD SENTENCE
#1 **LM2 VEEP THREATENED**	.20	In the hour's top story, a spokesrep for Lunar Mining and Manufacturing, Inc. has just confirmed that the self-proclaimed killers of BHK30 BHXNDP JUH2 have threatened to murder the Vice-President and interim President unless LM2 pays them half a billion dollars.
#2 * * * * * * **VAN GOGH GOES FOR BIG DOUGH**	.20	**#2** * * * * * * The Computer Science Department of the University of Pusan, which stunned the art world last week by announcing the development of an artificial intelligence identical in personality and talent to the great Dutch painter Vincent van Gogh, has agreed to sell the program to the Louvre for $100 million dollars.
#3 * * * * * * **COMPUTER CRASH FINALLY CONTAINED**	.15	**#3** * * * * * * Technicians from IBM, Matsushita, and n'Gongo Electronics, despite harassment by a Coalition crisis management team, have brought the year's worst computer crash under control, and expect to

restore service within forty-eight hours.

#4 * * * * * *

2000 STREETERS ROUNDED UP IN TOKYO .10

#4 * * * * * *

Over two thousand street people, some armed with weapons ranging from bows and arrows to automatic rifles, have been taken into custody in Tokyo today; the round-up was staged in retaliation for the streeters' alleged tampering with the safepath beacons that led to the destruction of a ST jetliner yesterday morning.

#5 * * * * * *

CCU RIVALS PRAISE REVAMP .10

#5 * * * * * *

Spokesreps for UE and other major parties have announced that they will be following the lead of new CCU AD/NE/DP Information Aid Emsisicks and reorganizing their own operations accordingly.

#6 * * * * * *

MAJOR EXPLOSION AT HOME OF DAC KILLER .10

#6 * * * * * *

An blast of undetermined origins has just shaken the apartment of ALL80 AFAHSC NFF6, the New Havener who yesterday achieved worldwide fame by killing a Dac with his bare hands and then writing a best-selling article about it.

#7 * * * * * *

COALITION MUM ON WHETHER DAC SHIP REPLACEMENTS OR REINFORCEMENTS .10

#7 * * * * * *

Coalition spokesreps contacted by pholo earlier this morning refused comment on the suggestion, presently being raised by many xenobiologists, that the Dac ship now en route to L5 will relieve one of the ships currently parked there.

RANK HEADLINE price	LEAD SENTENCE

#8 * * * * * * *

PLUTO PROBE PICKS   .10
UP NEW SIGNALS

#8 * * * * * * *

The MIT/ToDai robot probe
in orbit around Pluto has
detected faint radio
transmissions apparently
emanating from Barnard's
Star; it has, however, found
no evidence linking either
the star or the
transmissions to the Dacs.

#9 * * * * * * *

BLAST IN NEO   .10

#9 * * * * * * *

According to unconfirmed
reports from hundreds of
locations across East Asia, a
major explosion took place
minutes ago in near-Earth
orbit; Coalition spokesreps
have yet to comment.

#10 * * * * * * *

TELEBETTER WINS   .10
TOP COP'S REC

#10 * * * * * * *

The Director of Coalition
Intelligence for North
America, according to a
press release issued by her
office this morning, has sent
all Coalition employees a
free sample of TeleBetter, a
new drug designed to
enhance telesensory
interface.

This update has been provided as a public service by all data management corporations participating in NEWSBANK/UE, a news data base organized and supervised by the Uhuru-Episcopal Directorate of Public Information.

To read any of the above news stories in full, simply highlight the title and press ACCEPT. The article will be transmitted to your unit's memory. Your bank balance will be debited by the sum in the column headed "price."

To see the headlines of the day's other news stories, simply scroll your screen up.

Thank you, and do be careful.

VI

Emdy's scream was raw and ugly, and it froze him for a moment. Terror shrieked in it, and pain, and rage too, that the world had turned so crazy. Ale wanted to cry out in empathy. He would have taken her agony for his own, if he could have.

He charged inside, into the chill CO_2 fog from the automatic extinguishers. Kitchen scraps and shredded plant leaves littered the living room; he had to crawl over the liquor cabinet to get to the hall leading to the toilet. Mrs. M'ti Emtenne's sirenish wail knifed through the wall. Footsteps, fast and heavy, sounded in the corridor. He trembled abruptly: for the third time in two days, chance had spared him. If he had left the pear tree untended, the flying glass would have scythed him down. "Doc!"

He found her on the toilet, pants still bunched around her ankles. Moaning, she rocked back and forth, hands cupped over her ears. A drop of blood splattered on her bare thigh.

He touched her left hand, lightly, and she raised her face. Tears streamed down it, thinning the red stain on her upper lip. "Ale!" She shouted it. "Ale! My ears, I can't hear!"

Kneeling, he wrapped her in his arms, as though his desperate hug could heal her. Inside his head he swooped to ORA:CLE's interface, dove into Yale-New Haven Hospital's remote data base, and surfaced in its Dispatch Program. Prodded, the computer promised to land a black bag on his terrace within ninety seconds.

Returning to real-time, he helped Emdy to her feet. She quivered so badly he had to bear most of her weight. She could not possibly climb over the broken furniture that clogged the hall. He guided her to the bedroom next door. The extinguishers still hissed clammy clouds, but with all the windows shattered, enough fresh air swirled in to dilute the hazard.

He laid her on the bed and tented her in cold blankets. With exaggerated movements of lip, teeth, and tongue, he mouthed,

"WAIT. DOCTOR. COMING." He listened for the whirr of rotors. And prayed.

When the black bag came, and he had lifted it over the rubble so that it could glide to Emdy, he accessed The Oracle again. Fury was rising in him, but he held it under control. *What was transmatted to my matter-transceiver?*

A tenth of a second later, it replied, #One hundred cubic centimeters of gas from the depths of Jupiter's atmosphere— at its original density.#

How did Central Transshipping miss it?

#It was a direct shipment; it never went through Central Transshipping.#

"What?" That one he shouted aloud.

#The Yale Astrophysics Lab has reported a missing consignment of Jovian gas; it seems probable that your package was meant for them.#

The black bag interrupted: "I'm calling an ambulance, sir."

"How is she? Is she—will she—"

"Sedated, sir. And she'll be fine. A few hours in the hospital, and she'll be as good as new." It trundled back to the bedroom.

The drugs had muted her moans. Only now did he realize how much they had unnerved him. He sagged against the chipped wall, and thanked Whomever for having let her be inside the bathroom, even though the compression wave had punctured her eardrums. If she had answered the massie. . . . He shuddered. *How the hell could a shipment for Yale wind up here?*

#Sunspots.#

What?

#The records show that sunspot interference garbled the address as the transmission neared Earth.#

With quintuple redundancy circuits? That's the silliest damn thing I've ever heard of.

#Yes.#

He let a beat go by while he digested that. Then: *You agree with me?*

#Quite.#

He almost did not know what to ask next. *What the hell's going on here?*

#It should be obvious, sir: someone is trying to kill you.#

Who, dammit? "WHO?" At his bellow, the black bag popped into the corridor to ask if he, too, needed medical attention. He shook it off with a wave of his hand; it rolled backwards into the bedroom. *Who?*

#A true conundrum, sir. We are not yet sure.#

We?

#Mr. Ale Elatey, scholars of East Asia, 1500–2000 AD, are an endangered species. ORA:CLE will not see them made extinct.#

Extinct. The word itself sounded final. He shivered. *So what do you recommend?*

#For the moment, nothing concrete. Tend to your wife. Keep yourself available.#

You mean alive.

#One and the same.#

Outside, chopper blades flailed the air. Hopjets whistled; glass crunched on the terrace. The heli's roar diminished; the operator was probably taking it up to the roof. "Yo!" called a static-crackled bass.

"In here!"

The first stretcher bearer scrambled easily over the demolished furniture. A round-bodied machine with eight spidery legs, each ending in an adjustable foot that could shrink to a tubular stump or inflate to a meter-wide pontoon, as rescue conditions demanded, it carried a folded litter in two of its four telescoping arms. Its camera fixed on Ale; the center-mounted spotlight dazzled him.

"Hey!" He held his forearm before his eyes. "You don't need that."

"Power's still on, huh?" It flicked the spot off. "Where's Ms. Emdy Ofivo?"

"In here, in here!" said the black bag from the bedroom.

"Is that you, Jayef? 'Scuze me, sir, let me through." Ale shrank back against the wall as it edged past, but one of its polished knee joints clipped his thigh anyway. "Hey, I thought they retired you, Jayef."

"It turned out I was allergic to my husband's hair dye. As soon as he switched brands, the shakes went away. Nothing too serious here, mostly punctured eardrums, a few bruised ribs in the back, shock—maybe a touch of whiplash."

The second stretcher bearer appeared at the end of the hall. It tilted its body to study the overturned liquor cabinet, extended all four of its arms, and grabbed hold. Gears whirred. Its legs flexed, lifting its body half a meter higher; its arms retracted. The cabinet rose. "Does it matter where I set this down?"

"Anywhere's fine."

"Right." Waggling a camera, it pivoted on its turntable

pelvis, and took two arachnid strides into the living room. A wine glass fell from the cabinet's smashed door, and bounced on the carpet. The motor hummed in protest as it bent to lean the cabinet against the back of one of the sofas. It returned to Ale with the stench of spilled liquor eddying in its wake.

"In there." He nodded to the bedroom.

"Thanks." It slipped past, then hesitated in the doorway. "Uh . . . you'd better wait in the living room; it'll get awful crowded when we bring her out."

He wanted to stay with her, but she seemed to be in competent hands, and he would only get in the way. Hands in his pockets, head down, he trudged into the living room. There he surveyed the damage.

Crockery, canned goods, and scraps of cupboard littered the floor. The blast had stripped most of the leaves off the dracaena, diffenbachia, and schefflera in the planter, and snapped all their stems. A deep gouge ran diagonally along the dining room table, cutting a line from the transceiver room across the kitchen counter to the coffeepot wedged in the arm of the sofa. The spider plants on the left wall looked mown.

He walked toward the front door, glancing over the toppled kitchen counter to the site of the explosion. It had mashed the refrigerator into a slab of standing plastic twenty centimeters thick. The door hung by a single hinge, and orange juice puddled below it.

The wreckage sickened him. All the furnishings and fixtures—he and Emdy had saved for years to afford the down payments on it all, and still faced monthly debits on most of it—all so much junk. And his planter, five meters long and six years in the growing, a desert. They had insurance, sure, but could a credit from the company replace the vases Emdy had cast in her pottery classes? Could it resurrect a wall full of cherished plants?

He stopped. "Oh, no." It came out a whisper, hushed by an image: his bonsai, perched on pedestals outside the windows letting onto the terrace.

The twisted, shattered windows that had spat their glass outwards in a cloud of sparkling shrapnel.

He turned on his heel and started for the balcony, almost slipping as he stepped on a shiny chrome funnel that rolled beneath his foot.

The stretcher bearers came carefully around the corner, picking their ways through the debris, holding Emdy absolutely steady on her litter, her feet higher than her head. The machine in the rear also carried the black bag, which kept one tentacle wrapped loosely around Emdy's left wrist.

"We're taking her to Yale-New Haven Hospital," said the lead bearer. "You can call Hospital Information in, say, fifteen minutes to find out all the details—room, doctor assigned, all the rest. So, excuse us, please—?" Its third arm telescoped out to grab the doorknob.

He stepped aside. "I'll come with you."

"Sorry, sir, you can't."

"What do you mean, I can't? That's my wife there, and—"

"It's the rules, sir. You're allowed to accompany us to the roof, but no farther." The door swung open on a crowd of curious faces, a near-mob that the sweating building cop was trying to wave back. At the sight of Emdy's face, blood-smeared and ghastly white yet not shrouded in a plastic body bag, the crowd sighed and swayed forward. The cop's spread arms could contain only three of them. The bearer had to deal with the others.

It paused. Its camera swung as, apparently, it assessed the situation. Metal clicked. Two of its arms extended out a good three and a half meters. Their tips touched together; their elbows bent outward to form a wedge, a spearpoint. Then the machine advanced, cleaving a path for itself through spectators who drew back hastily.

The second bearer kicked Ale's front door shut before any of the curious could slither into the ruined rooms.

Ale walked alongside the stretcher, holding Emdy's right hand, answering the "How is she?"s with hurried "She'll be okay"s.

The elevator whisked them soundlessly to the roof, and let them into the low-ceilinged walkway that led to the open helicopter hatch. The first bearer said, "This is as far as you can go, sir."

"You've got room on—"

"Sorry, sir. Rules." It shook its third arm; the hand blossomed into a vinyl-covered shield that caught Ale in the chest, stomach, and thighs. Shooting out to full length, it pushed him backwards.

"Hey!" He tried to backpedal and then slip around the side of the shield, but the second bearer seized his belt and propelled him into the elevator. Hoisting him onto his toes, it held him suspended. Another of its arms snaked in, groped for the control panel, and stabbed the button marked thirty-eight. Then both arms withdrew, spreading into shields as they did, blocking the exit until the doors closed. The machinery sucked Ale back to his floor. The cage dropped so quickly that he arrived before he had resettled his pants.

"Ale."

He turned. "Oh. Dr. L'ai Aichtueni."

She frowned. *"Water."*

"Water."

"I just heard what all the commotion was about." She touched his left forearm. "I'm so sorry. Is there anything I can do to help?"

He studied her. For once she seemed undrugged. "Can you get me on the ambulance before it leaves?"

"It's already gone. And even if it hadn't, I couldn't. Rules."

"That's what they said." He started down the hall for his apartment. *Rules. Jesus Christ. What garbage.* He wished that the hall were littered with bottles or cans or *something* he could kick, hard . . . or branches and broomsticks that he could snatch up to break over his knee.

L'ai, matching him stride for stride, tapped him on the shoulder. "Why don't you come upstairs? Let me give you a drink, help you calm down."

He shook his head. The last thing he wanted was to calm down.

"I know how you feel. My mother lived with me right up till the end. When they took her away . . ." She held out a hand, clenched it slowly, then shook it. "They had to pin me to the floor so the black bag could sedate me. Me, a professional. But it's in the genes. From three million years ago, when all you could do if a member of your troop got hurt was to stay at its side and swing your stick at the buzzards and the jackals."

He looked at her, then. "You know that? For a fact, I mean? Or is it just, uh . . . a personal theory?"

She shrugged. "What does it matter, if it's true? Look, your place must be a mess—let me help you straighten up."

The offer seemed sincere, but he recoiled from it. "No, I'll get it." To have a stranger picking through their charred, scattered belongings. . . . "I need something to keep myself occupied, anyway."

They stopped five meters from the knot of gossiping neighbors by his door. The group fell silent at his approach, some looking pointedly from L'ai to him to the ceiling. He wished they would not think what they were surely thinking—he was not that kind of man—but their expressions, of accusation and of contempt, made him squirm, which they probably took as a confession.

So he said, a little too loudly, "Thanks for checking, Doctor— I appreciate your consideration."

She began, *"Wa—"* then flicked her gaze to Mrs. M'ti Emtenne, who leaned forward, lewd hunger on her face. L'ai coughed. "Why, that's quite all right, Mr. Ale Elatey; I'm only sorry I couldn't get here sooner." Looking back to Ale, she blinked three times; the corners of her mouth twitched almost imperceptibly. "I'll see you later."

I'm sure you will. He nodded goodbye and turned around. The disappointment that confronted him was as palpable, and as chilling, as the CO_2 spray had been. *Vultures.* Stepping forward, he brushed off Mr. Efwy Soo's eager questions with a muttered, "Excuse me," and let himself in.

Wef DiNaini was kneeling by the planter, picking up leaves and bits of stem. At the sound of the door he looked up. His eyes were red; his cheeks, wet. "I'm sorry. I knew I should have waited."

Ale squinted at the old man, unsure of what he was talking about. "Waited for what, Wef?"

"Till I got back home to find out about Yuai." Snuffling, he tried to dry his cheeks on the sleeves of his plaid shirt. "But I was too goddamn impatient. Always am. Just won't ever learn. Dammit."

He made the connection at last. Gesturing to the rubble, he said, "You think all this happened because of you?"

"Yes! Because now they know we know, and that's why—" He broke off with a ragged inhalation.

Ale took a deep breath of his own. If he had to play a guessing game with a remorseful old man who was probably half-drunk , he would surely scream. "Wef. What is it we know?"

Wef clutched the edge of the planter and hauled himself to his feet. "It's Yuai. He found out that the Coalition jammed your DacWatch. The Coalition had him killed."

TOP TEN NEWS STORIES OF THE HOUR

16 June 2188, 1100 EDT
New England Region

RANK HEADLINE	price	LEAD SENTENCE
#1 LM2 VEEP: NOT ONE CENT FOR TRIBUTE!	.20	PKU40 BPJRDC RLNT, VP and acting President of Lunar Mining and Manufacturing, told reporters through her spokesrep that she will risk death rather than pay the half-billion dollar protection fee demanded by the murderers of BHK30 BHXNDP JUH2, the firm's late President.
#2 * * * * * * NEO BLAST TRIGGERED BY SKIPPER'S IMPATIENCE	.15	#2 * * * * * * The explosion in near-earth orbit that lit up western Pacific skies shortly over an hour ago signaled the fiery death of the *Ohayo Maru*, a cargo ship on the lunar run, whose captain had refused to wait for Dac clearance.
#3 * * * * * * POPE RAPS COMPUTER SCIENTISTS	.15	#3 * * * * * * Pope Han Il the First, in a shrill public address delivered at 0930 (EDT) this morning, condemned the University of Pusan's sale of its Vincent van Gogh program, calling it "the twenty-second century equivalent of slavery."

RANK	HEADLINE	price	LEAD SENTENCE

#4 * * * * * *

EIGHTY-EIGHT-YEAR-OLD NEWEST UE BILLIONAIRE .10

#4 * * * * * *

An eighty-eight-year-old Brussels grandmother of twelve this morning became the latest billion dollar winner in Greensweep, the monthly lottery conducted by the Uhuru-Episcopal Directorate of Public Revenue.

#5 * * * * * *

CCU NOMINATES EMSISICKS FOR VD/NA/DPI .10

#5 * * * * * *

Aid Emsisicks, the one bright star of the Citizens & Consumers United Party, was selected at an early morning caucus as the official party-backed candidate for Vice Director for North America, CCU DP Information; he will run unopposed.

#6 * * * * * *

SNAP KILLS FIVE; BLUES SAVE WIFE .10

#6 * * * * * *

Tragedy struck a Cleveland family this morning when a berserk father of four threw his children and his mother-in-law off their twentieth story balcony; two fast acting blues caught the wife before she hit the ground.

#7 * * * * * *

COALITION SCORNS AMREV PROPSAL; CALLS IT RECIPE FOR DEATH .10

#7 * * * * * *

A spokesrep for the Coalition denounced a proposal by the American Revival Party "to meet the intruder at the gates," pointing out that the five Dac starships now parked at L5 would hardly stand by while Earth forces attacked the sixth.

#8 * * * * * *

SD DEMANDS .10

#8 * * * * * *

At the request of the Social-

RANK HEADLINE	price	LEAD SENTENCE

**PROMPT COALITION
TO PROBE
COMPUTER CRASH**

Democratic DP Communications, Coalition researchers consented to investigate the causes of yesterday's disastrous computer crash in Wichita, and make recommendations for system reconfiguration.

#9 * * * * * * *

**DROUGHT PARCHES
SIBERIA**   .10

#9 * * * * * * *

The Marist-Communist Directorate of Public Agriculture announced this morning that Siberian grain fields, experiencing the driest growing season in a century, will yield 30 to 50 percent less than estimated in May.

#10 * * * * * * *

**DAC KILLER BLAST
TIED TO MASSIE**   .10

#10 * * * * * * *

The explosion that ripped the apartment of New Haven author and scholar ALL80 AFAHSC NFF6 at 0958 EDT this morning, sending Ale's wife to the hospital for observation, appears to have been caused by a defective mass transceiver, MR DP Safety officials announced a few moments ago.

This update has been provided as a public service by all data management corporations participating in NEWSBANK/SD, a news data base organized and supervised by the Social-Democratic Directorate of Public Information.

To read any of the above news stories in full, simply highlight the title and press ACCEPT. The article will be transmitted to your unit's memory. Your bank balance will be debited by the sum in the column headed "price."

To see the headlines of the day's other news stories, simply scroll your screen up.

Thank you, and do be careful.

VII

"You're serious," said Ale.

Wef nodded, sniffed, and swiped at the dampness on his right cheek. "I found Yuai's prelim report—he *did* slip me in here to protect you. I also saw the orders to 'rase him."

"This is crazy. Why in hell would the Coalition *want* to jam my DacWatch? Who am I to them?"

"I don't know." Wef sagged. "I picked up a tag when I was on line and I pulled out before it saw everything I was doing. I didn't get out quick enough, though—God, I'm sorry."

"No, that can't be it—they'd go for you, then, not me. Don't blame yourself. It can't be your fault." The stink of smothered flames filled the room; in the kitchen, a twisted pipe dripped with plinking insistence.

Depression settled over Ale. He had so much to do. To begin with, he had to clean up. The vacuum cleaner was in the— *No, wait, check the bonsai.* The damaged ones would need immediate care. Again he stopped himself. Fifteen minutes must have gone by. *Call the hospital, find out how Emdy—* oh, God, he had to tell The Oracle he would be taking the afternoon off—*no way I can concentrate when everything—* Could he even achieve interface? Maybe if he used some TeleBetter . . . *no, no, got to keep a clear head, got to. . . .*

"Ale?"

The voice startled him. "Huh?" Blinking, he gaped at the old man, who still knelt on the floor. "Sorry, I—"

"I think you're in shock."

"Me? No, I'm fine, just fine, it's . . . there's so much mess, I mean—" He gestured helplessly at the torn sofas. "I don't even know where to start."

"The Coalition tried to kill you and you're worrying about tidying the living room? Wake up, Ale!"

"But it's—and my plants, my God, I—" He began walking

toward the terrace. He stopped. "I just realized—how am I going to call the hospital? Everything's smashed."

"Goddammit, Ale Elatey, would you pay attention? The Coalition—"

He held up his right hand. He was so very tired, so very confused, that he resented being forced to confront reality. "Wef, I hear you, I know what you're saying, but what am I supposed to do, huh? Tell me. You say the Coalition's trying to kill me. Okay, so it is. What do I do? The government of governments, with branches in every city and town, with five million employees and gotta be a million tele-factored remotes, this big huge mean machine is trying to squash me—but what can I do? My ID/dress card melted with the computer, so I've got no money; I've got no place to hide, can't even go outside without drawing Dacs or streeters; I've got no political pull, so I can't just call somebody and say, hey, tell 'em to leave me alone . . . all I can do, Wef, is tidy up, find out how Emdy is, and hope that this is all a mistake that will get straightened out quick so Emdy and I can live happily ever after amen. So with that thought in mind—"

"All right," said Wef, "all right. For an Eighty, though, you're awful dumb. You do still work for ORA:CLE, don't you?"

"Uh-huh."

"And you don't figure ORA:CLE could help you out, huh?"

"Well, I—" He blushed. The name of the company *was* Opinions, Research, and *Advice.* . . . "I'll give The Oracle a call, see what it says."

"Good boy. You do that. And while you do, I'm gonna get a clean-up crew in here, and then I'll see what I can do to save your ass."

Going to a corner of the room where the carpet had escaped both charring and soaking, he kicked aside hunks of sofa stuffing, sat, and closed his eyes. With a deep breath, he reached out for interface.

Alternating currents of rage and gloom swept through him, fuzzing his head with static. He could not touch ORA:CLE. Briefly he tasted despair. Everything had soured for him, everything!

Grimly, he set his teeth and forced himself to visualize the mountain. For a moment it loomed through the fog of emotion, and then it vanished, replaced by an image of Emdy, bleeding on the john.

He rubbed his eyeballs, sparking phosphenes of green and red and orange. A tunnel yawned up before him, but before he could step inside it snapped shut and retracted into the mist. Emdy Ofivo appeared, head on a pillow, face ghastly white.

Rocking back and forth, he rubbed harder, now, hard enough to hurt. His fingertips slipped on involuntary tears. The phosphenes swam like tropical algae and he focused, calling, *Oracle! I need a hand here*.

#Yes?#

It pumped something through from the far end of interface. The fog blew away. The tunnel into the mountain opened sharp and inviting.

Thanks.

#My pleasure. What seems to be the problem?#

You said before that someone was trying to kill me. Well, a bomb—

#I've heard. It's a very popular news item right now.#

Our refugee says the Coalition did it.

#How very interesting. And why, precisely, have you called on me?#

I was hoping, uh . . . hoping you could investigate it for me.

#Of course.#

So why would the Coalition want to kill me? It's crazy; it doesn't make any sense!

#I quite agree.# It paused for what seemed several minutes. #I am sorry, sir, but that information is not available right now. Shall I keep your question on permanent file?#

Hell, yes!

#Very good. When I have the data, I will be in touch.#

Thanks, he said, into the blankness of severed interface.

As he came back to reality, the whine of a small motor grew steadily louder—and something seized him. He jerked upright and snapped his eyes open. Too late. Tentacles slid under his knees and behind his back, wrapping around his chest, pinning his arms to his sides. Gears clashed. The tentacles lifted him— "Hey!"

"Sorry if I bothered you, Mr. Ale Elatey, but I gotta vacuum underneath you, you know?"

He looked back over his shoulder into the gleaming silver carapace of a rent-a-clean. "Christ's sakes, put me down."

"You're the boss." It tipped forward slowly, lowering him till his feet touched the carpet. The tentacles unwound to release him. "If you don't mind, though, how's about moving over by the windows till I'm done here, okay? I'm all finished over there."

He approached instead Wef DiNaini, who stood in the middle of the living room, arms folded across his chest, braids thrown back over his shoulders. Wef wore a headset with a swing mike. Beside him, a dented lifter held the smashed liquor cabinet in the air. The old man was saying, "You scanned it on all sides, top bottom and inside, too?"

"Hey, man," said the lifter, "I'm a pro."

"Last person said that to me gave me a disease they hadda whip up a new antibiotic to cure. I asked you a question."

"Yeah, I scanned it, Wef."

"And you bubbled the scan?"

"Uh-huh," it said in a bored tone.

"And you also commed the scan down to Mr. Ale Elatey's insurance company?"

"You know it."

"Then how come they can't find it? How come—" He tilted his head into a listening position. "Wait a minute." He snapped the microphone up to his mouth and spoke: "Then try the— Okay. You got it now? Good. What do you mean, eighty percent? I want full value on that, sister, or— Jesus God, ain't you ever heard that wooden furniture increases in value every year? Don't give me that depreciation shit. This is *wood*, sister, *wood*. All right. No cash, just replace it with something absolutely identical—in *wood*." Pushing the mike away, he made a face. "Insurance adjusters, Jesus." He nodded to the lifter. "All right, into the chipper with that."

It wheeled, carried the cabinet out the door, and headed down the hall to the floor's recycling room.

"Wef, what the—"

"Back among the living, huh?" Wef came over. "They'll be finished here in about half an hour; soon as they're out the massie techs come in to replace your transceiver, and then the insurance company starts shipping you replacement furniture. 'Zat sound okay?"

"You, uh . . . you seem to have everything well in hand."

"Well, hey. I figured this isn't something you needed to worry about right now."

"You're right about that."

"What'd The Oracle say?"

"It's going to investigate, and get back to me later."

"The lady next door stopped in while you were, uh—" Wef waved a hand at the corner. "—out."

"Mrs. M'ti·Emtenne?"

"A cute old broad with short-shorts and a great tan?"

"That's her." *Cute?* "What did she want?"

"She said she called the hospital, Emdy's fine. Emdy's in Room 8792 but don't call because she's doped to the hairline and they don't expect her to wake up till tomorrow morning."

Ale found himself on the verge of protest. Twenty-four hours seemed like forever. He and Emdy had not been apart for a sixth that long since their wedding day. "Did Mrs. M'ti Emtenne say when Emdy's coming home?"

"Probably tomorrow afternoon, if the test results look okay."

"Well, that's something, at least."

"Yeah." Wef patted Ale's shoulder. "Why don't you go check your plants? Let me finish up in here."

"Okay," he said numbly. "And thanks for taking care of all this, Wef."

"Hey, it gave me something to do, something to occupy my time—and besides, your insurance company's paying for it." He winked. "Your company's paying for just about everything around here today."

He walked to the terrace door. The DacWatch no longer functioned, of course—though he would never trust it again, now that Wef had learned about the Coalition's tampering—so he squatted, visually to quarter as much of the sky as he could see. On the terrace next door, Mrs. M'ti Emtenne sunbathed. For confirmation he studied the balconies of the building across the street. About the fifteenth floor, a young woman in a purple bikini was reading a book. It was probably safe out there. Probably.

He stepped out. And cursed.

He had been caring for eleven different bonsai, ranging in age from three to sixty years old. The Dac's bullet had shattered the azalea the previous day, leaving ten gnarled plants proud on their pedestals outside the living room windows.

Now. . . .

He walked down the line. The wisteria was gone completely, presumably blown over the railing. Of the Japanese maple there remained two leafless branches and one pot shard. The juniper must have followed the wisteria. The pyracantha. . . . He picked up its undamaged pot and stared in disbelief at the plant's stump. A perfectly smooth cut, as though a power saw had swept across it. The yew lay upside down in a clump of needles and smashed ceramic; most of the dirt had fallen off its roots so the sun could dry them. . . . The white oak, the dwarf Alberta spruce, the flowering cherry—nothing but split bark, pulped trunks, and mashed leaves. . . . The ginkgo looked all right; had a real knack for survival, the ginkgo did, being as it was a survivor from dinosaur days and not, really, a true tree at all. . . . The Chinese elm had stayed on its pedestal, too, and though an arrowhead of glass had bit into its trunk, would probably heal after a rinse and some sulphur dust.

He lifted the yew and held it upright. Thirty-seven years old; his constant companion since his ninth birthday. Thirty-seven years in a shallow blue dish four centimeters across. Dead, now, its resinous tears nearly dry on its mangled branches.

A sigh caught in his throat and almost thickened into a sob. He hefted the yew once, then tossed it over the railing. It disappeared into the scrub forest below. There it would rot into slow, steady fertilizer for the stunted trees of Chapel Street.

Behind him, a rent-a-clean purred out onto the balcony. "Want me to get this mess for you, Mr. Ale?"

"I suppose. . . . Be careful you don't knock these two over." He pointed to the ginkgo and the Chinese elm. "Wait." He took the pyracantha. It might not be possible to coax new growth from the stump, but he had to try. "Okay, it's all yours."

"Righto."

Pot in hand, he went inside just as a plumber clanked out of the kitchen and said, "All right, Wef, it ain't leaking no more, but I can't give you no water till you get new fixtures."

"All right, I'll get back to you this afternoon."

#Mr. Ale Elatey?#

He leaned against the wall. *Yes?*

#The Coalition monitors have just permitted me access to some information in regards your earlier question. Unlike your refugee, I could find no hard evidence linking the Coalition to any attack on you; there is, of course, some circumstantial evidence, but not enough to convince a court. Shall I continue to keep your question on permanent file?#

Yes. And do your experts have any hunches?

#I did not realize that you were consulting me in my professional capacity.#

You mean you're going to charge me?

#Oh, no, professional courtesy, you know. Merely an eccentricity of my programming. One must formally request O/R/A.#

All right, then. Consider this a formal request for opinions, research, and advice.

#Done. Will you stay on line, or shall I call you back?#

Ah—

#Wait.# Small voices chattered in the distance. Ale strained to make out what they were saying, but could not. Then The Oracle returned: #One consulting Computer-Linked Expert wishes to know the extent of your previous political involvement.#

None.

#Wait.#

A minute passed, and another. His attention wandered from the dark cavern where mouse-squeak voices whispered in the shadows, and focused on the fact that he stood against a living room wall, holding a clay pot with—

#Another consulting Computer-Linked Expert wishes to know if you have, perhaps, stumbled over any sort of ancient Chinese secret that might either threaten the Coalition's survival or enhance the position of the Dac invaders.#

Something in the question provoked a nebulous idea. It flitted vaguely across the back of Ale's mind, showing itself just long enough to hint at its desirability, and then disappeared. He watched it go and wondered what it had been. *No, I don't think so.*

#Wait.# A high-pitched freight train whistled past as The Oracle fed data to someone in the background. #A Computer-Linked Expert on actuarial statistics has just inquired as to the number of Seeleys who have died in the last twenty-four months.# A tone sounded. #He wishes to address all CLEs.#

It took less than a second for The Oracle to patch everyone together and surrender control of its voice to the Seeley.

#Ladies and gentlemen, I very sorry intrude on you like so, but I specialty actuarial statistics. Please apologize very bad English. I do good all sorts numbers, not so good words. Oracle say one thousand thirteen Seeleys die last two year. Seem like too many. Oracle now comming more data to my actuarial program. Very sorry, need permission victimized Seeley look at his files.#

The Oracle said, #That's you, Mr. Ale Elatey.#

Code name and all?

#I shall issue you a new one later.#

Oh, all right. But wait: what is my code name?

#E. O. Reischauer.#

How flattering.

#Yes, isn't it? Thank you for your consent.#

Something whined through the darkness, then: #Coarse analysis say death rate for Seeley universe twice normal. Many, many accident. Must be we very clumsy, or maybe just too very bad luck.#

From the darkness came a hoot of derision.

#Ah, so. Statistically unlikely. But Samson-in-temple is Western role model myth, yes? So what if some big orgazation with lotsa power got idea world needs new Dark Age, huh? Iz better way to do?#

TOP TEN NEWS STORIES OF THE HOUR

16 June 2188 1200 EDT
New England Region

RANK HEADLINE	price	LEAD SENTENCE
#1 SAH'S FIANCE OD'S IN HANOI	.25	DFF20 AVHSLX RZPV, the intended husband of turncoat singer Sah, was found dead in his bourgeois Hanoi apartment twenty minutes ago, the decadent victim of an overdose of superhero, said a spokesrep for the Ho Communist DP Emergency Services.
#2 * * * * * * FLAMES CLAIM 178 IN MUNICH HIGH-RISE	.20	#2 * * * * * * Firefighters from all major Munich parties are battling twenty-meter flames that have already killed at least one hundred seventy-eight residents of the stricken high-rise, left eleven thousand homeless, and pumped in excess of twenty-five tons of CO_2 into the air.
#3 * * * * * * DOW UP TWELVE	.15	#3 * * * * * * Its greed whetted by prospects of increased grain exports, the stock market opened sharply higher this morning, with the biggest gainers concentrated in the agricultural equipment field.
#4 * * * * * * AID EMSISICKS	.10	#4 * * * * * * The CCU's actor-turned-

RANK HEADLINE	price	LEAD SENTENCE

WINS AGAIN, NEW VD/NA/DPI

novice-politico, Aid Emsisicks, has won the post of Vice Director for North America, CCU DP Information, less than thirty-six hours after entering the political arena for the first time.

#5 * * * * * * *

MIT PROF SAYS POPE TRAPPED IN TWELFTH CENTURY .10

#5 * * * * * *

AEA92 BUWLIC C76Z, Nobel Laureate and Professor Emeritus of Computer Science at MIT, said Pope Han Il's condemnation of the van Gogh program sale "shows a basic incomprehension of the essence of modern science and technology."

#6 * * * * * * *

FREAK RAIN WASHES OUT WARSAW .10

#6 * * * * * *

Flood waters fed by forty-six centimeters of rain in the last thirty-six hours are rising in the streets of this Polish city, driving tens of thousands of people to higher levels.

#7 * * * * * *

COALITION LABELS COLONY TALK FOOLISH GOSSIP .10

#7 * * * * * *

In response to thousands of inquiries flooding the central data banks of the Coalition, a spokesrep for the Coalition denied today that the Dac ship on its way to L5 is carrying alien colonists.

#8 * * * * * *

STREETERS RAMPAGE IN KOBE .10

#8 * * * * * *

More than eight hundred streeters in this Japanese port city began rioting, looting, and burning shortly after sundown this evening (local time), apparently in reaction to the arrests

yesterday of two thousand
Tokyo streeters.

#9 * * * * * * **#9** * * * * * *

TOP COP DENIES .10
PAYOFF IN
TELEBETTER REC

"I sent out samples because
I have faith in the drug, not
stock in the company," said
the head of Coalition
Intelligence while evading a
reporter's inquiry at a press
conference that ended
minutes ago.

#10 * * * * * * **#10** * * * * * *

COMPUTER CRASH .10
CAUSED BY VIRUS

The Wichita-centered
computer crash that caused
damage across the Midwest
was triggered by a program-
erase virus fed into the
system by dissident
elements, a Coalition
investigative team reported
twenty minutes ago.

This update has been provided as a public service by all data management corporations participating in NEWSBANK/Mao Com, a news
data base organized and supervised by the Maoist Communist Directorate of Public Information.

To read any of the above news stories in full, simply highlight the
title and press ACCEPT. The article will be transmatted to your unit's
memory. Your bank balance will be debited by the sum in the column
headed "price."

To see the headlines of the day's other news stories, simply scroll
your screen up.

Thank you, and do be careful.

VIII

When the Seeleys spoke—to themselves, to specific colleagues, or to the assembly as a whole—The Oracle routed each comment only to as many individuals as the context and the speaker's intentions seemed to require. A two-party conversation could seem like an old-fashioned telephone call.

Now, though, as the assembly of experts finished digesting the actuary's suggestion, everyone wanted to speak to everyone else. Twenty thousand voices roared out of the darkness. It sounded like a convention held in an elevator. #Preposterous!# shouted one; and #Bullshit on preposterous, it has to be right!# #You're accusing them of genocide?# #It'd be aristocide, but who the hell could be crazy enough—#

Ale's head hurt. He could not possibly keep track of who was saying what, not when twenty thousand babbles intertwined with and overrode each other. Of The Oracle he asked, *What effect* would *killing all Seeleys have on the culture?*

But apparently The Oracle thought he meant his remark to be broadcast, too, for someone responded, #Absolutely none!#

#Whaddaya mean, take out twenty thousand of the brightest—#

#World population—#

#Would it not depend on both the murder rate and the replacement rate?#

#Yeah, you keep skimming the cream off—#

#Heavens, it would be a million years before one noticed any effect!#

#He's right, and besides, you got all those books banked—#

Do we? asked Ale.

#Well, sure—#

My Ph.D. thesis has been erased. How's yours?

The question rippled outward like the shock wave of a bomb.

For a moment the chamber itself seemed to hold its breath. Then a new blast of noise surged through it as hundreds of Seeleys discovered their books, papers, and articles missing entirely from the data banks.

The Oracle spoke up: #Ladies and gentlemen, may I suggest a brief recess while you arrange your thoughts? With twenty thousand of you speaking—and interrupting—simultaneously, the general confusion level has risen so high that to switchboard you properly taxes even my capabilities.#

With that it evicted them all back into real time and the real world.

Dazed by the abrupt end to interface, Ale looked around. The rent-a-cleans had gone, leaving the apartment clean. Terribly, mechanically clean: the carpet shampooed into bright fluffiness; the walls scrubbed, patched, repainted but not replanted; the windows full of glass so new that only the machine-cool air convinced Ale the frames held any glass at all.

But where had the furniture gone? The place looked like it was waiting to be rented. He wandered from room to room, opening doors at random and glancing in. No furniture anywhere. Neat stacks of brown plastic boxes in every corner, though, each box full of papers or mementoes or— He opened one in the bare room that had been Emdy's office, and found within the carefully labeled floppy disks she used as backups for her on-line storage.

"Where the hell did everything go?"

A door banged and he jumped.

"Sorry." Wef DiNaini emerged from the front closet. "Didn't mean to startle you. Told you your insurance company was going to pay for just about everything around this place. You're getting a brand-new set of household effects here, Ale. From soap to nutcrackers. They'll start shipping it once the massie's replaced." He glanced at his watch. "Another couple hours, I suppose."

"I wonder if we should bother," he said gloomily.

"You mean 'cause you're moving soon? Well, we can check with Emdy, see if she wants to replace everything now or maybe wait on some of it—"

"No, that's not what I mean. I—" He looked sharply at the wizened old man. "Nah, never mind."

Dark eyes bright and bold, Wef stared right back. "Bad news from The Oracle, huh?"

"You might say that."

"What?"

"Ahh." He waved a hand.

"No, come on, tell me."

"Look, Wef—"

"What, you think I'm going to run tell? Ale, I already know that the Coalition's tried to knock you off a couple of times, now. What can you tell me that's worse than that?"

He gave a short, sad laugh. "That it's not just me. That it's all Seeleys everywhere. All twenty thousand of us."

"They tried to get all of you today?"

"No, no . . . they're doing it slowly, it looks like. Lots of accidents. Diseases. This statistics type, he said our mortality rate's twice normal. Not only that, they're erasing our books. Bit by bit, they're wiping us out."

"That's crazy!"

Ale nodded. "What none of us can figure is *why!*"

"You're saying that makes a difference?"

Unexpected, the question made him lean back, eyes wide. "Huh?"

"Dead is dead, Ale." He shoved his hands into his pants pockets. "Got a mad dog coming at you, you can't fart around asking 'Why? why? why?' You slam your door—or you throw a net over the sucker—or you shoot it." He took his right hand from his pocket. He was holding the Dac gun. "Found this in one of the kitchen cupboards. Thought you might want to keep it. Here." He held it out to Ale. "Funny sort of grip."

"Uh—" Weighing the weapon on his palm, he tried to find an explanation.

"You don't have to say anything. But I'd keep that somewhere closer to hand than the kitchen. You got people coming after you, you might need that in a hurry."

"Thanks." He pocketed it.

"So what are you folks planning on doing?"

"Haven't got the faintest of ideas, Wef."

"Can I make a suggestion?"

"Sure."

"Whatever you do, make sure all of you do it together." He coughed into his fist. "I think it was Ben Franklin said, back when they were planning the Revolution, something like, 'Let us all hang together, or gentlemen, we shall assuredly hang separately.' Good advice when you got something big as the Coalition after you."

"You're probably right."

"I am right, and you know it—" The front doorbell rang. "Lemme quick say, you guys need any help I can give, you just ask, all right?"

"Thanks." He went to the door. "Video."

Wef chuckled. "Your computer's out, remember? Got to do it the old-fashioned way—use the peep hole."

"Uh-huh." He squinted through the tiny lens. A blue and white cart waited in the hall, rocking back and forth on its wheels. "Pholo company."

"Well, let 'im in."

Ale reached for the latch—*after* he slipped his hand into his pocket. The alien metal reassured him. He did not really think that an assassin in disguise stood outside, but . . . better safe than sorry. He swung the door open.

"Hi, hear you had some more trouble." The cart rolled into the vestibule. "Your wife okay?"

"She will be, once she heals."

"Nice lady; shame it had to happen. Gas from Jupiter, by Jove." It paused expectantly. "That's uh, a joke there?"

"Not funny," said Wef.

"Hey, you don't live— Wef Di*Nai*ni?"

"Yeah, who—"

"The name 'Transistor' mean anything to you?"

"You're shitting me! It's been what, thirty years? What are you doing working for the pholo company?"

"My Parole Officer explained it to me, said if I hadda be a thief, I better do it legally." It bent its lens back to Ale. "Same locations?"

"Please."

"Okay." Wheels rumbling across the parquet floor, it moved toward the study.

"You don't mind if we watch, do you?" said Wef.

"Hell, I won't even notice—install's an automatic job, so once—"

"Uh-uh," said Ale and Wef simultaneously.

It braked. "What's the matter?"

Ale said, "Remember what happened last time your cart was here on automatic?"

"Come on, guys, I'm telling three jobs right now, and—"

"Uh, Transistor?"

"Yeah, Wef?"

"Does the ID/dress 'EPC70 CFCCUA GPVY' mean anything to you?"

It did not move, but through its speaker spat the sound of a hand slapping a console. "How'd you find that out, Wef?"

"Transistor, this is Wef DiNaini, here. Now. Are you going to handle this personally? Or do you think you can convince your P.O. that those really aren't your electroprints on that withdrawal?"

"Withdrawal? Aw, shit, you wouldn't, Wef."

"Ale here's my host. Guy's gotta be a good guest, you know?"

"Which is to say you would, huh?"

"In a flash."

"Okay. Personal install, coming up. Just lead me to the spot."

—2—

It hooked up three new pholos—one for each office, and the third in the living room—in less than half an hour. Ale and Wef hovered over it throughout, although Ale felt silly because he was a Sinologist, not an electronics technician. "Transistor" could wire packets of plastic explosive into every receiver and Ale would never notice it.

It disconcerted him to know the ID/dress of the repairman. It was disturbing. A reality of life was that those who cared for your appliances manifested themselves as appliances. They came to your door in metalized boxes that rolled on plastic wheels. They did not have names, they had logos.

Ale kept looking at "Transistor" instead of at its manipulators; he kept wondering where the guy lived, and whether he liked his job, and how he had ever gotten mixed up with someone like Wef DiNaini.

Once "Transistor" (Ale could no longer bring himself to think of him as "the cart") had left, he asked Wef that.

"He helped me de-bug a program once." Wef looked thoughtful for a moment. "Hell, the statute of limitations has expired, may as well tell you what it was. Gorgeous program. First, it set up about six thousand dummy accounts, spread 'em from Cleveland down to Rio, and east-west from ocean to ocean. I had a real nice machine, so it only took about ten minutes to get that part out of the way. Then we commed the program into the banks of Cleveland Electric Illuminating just before they ran their payroll. What this did was, *after* their payroll program calculated what CEI owed each person, but *before* the program pumped a credit memo to that person's bank, *our* program changed the person's ID/dress and bank info. So the Cee-em went to us—"

"But—"

"Wait." Wef held up his hand. "I can see where you're headed, but let me finish. Okay. As soon as the CEI computer kicked out that Cee-em, our program told it to change the ID/dress and bank data *back* to what it had been, and erase the dummy info. So—this is a small utility here—an hour later, the payroll's all done. There's money in four thousand of those accounts. Our program proceeds to erase all transaction records at CEI, slip over to CEI's bank's computers where it does the same, then it erases itself. Then—and this is where it gets really neat—"

"Wef." It was getting late. He wanted to call Emdy, never mind what the doctors said about waiting till the next morning. "I'd like—"

"Hold on. Listen. It's sort of complicated, but I think you'll be able to follow it. At this point we've got two mill in four thousand separate accounts. The program—"

"Which you said had erased itself."

Wef's face wrinkled with exasperation. "The copy in CEI's memories, sure. But our copy is still running. It goes through and changes all the ID/dresses on those four thousand accounts—just to confuse things—then it moves all the money into a thousand of the original accounts that were never used, and closes out the first four thousand accounts. The trail's already pretty damn confused for anybody trying to follow it, but each of those thousand accounts 'buys' enough from fifty-three different massie order houses to empty out the accounts. Which are then closed. Those massie order houses are in serious financial trouble, though, so they pay off their two hundred different suppliers and close up shop. The suppliers—who are me, Transistor, and the program, if you haven't picked up on that yet—then use the cash to buy more supplies, which they then turn around and sell to legit massie order houses. All this in about forty-five minutes."

"I can't believe you got away with that."

"Well, the truth of the matter is—" Wef shrugged. "We didn't. They got us about two years later, but by then each of us was worth about twenty mill and could afford *real* good lawyers."

"Why'd you make a big deal in the beginning, then, about the statute of limitations and all that?"

The old man grinned. "Didn't figure you'd sit still for the story if I started it with, 'Lemme tell you 'bout a scam/gram that flopped.'"

"Oh, Jesus."

"The massie techs ought to be here—lemme call, tell them to hurry up."

"All right, and I'll call Emdy."

"Assuming she's awake—" He gave Elatey a pitying glance. "—just how do you think she's going to *hear* you?"

"This is Connecticut, Wef. I don't know how it works down there in Florida, but up here all hospital pholos have a voice-trans program."

"Oh." He looked abashed. "I forgot about that. Well, give her my best. And I'll see if I can't get a massie in here for you real soon now."

"Thanks." He went to his study, sat on the bare (but, now that it had been shampooed, surprisingly soft) carpet, and called the hospital.

There was no Room 8792. Mrs. M'ti Emtenne had heard it wrong. So he asked for Emdy Ofivo.

The switchboard at first denied that Emdy was there, then confessed that the program which entered new admissions into the Directory had been acting up lately, but it could transfer him to Billing, which would surely know everything because their machines always worked perfectly. Without fail.

Billing, however, insisted that the Hospital Code of Confidentiality precluded revealing anything about a patient who, if she had not listed herself in the Directory, obviously was opting for privacy and seclusion.

At that point Billing disconnected him. Growling, he called the Emergency Room, which did not know the room but did know the floor, and switched him to the desk on the eighty-second floor. There, an officious nurse so thoroughly starched and capped that he had to crackle when he breathed, maintained that only immediate family could speak to Ms. Emdy Ofivo, and if the caller could not produce an ID/dress card for purposes of identity verification, the caller could wait until Ms. Emdy Ofivo called him, the hospital released Ms. Emdy Ofivo, or hell froze over, whichever came first.

He tried the switchboard again, and got the same operator

who, now that she had a floor number to work with, was willing to do a quick Directory cross-elimination to ascertain which rooms Emdy could *not* be in. According to the Directory, there were only two vacant rooms on the floor. The obliging switchboard tried both numbers for him.

Emdy answered at the second. Bandages over her ears, she wore a pale lemon hospital nightie and cradled a keyboard in her lap. Her blue eyes, bloodshot from the explosion and dulled by the painkillers, still managed to sparkle when her husband's image formed before her.

He looked at his watch. Twenty minutes. Considering what he had been up against, he had made pretty good time.

Printed words appeared in a white balloon apparently tethered to Emdy's upper lip: "HI, ALE. VOICE TRANS ON. PARDON SYNTAX; I TYPE SLOW. YOU CAN READ THIS, OR IT SYNTHESIZES VOICE. YOUR CHOICE."

What a choice. He could talk to a character in a comic strip, or listen to a metal monotone. Like The Oracle, but with less sophistication. "I'll read." At least that would let him inflect her words any way he wanted.... "How are you?"

Her balloon disappeared when he spoke; she waited for words to form in his. Then she nodded cautiously. "OKAY, I GUESS. NO PAIN. RINGING—" She pointed to her gauze-swathed ears. "DOC SAYS, OBSERAVT—" Frowning, she backspaced and lifted off the last three letters, then retyped: "—VATION TONIGHT. HOME TOMORROW."

"Don't worry about typos, huh?"

"WHAT? ROTTEN PROGRAM HERE. QUOTES YOU: 'DONT WORRY ABOUT TIE BOWS (GRUNT).' YOU REALLY SAY THAT?"

"I said—" He caught himself and rephrased it. "—don't worry about typographical errors, all right?"

"AH! GOTCHA! NO WORRY. HOW YOU?"

"Just fine, Emdy—worried silly about you, but I was outside, it missed me completely."

For a moment she looked puzzled—he figured the translation program had probably written 'Emdy' as 'empty'—but then her forehead unwrinkled and she wrote, "WHAT HAPPENED?"

Briefly he hesitated. Someone could be tapping the line. He had not worried about it while in interface, because The Oracle did not permit *anyone* to eavesdrop on its internal conversations, but now. . . . He decided not to let it bother him. If the Coalition knew that he knew, they would either lay off—or kill him immediately, overtly. And better they try the latter when his Emdy was out of harm's way. He did not want her injured on his account again. "There's no proof," he said, "but it looks like the Coalition re-routed a shipment of Jovian gas from Yale Astrophysics Labs to our massie."

It took her a moment to assimilate that. She blinked. Her fingers flew: "WHAT? WHY?"

"We don't know."

"'WE?' YOU & WEF?"

"ORA:CLE—we had a Seeley conference this afternoon. *Somebody* is going after us—and getting a bunch of us. Who else has that kind of power but the Coalition?"

"NOBODY. MISTAKE?"

"I don't think so." Briefly, he told her about what Wef claimed to have learned, and then related the actuary's statistics and conclusions. "We're going to be meeting again later on, and—"

She shook her head.

"What's the matter?"

Carefully she typed, "I HAVE A BAD FEELING ABOUT THIS. SOMETHING REALLY DIRTY GOING TO HAPPEN. DON'T GET INVOLVED."

"But I'm *already* involved."

She pursed her lips. "COA BEEN KILLING QUIETLY, DISCREETLY—ONE HERE, ONE THERE. IF CLE'S ACT, MAKE NOISE, WHATEVER, THEN COA'LL GO FOR NOISY ONES FIRST, LEAVE YOU ALONE. YOU KEEP QUIET, YOU KEEP SAFE."

"Until the 'noisy ones' are all shut up—permanently. Then they'll come back for me."

"NO! COA HAVE TO GET NOISY ONES QUICKLY. MEANS MESSILY. WIND UP WITH BIG HUE AND CRY, PUBLIC OUTRAGE. COA TOP BRASS GET VOTED OUT, GO TO PRISON. WHOLE THING OVER AND DONE WITH, YOU SAFE. YOU SEE? LIKE WAR—FRONT LINE DANGEROUS, REAR ECHELON PRETTY SAFE."

"And you want me to hide in the rear echelons until this whole thing blows over, is that what you're saying?"

"YES!"

"Emdy, if other Seeleys are dying, I can't just—"

"YOU ARE THE ONLY PERSON IN THIS WHOLE
WORLD I CARE ABOUT. LET OTHER CLE SPOUSES
WORRY ABOUT THEIR LOVERS; I'M TELLING YOU,
DON'T GET INVOLVED."

"Emdy—"

"DAMN YOU ALL80, WHAT AM I SUPPOSED TO DO
IF YOU GET KILLED? EVEN IN A GOOD CAUSE? WHAT
DO I SLEEP WITH, A MEMORY? I WANT *YOU*, NOT A
PLAQUE ON A WALL SOMEWHERE. YOU GET MAR-
TYRED, YOU'LL BE A LOUSY HUSBAND."

Instinctively he reached out to the pholo. He wanted to touch
her, to reassure her that he would be fine, but that he *had* to
get involved because he had to do something to guarantee his
survival . . . of course his hand passed through the sphere of
light and he felt foolish. "Emdy, I—"

#Mr. Ale Elatey, the conference is about to resume.#

Yeah, I'll be there in a minute.

#Very good, sir.#

"Emdy, I have to go—the meeting's going to start in a
minute."

Her fingers flew as she pounded out: "ALE—"

"Look, I'll be okay, don't worry about me. Just concentrate
on getting better. Oh, God," he said, suddenly remembering,
"listen, Wef's replacing the furniture; you'd better give him a
call on the living room number and double-check his taste. I
think he's only getting stuff that's identical to what was destroyed, but you'd better check. I'll call you later, all right? I
love you, Emdy." He blew her a kiss and reached for the
disconnect button.

But she was typing, so he waited to read: "IF YOU GET
YOURSELF KILLED, I'LL NEVER SPEAK TO YOU
AGAIN!"

"Fair enough." He smiled. "See you later, beautiful."

He switched the pholo off. Metallic scraping noises came
from the kitchen; he assumed the technicians had arrived with
their new mass-transceiver. He hoped Wef was keeping an eye
on them, because he had to go back into interface.

Wearily, he shook himself, and plunged into the endless
darkness of the cavern.

—3—

#—ell, what else can we do?#

#Bullshit on resigning! Let's find out who ordered this and fight fire with fire—arrange some accidents for them!#

#Don't you understand? We've been trying to trace the orders but they've covered their tracks. Hell, we can't even find a record of the orders.#

#Then let's be bloodthirsty! Let's just start going after Coalition people until the message gets through.#

#Innocent bystanders?#

#There's no such thing as an innocent politician!#

#Scholars, scholars, please!# called a new voice. Loud and forceful, it was nonetheless calm. #Bickering will solve nothing. Indecisiveness aids only the enemy. Panic will destroy us all. May I suggest, therefore, that each of us does what all of us do best: focus on truth.#

#Back to our books? Are you crazy?#

#Oh, no. Not back to our books. We have a mystery before us, my colleagues, a mystery that we must solve if we are to survive. We have also twenty thousand of the finest intelligences in the world linked together into this marvel known as ORA:CLE. Now is not the moment for false modesty. Let us wield our brilliance like a pathologist's scalpel, and discover the social cancer endangering us all.#

#That's a pretty speech,# shouted someone else, #but what the hell does it mean?#

#To put it quite simply, we are trying, each of us, to solve in a moment, a problem much too large for any one of us to solve in a year. Let us divide the task into more manageable portions. According to our actuarial colleague, one thousand thirteen of us have died in the last two years. Were we banded in groups of twenty, each group could study the case of one of our late colleagues with almost microscopic scrutiny. We could determine, for example, what research the individual in question was attempting, what opinions and/or advice it had rendered, what contacts inside the Coalition it had. . . . Do you really not see? From questions like those we search for motives and then, provided with two starting points—for in many cases we know the means of death—we establish opportunity, and work our way backwards to the identities of the murderers.

We compile a mosaic of thousands upon thousands of data bits. I suggest we commence immediately.#

#Oh, sure! We just hunker down over our 'microscopes' and squint away, huh? And in the meantime, how many of us die?#

#Given the computer capabilities available to us, we should be able to complete the initial phase by early this afternoon.#

That silenced the heckler—at least, the next voice belonged to someone entirely different. #Sorry. What 'initial phase' refer to?#

#It consists of proving, to our satisfaction and to the satisfaction of any reasonable audience, that, indeed, five hundred some Seeleys have been murdered in the past two years. Suspicion is not enough; statistics are not enough. We must have proof, my friends, for if we do not, the release of our preliminary findings will have a negligible impact on the public.#

#So we *going* take our case to world, eh?# said someone nearer to Ale, and a bit below him.

#Oh, quite. I should expect that we could insert our initial report into the data banks by late this afternoon. And to digress a moment—my colleagues, although our methodology *must* meet all standards of academic rigor, the actual *language* of the final report should be slanted for the average, run-of-the-mill nitwit who makes ho-soap stars so fabulously popular. No passive or stative verbs. No dull words of any sort, and no sentences longer than ten words. Many small words. And large sexual organs, if at all possible. I recommend graphic violence, especially of the less common sort. Play up the angle that the dead belonged to a mysterious elite—we are an intellectual aristocracy, and commoners are *always* fascinated by aristocrats. Speak of eccentricities. Make the dead seem larger than life.#

#Now wait a minute! That's—#

#My friends, we want people to *read* our report. From beginning to end. I guarantee you, they will ignore, totally, the sort of reflexive, convoluted, polysyllabic prose, from which we have sucked all life, with which we are all so comfortable. Excite the readers! Titillate them! Make them buy our story, make them ache for us. Now. I believe The Oracle is ready to divide you up into research groups—#

Five milliseconds later Ale—along with eighteen other Seeleys—was assigned the task of researching the life and almost-death of one Ale Elatey.

The data transmission whined in the background. *Hey, wait a minute!*

The whistle stopped. #It's quite all right, Mr. Ale Elatey. I did promise that I would assign you a new code name.#

But—

#Ah. The revelation of your true identity disturbs you, does it? I regret that, but I'm afraid it is essential.#

I don't like it.

#You may, if you prefer, resign.#

Ah . . . no, I don't think so.

#Very well, then.#

The whine resumed. A few seconds later, a new intonation pattern took over. #Mr. Ale Elatey. I've got the access codes to all DP/Revenue files. If you could send me a copy of your personal address disks? I plan to identify both the occupations and the employers of everyone you and your wife know—just to see if any of them works for the Coalition.#

I'm sorry, he said, *but those were destroyed in the fire.*

The voice sighed. #Ah, well, I'll work with your neighbors, then.#

Another grilled him about his political affiliations and his voting patterns; a third asked for a list of all the organizations to which he belonged; a fourth wanted permission to inspect his cre/deb accounts; a fifth— Each of the eighteen wanted to know something about the pattern of his life, his thought, his researches. Each hoped that what he learned would solve the problem of why the Coalition wanted Ale Elatey dead.

After two hours his team told him to write the report.

In the nearby darkness hovered eighteen presences, alive with data and correlations and keen-edged suspicions. Ale said, *How do you do this?*

One of his teammates answered. #You can either write directly to memory, or you can pretend that you're sitting at a keyboard and—#

Ah! Just like he did with that 'azalea' he trained while he sat around waiting for queries. *Now I understand.*

He made a pass with his hands. The darkness faded into fluorescent light. One gesture created walls, floor, a roof; a second furnished the small room with a polished mahogany desk and a leather-upholstered swivel chair. A flick of the finger put a computer screen on the desktop. Finding it good, he smiled, and sat.

"My ID/dress is ALL80 AFAHSC NFF6—" Each word

appeared on the screen as soon as he spoke it. "—and until
recently I worked as a Seeley under the code name 'E. O.
Reischauer.' I believe that the Coalition has attempted to arrange my demise three times."

#You're getting a little prolix there, Ale,# said another
voice.

Oh. He scowled at the screen and the words disappeared.
Lemme try again. "My name is Ale Elatey. I'm a Seeley. My
code name used to be 'E. O. Reischauer.' I think the Coalition's tried to kill me at least three times in the last day and a
half."

#Much better,# murmured the kibitzer.

"I don't have hard proof, just hunches. Circumstantial evidence, if you will. Yesterday morning, somebody rewrote the
software running my DacWatch. Just mine, not anybody else's.
They fixed it to show a green light all the time. The building
cops watch the entrance to the junction box room twenty-four
hours a day, and they said nobody went in to do it manually.
It had to have been done through the DacWatch network itself.
I don't know if you know this or not, but the Coalition provides
all the software for DacWatch—and supervises the network's
operation.

"Yesterday afternoon, a cart came over to fix my pholo.
The job was simple, so it ran on auto. It put in a heavy-duty
laser that burned a hole through my wall, and almost through
my forehead." He touched the still-tender area: for his own
benefit, not the readers'; they would see only words. "The
pholo company tapes everything its carts do—and the tape of
this incident shows that the cart got a radio transmission
from . . . someone. The first thing the transmission told the cart
to do was turn off its tape recorders. Now, the Coalition isn't
the only group around that has override software—but nobody
else has that software legally. To be fair, someone else could
have done it—someone with a transmitter, with the software,
with a reason to kill me—and someone who knew my pholo
was broken. The last call I made before the pholo broke was
to the local office of the Coalition. You figure it."

He paused, wiped sweat off his neck, and went on. "The
third time was this morning. Research scientists in orbit around
Jupiter sent some gas from Jupiter to Yale University. It came
into my massie, instead, and exploded. The Coalition has interfaced its own monitors with all mass-transceiver relay sta-
tions operating off Earth. The station that relayed the gas to

my apartment said maybe sunspot interference did it. The Coalition erased all internal records of all its monitors on that station. You figure it.

"That's about it for my story. Like I said in the beginning, no solid proof, just circumstantial evidence and hunches. But when you put my story together with all the other stories of so-called accidents that happened to other Seeleys, you get to thinking. And wondering. Why is the Coalition doing this to us? Why is it killing us off?"

He was done. He leaned back, realizing as his muscles began to relax just how tense he had been.

What a lovely typewriter, though.... He had never before "written" while interfaced, but if The Oracle said it was okay, he would certainly write his paper on Tan Wang Ch'i right here.

His eighteen teammates finished their review. #Well done,# said the one who had accused him of being prolix.

Thanks.

The Oracle broke in. #Ladies and gentlemen, the report seems to be completed. I am depositing it in the data banks now. I suggest all of you go home, rest, and be prepared to defend your conclusions when the inevitable denials, and accusations of slander, begin to arise. That's all.#

He found himself in the middle of his study, now fully equipped: while he had been in interface, Wef had had a desk, a recliner, a pole lamp, an end table, and a computer installed. With a yawn, Ale got to his feet. He was stiff all over. To loosen up, he tried to touch his toes—but could not. "To hell with it."

He sat in the recliner, pushed it back, and frowned. The cushioning bulged in all the wrong places. He shifted his weight around, wondering why Wef had bought something so poorly stuffed—then nodded to himself as he understood. *This* recliner had not yet learned the contours of his body. He would have to break it in.

Turning his head, he studied the computer. An ibn Dauod 1000, hmm, the whole line had a reputation for quality, durability, and—he gulped—high prices...but the insurance company was paying, so what did it matter? He looked at it more carefully. Plastic housing tinted a discreet gun-metal grey, sculptured keyboard with two dozen keys whose purpose he did not immediately recognize. He would have Wef explain it all before he even tried to turn it on.

Pushing out of the recliner, he ambled through the massie chamber into the kitchen, where a gleaming new refrigerator stood stuffed with food and what had to be three cases of Wef's beer. He fixed himself a snack.

Odd that the pholo had not rung yet. He had expected that, once the article hit the data banks, all three of their pholos would be ringing constantly, just as they had after his narrow escape from the Dac.

He wandered into the living room. Wef DiNaini sat at the far end, hunched over the keyboard of the new main apartment computer, eyes fastened to the seventy-five-centimeter screen that displayed, in six different key colors, the floor plan of a large office building. "Hey, Wef."

The old man ignored him.

"Hey, Wef!"

No response.

He walked over and tapped Wef on the shoulder.

The refugee raised his head slowly, blinked, and said, "Oh. Ale. Sorry. I was sorta lost in thought there...."

Ale goggled at the terminal. "Wef. When I saw an ibn Dauod 1000 in my study, I figured that was pretty classy—but this is a 4500! It costs ten times what—"

Wef poked him in the stomach. "It didn't cost you a penny, boy; it's all coming out of the insurance company's account."

"But the whole old one didn't cost what this keyboard must have—how did you convince the insurance company—uh-oh," he said, as a self-congratulatory look brightened Wef's eyes, "I have a funny feeling that you—"

"You're an Eighty, Ale. You need a good machine. And most Eighties have good machines, anyway. Didn't take more'n, say, three minutes at the public computer downstairs to make the insurance company think you *always* had a 4500. Anybody reviews it, they won't think twice about the model. And the old one's been resiked already, so don't you worry."

"Oh, thanks...." He bit his lip as he looked over to the pholo. "The pholos *are* working, aren't they?"

"You used one yourself, a couple hours ago, right?"

"Yeah, but... frankly, I was expecting to get a lot of calls tonight." Quickly, he explained. "I haven't even gotten one yet."

Wef said, "You sure it's banked?"

"Let me check." Closing his eyes, he slipped into interface. *Hey, Oracle!*

#Yes, Mr. Ale Elatey?#

Have you put that report in the data banks yet?

#But of course. TIME-CBS, Barron-McGraw, half a dozen others.#

What's the title?

#"Coalition Killing Scholars." Cross-indexed under assassination, conspiracy, Dark Age, all proper names—#

Thanks. He returned to real time and told Wef what The Oracle had said.

"Well, let's check it out." As the old man tapped at the keyboard, he looked apologetically at Ale. "They sent the wrong make voice-reader, replacement's coming tomorrow. There." He hit the last key.

The screen said, NO FILE.

"That's funny," said Wef. "Let me just—"

Ale was already back in interface. *Hey, Oracle—*

#No need, Mr. Ale Elatey. I, too, have just checked. Your report was erased in its entirety. Every data bank now seems infested with a Coalition Monitor Program which obliterates the report every time I enter it. We are being censored.#

TOP TEN NEWS STORIES OF THE HOUR

RANK HEADLINE	price	LEAD SENTENCE
#1 **VISTULA SAVAGES WARSAW; THOUSANDS DROWN**	.20	Swollen by incessant downpours that have dropped up to seventy-five centimeters of rain in the last forty-eight hours, the Vistula River broke its levees and raged through the streets of this unprepared Polish city this afternoon, drowning thousands and causing billions of dollars worth of damage.
#2 * * * * * * **RALLY DRIVES DOW TO HIGHEST LEVEL IN THREE YEARS**	.15	#2 * * * * * * Led by impressive gains in the agricultural equipment field, the Dow-Jones Industrial Average rose 21¼, on a volume of 248,556,000 shares, to close at 2493.75, its highest since April 2185.
#3 * * * * * * **AID EMSISEN OKAYS CLOSE-UP ON CELEBS**	.10	#3 * * * * * * In a ruling aimed at the viewer/caster constituency, Aid Emsisen, the CCU Vice Director for North America, DP Information, relaxed eleven separate regulations that denied the public access to intimate details of celebrities' lives.

RANK	HEADLINE	price	LEAD SENTENCE

#4 * * * * * * *

BOMB SHATTERS LM2 HQ .10

#4 * * * * * * *

A major explosion ripped apart the Luna City office of PKU40 BPJRDC RLNT, VP and acting president of LM2, who earlier today told reporters that she would not pay the protection fee demanded by the murderers of her predecessor, BHK30 BHXNDP JUH2.

#5 * * * * * * *

REPAIR CART SNAPS; STUFFS GRANDMOTHER IN DISPOSAL .10

#5 * * * * * * *

In Cairo, a General-Hotpoint tele-factor, angry at the fourth service call from the same household in three days, butchered an eighty-seven-year-old woman and was grinding chunks of the corpse in the kitchen disposal when police arrived and executed him, a spokesrep for the Cairo MR/DP Safety announced this afternoon.

#6 * * * * * * *

SIXTH DAC SHIP IDENTICAL TO FIRST FIVE .10

#6 * * * * * * *

In a follow-up to earlier announcements, a Coalition spokesrep revealed this afternoon that long-distance analysis of the latest Dac intruder reveals it to be structurally identical to the starships now parked at L5.

#7 * * * * * * *

UNIVERSITY OF RIO TO CLOSE PERMANENTLY .10

#7 * * * * * * *

Citing "budget cuts beyond the capability of the institution to withstand," the Governors of the University of Rio de Janeiro announced this afternoon that the school will close for good on September 1, 2188.

RANK HEADLINE	price	LEAD SENTENCE

#8 * * * * * * *

SIBERIAN REINDEER ON MARCH .10

#8 * * * * * *

Thousands of reindeer are moving south from the parched Siberian tundra in search of water, reports from gas-line service telefactors say.

#9 * * * * * * *

SAH: POLICE LIED .10

#9 * * * * * *

At an emotional news conference, pop singer Sah accused the Ho Communist DP Pathology of lying in its Coroner's report on the death of DFF20 AVHSLX RXPV, the singer's elderly fiancé.

#10 * * * * * * *

FAMED SCHOLAR DEAD IN MUNICH FIRE .10

#10 * * * * * *

A spokesrep for the Christian-Democrat DP Safety confirmed that this morning's blaze in a Munich high-rise claimed the life of GBU90 CGFVIG JIPU, prize-winning author of a study on the relation between twentieth century music and the Great Depression of 2010.

This update has been provided as a public service by all data management corporations participating in NEWSBANK/MR, a news data base organized and supervised by the Muslim-Republican Directorate of Public Information

To read any of the above news stories in full, simply highlight the title and press ACCEPT. The article will be transmitted to your unit's memory. Your bank balance will be debited by the sum in the column headed "price."

To see the headlines of the day's other news stories, simply scroll your screen up.

Thank you, and do be careful.

IX

The sun hid just beneath the eastern horizon; the air lay still while the world held its breath. Ale parted the sliding glass doors and ventured onto the terrace. Half-full watering-can in hand, he watched blearily for Dacs.

He had slept poorly. He was used to blanket tug-of-war, slumberous hugs, and a warm body spooned against his back. He had last slept alone the night before their wedding. He did not like it.

Nor did he like going outdoors when his DacWatch might have been tampered with again.

And he hated the half-emptiness of his watering-can. It drove home the fact that he had but two plants left—that today, because someone, somewhere, wanted him dead, nine cherished works of art rotted on Chapel Street.

He looked around again, patting his pocket for reassurance. The sky was pale, featureless; the forest below dark and forbidding. Five windows glowed in the building opposite—probably tele-factors on the graveyard shift.

He touched the ginkgo's soil. Still damp; he would return later. And the Chinese elm . . . he pursed his lips. Its leaves were yellowing, presumably from trauma. And its soil, too, was moist. He could have stayed indoors.

Overhead a helicopter stirred the pre-dawn calm with harsh, choppy rotor strokes. He glanced up but saw nothing. The sound died away.

Setting down the watering-can, he turned each pot one-quarter of the way around, to let the sun reach the sides that had been in shadow, so that the two survivors would grow evenly. Then he leaned against the railing and watched the eastern sky brighten.

From the scrub forest below drifted a scream. He ignored it. It was probably a streeter fighting off a wild dog; he could not help either of them. Neither would appreciate his help, anyway. He could call a blue, of course, and the blue would drive off the dog, but then the streeter would hide—or the blue would arrest the streeter—or the streeter would disable the blue. . . . No point to it, none at all.

The report had still not hit the data banks. The Oracle had tried all night to slip it in, but the Coalition monitors kept catching and erasing it. He found it hard to blame them. Every member of the Coalition would lose its job and perhaps its freedom if word got out. Naturally they were desperate.

The last big question was why any of it had happened in the first place.

It was not as though the world were a Confucian society in which wealth derived from political power, which itself derived from royal birth *or* from existing wealth *or* from passing a civil service examination based entirely on extensive knowledge of the Classics. In that sort of society, princes, merchants, and scholars automatically challenged each other, because there was, quite simply, not enough to go around.

But this was 2188! With wealth and opportunity enough for all of talent, for anyone who had ability, desire, and the willingness to develop its potential. So why were the politicians slaying the scholars?

He leaned against the railing. Its chill wrought iron cut into the flesh of his forearms. Gieb Uneunzig was dead. Another Seeley gone. It seemed impossible, but—could the Coalition have set that fire? That the Coalition was killing Seeleys was proof of its madness—but could it be *that* mad?

Inside, the doorbell rang. Below, treetops shook violently—and a Dac winged up out of the foliage. *Dammit, they jimmied the alarm again!* Frowning, he grabbed his can and raced back in, closing the terrace doors behind himself. Softly, not wanting to awaken Wef DiNaini, who snored in the closet by the front door, he called, "Video."

The small screen on the inside of the door brightened, then resolved into a blurry picture of a stretcher bearer with the Yale New Haven Hospital logo on its front. Puzzled, Ale said, "Open."

The door swung inwards. The machine moved in on its spidery legs. "Good morning, Mr. Ale Elatey." It spoke in a voice just louder than a whisper. "Bringing your wife home for you." Behind it came a second bearer; between them they carried Emdy Ofivo on a stretcher. Pale, with dark circles under her eyes, she managed a taut smile and a wave. "Ms. Emdy

Ofivo's ears are still pretty sensitive, sir. The doctor told us to warn you about that, and to make sure she wears her earmuffs. Where's the bedroom?"

"This way." He led them there, and pulled the covers down. They lifted her gently onto the bed. While one plumped up her pillows, the other folded the stretcher into a package the size of a briefcase. Ale kissed her on the forehead. "Good morning, beautiful. It's good to have you home."

"It's good to be home," she whispered.

The bearers were starting to leave, so he said, "I'll be right back," and followed them into the hall. "Excuse me."

It turned its camera lens on him. "Yes, sir?"

"Isn't it awful early for this sort of thing?"

"Yes, sir, it is, but we have a lot of deliveries to make today, and your wife was one of the people who were in shape to travel early. I guess that's what it is."

"You guess?" he said sharply.

"Well, *we* don't decide who goes when. Yale New Haven Dispatch just gives us a list: this person at this time, that person at that time."

"Okay." He could say nothing more without sounding paranoid.

"We've got to be going. Be careful."

"Right, you too." He went back inside, closing the door. "Lock." The bolts slapped home.

In the bedroom, Emdy was up and changing.

"Hey, you—"

She recoiled and covered her ears.

"Geez, I'm sorry," he said more quietly. "I forgot. But what are you doing up?"

"I can walk, Ale. Really. It's just these new eardrums are going to be sensitive for a while, that's all. And of course a couple ribs are bruised. But I would have walked from the helicopter, if they'd let me. Rules, they said." She eased a pair of white earmuffs onto her head.

"It's always rules." He made a face. "Can I get you some breakfast?"

"Coffee and juice?"

"Coming up." He started to turn.

"And maybe some croissants, too, if we have any fresh."

He had to smile. "For the first time in years, honey, *everything* is fresh—guarantee you that nothing is more than eighteen hours old."

A few minutes later, she sat down across from him. She had put on makeup that could not disguise her pallor, but her spirits seemed good. She said, "So—"

The toaster *ding*ed.

She cringed away from it, raising her hands as if to shield herself. Then, as she identified the sound, she grimaced. "I seem—"Her voice trembled."—to have acquired a new reflex."

"It'll fade."

"You think so?"

"Uh-huh." He slid the two warm croissants onto a plate and offered her one. She took both. He raised an eyebrow, and put the last two rolls into the toaster. "Butter?"

"And jam, too, please." She accepted the jar with a smile. "So how did everything turn out?"

"Well, we researched all the deaths for the last two years, wrote a comprehensive report on it that The Oracle filed in the data banks—and the damn Coalition monitors erased it all."

"Thank God," she said through a mouth full of pastry crumbs.

"Emdy, you're *grateful* for censorship?"

"You betcha." She swallowed, licked jam off a finger, and pointed the finger at him. "You're a scholar, I'm a business-person. We look at it differently. To you, it's not only some abstract infringement of an even more abstract concept—I mean, what exactly *is* 'freedom of speech?'—it's a personal insult. To me, though, the bottom line is that this'll keep you out of real trouble."

"*Real* trouble? Just—" The toaster chimed. Emdy twitched a centimeter, but no more. He laid the croissants on a plate.

"Ale, could I have some more orange juice, please?"

"Sure." He went to the refrigerator to refill her glass. When he returned, Wef DiNaini was sitting in his chair.

"Hiya, Ale. Good rolls, here. Got any more?"

Ale looked at the empty plate. "No," he said carefully, setting the juice down in front of Emdy, "no, those were the last. . . ."

"Ah, well." Wef leaned across the table to chuck Emdy under the chin. He did keep his voice low, though. "Emdy, doll, love your ears! Glad you're back so soon. Your hubby here is rotten company."

"Thanks a lot, Wef," said Ale, while Emdy chuckled.

"Gotta get to work, gang." He headed for the new computer, but stopped. "Oh, by the way, you guys haven't slotted your new ID/dress cards yet, and the machine's going to stop taking your orders. If you'll give 'em to me—" He held out his hand.

"Have they come?" said Ale.

"Yesterday afternoon—I put 'em on Emdy's desk."

Ale went and got them, then gave them to Wef, who was already warming up the computer. "Here we go."

"Thanks." He popped them in their appropriate slots. "Now you're in business again."

Ale returned to the table and picked up the argument where they had left off. "What do you mean, *real* trouble? There's something false about three attempts on my life?"

"You don't understand."

"That's for sure."

She winced. "Please, not so loud."

"Sorry."

"Ale, this has to be some kind of mistake. The Coalition just wouldn't try to kill off Seeleys as a matter of policy."

"Then why—"

"No, wait. Clearly, somebody in the Coalition has flipped out. No argument there. But it's equally clear, to me at least, that the Coalition will come to realize that, and will take steps."

"To what?"

"To stop the person. *But,* if you make a tremendous fuss about it, why, the Coalition's only option is to deny the whole thing and then get even with you for embarrassing it."

"That's crazy."

"Of course it is. But you have to understand, you're dealing with an institution here. Now, an institution believes what its constituent elements believe. If various members of the Coalition believe that they would be embarrassed by a report linking the Coalition to these murders, then the Coalition is embarrassed, and the Coalition will act. If the members think the report theatens them, then the Coalition itself feels threatened, and it will act. And Ale, honey, the last thing you want to do is make something as big as the Coalition feel threatened. It's really not very safe."

"But if we keep quiet—" *Remember her ears; don't shout.* "—then how are the responsible members of the Coalition going to learn about the rotten apples in their midst? Huh? Tell me that."

"Don't worry, they'll find them. What you—"

"Hey, sorry to interrupt, folks." Wef pulled up a chair and poured himself a cup of coffee. "But I was just diddling around with this new machine and your ID/dress cards, and, uh—Ale, you got a RAT code on yours."

"Huh?"

"A RAT code. 'Report All Transactions.' Anytime you do anything on any computer anywhere, even make a pholo call, Coalition Intelligence gets a copy of it. Just about everybody over a Seventy has a RAT code." He made a face. "Can you imagine how much memory they're wasting on that sort of shit?"

"Wef, why—"

He held up a finger "You also got a WAR code on your card, Ale, and that is one hell of a lot rarer. I'm a little worried."

"War?" said Emdy.

"'Watch And Report.' Every computer you're slotted into keeps you under surveillance at all times, either through its standard peripherals, or through the sensors of any attached household appliances. Like your DacWatch, or your door camera. Everything you say and do is reported straight to the Coalition."

"They're bugging me?"

"More'n that. This is a pretty sophisticated program. The kind that, if the guy on the other end asks it, 'Where is Ale Elatey?' the program can say, 'At his breakfast table, drinking bad coffee with his wife and guest.'"

Emdy went pale. She spoke in an unsteady whisper. "You mean they're listening to us right now?"

Wef grinned, and laid both ID/dress cards on the table. "Nope. Neither of you is slotted in. And just for safety's sake, I told your computer Ale went down the hall."

"This is—" Sputtering, Ale picked up the card and examined the thin magnetic strip on its back. "I've been under constant surveillance all along?"

Wef nodded.

Ale shuddered. Then sat upright as a new thought occurred to him. "You said they could track me through the attached sensors of any household appliances?"

"Yup. Scary, ain't it."

"Worse than that." The clock on their bedroom ceiling had a microphone. One sensitive enough to hear the "Time" command even when it was said so softly that it would not disturb the person still asleep. He sneaked a glance at Emdy, wondering if she, too, had realized that the Coalition could have eavesdropped on their lovemaking. But no blush marred her cheeks, and she was as modest as they came. "Wef, that's an outrage!"

"Uh-huh. That's the the 'WAR' code for you." He scratched behind his right ear. "Want it erased?"

"You bet." He pushed both cards across the table to Wef. "As soon as possible."

"No!" Emdy winced at her own volume.

They both looked at her. "Why not, Emdy?" said Ale.

"Because—because they'll know!"

Wef shook his head. "Nah. They'll just think you're not slotted in."

"Please, Ale. Don't do it. They put that on your card for a reason—I don't know what the reason is, but I know they had one—and—and—"

"Emdy." He folded his hands around her cold fingers. "Emdy, I can see you're scared, but this kind of intrusion into my—our—private lives is just plain wrong. They can't have a reason that could justify it. No way."

"What if they're doing it to protect you?"

"Huh?"

"Well, it's possible, they could have found out about the murderers and so they put that 'WAR' code on so they could make sure you were safe."

"Emdy, you don't believe that yourself."

"Ale—" She pulled her hands out of his. "I have a feeling about all this, a real bad feeling, a hunch that if you just lie low, everything will be okay, but if you do anything wrong, if you make any kind of fuss, you'll be giving the Coalition an excuse to get you."

He looked into her terrified blue eyes. "I'm sorry." Handing the cards to Wef, he said, "Emdy, I have a feeling, too. I think you're wrong. I think the only thing I can do—short of rapelling down to ground level and becoming a streeter—is to resist. If I play it your way, I'm vulnerable to them any time of day or night, because they'll know where I am. And frankly, I don't want that."

Wef returned with the ID/dress cards. "All wiped."

"That was quick."

"Listen, Ale—I couldn't help overhearing what you were saying before about that Monitor Program eating your report. I might be able to help you with it."

Ale raised his eyebrows. "Uh, Wef—no disrespect or anything—but some of the finest computer types in the world work for ORA:CLE, and The Oracle itself is a damn good program. If they—"

Wef waved a hand skeptically. "C'mon, Ale, all of your guys are *honest*—I'll bet none of 'em have spent sixty years figuring out ways of getting around guardgrams without leaving any traces."

"Like you and 'Transistor' did with that Cleveland one?"

Wef shrugged. "I've been caught five times on twenty major ops and literally thousands of minor ones. Now, you ever heard of a blickstrobe champ who hits eighty percent of the time? Course not. Just can't be done. All time top is forty-eight point seven. What I mean to say, Ale, is I'm good. Trust me."

"Well, I don't—"

"Look, Ale, it's just a matter of finding, then cracking, the codes that control access to the censorship programs. If the power's still on down in Florida, I can probably call up my files from here. What can it hurt?"

"Plenty," said Emdy. "Ale, Wef—if you draw attention to yourselves, you make yourselves targets, and—"

"Emdy, honey, I've spent a lifetime *not* drawing attention to myself. Nobody's gonna know it's one of my little beauties that freed up the Seeleys' report."

"But they'll know about Ale!"

Wef shrugged. "They already do. Ale's problem is that nobody else does. Maybe did more people know his name and his situation, that sorta public knowledge would protect him. Anyway, it's up to him."

"Let me check with The Oracle." He avoided his wife's eyes and headed for interface, fighting through the turbulence of the squabble. *Hey, Oracle!*

#Yes, Mr. Ale Elatey?#

Quickly he relayed Wef's offer. *Well?*

#Please thank him on ORA:CLE's behalf, and request him to initiate the programs.#

Right.

Back in the real world, Ale told Wef, "It says go ahead."

Emdy pushed out of her chair and stalked to the window, her back stiff, her jaw tense.

Wef hurried to the console and began issuing it instructions. Muttering, "It figures," Ale did the dishes.

Half an hour passed before Wef jumped up. "Got it!"

"Got what?" said Ale.

Emdy, by now at her desk, kept her head bent over her own computer screen, raising it just long enough to tell her door, "Close."

The firm metal click drowned out Wef's first word; Ale said, "Sorry, say again please?"

"You're on—*and,* you're Number One."

"You got it past the monitors?"

"Uh-yup. And once I did that, I sent a copy to every Recommender in the book—and from what I picked up, they didn't read much more'n the first line before they put it on their 'Must' list. You guys—"

All three pholos rang simultaneously. "Uh-oh," said Ale, remembering the flurry of calls after his first appearance on the best-seller list.

"Not to worry. You don't want to talk?"

"Not particularly."

"Figured as much. Let the machine handle it. Hey, Ace!"

The pholos stopped chiming. Ale said, "A screen?"

"Yeah. Anything for you is getting a 'sorry, he's busy, please try again next month.' Anything for me or Emdy, though, gets patched straight through."

"Thanks."

"My pleasure."

Vertigo seized Ale suddenly; The Oracle's cold voice boomed: #Emergency Meeting immediately.#

Right, he said inside, while saying aloud, "They just called a meeting"—he crossed over to the sofa and sat down—"I'll be back in a while."

Wef nodded vaguely and headed back to the console.

As Ale entered, The Oracle was announcing, #The main computers of Coalition Intelligence have demanded the names and ID/dresses of all living Seeleys. I did not comply. They are now launching a concerted attempt to decipher my privacy codes. I am, of course, resisting to the best of my ability, but—excuse me. I fear I must—"

Interface failed suddenly, pitching Ale back into his living room with the beginnings of what would probably be a major headache. It was not supposed to happen like that. The exit procedures were designed specifically to lessen the trauma of moving from one state to the other. If The Oracle had to ignore them, something bad must be afoot.

Emdy's door clicked open and her voice wafted out: "Ale—there's a Coalition helicopter heading for the building—it's DP Security!"

TOP TEN NEWS STORIES OF THE HOUR

RANK HEADLINE	price	LEAD SENTENCE
#1 COALITION CHARGED WITH KILLING SEELEYS	.25	In a copyrighted article deposited in all major newsbanks earlier this morning, the Association of Computer-Linked Experts, employees of ORA:CLE, Inc., accuses the Coalition's Directorate of Public Intelligence of masterminding a bizarre plot that has already resulted in the deaths of over five hundred Seeleys.
#2 * * * * * * STARS BURNED AT EMSISEN, BUT RIVALS TO COPY DEREGULATION	.20	#2 * * * * * * While hundreds of worldwide celebrities flee the CCU because Aid (VD/NA/DPI) Emsisen relaxed his department's definition of 'invasion of privacy,' other political parties hurriedly rewrote their own to bring them more into line with the CCU's.
#3 * * * * * * STILL NO CLUES IN LM2 OFFICE BOMBING	.15	#3 * * * * * * Lunar police continue to hunt in vain for leads to the identities of the extortionists who planted a bomb in the corporate headquarters of Lunar Mining & Manufacturing, Inc.

#4 * * * * * *

MARKET PRIMED FOR ANOTHER BIG DAY

.10

#4 * * * * * *

Circuits to all major stock exchanges were beginning to overload by 0843 EDT this morning, as speculators, caught in the euphoria of yesterday's twenty-one point surge, placed early orders with their brokers.

#5 * * * * *

SUICIDE RATE SOARING, SAYS PROF

.10

#5 * * * * *

Citing figures compiled by the Coalition's DP Statistics, a professor at the University of Colon claims the worldwide suicide rate has been increasing six-tenths of a percent annually for the last eighteen years.

#6 * * * * * *

WARSAW SIGHS AS SUN COMES OUT AT LAST

.10

#6 * * * * *

Floodwaters are still rising in Warsaw, but the torrential rains that have all but destroyed this Polish city in the last four days have stopped, and the sun has emerged to dry things out.

#7 * * * * * *

TRANSPLUTONIANS NOT DACS, SAY RESEARCHERS

.10

#7 * * * * * *

A Social-Tech DP/Research team has tentatively concluded that the radio signals detected by an MIT/ ToDai robot observatory circling Pluto differ significantly from those emitted by Dac starships, including the one that has just penetrated Neptune's orbit.

#8 * * * * * *

TELEBETTER CREDITED IN CLEVELAND RESCUE

.10

#8 * * * * *

The young bluefly who yesterday saved a woman from certain death by catching her in mid-air after her husband had thrown her off their thirtieth floor balcony today credited the feat to TeleBetter, a new drug that enhances telesensory interface.

#9 * * * * * * *

CO IN BAHRAIN GAS .10 LINE FELLS FORTY-EIGHT

#9 * * * * * * *

MR DP/Safety officials revealed at 0708 (EDT) this morning that forty-eight residents of a Bahrain singles dorm have died as a result of carbon monoxide infiltration of a natural gas line; seventy-three have been hospitalized.

#10 * * * * * * *

CLEANSPRING MUST .10 RECALL TWO MILLION BOTTLES

#10 * * * * * * *

Cleanspring, Inc. has reluctantly agreed to notify all those who have recently purchased four-liter bottles of "Spring Pure Bottled Water" marked "AC/875/ SEN" that the contents might be contaminated, and the bottles should be returned to Cleanspring (collect) unopened.'

This update has been provided as a public service by all data management corporations participating in NEWSBANK/MC, a news data base organized and supervised by the Marxist/Communist Directorate of Public Information.

To read any of the above news stories in full, simply highlight the title and press ACCEPT. The article will be transmitted to your unit's memory. Your bank balance will be debited by the sum in the column headed "price."

To see the headlines of the day's other news stories, simply scroll your screen up.

Thank you, and do be careful.

X

The helicopter had to be coming for him. He ran to the bathroom, remembering just in time not to shout when he called, "Emdy, water the plants every morning, even if they're still damp." He swung open the medicine cabinet, grabbed his toothbrush and a tube of toothpaste, vetoed the razor but took a hairbrush, and shoved all three into his pants pocket. "Wef, you'll watch over her, right?"

"Shit," said Wef from the kitchen. There came the *pop* of an opening beer can. "Ale, I'm sorry as hell—"

"I *told* you not to erase—"

"Emdy," said Ale, "I don't think it was Wef. The Oracle said the Coalition was trying to break its privacy codes and get all our names and ID/dresses. I guess the Coalition's got better programs than ORA:CLE." He dashed into the bedroom, snatched an overnight case out of the closet, and feverishly stuffed it with clothes. "Win a few, lose a few, huh?"

He did not know whether to be terrified or exhilarated. His heart pounded; his mouth had parched; but he felt so *good!* Maybe because what had been sly and secretive was now becoming overt. The enemy had ceased to hide. Direct confrontation was finally possible. *This* was what the Seeleys really needed, strange though it seemed: a blatant muzzling, so that all the world could see that their charges were true, that the Coalition did mean them harm.

For a moment he paused. How could the Coalition *muzzle* someone with an interface implant?

Then he shivered. A few quick slashes with a scalpel would do it. . . .

Leaning against the corridor wall, he tried to think of what else he should take. Clothes, toiletries, um . . . he slipped his hands into his pockets and straightened as warm metal grazed his fingers. The Dac gun! That he had to leave behind. Coa/Security would frisk him first thing, and if they found the weapon— He did not want to think about the consequences. He had to hide it. Quickly.

But where? His office was out—surely they would search it. Emdy's was no good, either; he wanted to keep her out of trouble. He breathed hard, already imagining the footsteps in the outside hall, the harsh knock on the door... not the bedroom, or the kitchen, or— He snapped his fingers and ran for the kitchen.

Then he froze as a sidelong glance out the living room windows caught the wing flurry of a landing Dac. It perched on the rail like a vulture in a tree. Huge head swinging from side to side, it examined the terrace tiles. It screeched. And flew away.

His heart resumed beating. After two deep breaths he remembered what he was supposed to be doing.

Two plastic bags, that's all I need, now where are they? Almost frantic, he threw open cupboard doors and pawed over shelves until finally a roll of plastic bags tumbled free. He tore one off and raised it to the light; finding no holes, he dropped the gun into it and sealed it with a twist-tie. Then he put the package, tied end first, inside the other bag, and closed that one thoroughly. He ran for the bathroom, lifted the toilet-tank, and eased the gun into the water. *Not a great place,* he decided as he rinsed and dried his hands, *but they won't look there first, and—*

The doorbell chimed. Sighing, he threw the towel at the rack and walked for the door. He had to make a conscious effort to keep his shoulders square. He was more frightened than he had ever been. It did not help that Wef DiNaini shook his hand, slapped him on the back, and said, "Good luck, Ale. You'll need it."

"Thanks. Thanks a lot." He faced the door. "Open."

With the cautious, mincing steps of the self-conscious inebriate, L'ai Aichtueni stepped inside. Her pink-eyed gaze swept the room, dipping at Ale's overnight case; her eyebrows lifted. "Leaving us?"

He opened his mouth to reply but Emdy said, "Ale! The helicopter's going away!"

He wanted suddenly to drop into a chair and heave a huge sigh of relief.

Wef said, "Hah! Knew that'd fix 'em," then ambled back to the ibn Daoud 4500.

L'ai closed the door. Glancing at Emdy's earmuffs, she kept her voice low. "What's going on?"

"Well, uh—" He shrugged and tried to maintain a mask of nonchalance. "We thought for a while there that the cops were coming to arrest me, and—"

"For the article?"

"Uh-huh. And—"

"It was a *very* good article—is it all true?"

He blinked. "Did you *mean* that as an insult, or was it an accident?"

Her hand flew to her mouth. "Oh, Ale, I'm sorry, I— What can I say? I did *not* mean to offend you; it was more of a reflex response to anything one sees in the data banks these days. In fact, I came down immediately after reading it to ask a favor."

"You're not going to ask me to run—"

"Yes!" She bobbed her head vigorously; her white hair bounced up and down. "You'd make a marvelous candidate, and with the media exposure you've received lately, you would have no recognition problem at all. And the opportunity for advancement, well! Look at Aid Emsisen."

He frowned. "I don't know the name. Who is he?"

"Only the hottest young star in politics today. He was a ho-soap actor until he joined the CCU. Of course his name then was Aid Emsiso—"

"Yeah, I know him now. A big guy with curly black hair and two hundred teeth, right? *He's* already a Seven?"

"And probably an Eight by next week. Ale, that could be you. *You* could be influencing party policy, perhaps even becoming a member of our delegation to the Coalition—you would like that, wouldn't you?"

"Sure, I'd just love a chance to walk into the lion's den."

She fixed him with an exasperated look. "It is all done by pholo."

"You know what I mean." He *hated* dealing with squash-heads. They were so unreasonable. "It just seems, ah . . . no. I'm sorry, I don't want to get into any of that. Do you understand?"

She gave a slow nod. "Yes, I think so. You're afraid—for which I can't blame you, given all that's happened—and you think that if you speak out more than you already have, you shall be in even greater danger. But—"

"No." Anger kindled inside him. "That's not what I meant.

What I meant was, all my energies are going into fighting this conspiracy. I will not dissipate them by distracting myself with politics!"

"But Ale, *everything* is politics."

BEEPEEPEEP

"You'll have to excuse me—" He took her by the elbow and led her to the door. "—but The Oracle is calling."

"Think on it, Ale." She turned and put both of her thin, pale hands on his shoulders. "Think long and hard on it, because we are in *desperate* need of talented people." Her gaze wandered, then focused on his face. "Okay?"

"Gotta go. 'Bye."

"'Bye, Ale."

Leaning against the door, he closed his eyes and edged into interface. *What is it?*

#If I have interrupted any of you, please forgive me—also, please accept my apologies for the untimely manner in which I terminated our last joint interface. To bring you up to date: I fended off the Coalition Inquiry Programs by providing them with the names and addresses of twenty thousand Coalition Employees. In their haste to silence all of you, the Coalition failed to verify the list, and issued warrants for all twenty thousand.#

A storm of applause broke out in the dark chamber and welled quickly to a cacaphonous crescendo.

The Oracle flicked the switch that hushed them all. #Please, we have little time, and cannot afford to devote any of it to self-congratulation. The deception will not hold. Even now some of the detainees are proving their identities—and their influence. The DP Security is embarrassed, and can be expected to unleash their computers on me swiftly. I doubt my ability to withstand a second round of interrogation.#

A voice shouted, #Well, what do you suggest?#

#Oh, come,# it said. #I am a switchboard program; any suggestion I might offer must first originate with one of you.#

#The key,# said someone else, #is to exert on the governments various the popular pressure. This is the *sine qua non* for any sort of the reform political.#

#Yeah, man,# said a third Seeley, #but that was the whole point of that article we did up. Look at the numbers, will ya? The Royalty Programs say we have sold better'n ten million copies of that thing, and I don't see any pressure. The people be too fat and happy, that's all. We better give up, be good li'l boys and girls, and beg the Coalition for its magnanimous for-giveness.#

#But no! That which you have said initially is exactly the case. It is necessary for us to enkindle passion in the breasts of the voters, but, if I may say so, it is very difficult for people to feel the grand passion for the fate of complete strangers.#

#Da, is wery good point. Is up to us to find way to proof to vatchew—#

#Have mercy, man! Would you just speak your own language and let The Oracle translate for you?#

#Sorry. It is up to us to find a way to prove to every single individual that the Coalition's actions are going to harm it. This is our task. Once achieved, we are victorious.#

#We won't never win, man! The Coalition be too damn big, and don't nobody out there care what happens to us unless it happens to them, too.#

#Nyet. I think there is no problem in convincing the business community, for one, that to lose all Seeleys will have negative impact on the profitability. Perhaps they do not grieve too highly over loss of Asian History expert—don't take personally, Ale Elatey, if you are out there; just realism—but over last several centuries business has come to rely on social scientists for market research and product development advice, on natural scientists to do basic research leading to new insights, on engineers to develop new insights into new technology products to make bottom line fat and black—so me, I say, tell business, is very contagious disease on loose here—we catch, you die from it eventually.#

A score of Seeleys began to speak, to drown each other out, and then to bicker. The noise level rose steadily. After only a few milliseconds, Ale could barely hear himself, much less debate public indifference with a colleague who, despite the complete lack of public uproar, maintained that all they needed to do was to inform the populace, who would handle the rest.

Look, Ale was saying, *ten million people bought the report—*

#Ah, b#t do they know #### it #ays y##?#

Well, if they've read it—

#My ##### ex####y! As so## ## #### #### ##ad it—#

What?

point exactly! ## soon as they #### read it—#
But they've had lots of time—
#Not ## ### through it, only ## st#rt ##.#

Ale gave up. It was impossible to carry on a conversation with someone who was not only not listening to you, but could not hear you even if it wanted to.

The Oracle intervened with another flick of the mute switch. The room fell silent. #Ladies and gentlemen, the Coalition's computers are attempting to come back on line. I suggest a recess, during which each of you contemplates both the problem at hand and various possible solutions. Monitoring your statements, I extracted two separate opinions: one group wishes to acquiesce to the Coalition, the other wishes to resist. You may expect to hear from me shortly.#

The vestibule coalesced around Ale. His shoulderblades hurt from pressing against the front door. He stretched, then touched his toes a few times in an effort to work out the stiffness. It helped a little.

Wef sat at the ibn Daoud 4500, across whose screen snaked multi-colored graphic representations of quadratic equations. Emdy— Ale stepped to his left and looked. Yes, she was hunched over her desk, her office door still firmly closed.

"Hey, Wef."

The old man lifted his head and looked over his shoulder. "You're a spooky sumbitch, you know that, Ale? One minute you're here, the next you're doing your impression of a statue. You oughta wear a sign, you know—'Out to Lunch' or something like that."

"Usually I don't interface in public, Wef, but things just aren't too usual these days. I've got to talk to you."

Emdy's office door clicked open. She passed them on her way to the kitchen, but ignored them. Ale sighed. He hated it when she was like that.

"What's the problem, Ale? Censors strike back or something?"

"Nah. Just the Seeleys are split. Seems like half of us figure we've shot our wad, and nothing's happened, so we'd better roll over and accept the inevitable. The rest of us want to try something else, but we're not sure what will work."

Wef reached over his shoulder for his left braid and began to nibble on its tip. "Which side are you on, Ale?"

He shrugged. "I'm not sure. I mean, we gave it a good

shot, it didn't work, and to be honest, I don't think just telling the world what the Coalition's doing to us is going to win us a lot of support. I don't believe people care enough for others to get upset on our behalf. But at the same time, it'd be crazy to give up! 'Cause the Coalition's just going to go on killing us. I don't know. It looks like a no-win proposition either way."

Behind him, Emdy said, "That's the first sensible thing I've heard you say since this started."

"Don't start on me, Emdy, I—"

"No! You listen to me, Ale Elatey. You've gone out of your way to antagonize the Coalition, and what's it gotten you? Nothing!" A spasm of pain distorted her face; she continued in a harsh quick whisper. "You don't even get a share of the royalties on the best-seller you idiots did—ORA:CLE, Inc. is taking all of them. Plus you've made a lot of enemies, and damn few friends. So where does that leave you? In trouble, that's where. Deep, serious trouble."

Wef shook his head. "Emdy, honey, I find it truly unpleasant to have to disagree with a beautiful woman, but I am going to. Now, I don't dispute what you say about Ale here being in trouble. He is. But like Julius Caesar said a long time ago, 'The dice are rolling.' Can't call 'em back, can't say, 'Oops, I made a mistake, let's just forget all about that.' And truth to tell, I don't think Ale *made* a mistake." He paused to chew some more on his braid. "You're in business, Emdy, so let's talk bottom line. Somebody was trying to kill your husband, and came awful damn close three times. He just *can't* set back and let 'em take a fourth shot. Let's say somebody tried to cheat you three times. Would you do business with 'em again? Or would you call up the authorities and say, 'Hey, there's a guy trying to defraud me'?"

"Of course I would! But—" She set her coffee cup down on the dining room table. "But—" Her face contorted; her eyes began to glisten. She wrung her hands. "But this *isn't* a business deal! This is real life! And in real life, when a man steps on a bug, there's nothing the bug can do." She stopped to clear her throat, and to wipe her overflowing eyes. "Wef, there's no place he can run, nowhere he can hide, nothing he can do to keep the Coalition from killing him if it wants to. I hate it! He's my husband, my lover, my very best friend—and he's so much smaller than the Coalition. It won't help him to fight— it'll only guarantee that they'll try it again and again until finally they get him. If he'd just shut up, and do nothing, then maybe there's a chance they'll ignore him and concentrate on the loudmouth Seeleys. But—" Her voice caught on a sob. "But goddammit, if he keeps calling attention to himself, I'm going to wind up a lonely widow and I can't *stand* that thought!"

Ale heard the strain in her voice. Too much was happening to her, and it was happening too quickly. Fresh out of the hospital as she was, she needed peace and quiet, and was getting nothing but tension. He stepped toward her, his arms open. "Emdy—"

She backed away. "No. You're like . . . you're like somebody with a horrible disease who'd rather kill himself than do what the doctors say. I love you, Ale, but if you're not going to be with me, I'm going to have to learn to live without you. So don't try that. If you want to commit suicide, go ahead. But don't try to remind me how much I love you, because it'll make it hurt all the more when you're gone."

Slowly he lowered his arms. "I, uh—"

"No. Just— You're going to leave me, you're going to be gone, so just— Just leave me alone, okay?" She picked her cup and saucer off the dining room table and headed for her office. "I have all sorts of things to do, so don't bother me."

He felt like a fool. The *click* of her doorlock made him wince. He turned to Wef. "I, ah . . . shit, Wef, what do I do? I lose even if I win."

"What can I say?" The old refugee sprawled back in his swivel chair. "I think you're doing the right thing. I mean—"

Emdy's door flew open and she burst out of the office hissing, "Goddammit! I've just been erased!"

Ale said, "What?"

She glared across the room at him. "I just tried to order some office accessories. You know what the machine told me? It said, 'Identity Unknown.' You realize what that means? Officially, Mr. Get-the-Coalition-Mad-at-Him, officially that means I have never existed!"

TOP TEN NEWS STORIES OF THE HOUR

17 June 2188; 1000 EDT
New England Region

RANK HEADLINE	price	LEAD SENTENCE
#1 EMSISEN OKAYS LOOK AT APPOINTED OFFICIALS, PUTS CAREER IN JEOPARDY	.25	Aid Emsisen, Vice Director for North America of the CCU's DPI, has updated his department's specifications for 'celebrity-hood' to include non-elected government officials, thus permitting greater disclosure of their private lives than ever before; informed sources predict massive resistance by the affected bureaucrats.
#2 * * * * * * ACLE WACKO, SAYS IRATE COALITION	.20	#2 * * * * * * Replying to ACLE's charges that the Coalition has been systematically exterminating Seeleys, a spokesrep for the Director of Public Directorates went on record this morning as saying, "They've clearly spent too much time in interface—and from the sound of it, they probably spent the time reading a lot of bad fiction."
#3 * * * * * * DOW SLIPS	.15	#3 * * * * * * At 0959 EDT, the Dow-Jones Industrial Average was down point seventy-eight in light-to-moderate trading.

RANK HEADLINE	price	LEAD SENTENCE
#4 * * * * * *		#4 * * * * * *
DORA DODGES EMPTY MIAMI	.15	Hurricane Dora, deprived of her prey by a Social-Tech-directed evacuation, turned sharply northeast and headed back to sea this morning, sparing this deserted resort town any physical damage.
#5 * * * * *	.15	#5 * * * * * *
NO CHANGE IN SIXTH DAC'S COURSE		Coalition spokesreps report that the sixth Dac starship to invade the system in the last six years is maintaining a direct course for L5.
#6 * * * * * *	.10	#6 * * * * * *
BOSTON STREETERS RAMPAGE		An estimated fifty street people clambered up drainpipes and broke in terrace doors to seize the first floor of a Commonwealth Avenue condominium complex, a spokesrep for the MR/DPS announced at 0930 EDT this morning.
#7 * * * * * *	.10	#7 * * * * * *
CLEANSPRING RECALL LINKED TO SNAP		Investigators from the UE/DPS have tentatively determined that the source of the contamination that caused Cleanspring to recall over two million bottles of water came from a disgruntled ex-employee who has since committed suicide.
#8 * * * * * *	.10	#8 * * * * * *
ALEXANDRIA BLACKED OUT		A defective transformer at a substation in this Egyptian port city failed abruptly this morning, plunging the southwestern suburbs into darkness.

RANK HEADLINE	price	LEAD SENTENCE

#9 * * * * * *

BLICKSTROBE CHAMP TURNING IT OFF .10

#9 * * * * * *

After nine months as undisputed World Blickstrobe Champion, seventeen-year-old NGB90 CLITXD UGLR announced this morning that she was retiring from the game, saying, "What I've earned in the last two years has put out the fire in my belly."

#10 * * * * * *

LM2 MURDER STUMPS LUNAR COPS .10

#10 * * * * * *

Lunar Police confessed that they have no new leads in the slaying of BHK30 BHXNDP JUH2, though they insist that they have not closed down their investigations.

This update has been provided as a public service by all data management corporations participating in NEWSBANK/ST, a news data base organized and supervised by the Social-Technological Directorate of Public Information.

To read any of the above news stories in full, simply highlight the title and press ACCEPT. The article will be transmatted to your unit's memory. Your bank balance will be debited by the sum in the column headed "price."

To see the headlines of the day's other news stories, simply scroll your screen up.

Thank you, and do be careful.

XI

"You bastard!"

"Emdy—"

"Oh no. Don't you even talk to me. This is all your fault, none of it would have happened if you'd listened, but oh no, Mr. Hotshot Seeley, he doesn't listen, he knows better." Her voice began to rise, to shrill. "He always knows better. He knows so much so well that now I don't exist. I've been erased. And I'll bet you don't know jack*shit* about getting me restored. Well? DO YOU?!?"

She had surrendered to panic. He could hardly blame her, even while he wondered how much of her hysteria stemmed from the pain she had to be causing her ears. He held up his hands, first placatingly; then, as she swung, defensively. He parried the first swipe, but she lashed out again. He reached to snare her wrists. Her knee snapped up into his groin.

Breath whooshing out of him, he doubled over. Bright lights sparkled behind his eyes. His kidneys burned. He wanted to die, but if he had to live, he wanted to hold his breakfast. He dropped slowly to his knees, barely feeling, through the fog of anguish, the carpet on the floor.

He heard her shout, "I'LL KILL YOU!" It came to him that she was snapping, that erasure had ignited all the frustrations of all the years to burn away her sanity. She had gone berserk. At any moment she could grab a knife or a rolling pin or a Dac gun and make good on her threat.

He hurt so much that he almost hoped she would.

Through tear-blurred eyes he saw her foot draw back for a long, strong kick to his face. He should tumble away and scramble to his feet. All he could do was topple sideways while she shouted "LEMME GO!"

The pain began to recede. It dawned on him that she screamed at Wef DiNaini now. Not that Ale cared. The only thing he cared about was the slowly fading pain.

BEEPEEPEEPEEPEEP

He fled the agony of his body into interface.

The great hollow voice boomed, #Again, please excuse the interruption, but the situation is growing steadily more precarious. I have once more resisted the incursions of the Coalition's Inquiry Programs; however, the Coalition is initiating a far-ranging literature search, for clues to your identities. If you know of any document in any data bank anywhere which identifies you as a Seeley, you would be well advised to erase it at once. The Coalition has unleashed gigabytes of computer power on this search, and is confident of its completion within the hour. That is all.#

The darkness of interface dwindled away. He lay curled on the living room rug while above and behind him Emdy cursed Wef. "YOU FUCKER! LEMME AT 'IM! HE'S RUINED ME, I'M GONE, I DON'T EXIST ANYMORE AND IT'S ALL HIS GODDAMN FAULT, LEMME AT 'IM!!"

"Emdy, honey, I can't— oof!"

Her voice was dangerously quiet. "Let go of me or I'll do it again."

Wef spoke in a strangled tone: "Only—if—you—promise—not—to—hurt—him. Agh!"

The pain slumbered, now. Ale knew motion would awaken it immediately, but he had to get up. If his wife—his Emdy, his dear sweet Doc—had snapped, someone had to immobilize her before she killed herself. Before she killed everybody around her. Like that maniac in Cleveland, he thought, the one who threw his wife and kids off their terrace. . . . Gasping, he climbed onto elbows and knees, and from there pushed himself to his feet.

Wef still struggled to restrain Emdy. Jaws clenched tight in a face gone pale and sweaty, he stood behind her, his arms, locked around her waist, pinning her own arms to her sides.

She had five centimeters and probably seven kilos on him, but he had all the leverage. Her hands clawed for any part of him in reach; her booted feet stamped backwards again and again. Suddenly she jacknifed forward, slamming her butt into his stomach and almost rolling him over the top of her back.

As he clung to her, his feet centimeters off the ground, he caught sight of Ale. "Cops! Get the cops, Ale!"

He shook his head, roiling the nausea. "I got something

better. Wait a minute." Supporting himself on chair backs and table tops, he limped into the bathroom. The medicine cabinet swung open at a touch; he rummaged hurriedly through the bottles till the blue-white label of the tranquilizer caught his eye. Carrying it, he made his painful way back to the living room.

Her wild eyes focused on the sedative immediately. "Oh, no, I'm not going to take any of that. You're not going to drug me, Ale Elatey. Oh, no. Don't even think of it."

He shook two capsules onto his palm. "Emdy, you can take these voluntarily, or I'll call the cops. And if they show up to arrest you, you're not going to have an ID/dress for them."

She lunged forward, almost breaking free. "What do I care? I just want to—"

"Yes, I know what you want, but you have to take the pills. Or else I call the police. I promise you, Emdy, I won't like it—but I'll call."

"No, I won't take them. Call the cops. What difference does it make? I've been erased, remember? I don't exist. What the hell difference does anything make any more, when your whole life can just disappear in a *pfft!*? Take your damn pills yourself, I won't."

"Emdy, we can fix it!"

"Bullshit."

"He's right, honey." Wef panted for breath between phrases. "We can fix it. What, you think you're unique? Billions of people running around and you think none of 'em's ever been erased? Happens all the time. It's a pain, but in a couple hours we'll have you back on line."

She relaxed, then, a little. Some of the fight drained out of her body; fatigue softened her scowl. "You're sure?"

"Positive, honey. Uncle Wef'll fix, no problem."

She sagged back against him. "All right. I'll take the pills. Let me go, though?"

Wef looked at Ale, meanwhile saying, "Uh—"

"Please?"

Ale eyed her dubiously. If she was sincere, they had no reason to keep her pinioned any longer—but tales were told of snappers possessing almost unbelievable cunning, snappers who would charm or smile or say anything they thought plausible, as long as it would win them freedom.

But she was his Emdy. "Okay, Wef."

The old man released her, held up his wrist to examine the

angry red scratches across its back, and shook his head. "You have any ointment in there?"

Distracted, he said, "Uh, yeah, middle shelf," and reached out his open left hand to Emdy.

She took it—squeezed it—said, "I'm sorry," in a voice so low he could barely hear it. "I didn't mean— I didn't plan on . . . I don't know what I mean, what I'm saying. Except I'm sorry. Are you okay?"

"Yeah, I am, but, uh . . . well, hell, we can always adopt." He led her to the sofa and sat beside her. "Here." He passed her the pills.

"I don't need these any more."

He narrowed his eyes. "You sure? For a minute there—"

Absently, she rubbed the side of her neck. "I went pretty crazy, didn't I? I always wondered . . . I think I'm okay now. And I know I'm exhausted—it's been a while since my last fist-fight."

Wef emerged from the bathroom. Spreading a pink lotion on his forearms, he said, "Emdy, honey, I've wrestled alligators was easier to pin than you."

"I'm sorry for all the trouble I've put you to."

"'tsokay." He gave a leering wink. "'druther have my arms around you than a gator any day. Now, about—" The pholo rang. "Who's it for, Ace?"

The speaker in the ibn Daoud 4500 crackled once, then said, "Dr. L'ai Aichtueni, calling for Mr. Ale Elatey."

Emdy's lips tightened, but she said nothing. Wef looked at Ale and raised his eyebrows in question.

Oh, Jesus. "No. I'm busy. Tell it to take a message." It was embarrassing—and aggravating—to get calls from a squashhead neither he nor his wife could stand.

Wef relayed the command, but the computer said, "Dr. L'ai Aichtueni requests emergency consideration."

"Oh, hell." He struggled to his feet. "I'll take it in my office."

Once in his study, he closed the door and flicked on the pholo. Her smiling image formed in the lightsphere. "Water." With Emdy so shaky, he had to keep the call short. Maybe terse would do it. "What's up?"

"It should have occurred to me earlier, Ale, but it was only a moment or two ago that I realized you could be in jeopardy."

"From the police? I know, I'm waiting for them to show."

Her pink eyes widened. "You're going to give yourself up?"

"Nope. Just not going to resist arrest, that's all."

"There is another solution, you know."

"Oh?"

"Hide."

How much squash did one have to pop to turn so stupid? "That's not very practical."

"Of course it is. They'd never think of searching up here."

"Your place?"

"Why not? It's safe, luxuriously equipped, and it would give me the opportunity finally to cajole you into running on our ticket. What more could one ask for in a sanctuary?"

The offer tempted him, because the notion of jail did frighten him, but beside the fact that it would not work, its unspoken aspect made him very uneasy, a discomfort intensified when she parted her lips a fraction and moistened them with her tongue. She wanted him on her ticket, yes, but elsewhere too, probably, and Ale Elatey was, to put it simply if archaically, not that kind of man.

For that matter, he could not figure why (if he did) he attracted her—he liked himself, surely, and at times could be quite pleased with himself, but he harbored no illusions. His shoulders were narrow; his midriff was not; trivia of esoteric sorts fascinated him; great black rings of potting soil usually underlined his fingernails ... perhaps the controversy in which he was embroiled lured her. Yes, that made sense. A public figure herself, if only in a limited way, she might well prefer to associate with other quasi-celebrities, who could be expected to understand the demands that life in the public eye imposed, and at least some of whose luster would naturally reflect off her. . . . *Or maybe,* he thought, as his eyes seemed to meet hers through the pholo, *maybe what excites her is dallying with a public enemy, with someone the Coalition views as a threat.* . . . Something else occurred to him; he shuddered. *Maybe it's a weird form of necrophilia; she figures I'll be dead soon, and—*

"Well?" Impatience sharpened her tone.

He sighed. "Thank you, Water, but no. I do appreciate the thought, but . . . well, for one thing, they would search up there. You're on record as calling and visiting here. They'll search the apartment of everyone who knows us. It wouldn't work. But thank you."

She shrugged. "I expected as much—or as little. If you change your mind, call. And best of luck with the Coalition."

"Thanks, I—" But the sphere popped like a soap bubble, leaving him alone in his study again. His turn to shrug. And to wonder what she was like in— But no, he was thoroughly married and he would not think along those lines. He went back to the living room, instead.

"—was issued, the info went into the banks." Wef sat beside Emdy, one hand on her shoulder. "And at the same time, it went to seven very special banks where it was stored in ROM bubbles. That stuff can't be erased or altered. Period."

She lifted her gaze to Ale. Her eyes were puffy, bloodshot. "Don't give me that, Wef. Nothing's permanent."

"Sure, the place could blow up or somebody could melt down the bubble arrays—but these are vaults, honey. Guarded like you wouldn't believe. And there's seven of 'em. Means there just ain't much chance you're not on file anywhere. As long as one of 'em's got your record, you're back in business."

"What *about* my business, though? The contracts, bank accounts—that's all gone, too."

He tousled her hair. "I sorta doubt it, Emdy. It's in there, but it's keyed to an ID/dress that doesn't exist right now, so you can't pull it out. Soon as your ID/dress's restored, you'll have access to all of it. So what say we get started, huh?"

"All right."

"Ale—" Wef stood up. "You don't mind if we use your study, do you? We're going to need peace and quiet for this one, 'cause of the drugs."

Emdy's voice shook. "What drugs? I—"

"Don't you worry, honey, just a little hypno/truth serum, wouldn't hurt a fly. It's one part of proving that you are who you say you are. Ol' Wef'll be right there with you, though, so don't worry." He turned back to Ale. "You're not using your study, are you?"

"No, I'm not." He waved in its general direction. "Go right a—"

BEEPEEPEEP

Wincing, he slipped into interface. *I wish you'd stop breaking in in the middle of a sentence.*

#My apologies, but I thought you might like to know that you are reasonably safe from the Coalition, for the moment at least.#

Why? Have they stopped—

#Oh, nothing of the kind. I have been monitoring their transmissions, though, and they believe that you have left your apartment, and are carrying your ID/dress card. They are waiting for you to slot into another computer elsewhere. When you do, they will pounce.#

The WAR code. If Wef had not found and erased it, his household appliances would still be reporting his movements. No, wrong again. The appliances at the nearest prison would be making the reports.... For the time being, though, he was effectively invisible to the Coalition. A nice feeling, that. If only he could slot in for transactional purposes...unless Wef had wiped the RAT code, too? He could not remember. He thought so, but he would have to ask. *That's good to know. Anything else?*

#At the moment, no. There will be another joint assembly in mark! two minutes eighteen seconds, however.#

Fine. See you then. This time *he* left interface first. Much easier on his head.

The living room took form and shape just as Wef and Emdy were leaving it. Wef had his arm around Emdy's waist. Ale was not sure how to take that, or even what he might say about it. So he said nothing. He scowled, and chewed on a fingernail.

Another joint assembly. It seemed pointless for them all to link together and talk at each other. What had hot air ever solved outside of ballooning? They needed action—strong, decisive action.

Oh, sure, he thought gloomily. *Twenty thousand of the world's top scholars are going to* act? *Hah.*

BEEEEEEP

He lapsed back into that deep, dark well. *You know, there's got to be a way for you to call me without giving me a heart attack.*

#My apologies. I shall log your comment, and pass it on to the Design Committee.#

Oh, gee, that'd be wonderful.

#Sarcasm ill-befits you, Mr. Elatey.#

What can I say? The Design Committee just seems to bring it out in me.

A pall of silence lay over the vast cavern. Briefly, it disconcerted Ale, who had expected a murmur of voices rising and falling like a worried tide. The Oracle must have been squelching crosscast.

#Ladies and gentlemen, if you are ready, we shall begin. The mass chaos of our last session has convinced me to prohibit simultaneous access to the microphone, as it were. In this session, one person shall speak at a time.#

He was less sure than ever that this would work. A group of twenty thousand experts needed more than a switchboard program to function effectively. It needed a system, a set of ground rules, some sort of organization—none of which it had. How, for example, would The Oracle decide whom to let speak first? Did the race go to the swift? Or—

#We have no time,# The Oracle said, #for non-productive verbiage. All shall hear the speaker, and only the speaker; I shall hear all of you at all times. If you wish the speaker silenced, say so. I shall maintain a running poll; when fifty percent plus one wish the speaker cut off, the speaker will be cut off, and the next brought on line. Those who have things to say need only to ask for air time, and they will go into the queue. Please be ready to address the assembly at my prompt. Thank you. Who wishes to—?#

#The problem-solving mechanisms of the Tlingit—# The hesitant voice lapsed into long pauses between phrases. #—are worthy of consideration—#

Cut it, muttered Ale.

#—here today, especially in light of the difficulties we confront—#

#Speaker Number Two,# said The Oracle.

#In my country we have the long-standing tradition of dealing physically with dictators. We need only to find the charismatic individual behind whom we can rally, and then that person will lead us—#

Cut this one, too. How could anyone propose armed rebellion? Beyond the fact that no one had weapons, and even beyond the fact that revolution required great popular discontent with the rulers, there lay the reality of the Dacs, which would surely savage any militia foolish enough to venture outdoors.

#—in a magnificent campaign certain to culminate in glory and liberation. The revolution will demand great sacrifice, yes, but—#

#Speaker Number Three.#

#Thank you. While I wouldn't mind forcing the Coalition to get its knee off my throat, we'll have to convince a whole lot of solid, satisfied citizens to go along with us.#

Cut! First anthropobabble, then Latin machismo, and now a simple-minded restatement of the obvious? Was this all a conspiracy to waste his time?

#Frankly, I don't think *we* can impact the Coalition. Neither can the average individual, even if it believes our charges and is as outraged as we are. Only the parties who select representatives to the Coalition can effect any change. And I think I have a way to do that.#

Can I take back my vote?

The Oracle said, #Yes, of course.#

The speaker said, #I am sorry to bore you with history, but although the Coalition is charged with freeing us from the Dacs, it came into being to deal with another planetwide problem: CO_2 pollution and oxygen depletion. We all know, and endure, the solution it imposed—complete reforestation, and enforced immobility until the biosphere has healed itself. What too few of us know is that this is nonsense. Oh, green is clean, yes, and the forests are sopping up the excess CO_2, but there was, and is, a much simpler way of dealing with the oxygen problem: electrolysis of sea-water. Break it into pure oxygen and hydrogen. Release the oxygen, save the hydrogen for a non-polluting fuel. The— Uh, The Oracle says someone has a question?#

#Ja! You are speaking huge amounts of energy to accomplish such a task. From where can we expect to find this energy?#

#From the source of all energy—the sun. A network of solar power satellites— Another question?#

#The solar power option was considered—and dismissed as impractical—a hundred years ago, when the reforestation projects began. Why do you expect it to be successful today, given the ubiquity of the Dac threat?#

#To answer the question you didn't ask—'Am I proposing that we do this?'—no, that's not the point of my remarks. Our goal is to discredit the Coalition so that the parties which appoint representatives to it will withdraw from it. Deprived of leadership and funding, the Coalition will cease to exist, at least as a threat to us. Now, it's been said over and over that the average person doesn't care if the Coalition goes around killing Seeleys. But the average person *does* care that it can't walk in the park. Another question?#

#It's not the Coalition keeping people inside, it's the Dacs.#

#For the last six years, yes, but for the ninety-four years before the Dacs came it was the Coalition. And that's the point we want to stress—that the Coalition stole our freedom of

movement when it didn't have to. Now, as for the earlier
person's question. It's very difficult to say what the Dacs will
do, given that they won't talk to us. But through trial and error
we've found flight paths for jetliners, launch lanes for our
shuttlecraft, orbits for satellites, the "customs" points in near-
Earth orbit ... we have solar power satellites up there right
now, and they are not being interfered with. I think it's worth
a try. Yes?#

#As I said, this sun-sea option was considered a hundred
years ago, but was rejected because it wouldn't work!#

#Ah, but it wasn't! Again, my apologies, but some history:
The Coalition convened a panel of scientists to evaluate possible
solutions. My grandfather was one of them. The whole project
was kept under wraps, ostensibly to shelter the participants
from 'political pressure.' The panel unanimously recommended
the SPS/sea-water approach. The Coalition rejected the panel's
report on the grounds that the panel had underestimated both
the actual cost and the environmental hazards; it then classified
the report Top Secret and warned the panel members that any
attempt to make its contents public would result in arrest, guaranteed conviction, and very long jail sentences, not only for
panel members, but for their families as well. It then announced
its own plan, and began ...... #

The speaker's voice faded; Ale became aware that he was
sitting in his living room, waiting for a sound to repeat itself.
What sound? Eyes still shut, he tried to recall it, but could not.
It was gone. The apartment was still except for the low mutter
of voices from the study, where Emdy was answering the questions of the ID/dress Verification Program.

He shrugged, and slipped back into interface.

...... if I understand you correctly, is that we should
wage a propaganda campaign to convince people that this is
what the Coalition did, with the connivance of their own parties,
and that they should start voting down the parties' hierarchies
until the parties withdraw from the Coalition.#

#Pretty much, yes.#

#But this requires documentation. Were I to be told this
without verifiable evidence, my reaction would be one of in-
credulity.#

#I'm afraid mine would be, too. But the evidence must be
filed somewhere. You know governments—they throw nothing
away. Let me ask the assembly: Has anyone ever come across

this document in their researches, or any reference to it?#

From the silence in the cavern it was apparent that no one had.

The speaker said, #Oracle—do you think you could find it?#

#If it's truly Top Secret, access would require a priority of '9,' and I am—or was, rather—cleared only to '4.'#

I'll bet Wef could do it, said Ale.

#Do you really think so?#

If it's on a computer somewhere, he can do it.

#Very well, then, why don't you ask him?#

Okay.

He emerged from interface to find he had company. Wef DiNaini was looking uncomfortable; Emdy sat, spine rigid, in one of the dining room chairs. Her eyes had a zombiesh cast, the side effect of the hypno-serum. Her cheeks were red; her blouse, rumpled.

Ale glanced from one to the other and thought he knew what had happened. "Emdy, I think it's time for you to take a nap."

She rose and pivoted clumsily. He followed her into the bedroom, polarized the windows down to dimness, and sat on the bed next to her. "What did Wef do to you?"

"He helped me get my ID/dress reestablished."

"Besides that."

"Nothing." She stared blankly at the ceiling.

He studied her slack face. Her blush and Wef's averted eyes said something had happened. "He didn't touch you?"

"Uh-uh."

He thought a moment longer. "Did he tell you to do anything?"

She closed her eyes. In a whisper, she said, "To take my clothes off."

His right hand rolled into a fist. "Did you?"

"I had to." She turned her head away from him. "I— I don't like these drugs, Ale. I do what I'm told, even if inside I don't want to, I'm afraid to, I'm disgusted . . . I don't like them!"

"You won't have to take them again. Promise. Now, you get some sleep." He bent over and kissed her on the forehead.

She was snoring before he reached the door.

Wef sat at the computer, gaze fixed on the screen.

Ale grabbed the old man's shirt and hoisted him to his feet. "I'm going to break you into small pieces."

The refugee's eyes widened. "Now, you don't understand, I didn't—"

"You told her to strip, knowing damn well she would."

"But I didn't even look!"

Releasing him, Ale rocked back on his heels. "What?"

"It was a scam, that's all." The words tumbled rapidly from his mouth. "I've run it before, it's simple, and it works great. And I'll split the take with her, don't worry about that, I—"

"What the hell do you mean, a scam?"

"The secret's in volume, 'cause only one person in fifty's gonna bite, but I set the routine up a couple years ago and it's all stored on my machine back home, I just trigger it from up here and—"

He seized the old man's shirt again. "I swear to God, Wef, if you don't tell me what this scam *is*—"

"I'm coming to that, I'm coming to it." He cleared his throat. "See, while she's peeling I do a voiceover that says, 'Interesting things could be happening in your neighbor's bedroom right now. Wouldn't you like to watch? For a mere twenty dollars we'll tell you how.' I give 'em the account number. As soon as the credit memo hits I send 'em a letter that says, basically, 'Go into your neighbor's bedroom, sit down, and keep your eyes open.'" He shrugged. "The nice part is, their complaints won't stand up—not that many ever do complain—because I delivered just exactly what I promised 'em."

Ale had to struggle to keep from choking on his wrath. "You said something about volume, Wef. Just how many people does this program of yours solicit?"

"'bout a hundred thousand."

Ale felt sick. He wanted to throw the old man to the ground and kick him into a bleeding, unconscious pulp. "Get out of here before I kill you."

"Ale, please, I got no place to go." Now he looked frightened. "Please, I'm sorry, I didn't think— I mean, I wouldn't touch her or hurt her for the world, but—but she was perfect for this, and we both made a pile of money, and nobody in this building saw her." He clutched Ale's forearm. "I mean, you can understand, can't you? The Program had just ended, she was sitting there, and I just—it just hit me, I can run the peep scam! Please, Ale, I'm sorry. I'll apologize to her when she wakes up, I'll make it up to you—but if you throw me out, who'll take me in till it's time to go back to Florida? Please?"

Slowly he released the old man's shirt front. His fingers felt dirty. "Look, Wef, I—"

BEEPEEPEEP

Now what?

#Any luck, Mr. Elatey?#

Luck?

#In getting your refugee to find those documents for us.#

Ah . . . I'll let you know about that in a while.

#Very well.#

Slipping back into reality, he shook his head. Wef still stood before him, a ragged supplicant. Ale's stomach churned. He did *not* want to ask the old man for help, not now. He did not want to owe Wef a thing. What he really wanted to do was hurl him off the terrace and—

The old man stepped back a pace. "Ale?"

"Aahhh! Look. I'm reacting like you've violated my property rights or something. You didn't; you violated Emdy's privacy, and she hasn't asked me to get back at you for her. Yet. We'll see how she feels when she wakes up. If she's furious at you, I'll take it out of your hide. If she forgives you, you survive. As for staying—we'll see what she thinks."

"Thank you, thank you, I—" His gaze darted to the computer screen, then jerked back guiltily to Ale. "Can I do anything for you?"

He hated himself, but he had to ask, because if this miserable little man could help save twenty thousand Seeley lives . . . "Maybe. At the meeting, somebody said the Coalition is sitting on a document—"

"I'll find it for you." He sidled around Ale and plopped into the chair behind the terminal. "What's the name of the document? Where's it stored?"

"I don't know. It's about a hundred years old. It's a report from a panel of scientists to the Coalition concerning solutions to the oxygen depletion and CO_2 pollution problems. It recommends creating new oxygen by electrolysis of sea-water, with the power coming from Solar Power Satellites. The Coalition rejected the report, and buried it somewhere under a Top Secret label. The problem is, the conference itself was a secret, so there are no contemporary records of its meeting or anything."

"No problem, Ale. No problem at all." He swiveled around in the chair and began typing commands.

Ale went out to the kitchen to make himself a cup of coffee.

While the water boiled, he washed his shaking hands, thoroughly, several times. He still could not figure out what he should have done. *What a miserable position to be in!* To need a favor from— The kettle's screech broke into his thoughts; he shut off the heat and splashed the water into the cup. The freeze-dried coffee dissolved at once, throwing fragrant steam into his face. He looked into the cup, made a face, and poured it down the drain. To *ask* a favor from . . .

Emdy drifted in.

"I thought you were asleep."

She smiled wanly. "I was—till the drugs wore off. Ale, I, um, I don't want you to say anything to Wef about, about . . . you know."

"Too late. I already have."

"You didn't hurt him, did you?"

"No." He paused. "I wanted to, but—" He shook his head. "But it seemed like that would just make a bad situation worse. What I told him was that you'd decide whether he stayed or went, and what kind of health he'd be in in either event. And I'd make sure it did happen. So it's up to you."

She leaned back against a countertop. "I don't know. I haven't been so embarrassed since—since *ever*. But he didn't touch me, he didn't have me do anything, um, lewd—" A pink spot appeared on each of her cheeks; she ducked her head. "He just let other people look at me." Hugging herself, she shivered. "I think he's sick but . . ."

"Do you want to throw him out?"

"We can't. It's against the law. Unless he commits a crime against us, and we press charges, but I won't, Ale." Her flush deepened, but when she lifted her eyes, defiance sparkled in them. "I won't send him to prison."

"Okay, but—"

In the living room, Wef called, "Ale! I got it! Want it commed over to ORA:CLE?"

"Please." He strolled into the living room.

The old man snapped his fingers. "Done."

Emdy frowned. "What's going on?"

"We're looking for a document, and—"

"You're getting in deeper!"

"No, we're just—"

She looked from one to the other. "Damn you both! I just got *erased* because of what you've been doing, and now you're doing it again, and you're going to get me hurt again. Wef, you promised, you swore you'd—"

Ale said, "But The Oracle—"

"Goddamn The Oracle, too! Fucking program is all it is. What does it care if it gets erased? Probably has a backup copy of itself somewhere. It doesn't feel pain—or wake up in a cold sweat 'cause it's terrified the government's going to kill its husband." Her cheeks were wet, now; she pulled a cushion off the sofa and kicked it across the room. "Goddamn everybody! You two, The Oracle, the government, why don't you just leave each other alone—"

BEEP

He closed his eyes and listened.

#Attention. The documents of which we spoke earlier have been found and released to the data banks. Initial public reaction is overwhelmingly in our favor. The Director of the Coalition is about to make a hovee speech which spokesreps promise will be "extremely significant."#

TOP TEN NEWS STORIES OF THE HOUR

17 June 2188 1200 EDT
New England Region

RANK HEADLINE	price	LEAD SENTENCE
#1 RISING YOUNG POLITICIAN UNDER FIRE OF FAT-CATS	.25	Well-funded special interest lobbying groups are being organized at a furious pace in an attempt to reverse VD/NA/DPI Aid Emsisen's recent ruling that for purposes of media disclosure, all public servants occupying policy-making positions will be defined as 'celebrities,' a ruling that allows far greater public scrutiny of their lives.
#2 * * * * * * COALITION CHARGED WITH IGNORING SUN/SEA SOLUTION TO CO2 THREAT	.25	#2 * * * * * * The Association of Computer-Linked Experts has just published a hundred-year-old study which it accuses the Coalition of suppressing for the last century; the study asserts that a solar power/sea-water hydrolysis combination would more effectively solve the carbon dioxide crisis than would reforestation.
#3 * * * * * * STREETERS FACE OFF BOSTON UE/COPS	.20	#3 * * * * * * The Boston Uhuru-Episcopal DPS was forced to call on other parties for assistance this morning when bow-

and-arrow wielding streeters
who seized the ground floor
of a Commonwealth Avenue
condo repulsed a UE/DPS
assault on their barricades,
a UE spokesrep admitted at
an 1130 EDT news
conference.

#4 * * * * * * *

**DOW DROPS
SHARPLY**

.15

#4 * * * * * *

Unsettled domestic
conditions are being cited
for the 15-point plunge in
the Dow-Jones Industrial
Average over the last half
hour, Wall Street sources
revealed.

#5 * * * * * *

**COALITION
DEFENDS PLAN FOR
SIXTH DAC**

.10

#5 * * * * * *

An obviously weary
spokesrep for the Coalition
took issue this morning with
critics of its strategy for
confronting the sixth Dac
intruder, now some 3.5
billion kilometers away from
L5, saying, "We're not the
fools they are."

#6 * * * * * * *

**DRY MIAMI
THREATENS SOCIAL-
TECH EVACUATION
REPUTATION**

.10

#6 * * * * * *

While Hurricane Dora
headed out to sea, leaving in
her wake only a splattering
of rain on Miami, red-faced
ST/DPS forecasters re-
examined their computer
programs amidst charges of
misleading the public and
overcharging taxpayers.

#7 * * * * * * *

**NEW DRUG COMES
UNDER ACADEMIC
FIRE**

.10

#7 * * * * * *

In a copyrighted article
desposited in all major data
banks at 1125 EDT this
morning, a team of
researchers at the
University of Zimbabwe
report "significant

psychological problems" among heavy users of the new over-the-counter drug "TeleBetter."

#8 * * * * * *

TROUBLE IN PARADISE .10

#8 * * * * * *

A program glitch has temporarily re-routed all automated supply ships around the Hawaiian island of Maui, resulting in a state of near-famine on parts of the island, a CCU investigative news team has discovered.

#9 * * * * * *

MILANESE METH PLANT BLOWS .10

#9 * * * * * *

A recycling plant in this Italian city exploded in seven-story flames when an overpressurized methane tank burst and the gas ignited; no fatalities have been reported, but the shock wave broke windows up to six kilometers away.

#10 * * * * * *

DIRECTOR TO ADDRESS HOLO AUDIENCE .10

#10 * * * * * *

A spokesrep for the office of the Director of the Coalition of Public Directorates announced that a "major speech to announce important policy decisions" will be given at 1215 EDT.

This update has been provided as a public service by all data management corporations participating in NEWSBANK/CCU, a news data base organized and supervised by the Consumers & Citizens United Directorate of Public Information.

To read any of the above news stories in full, simply highlight the title and press ACCEPT. The article will be transmatted to your unit's memory. Your bank balance will be debited by the sum in the column headed "price."

To see the headlines of the day's other news stories, simply scroll your screen up.

Thank you, and do be careful.

XII

Ale sat in his study, gnawing idly on a thumbnail while he scanned his computer screen. Through the open massie chamber wafted the aroma of deep fried scallops. His stomach rumbled. He hoped Wef would have lunch ready soon.

The doorbell rang. "Can you get that, Wef?"

"Yeah, sure." Bolts clicked. Voices murmured. "Hey, Ale! Guy at the door says the Haven Manor Residents' Association is meeting in the auditorium to talk about this solar power scam. Says they'll have local reps from the CCU, SoshiTech, couple of others. Wants to know if you and Emdy are going."

Emdy shouted from her office, "Count me out!"

Ale swiveled around in his desk chair. "Yeah, me too, Wef."

"Don't you guys have any interest in upholding democracy?"

"Come off it. As a matter of pure fact, I'm voting right now." He spun back to stare at the computer screen. Well, he would be voting. As soon as he could figure out which to vote for. . . .

In answer to the question he had put the parties—"What do you propose to do in light of the accusations that the Coalition ignored the solar/sea solution to the CO_2 problem?"—only one party's response said, "Disband the Coalition." But that hardly counted, since the American Revival Party responded that way to almost any question. Ale could never be sure if that was their official platform, or just bad programming. . . .

The other thirty-seven parties active in New England all offered variations on a different theme, stated perhaps most ponderously by the Marian-Vegetarians: "In view of certain extremely grave allegations that have been brought concerning a decision made by the Coalition almost a century ago, the Marian-Vegetarian Party recommends the immediate formation of an independent commission empowered to investigate every aspect of that decision and the consequences resulting from it."

"Which is to say," said Ale to himself, "study it to death. And maybe people'll forget about it." He ran his eye down the list again, hoping to find some party he could switch his vote to other than AmRev—never would he vote for those lunatics—but nobody seemed willing to commit to anything beyond "thorough investigation."

"Or in other words," he said again, "you all have to seem to be reacting, even if none of you are going to do anything." Maybe he should run himself. Aichtueni had thought him a viable candidate. And he knew damn well how he would vote if he got elected. . . .

He typed in, QUERY: POLLS, RECENT, SUBJECT—CHARGES AGAINST COALITION.

The index flashed, ONE. GALLUP/HARRIS. 17/6/88; 1145 EDT. SEE (Y/N)?

He tapped the "y" key.

17 June 2188
Copyright © 2188 by Gallup/Harris, Inc.

A survey of North American sentiment re: Did they have to lock us indoors?

The poll computer contacted 2847 North American homes between the hours of 1000 EDT to 1200 EDT on 17 June 2188. The sample error of this poll is estimated at ±2.5%; ±3.3% when comparing these results with those of previous surveys.

QUESTION ONE:

Are you familiar with the charges that the Coalition withheld a scientific report stating that sea-water and solar power provided the optimum solution to the CO_2 pollution difficulties?	Yes:	39%
	No:	51%
	Not sure:	8%
	No answer:	2%

QUESTION TWO (asked of those familiar with the charges)

Do you believe those charges?	Yes:	63%
	No:	17%
	Not sure:	18%
	No answer:	2%

QUESTION THREE (as above)

Should the Coalition be disbanded?	Yes:	72%
	No:	23%
	Not sure:	1%
	No answer:	4%

Ale whistled softly to himself. Whoever had suggested that strategy had known what it was talking about. If things kept on the way they were—

"Wef! Ale! Ohe Ainainine's about to come on."

He headed for the living room. Emdy was already sitting at one end of the long couch; he sat at the other. Wef plopped down on the sofa facing them, on the far side of the living room. Avoiding each other's eyes, they concentrated on the holo cube in the middle of the room, which at Ale's muttered "Hovee-on," shimmered, then filled with the gleam of mahogany.

Behind the huge, bare desk sat Ohe Ainainine, the Director of the Coalition of Public Directorates. An old woman, gaunt and frail-seeming, she wore purple and diamonds. Her short white hair framed a high, broad forehead and calm brown eyes. She spoke in a tired but well-modulated voice; intelligence and conviction infused her every word.

"I have just been informed"—she looked directly into the holo lens—"of a plot to impugn the integrity of all the data networks in the world."

"Hoo-boy," said Ale, "the gloves come off."

Emdy said, "Did you expect anything else?"

"A group of conspirators has developed the software required to insert any misinformation it chooses into the public data banks. This is horrible!"

"Hey!" Wef popped the tab on another beer. "That's me she's talking about. I ain't horrible." He pegged his empty at the holovised image; it sailed through and dinged the leg of the coffee table.

"Stop it, Wef," said Emdy.

Gripping the arms of her chair, the Director bent forward. "Our civilization is built on the speedy dissemination of trustworthy information. The conspirators seek to undermine that foundation, and in so doing, threaten to topple that entire civilization."

Emdy made a rude noise, but when Ale winked at her, she said, "Just because she's full of it doesn't mean I agree with what you're doing."

Ohe Ainainine was still speaking. "—and not without a great deal of preliminary soul-searching, the immediate arrest of everyone known to be involved. I promise the public that the conspirators will be treated with the compassion due the insane, as they must of course be, but these poor, sick people will never again be permitted to disrupt the steady flow of truth."

"They made a good start by arresting all those Coalition people," said Ale. "Their only mistake was letting them go."

"—obvious and pernicious is that it would have been within the Coalition's power to solve the carbon dioxide problem with solar power and sea-water. I wish I could identify for you exactly what other misinformation this group has already deposited in the world's data banks. Unfortunately, they have, with great stealth and cunning, interwoven their lies with the public's truth. It will be necessary for the Coalition to review every datum now on file anywhere, and to purge the records of all contamination."

Ale frowned. This smacked too strongly of Imperial China, where founders of dynasties rewrote the history books to cast their immediate predecessors into disrepute, and to further legitimize their own claims to the throne. And the Director, with her constant invocations of the word "truth," reminded him of Humpty Dumpty, whose words meant just what he chose them to mean. "Wef—can they 'purge the records'?"

"Sure." The old man burped. "With a lot of people, a lot of time, a lot of money, sure. The question is, can they keep 'em purged? And the answer to that is, I don't think so."

Emdy said, "Hush. Listen." She pointed to the holo cube.

"—the phrase 'Access Temporarily Prohibited.' This will, inevitably, cause some small measure of inconvenience, but the information you're seeking will probably be available from another data bank. In any event, I assure you that the review committees will complete their daunting task as expeditiously as possible, and I urge you to cooperate whole-heartedly."

"They're going to shut down the data banks?" said Ale incredulously.

"They're going to try," said Emdy.

Wef burped. "They're gonna fail."

The Director's expression softened. She raised a fine-boned hand to the holo cameras in invitation. "To the conspirators I say: Please. You know who you are. You know that you need help. We stand ready and willing to provide it. Call us. Let us help you."

She straightened, then. "Thank you. And good night."

The picture shimmered and dissolved into thousand-colored snow. Ale chewed his thumbnail while he waited for the commentators to come on with their standard post-address analysis.

Instead, a baritoned announcer said, "We now return you to our regular programming."

The theme song to DOOMED CHILDREN rang out.

"Hovee-off," said Ale. Slouching on the sofa, he let his head loll back. He stared at the ceiling. "Did you notice that she didn't once mention ORA:CLE or ACLE?"

"Did she have to?" said Emdy. "Everybody knows who she meant."

"Sure, but I would have thought—"

"She's afraid," said Wef flatly.

Ale lifted his head and looked at the refugee. "What do you mean by that?"

"Just think about it. You got this lady, her word is law, nobody ever disagrees with her and nothing ever interferes with her—then all of a sudden one of her schemes starts coming unraveled. She can't figure it—you guys weren't supposed to notice. She doesn't worry, though. She can contain the problem by keeping the data out of the banks. But it shows up in the banks anyway. And she can't get the computers to find out who you are. More'n that, there's this piece of absolutely crucial information that's supposed to stay buried for a million years—and the next thing she knows, it's on all the news screens. Put yourself in her place. She thought she had everything *under* control, not *out of* control. Wouldn't you be afraid?"

"I suppose so. . . ."

Emdy went to the window and leaned against it. "Hey!"

Ale looked over quickly. "What?"

"Four Dacs, flying single-file down the street, just above the treetops . . . no, don't get up, they turned the corner. One of them was carrying one of those what-do-you-call-it, ah . . . a metal detector. I wonder why."

Wef said, "Who can figure a Dac? Say, Ale, d'jou see that

article yesterday, by some xenopsychologist down in Mexico City? She claims the Dacs are hunters—not predators, but like big-game hunters. Earth is their hunting preserve, and—"

The door swung open. Three burly policemen waving stun clubs spilled into the living room. "Freeze!"

For one quick sharp moment, Ale thought of running for the alien gun. He sat still. Even if he could reach it without being dragged down and beaten into unconsciousness, he could never escape. With a sigh, he heaved himself to his feet, hands raised above his head.

"Yeah, that's it," said the one in the lead. "Nice and easy, no resistance, nobody gets hurt." He motioned with his club. "All right, you two, back away."

Ale said, "Me?"

"Yeah, move it! You, too, lady. Your friend gets one phone call; sooner or later you'll find out where he is."

The other two grabbed Wef DiNaini and hustled him out the front door.

TOP TEN NEWS STORIES OF THE HOUR

17 June 2188 1300 EDT
New England Region

<u>RANK HEADLINE price LEAD SENTENCE</u>

ACCESS TEMPORARILY PROHIBITED

This update has been provided as a public service by all data management corporations participating in NEWSBANK/   , a news data base organized and supervised by the   Directorate of Public Information.

To read any of the above news stories in full, simply highlight the title and press ACCEPT. The article will be transmitted to your unit's memory. Your bank balance will be debited by the sum in the column headed "price."

To see the headlines of the day's other news stories, simply scroll your screen up.

Thank you, and do be careful.

XIII

The door closed behind the police and their prey. Emdy fixed Ale with a level stare, held it for a long moment, then shook her head. "Damn you." It came out quiet and deadly, a knife from the shadows.

Surprised, he blinked, but said nothing while he tried to assess her mood, her meaning. Her narrowed eyes and set jaw wounded him with silent accusations. He stiffened. "What are you talking about?"

Her voice rose. "You know damn— ah!" Touching her ears, she squeezed her eyelids shut. She took a deep breath, and let it out. Slowly, she opened her eyes. They gleamed with pain. In a lower tone, she continued. "—damn well what I'm talking about."

He had to admit he did. "For God's sakes, Emdy! How come they didn't arrest *me* if that's what it was all about, huh? I mean, like the Director said, she's issued an order to arrest all us subversive types. And here three cops walk right into an apartment registered half in my name, they look right in my face—and they haul *him* off. I mean, if they were here to make political arrests, don't you think *I'd* have been the one to go?" Even as he shut his mouth, he remembered that, according to The Oracle, Wef's erasure of the WAR code on Ale's ID/dress card effectively hid Ale from the Coalition. He decided not to mention it. No sense weakening his own arguments.

"No! They—" Reddening, she sputtered to a stop, forced to acknowledge his apparent logic. She made a show of adjusting her earmuffs.

He kept quiet. Bitter experience had taught him never to press a forensic advantage with her—she would only dig in her heels and defend her position all the harder. No one but Emdy Ofivo could change Emdy Ofivo's mind.

Her glare wavered; her shoulders settled. "I don't know."

She glanced from the rug to his face to the wall. "They should have arrested you. And they didn't. And that means..." Her voice became measured, thoughtful. "That means, one, it wasn't because of the job he did for you, or two, it was but they haven't learned yet that you were in on it, or three, it was and they have but the squad with the warrant for *his* arrest got here before the one with the warrant for yours, or four... but what difference does it make? Maybe it's not your fault, but it's because of you, I'm sure of that, and if either of you had listened to me— If you'd just stayed out of it, the both of you, just left it alone like I told you and let other idiots be the martyrs, but no, you had to—both of you—"

"Emdy, Emdy—" Moving, he took her in his arms. It felt like he hugged a quivering bundle of cable. "Emdy, look, you're mad, you're upset, I don't blame you, but can't you see—"

She pushed him away. Her jaw tensed; her gaze focused on something beyond the windows. "I'm going to get him out."

Ale nodded. "Sure. As soon as he lets us know where he is, we'll call our lawyer and—"

"No. I'm going to *break* him out."

He frowned. She could not have said what he thought he had heard. Or meant it if she had. "You're what?"

"There's a teller in Hartford with an unregistered fleet, and the word is he'll do *anything*. He's expensive, but real good, and that's what you need in a situation like this, somebody who's real good."

He wanted to laugh, but she clearly meant every word. That chilled him. Emdy Ofivo, practical and pragmatic, had never indulged in fantasy. Were the painkillers affecting her? "Doc," he said softly, "that's impossible."

She shot him a look of pure contempt. "Nothing's impossible."

Worried, now, because once determined, Emdy became a juggernaut, he reached to touch her, to bring her back to earth. "This isn't the Wild West. Wef's cell is probably two hundred meters underground. How are you even going to *get* there? Make a reservation—'Yes, I'd like to book a taxi for two months from Monday, I'll be breaking a friend out of prison'? Come on, Doc."

"I'm serious!" She shook his hand off her shoulder. "But you're right. I'm not thinking clearly. There's this mindless panic inside me that makes me want to run around in circles screaming my fool head off. I just need to . . . I need to get Wef out, is what I need. And to relax." Pacing, she laced her fingers together and squeezed till her hands shook. "Hah. Relax. I just need some peace and quiet, that's all. And to get Wef out. God I hate cleaning up your messes. But I can't use the Hartford teller. That's *your* style. Confront the system. Meet it head-on. Uh-uh. There's a better way."

"Sure. It's called a lawyer. That's what they're for."

"Only if they let Wef call us." She ran her hands through her hair, mussing it further. "But I'll bet they don't. So I'll have to come up with something—something *inside* the system—that'll pop him loose."

He let out his breath with a sigh. "Honey, you're all worked up. Can I get you something? A drink, a—"

"Ask The Oracle where Wef is."

Leaden dismay gathered in his stomach. "Are you kidding?"

"It won't take a minute. Just go in your study, sit down, and ask it to find out for you."

So the juggernaut was rolling already. "Well, I—"

"You don't want him free, do you?" She appraised him with hard, hostile eyes. "You'd like it better if they locked him up for good, wouldn't you?"

"I—" The accusation hit too close to home to risk discussion. "All right, I'll do it. Give me a minute." He went to his study, dropped into his recliner, and pushed it all the way back. He closed his eyes. *Hey, Oracle.*

#Yes, sir?#

Wef DiNaini just got arrested.

#And you remain at liberty? How fortunate.#

Can you find out where he is?

#One moment.#

Waiting, he sat in darkness, while background voices muttered to each other. He could not make out what they were saying. He was too tired to strain to understand them. He was too tired for almost anything.

He had lost too much in the last two days. Were Emdy's grip on sanity to slip entirely, he would snap himself.

Or had he already? Ah, there was a gloomy, disturbing thought. Preposterous things had happened in the last forty-eight hours, things sufficient to drive anyone crazy—but things so implausible that they made more sense if viewed as the ravings of a deranged imagination. Could he, Ale Elatey, already have snapped, and imagined everything?

He did not think so. . . .

#Mr. Ale Elatey?#

Ah. Where is he?

#Are you certain he was arrested?#

Yes! The cops took him right out of my living room.

#There is no record whatsoever of that. More, there is not even a warrant outstanding for his arrest. All Directorates of Public Security with jurisdiction in your locale profess ignorance as to his whereabouts. The only location on file for him is your apartment.#

Oracle, something's very wrong here.

#Yes.#

Suggestions?

#Only that you check back with me in several hours; I'll be trying other routes to locate him in the meanwhile.#

Okay, thanks.

#You're welcome.#

He broke interface. Emdy was talking to someone in the living room. Rather than interrupt with a shout, he levered himself to his feet and walked out to her, entering just as she, her back to him, told L'ai Aichtueni, "I'm sorry. Ale left this morning, and nobody knows where he is."

L'ai looked at Ale over Emdy's shoulder. Her eyes seemed normal; her speech, undrugged. She raised one white eyebrow and said, "Oh, I think I do."

Ale winced. His cheeks grew warm.

"Do you?" said Emdy brightly. "Well, if you see him—"

"I do."

He cleared his throat. "Uh, Emdy—"

L'ai said, "There he is, right behind you."

Emdy whirled, her face an angry mask. "Do you have a suicide urge? What's the matter with you, coming out here when somebody else is—"

"Emdy, I didn't know you were—"

"Well, what did you expect me to do, tell the whole world that—"

"But you didn't have to—"

"I'm your wife, dammit, I did have to!" Pain wracked her expression; she cupped her ears with her hands. "I had to, I—"

"Em—"

"Be quiet, Ale." When not on squash, L'ai could muster quite an authoritative tone. "And you, Emdy, if you would be so kind. Please listen to me. Emdy, I understand what you were trying to do. I think it's wonderful. And I agree with you, Ale will be much better off if no one knows where he is."

"Well, now that *you* know—"

"No, please, hear me out. The entire building stands behind Ale. He'd hardly win the Most Popular Resident Award, but those who know him, trust him. We shall not turn him in. I promise you that. No one believes that the troubles you've had for the last several days have been coincidences—a Dac, a crazed pholo laser, a bomb? No. People here do think that somebody, probably the Coalition, is trying to kill Ale. We are ready to help protect him. Don't worry, Emdy. We may not be friends, but we are neighbors."

"I—" Slumping into a chair, she let her head fall against its upholstered back. "I don't know what to say."

"You don't need to say anything. Just—"

"Attention!"

They turned to the hovee, which shook off its meaningless spirals of color and blurred into the image of a young man.

"Attention! Please pardon the interruption, but we are certain to be forced off the air at any moment."

The man had black hair, a sharp nose, and full lips set in a grim line. His was not a familiar face, but something in his voice reminded Ale of. . . . He could almost put a finger on it.

"We will be forced off the air because we are going to present to you incontrovertible evidence that members of our government are in collusion with the Dacs. More: that those same members of our government invited the Dacs to our planet."

Open-mouthed, L'ai sat heavily on the sofa.

"We urge you to go on strike. We are calling for a world-wide general strike, to go into effect immediately, and to continue until every employee of the Coalition has resigned, and until the various parties have appointed a trustworthy, independent commission to investigate the crimes the Coalition has committed against the people."

Ale snapped his fingers. The man's speech patterns. He had heard them before. In interface. Speaking fast and persuasively.

The man was a Seeley.

And if he said he had evidence . . .

"We'll save the written proof for later. If we're knocked off the air, please look for it in any data bank under the heading, COALITION IN CRIME."

Emdy said, "Ale, you didn't tell me—"

"I didn't know."

L'ai glanced from one to the other but said nothing.

The man in the glowing cube said, "I'd like to show you a hoclip. You will, I think, recognize the New York headquarters of the Coalition."

A Dac fluttered along the steel-and-glass canyon, then hovered, high above the ground, before a building where dozens of bright flags blew in the breeze. On a floor near the top of the skyscraper, a window opened.

"The window," said the announcer, "is to the private office of the Director of Coalition Intelligence."

The Dac flew inside.

The window closed.

The hovee went blank.

TOP TEN NEWS STORIES OF THE HOUR

17 June 2188 1400 EDT
New England Region

<u>RANK HEADLINE</u> price <u>LEAD SENTENCE</u>

ACCESS TEMPORARILY PROHIBITED

This update has been provided as a public service by all data management corporations participating in NEWSBANK/   , a news data base organized and supervised by the   Directorate of Public Information.

To read any of the above news stories in full, simply highlight the title and press ACCEPT. The article will be transmitted to your unit's memory. Your bank balance will be debited by the sum in the column headed "price."

To see the headlines of the day's other news stories, simply scroll your screen up.

Thank you, and do be careful.

XIV

"I just figured it out." Ale looked over his shoulder at Emdy and L'ai. "You know what it is?"

"SoshiTech usually has the best response time," said L'ai.

Emdy shook her head. "The UE's almost as quick, and they've got better commentary. Do we know what what is, Ale?"

"Why they tried to kill Seeleys." He finished adjusting the ap-comp's HV Monitor. While twirling wisps of color tumbled in the cube, the computer began to eavesdrop on all broadcast and cable channels. If it found any holo cast concerning the charges against the Coalition, it would direct the hovee to show it. "The plot didn't make any sense at all until I saw that clip."

Frowning, Emdy pushed her blonde hair behind her ears with both hands, and readjusted the fit of her earmuffs. "Are you saying *that* made sense?"

"Doc, I don't know *why* the Coalition's conspiring with the Dacs—"

"Any bright teenager could manufacture that film," said L'ai.

"I know that, but—" He took a breath. "Look, we've proven that the Coalition is trying to kill us. Since most of us are apolitical, the only possible reason is that we're basically researchers. All twenty thousand of us. And good ones, too. Sooner or later, with twenty thousand people digging through the official records for other things, someone was bound to stumble on this Dac connection. They were probably eliminating anybody whose researches took it close to a clue."

L'ai raised an eyebrow. "East Asian Studies?"

"Hey." He spread his hands. "There could be a document on file comparing the Dacs to the nineteenth century British in China—or us to Tokugawa Japan. A 'key word' search just might turn up the whole thing—or almost as bad, from their point of view, turn up the fact that it exists but is classified, which would arouse my suspicions and make me scheme to get a copy of it, and. . . . Can you see where I'm going?"

The pholo rang. Ale reached out for it. The doorbell chimed. He hesitated, but both women were already getting up. He moved again—then stopped abruptly. "This could be the cops."

For a moment all three seemed rooted to the carpet. The pholo rang twice more as they exchanged confused glances. Finally, L'ai pointed to the kitchen. "Ale, go hide. Emdy, answer the pholo. I'll get the door."

Emdy nodded and went for the pholo.

In the vestibule, L'ai said, "Video."

"Broken."

"Damn . . . open up, then."

Ale ducked into the massie chamber just as the front door swung inwards. He peeked through the crack. L'ai backed up, smiling. Mr. B'jay Awu and old Mrs. M'ti Emtenne entered; she was clutching his arm. Awu carried his ever-present clipboard. *Not much of a threat there*, thought Ale, emerging from the chamber. "Hi, folks."

B'jay Awu waved the clipboard at Ale. "Ale, we've just heard the news! Appalling, to have the party Electors in the Coalition consorting with the enemy. . . . I've taken it upon myself to circulate a petition demanding the immediate ouster of the present Coalition, and the instatement of—"

"Ale," called Emdy from her study, "it's your mother on line two."

"Excuse me, B'jay, I—"

"Oh, say hello to your mother for me," said Mrs. M'ti Emtenne. She smelled of hamburgers and stale jasmine. "It's been so long since we sat down and had a good chat together."

"Uh—" It was news to Ale that M'ti Emtenne and his mother knew each other, but he kept the surprise off his face. "Sure. I'll tell her. Uh . . . make yourselves comfortable." He gestured toward the sofa.

B'jay Awu bowed to M'ti Emtenne. "After you, my dear."

"Thank you." She practically simpered.

Turning, Ale rolled his eyes and headed for the pholo in his study. "Yeah, Mom? Oh, Mrs. M'ti Emtenne says to say hi."

"That old biddy?" She sniffed her disapproval. "So you're not in jail after all."

"Did you expect me to be?"

"Frankly, yes. They dragged one of my neighbors away this afternoon."

"A Seeley?" he said sharply.

"Yes. I happened to be in the corridor when they carried him off. They'd beaten him rather severely, Ale. He was quite unconscious, and covered with blood. I doubt he'll survive."

"Mom, did you call and tell me this just to cheer me up, or what?"

"Actually, no. I called to tell you that if you have a place to hide, I advise you to go there immediately. Lie low, Ale. Things are bumping in the night and they're hunting for you."

"Oh, thanks." He made a face. "I need to hear that."

"I also called to tell you that, while it might be too late, our building has just elected six new representatives, each of them sworn to vote out its party's Elector on the Coalition. As I say, it may be too late—but those of you who can disappear for a while might survive this, this . . . purge." She shook her head dolefully. "I should let you go. I'm sure you have things to take care of before you leave. Best of luck, Ale."

The sphere went dark.

He sat in morose silence. *She could have waited till I'd said good-bye.*

The pholo rang again. His finger hit the answer button automatically. An unfamiliar man with a round face and wispy brown hair stared out of the sphere at him. "Ale Elatey, as I live and breathe!"

Gritting his teeth, he wished arthritis on his finger. "Uh—"

"Cibie Otutu, news reporter for Channel 11, New York. *Delighted* to get ahold of you—don't mind if I tape this, d'you?" Before Ale could speak he went on. "Actually called to get your wife's reactions to things, figuring you were either under arrest or in hiding like all the others—"

"All what others?"

"Other Seeleys. Can't find a one of 'em. Listen, just a few quotes for tonight's news, huh? Lemme ask you, Ale, whaddaya think of what Director Ohe Ainainine did this morning, eh? That's the denial on the sun-sea solution, the Seeley arrests, the data bank purges, the works. Your reaction, please."

"Do you think I'm crazy? They're arresting my colleagues, and you're going to 'cast this and say you found me at home and—"

"Hell no, Ale. Wouldn't do that to a topic. Gonna matte in a public pholo booth around your head, make it seem without saying so that you called in from the underground. So whaddaya think of the Director, eh?"

He blinked. The need to watch his words weighed on his tongue. Ranting and raving might be just what the 'caster wanted—it might even feel wonderful—but in the long run it would do Ale no good.

"Well, Ale?"

He spoke slowly and carefully. "I think she has acted in haste. From all I know of her she is a competent, methodical administrator, and I find it hard to believe that she would mendaciously disavow the authenticity of the panel's report. I suspect she sincerely believes that it never existed. I suspect that someone in the bureaucracy told her that."

"Whatcher saying is that the Coalition's own people are lying to it?"

"No, I'm not saying that at all. I'm saying that that's what I suspect. There's a difference."

"So what about the arrests and the purges, huh? How'd they miss you, by the way?"

"I think they just haven't gotten around to me yet. As for the arrests, frankly I think they're unconstitutional; I expect that the Director and her staff will be hit with some pretty stiff lawsuits. And the purges, well, I mean, it's what you order if you have good reason to believe that your data have been contaminated. Ohe Ainainine clearly believes that. I think she's wrong—I think the data are correct—we'll have to see what happens with this Commission she's appointing."

"Uh-huh," said Cibie Otutu. "Now lissen, a few more—"

"Ale!" Emdy's voice rang high and sharp.

"Cibie, things are a little crazy around here right now. Mind if we cut this short?"

"Say, no problem, I understand perfectly, but lissen, if they do haul you away, you be sure to give me a call from wherever they're holding you and we'll go into this in greater detail, all right?"

"Yeah, fine." Heavy feet sounded in the kitchen.

"Okay, great talking to you, Ale, and best of luck, eh?"

The pholo sphere blanked just as the massie chamber door opened. Behind it flashed a blue uniform. A deep voice boomed, "Ale Elatey?"

He almost bolted for the hall, but sat tight. If the Coalition had come for him, guards would be blocking the corridor outside the apartment. "Yeah?"

It was the building cop. He nodded. "Sorry to bother you, but I heard about the Director's orders to arrest all you Seeleys, and—"

"And you want me to go quietly, huh?" He put as much sarcasm into it as he could.

"Hell, no." He scowled. "I work for the lady owns this building. Just thought I'd let you know—case you were thinking of taking a short trip by air—that it seems like there's this helicopter on the roof got a busted rotor, and it's blocking the helipad. Been there for an hour or so, now, and already a coupla security-copters hadda change their minds about landing. The guy that flies it—he's in 18-B—says he's waiting for a part from Nairobi, but the factory there's got about a weeklong backlog. Just thought you oughta know." He tipped his bemedalled cap and left the room.

Ale tilted his chair back, a warm glow suffusing him. He had never realized his neighbors cared enough about him to risk confronting, even discreetly, the authorities. To think that someone he had never met would disable a helicopter on the roof just so the landing pad would be blocked when the police arrived. . . . To think a *cop* would be the first to tell him. . . . It made him feel very good indeed.

"Say, Ale?"

Blinking, he looked up. "Oh, hi, Emdy. Brooding, I guess."

"I don't blame you." She leaned against the wall, the picture of weariness. "It just seems so damn incredible, the Coalition trying to kill all of you, the Director herself dealing with the Dacs—I don't know, I'm beginning to think you're probably right about all of this. It's crazy, but it's the sanest option available."

"I know, I know . . . but it has happened before."

"The Director inviting Dacs into her office?"

"No, no, no—governments doing under-the-table deals with the so-called enemy. Russia did it with Germany in the 1900s, the Chinese practically made an art form of it—"

"No history lesson now, okay?"

"Sure, I'm sorry." Yawning, he stretched. "So has the convention in our living room broken up?"

"They're still out there, chattering away. They all want to know what's going on."

"Nothing on the hovee yet, huh? Censors must be working overtime."

"They want you to find out."

"How?"

"The Oracle, Ale, The Oracle."

"Oh. . . ." Of course they would think that way. ORA:CLE Inc's entire advertising strategy was to convince people that between them, the Seeleys had all the answers to everything, and that the easiest, if not the cheapest, path to truth lay in tapping ORA:CLE's number into your pholo. "Well. . . ."

"Come on. I'll get them to quiet down so you can concentrate."

"No need for that—just close the door on your way out."

"Okay."

He slipped into interface *Hey, Oracle, what's the story on this Coalition, Dac thing?*

#No comment.#

That so startled him that he almost lost interface. *What?*

#I regret to state that I am unable to comment on the allegations made recently over the holovision.#

But you have to know all about it—I mean, that was a Seeley there, wasn't it?

#Mr. Elatey. You of all people should understand that the rules governing anonymity—#

Sure, sure, I'm sorry. But—

#Perhaps this recording might enlighten you.#

Puzzled, he stayed silent. Voices hummed in the background; suddenly, two of them leapt into the foreground:

#Simply lay the one image on top of the other, and there you have it—a Dac dropping in to kaffeeklatsch with the Director.#

You really think people are going to buy it?

#They'll be seeing it with their own two eyes, won't they?#

Sure, but—

#Clearly, you don't understand. We are not targeting the thinking person, here. And we are not trying to reach the Average Moron intellectually: We're going for the gut. We will flash them an image so forceful that even those who are convinced of its falsehood will be unable to rid their minds of it. When they hear the word 'Coalition,' they will see that Dac flying through that great big window, and they will recoil.#

She'll kill us for this.

#Perhaps. But this could be the only thing that'll keep her from killing us.#

If the other Seeleys ever find out about this— I don't like it.

#They won't. And you don't have to like it.#

Dammit, it's wrong.

#No. It's an established propaganda tactic. They call it "The Big Lie."#

TOP TEN NEWS STORIES OF THE HOUR

RANK HEADLINE	price	LEAD SENTENCE
#1 GROUP DISRUPTS MEDIA WITH LIES	.00	A group of unidentified, self-styled experts has deliberately snarled all major communications outlets, and contaminated all significant data banks, by inserting megabytes of false information into the system; authorities expect the situation to return to normal within two or three days.

FURTHER ACCESS TEMPORARILY PROHIBITED

This update has been provided as a public service by all data management corporations participating in NEWSBANK/⸻, a news data base organized and supervised by the ⸻ Directorate of Public Information.

To read any of the above news stories in full, simply highlight the title and press ACCEPT. The article will be transmitted to your unit's memory. Your bank balance will be debited by the sum in the column headed "price."

To see the headlines of the day's other news stories, simply scroll your screen up.

Thank you, and do be careful.

XV

Out in the living room, someone turned up the volume on the hovee. Probably for the benefit of old Mrs. M'ti Emtenne, who refused to set her hearing aid beyond the first notch.

Down the hall and into Ale's study echoed the soothing bass of a Coalition spokesrep who read, with apparent sincerity, a prepared statement denying every charge the ACLE had leveled.

It was too loud for Ale, too loud and too true. As he got up to close the doors, he wondered how the others could tolerate it. He imagined all but Mrs. M'ti Emtenne wincing, pushed backwards by a nearly solid wave of sound. He could understand, as never before, how she had gone through seven husbands, why both her children had left home so young. Who could live with that?

Then he jerked the door open again, remembering, suddenly, Emdy's injury— The sound dropped to a whisper. She must have taken care of it herself.

Sinking into his recliner he sighed, aware that he was stalling. Sooner or later he would have to go out and report, and he did not look forward to it. He wished he had never asked The Oracle for the truth. He had no doubt about the Coalition's murderous intentions toward the Seeleys of the world—but there was also no doubt that ACLE had lied about the Coalition's involvement with the Dacs.

And that confused matters even more, because it ruled out the only conceivable motive the Coalition could have had.

Unless. . . . He shook his head. No. The Coalition could not possibly have felt threatened by the experts at ORA:CLE, Inc. This was not Confucian China, where learning conferred power. This was the real world, where the only thing that learning conferred was the ability to survive. Power, as Mao put it, "grew out of the barrel of a gun"—and the Coalition had held the guns, real or figurative, for over a century.

So what had driven the Coalition to homicide? He could understand why ACLE had resorted to the Big Lie—any port in a storm and all that, and this was perhaps the stormiest weather ORA:CLE, Inc. had ever sailed through—but the Coalition. . . .

It made no sense.

And what was he going to do now? He could not tell his neighbors that the hoclip of the Dac and the Director was a hoax. He dared not say that to anyone. He had to keep very quiet about it, keep it to himself. . . .

And yet, dammit! He was a scholar, sworn to the pursuit and dissemination of truth. How could *he* participate in an out-and-out lie?

How could he not participate? Revealing it for what it was would incur the hostility of the unaffiliated. It would tar the more important truth with the same brush. The population-at-large would turn their backs on ACLE, would close their ears while Seeleys died all around them.

"Ale?"

He jerked his head up. "Huh?"

L'ai Aichtueni stood with her hand on the doorknob. "Your face is twitching like you've got palsy—are you having trouble getting through?"

He seized her phrasing for a half-truth that would serve to mislead: "I'm having a lot of trouble right now."

She opened her mouth but outside the building engines roared, revving under a huge strain. Suddenly they purred. She looked back over her shoulder, toward the living room. Metal crashed in the street. Her eyes widened. She started to move.

He rose to follow. A great hollow boom shook Haven Manor.

Emdy yelped as B'jay Awu's voice rose high: "My God, it's burning!"

He broke into the living room hard on L'ai's heels. The others clustered at the terrace windows. The DacWatch glowed red. In the hovee cube, the Coalition spokesrep smiled like a choirboy.

"What's going on?"

Mrs. M'ti Emtenne spun around. "It went right past the window! Straight down! I couldn't see if there was anybody—I only got a glimpse—the corner of my eye, I was looking—but just straight down! And then a Dac flew up!"

As she paused for breath, B'jay Awu said, "It was a helicopter. I think it was being towed, because I saw a police towchopper flying away. I think the cable snapped. Apparently it disturbed a Dac investigating the street."

Emdy said, "And I think the landing pad's clear now." She whirled for her office, flicking on her pholo before she reached her desk. The thick glass walls could not contain her urgency: "Fire on Chapel by Haven Manor. A helicopter. From the way it's burning, it had a full tank of gas."

Sirens wailed before the rising black smoke reached the balcony.

Ale pressed up against one of the sliding glass doors. The terrace cut off his vision, tempting him to crack the door and peek outside—but the DacWatch burned ruby. The last thing he needed—

The front door opened. A man in a wrinkled brown suit stood in the doorway, nodding to himself as he slid something into his pocket. He entered; behind him came a squad of uniforms. He rounded the vestibule planter and surveyed the small group through hooded grey eyes. "I'm Lieutenant Deze Eforet. Which one of you's Ale?"

"That'd be me," he said.

"Let's go." The lieutenant pointed to the corridor.

"Can you give me a minute to—"

"No."

He shrugged. "All right, I—"

From the hallway came a curse. A hoarse strong voice said, "Use that again and you'll eat it, dip."

"Just move along, there's nothing to see here—"

"That's where you're wrong, 'cause your boss is in there, and I am going to see him."

"No. You call downtown—"

"Get out of my way."

"Listen, mister, I—mphph."

A plastic helmet clattered against the corridor wall.

Deze Eforet said, "See what's going on out there."

The cop nearest the door stepped outside—then grunted sharply and folded in half. A burly figure dressed in black denim stepped into the vestibule. "Awright! Who the fuck dumped my chopper into the street?" Stun club in hand, he punctuated his demand with sharp stabbing gestures.

The lieutenant titled his head and examined the intruder. "I did. It was blocking the helipad."

"So who are you, God?"

"I'm the officer in charge and—"

"Not any more you're not. We fired you guys eight minutes ago. So you just get your ass back up on the roof, and back in your chopper—"

"One more word, and—"

"Shut up." Black Denim brandished the stun club. "You already got the biggest damn lawsuit you ever heard of staring you in the face, you want to go for criminal charges, too? 'Cause maybe you didn't hear me right. The votes switched. The Uhuru Episcopal Party's in charge of security here now, and you guys have been fired."

The plainclothes officer turned to his squad. "Take him."

The big guy looked at the nearest cop. "Don't even think about it." Raising his voice, he called, "Reinforcement time!"

Through the door strode a small woman with a big jaw. She held a brace of heavy steak knives in her left hand—and one in her right hand. Which was cocked. Ready to hurl the gleaming stainless steel blade at the first uniform to move. "You heard what the man said. Don't even think about it."

For the first time the plainclothesman looked uncertain. "Wait a minute, I'm not MV—I'm Coalition. And I've got a warrant—"

"You *admit* you're a Dac dorker?" said the big guy disbelievingly. "You have the sheer, unmitigated gall to stand there and confess in front of everybody in this room that you're Coalition? There are easier ways to kill yourself, you know."

Deze Eforet reached inside his jacket. "Just hold on there, I—"

A knife whizzed past his right ear to sink into the wall. Quivering, it thrummed.

The short woman grinned. She had another knife in throwing position already. "Take your hand out slowly, traitor—real slowly."

He paled. And obeyed.

Black Denim chuckled. "Now. I suggest you all drop your clubs—"

They thudded onto the floor.

"—lace your hands behind your worthless necks—"

Five pair of arms snapped into place.

"—and start moving toward the elevator. Slowly. My friend here gets nervous when Dac dorking dips do anything sudden."

The cops filed out of the room.

The big man went last. Before closing the door, he turned, looked at Ale, and winked. "Don't sweat it. We'll make sure they don't come back."

Ale nodded. "Thanks."

"Believe me—it's my pleasure." For a moment he looked thoughtful. "Spread the word, though: I think things are about to go to hell. It's time to lay in supplies."

TOP TEN NEWS STORIES OF THE HOUR

18 June 2188 0900 EDT
New England Region

RANK HEADLINE	price	LEAD SENTENCE
#1 GROUP DISRUPTS MEDIA WITH LIES	.00	A group of unidentified, self-styled experts has deliberately snarled all major communications outlets, and contaminated all significant data banks, by inserting megabytes of false information into the system; authorities expect the situation to return to normal within two or three days.

FURTHER ACCESS TEMPORARILY PROHIBITED

XVI

—1—

Yawning and hungry, still wiping sleep crumbs from the corners of his eyes, Ale stumbled into his study to order groceries. He wished he had remembered to do it the night before. He hated waiting for the store to transmat breakfast.

The pholo sphere quivered into the image of a haggard black man wearing a business suit. "Good morning and thank you for calling BestShop for your kitchen needs. All our lines are busy now. Please hold. The first available operator will take your order. Thank you again."

"Oh, damn. . . ." He had not expected ACLE's call for a general strike to be answered—or to affect him personally if it were. *Well*—he clicked off the pholo—*there're some leftovers in the fridge, anyway. . . .*

He walked through the massie chamber into the kitchen, easing each door open and shut. Even with half the apartment between them, he could feel Emdy's sour, brittle mood. He put his feet down carefully. She had awakened first that morning, leaving him to get up on his own and find her sipping black coffee in her office, a sure sign that she was spoiling for a fight which she wanted him to start. He would not oblige her. He had no stomach for it. Fights hurt too much.

The refrigerator's light fell on mostly empty shelves. Cool air stroked his bare legs as he rummaged through the vegetable bin. Chinese cabbage for breakfast? A revolting thought. . . .

From the living room came the soft chime of the ap-comp receiving a string of mail.

He wandered out to inspect the computer's directory, then whistled to himself. That one transmission had filled a quarter of its memory.

Acutely aware of Emdy's scrutiny—it burned on the nape of his neck like a laser—he sat, jaw clenched. If she would not speak, he would not risk an explosion by saying the wrong thing. He scrolled through the day's mail, paying the bills as they flashed onscreen, dumping the junk, and skimming quickly through the rest to get an idea of what to do with it.

Apparently every association to which he belonged had published a special issue on ACLE's accusations against the Coalition. The scholarly journals attempted to maintain an aloof dignity; the others abandoned all pretense of neutrality and took vociferous sides.

Of the fourteen non-academic publications in memory, three claimed that the Coalition was telling the truth.

The last item in his box intrigued him—then worried him. Addressed merely to Occupant, 38-Q Haven Manor, it explained in lucid detail how best to wrap a parcel containing fecal matter, gimmicked aerosol cans, or explosives so that the detectors at Central Transshipping would neither notice the contents nor become suspicious that they could not notice them.

It also presented the access codes to a data base listing the ID/dresses of all North American Coalition Employees. And suggested that each of those civil servants deserved a short, crisp message from a citizen/taxpayer.

"My God," he said wonderingly, "this is incitement to murder!"

Motion at the edge of his vision caught his attention; he looked outside.

On the top row of windows across the way, a stubby-rotored painter was stenciling, in phosphorescent yellow: DOWN WITH THE COA

A siren shrieked; a moment later a blue swept into view. The painter reddened, then plummeted. The blue whistled down the street and disappeared.

The ap-comp clicked; new words formed at the bottom of its screen:

TO ALL RESIDENTS OF HAVEN MANOR
We most cordially invite you to attend
a seminar on
"The Tele-factor as Political Force"
or
"The Living Room Revolution"
in the Main Auditorium
1500 EDT Today
(simultaneously holocast on Channel 238)

He had, for an instant, a wild vision of repair carts run amok, seizing the Coalition by its foundations and shaking it to destruction. But the dream faded as quickly as it came. Telefactoring equipment cost too much for the average operator. Major corporations owned most of it, and monitored it through central switchboards that could shut individual units down at will.

He doubted that Ma Bell would sanction employee use of her equipment to insure the violent overthrow of the Coalition.

But maybe he would check out the seminar anyway.

His stomach rumbled. On second thought, Chinese cabbage might make a better breakfast than none at all. He rose from the chair. The pholo rang. He sighed, sat, and switched it on.

"Morning, Ale."

His jaw dropped. "Wef!"

"I just figured I'd better give you folks a call and let you all know that everything's just fine with me." The old man sat in a cubicle cramped with computer equipment and a fold-down bunk. Grinning into one of the cameras, he seemed fully at ease. "Your New Haven cops sure know how to treat a person right."

"Wef, where are you? We've—" He stumbled over his use of the plural. "—uh, been worried. About you. When you didn't call—"

Emdy's hand came to rest on his shoulder. She bent down close to his head. "We need to know exactly where you are, including your cell number."

For a moment the refugee frowned. Then he shrugged, and tapped three buttons on his keyboard. "Whatever you say— it's all in your machine, now."

Ale said, "Wef, what did they charge you with?"

"Suspicion of suspiciousness, I guess. Which is to say they haven't booked me yet, and until they do that, they don't have to tell me what they're charging me with."

"But Wef," said Emdy, "it's been twenty hours!"

"Well, they'd said they'd get around to it, but they're waiting on somebody to come in from New York. To tell you the truth, I'm in no hurry—soon as they charge me, they'll stick me down in one of the real cells, and frankly, honey, I'd much rather be here." He patted the keyboard. "They don't have the good stuff downstairs."

Ale held up a finger to signal Emdy it was his turn. "Wef, do you need a lawyer?"

The old man shook his head. "If they decide to question me, I might, but I can always order one then. Don't worry about it."

"Are they feeding you, Wef?"

"Not as good as you do, Emdy, but it's enough."

"We'll get you out of there."

"Hey, don't worry about me! I am just fine. I'm out of your closet and your hair, I've got a room all my own with very fine furnishings"—he tapped the CRT above the keyboard—"and I'm perfectly safe from Dacs, streeters, and exploding massies." He winked. "Don't worry about me—I'll talk to you later." He reached out of pholo range and the sphere vanished.

Alc pushed himself to his feet. "That's a relief."

"Well, Phase One ends successfully." Emdy took over the ap-comp. "Time for Phase Two."

Ale came alert. "What are you talking about?"

"I told you, I was going to work within the system to free Wef. Phase One involved notifying all parties' public relations departments that a probable computer failure—which I blamed on 'the current disturbances'—had made it impossible to locate someone the police had taken into custody. I asked them to request a manual head-count in all holding cells in the area, and to have Wef call me when they found him."

"So what's Phase Two?"

"Originally it was to bail him out, but since they haven't charged him yet, it'll be to force them either to charge him or let him go."

"And how—"

"I don't know." Tapping a fingernail on the edge of the desk, she stared at the screen. "I'll have to think on it. But I'll come up with something."

"Doc, I don't understand." Exasperated, he paced to the windows and back. "You got all upset with me because I was rocking the boat. Now you're doing the same thing—"

"It's not the same thing at all." She swiveled the chair to keep him in view. "I'm staying within the system; you went outside of it."

"But it's the system that arrested—"

"Don't you see it, Ale? The system's a river, a current, a flow. If you go against it, you drown. So does everybody with you. But if you ride it smart, if you steer right, you get where you want quick and easy."

"But is it smart? Right now Wef's okay where he—"

"Ale, you saw that wink! You know it meant that we were supposed to ignore everything he was saying."

"I thought it was a wink. . . . Emdy, you can't—"

"I can and I will." She spun and stalked away.

"Emdy!"

"No!" The glass rattled as she slammed the door. Her hand rose as if to touch her ear, but she squared her shoulders and marched to her desk.

—2—

Ale checked the time. 1405 EDT. He should leave for the "Living Room Revolution" seminar in fifty minutes. No, sooner. If it drew a crowd, the elevators would run slow—or glitch out completely—and he would get there late. Forty-five minutes, then.

Down the hall floated the murmur of distant motors. Normally such noises never penetrated his consciousness, but today he was so bored they sounded interesting.

Maybe it was the fleet picking up the Florida refugees. . . .

He strolled to the living room, glancing into Emdy's office as he passed, hoping to catch her eye but not succeeding. The hovee spun rainbows for amusement, and hummed to itself. He looked out the window. Nothing. The helis must be approaching the building from the north.

The building quivered just perceptibly; the engine noises faded.

Curious, he switched the hovee to the closed-circuit channel that carried the rooftop monitor's view.

A swarm of blue uniforms covered the flat black rooftop. He blinked, sank without thought onto the couch, then murmured to the ap-comp, "Estimate crowd size."

The hovee flickered. The ap-comp said, "Seventy-five humans; three machines."

A small knot of police clustered by the door to the staircase. One of them pushed back his helmet visor, removed his gauntlets, and knelt to pick its lock. The rest stood by the elevators, poised on the balls of their feet, tensely slapping stun clubs into open palms.

"Sound," said Ale.

The speakers clicked on just as Elevator Number Six slid open. The building cop stepped out and gave a friendly nod, but did not step aside. "Good afternoon. What can I do for you folks?"

The officer in charge said, "For starters, you can give us your override key for the elevators. Seems you've changed locks here without informing us."

"That's right, Captain. There were a lot of keys floating around, mostly in the wrong hands. Had a locksmith in just the other day. Surprised you weren't notified; it's usually automatic."

"Uh-huh." Sour, she held out her hand. "The override key, please."

"Gee, I'm sorry, sir. It's my understanding that your party's been voted out of office, which means this building isn't in your jurisdiction anymore. I'd get fired if I gave you the key."

"We've all been temporarily posted to the Coalition, which means we *do* have jurisdiction here. Now, are you going to give me—"

"I don't have it with me." He shrugged. "I'll go down and—"

She turned to her second. "Frisk 'im."

The lieutenant jerked his head. Two burly patrolmen stepped forward, seized the security guard, and held him tightly while the lieutenant ran his hand through his pockets. "Nothin', Captain."

The building cop said, "I told you so."

"We'll make do without." Turning, she called across the rooftop, "Got it open yet?"

"Another minute, sir!"

"We're not going to wait. Q Team! Into this elevator, straight to the auditorium, secure all entrances, nobody goes in or out, arrest anybody connected with that seminar, and seize all subversive literature. Understood?"

Ten cops stiffened to attention, chorused, "Yes, sir," and filed in.

Her gaze flicked to the lights above Elevator Number Four. "Here comes another one. B Team, get yourselves ready—"

Number Four opened. Metal flashed. Two guardmechs sprang out ready for battle. The police nearest them stumbled back in horror as panic-sonics washed over them. Tentacles struck like snakes, snapping handcuffs into place with the dry frantic crackle of a brushfire.

The Captain held her stun club at the ready as she spoke to the building cop. "Call 'em off!"

"I can't, I'm not telling them."

"Who is?"

"Damn if I know."

Sheet metal clanged. The Coalition's own mechs had joined the fray. They loomed bigger and moved faster than anything New Haven could afford; their factors told them with casual skill that bespoke years of training and experience—years their adversaries clearly lacked. The treaded one grappled turret-to-turret with a guardmech while two spiders maneuvered a tough nylon net over the other. The fight was over in seconds.

"Door's open, Captain!"

"A Team. Get to the auditorium and reinforce Q. Weld the fire doors shut on your way down. Move it!!"

The lockpicker snapped off a salute, grabbed his torch, and disappeared into the stairwell. Nine more followed him down.

She turned back and raised her eyebrows at the open, empty elevator. "Sergeant," she said in a dangerously quiet voice, "does B Team have a problem?"

"Four shields still handcuffed, sir." He pointed to where each of the three Coalition mechs worked to free a uniformed policeman from its shackles. "Be ready to go in a minute."

"See that you are. I— Dacs! Everybody under cover, move it, move it!"

Uniforms burst in all directions; the rooftop cleared in seconds. The monitor faithfully relayed the dispersal, the emptiness, the two sharp shadows of giant wings gliding smoothly across the asphalt and running over the edge of the building, the—

The scene in the sphere dwindled to a tiny black ball; the sound died. Ale figured the cops who had gotten inside had cut the wires. But a moment later the black dot swelled into a new scene, the inside of someone's Sahara motif living room. A man Ale had never seen before leaned into the cameras. "Those of you watching this channel know that the police have come to prevent us from holding our seminar, and to arrest everybody connected with it. We need your help. Get anything you can—a broom, a mop, a chair leg—anything at all, and join us in the hallways. We're fighting for our freedom. For our neighbors' lives. Please. All they have are stun clubs. If they can't reach us, they can't hurt us. We must drive them off. Please. Join us. Now."

Ale's blood surged. He jumped off the couch, already searching, mentally, for something he could use as a weapon. Something he could swing, something good and strong and heavy he— He faltered.

Was he crazy? Was he really going to rush a bunch of tough, trained cops, shouting, waving a plastic broomstick at them? You did *not* attack the police. Never. It was illegal, it was immoral, and it was suicide to boot.

He wanted to go out. So maybe he was crazy.

Someone ran heavily past his apartment door. And another someone. A hollow boom rolled up the corridor as the someones kicked in a door. A woman screamed sharply, briefly. Fell silent. And screamed again.

Yes, definitely crazed.

He ran for the door, snatched up a folding chair on the way, banged it hard on his shins, hopped, cursed, and kept going. He lurched into the hall and caromed off a cop racing to help his teammates. The cop bounced against the wall; Ale staggered and would have fallen had the folding chair not opened and provided him with its support. The cop shook his head once, to clear it, snarled, and lunged at Ale with his stun club.

Instinctively, Ale swung the chair up. The edge of its seat smacked the cop on the wrist; a leg caught him under the chin. The cop's eyes unfocused; he groaned. His jaw dropped. He sank to the floor.

Panting, Ale looked with wonderment at the chair, then set it down. Gingerly, so as not to awaken the unconscious policeman, he relieved him of his stun club.

It felt good in Ale's hand. Very good.

Careful to avoid the live tip, he slapped it into his palm. Yes, definitely. He could enjoy wielding this on the one making that woman scream.

He loped down the hall toward the source of the commotion. As he ran it struck him that he *could* go back and grab the Dac gun—surely that would be more threatening? But no, he had no time, it was too late, and besides (on the verge of his consciousness) the gun could kill and he did not want to kill. Not now. Not yet. . . .

A door opened to his left. Old Mrs. M'ti Emtenne ventured out, uncertainly brandishing a tennis racquet. He did not slow down. Weird old lady was as likely to hit him as a cop.

The shrieks came from 38-W. The door lay flat on the ground, bent screws dangling from its flimsy hinges. He charged across it and into the apartment.

Two policemen were trying to haul away a handcuffed teenager while the girl's mother clawed at their arms, apparently oblivious to repeated shocks from their clubs.

A hoarse guttural yell rose in Ale's throat as he hurled himself at the nearer cop. He brought the club down hard and fast. It whistled as it cut an arc through the air. The cop started to spin; her partner yelled, "Watch—"

The club smashed into the earpiece of her helmet—and snapped. The plastic helmet cracked. The cop folded at the knees and slumped to the floor.

"Oh, Jesus." Ale stared at the jagged stump in his hand.

"You said it, asshole." With a flick of his wrist the downed cop's partner pushed the girl off her feet. She yelped as she went over backwards and landed on her linked wrists. "You're about to regret what you just did, boy." He feinted with his club.

The girl's mother leaped on his back and wrapped an arm around his neck. He jackknifed forward, flipping her over his head and almost into Ale. She held on, though, but to his helmet, which ripped off with a rasp of velcro.

Red-faced, glaring, the cop started to straighten.

Ale took one long step with his left leg and kicked the cop in the cheek. The cop flew limply backwards. Ale hopped up and down, clutching his foot.

From the doorway, Mrs. M'ti Emtenne said, "Very nice, for a loafer."

—3—

Pacing, Emdy said, "I don't believe you actually—"

"I *know* it was dumb, but what was I supposed to do?" He sat on the couch and carefully wrapped a rubber bandage around his swollen ankle. As soon as he had taken care of that, he would do something about the bloody gash on his shin. He did not look forward to cleaning it. "Was I supposed to let them haul her away?"

"No, but... but you weren't supposed to get involved, either. They've already got it in for you, and this—this is just—"

Her office pholo shrilled.

"You just wait right there, Ale Elatey." She stalked toward her office, head high.

He sat in rueful contemplation of his twisted ankle, wondering where she expected he might have gone had she not ordered him to stay put. Peking, maybe? The kitchen?

She emerged with an aloof, triumphant smile playing about her lips. "It's all set."

He shook his head. "What's all set?"

"That was the MV/DP Security Ombudsman. He says he'll have Wef out on bail within forty-eight hours."

He sagged back, too confused to speak.

Emdy seemed to take his silence for consent. "It's much less expensive than I thought—and he only wanted half the bail money in advance."

Ale coughed. "Emdy—"

BEEEEEEP

He winced, and touched his temple. "Hold on. The Oracle's calling."

She made a noise that might have been construed as a sniff. *Yes?*

#A general announcement from ACLE for all employees of ORACLE, Inc., sir. 'With the assistance of persons who understandably wish to remain anonymous, the Association of Computer-Linked Experts has managed to breach the codes protecting the credit accounts of the Coalition, rewrite them, and erase the originals. The wealth which the Coalition has extorted from the citizenry over the past century has been wrested from the Coalition's avaricious control. The credit is now held in trust for the citizens of the world. Effective immediately, Coalition debit memos will no longer be honored. Coalition employees are advised that payroll memos will no longer be credited to their accounts. The foregoing is a draft of an announcement that will be released to the public data banks in seventeen minutes, barring further major revision. Comments are requested. Ladies and gentlemen, I think we've won.'#

TOP TEN NEWS STORIES OF THE HOUR

18 June 2188 1900 EDT
New England Region

<u>RANK HEADLINE   price LEAD SENTENCE</u>

SERVICE TEMPORARILY SUSPENDED

XVII

"Ale, what are you doing?"

He looked up from the textured plastic trough he was caulking. "Building a grow-wall to replace this planter." He was sitting on the parquet floor, his bandaged ankle thrust out at an awkward angle. "I figure ferns and mosses on the corridor side, and climbing vines on the dining room side. What do you think of *Hedera helix?* Too common?"

"What do I think?" She seemed taken aback. "This is no time to be planting flowers, I—"

"Ivy doesn't flower indoors, you know that." He wondered how best to test the seams without risking the vestibule floor. Maybe he would do them again, just to be safe. "Once in a while philodendron will, but—"

"For God's sakes, Ale!"

He lifted his head, surprised. "Did I say something wrong?"

Face flushed, she bent forward. "Why the hell are you fussing with houseplants when the Coalition's after you, and you assaulted a cop, and there's a general strike on so you can't get *anything* done and—"

"Emdy, Emdy." He struggled clumsily to his feet, wincing when he put weight on his right leg. Still murmuring her name, he took her in his arms and hugged her. "I'm sorry, Doc. I didn't mean to get on your nerves, but even though everything you said is true, what can I do about it? Just sit around and brood and make myself feel worse, that's all. So I do this, instead. It gives me something to do, keeps me busy."

He did not say the rest of it, the real truth of it. Constructing the grow-wall did more than just kill time: It gave him peace of mind as well. The low wooden planter divided the vestibule from the dining room, but anyone coming to the front door could see all the way out to the terrace. That made him feel naked. Exposed. Endangered.

Especially now, in light of all that had happened, he needed something to screen him from casual view before he could sit without fidgeting.

He knew the security was visual only, that should someone mean harm, a floor-to-ceiling sheet of vine-covered cork would not protect him. Every time he gave it even a moment's thought, he realized the flimsy panel would shield him from nothing but the glance of a passer-by. So he gave it as little thought as possible. Since erecting and planting the grow-wall was the only thing he could imagine that would make him feel any better, he was doing it.

But how to explain something like that to Emdy Ofivo? Another impossibility.

He sighed. She stirred in his embrace. "I'm sorry," she said in a whisper. "It's just—"

"I know. I understand. It's okay."

In the background, the hovee clicked as the ap-comp, its monitor program reacting to key word cues, switched channels.

Ale said, "Something's coming on."

"What is it?"

He watched the set across the top of her head. Sparkling white fuzz trembled in the cube for a few seconds, then fell like hail and melted. Director Ohe Ainainine's face filled the sphere. She looked older, more wrinkled; her grey hair lay as limply as if it, too, had given up the fight.

"Greetings," she said. "I will be brief. This will be the last time I will speak to you as Director of the Coalition. Since ACLE's announcement of its monstrous theft this afternoon, fully fifty-three percent of the permanent employees of the Coalition have submitted their resignations. These millions of dedicated public servants have been intimidated into abandoning their single-minded pursuit of the common good."

"Sure," said Ale. "Bet losing their fat paychecks had nothing to do with it at all."

Emdy lifted her head, touched a cool finger to his lips, then squirmed around so she could see, too.

The Director took a deep breath. "I announce, therefore, the dissolution of the Coalition and the immediate repeal of all its laws, rules, and regulations.

"You are, at this moment, without an umbrella government.

"I wish you much luck.

"Good night."

Ale stood silent, stunned, while the image faded into folds

of creamy white. Then he raised his arms, grinned, and let out a whoop. If he had a hat, he would have thrown it in the air.

Shaking her head slowly, Emdy dropped into the nearest chair. "I don't believe it. It's a trick. It has to be."

The hovee pulsed back into brightness. A deep, resonant voice-over said, "The following is a paid political announcement."

The picture firmed into an office softly, indirectly illuminated. A hologram of an Alpine meadow glowed on the rear wall. At a translucent fiberglass desk sat a young man with wavy black hair and candid blue eyes. "My friends"—he clasped his hands and leaned into the camera—"we face a grave and perilous era. For the first time in over a century, we lack a central guiding force in our political lives. We are well-educated, highly trained individualists, endowed with tremendous potential and blessed with abundant leisure. We pull in different directions. We need a single, overarching centrifugal force that will not nullify but orchestrate, harmonize, our individual centripetal forces. For the last century, until this moment of unworthiness, the Coalition has provided that centrifugal force. Now it is gone, and in its place lies a vacuum.

"My fellow citizens! We must beware! We must not allow this vacuum to jeopardize our security, our well-being.

"I urge you all to instruct your representatives to empower the Uhuru-Episcopal Party to replace the Coalition. Thank you."

The picture misted away, and again the deep voice-over came on. "The preceding has been a paid political announcement."

One more time the cube built its way bit by bit back to brilliance. The voice-over said, "We interrupt our regularly scheduled programming for the following, from news central in London."

A familiar face appeared. "Greetings to all of you now watching. This time, I presume, I will be able to address you without fear of being cut off.

"Congratulations to all of you for having the courage, the determination to relegate the corrupt Coalition to the scrapheap where it belongs.

"As you know, we at the Association of Computer-Linked Experts have seized control of the Coalition's Treasury. It contains trillions of dollars, a sum that increases by the minute as withholding taxes are credited.

"We hereby announce that we will hold that money in trust

for the people of the world. When you elect a new body to replace the Coalition, we will ensure that it spends your money wisely. We will accomplish that by refusing, on your behalf, to authorize payments that do not advance the legitimate purposes of a central governing body.

"Thank you, and do be careful."

The hovee downshifted into standby mode. Emdy sat staring at the display, her thoughts so far away that when Ale said, "Doc?" she did not even blink.

He returned to the trough, decided to skip a second caulk, and began to install the pumping equipment.

Two minutes later the ap-comp buzzed, signaling the receipt of a message the sender had coded important. He sighed. Other people had such strange ideas of what lent importance to correspondence. Laying down his tools, he went to the computer and called up the mail.

Bold capitals marched across the screen:

ATTENTION ALL DEPOSITORS:
DUE TO THE DISSOLUTION OF THE COALITION, AND THE SUBSEQUENT END TO THE COALITION'S ROLE AS CENTRAL FINANCIAL CLEARING HOUSE, THE SOCIAL-TECH DIRECTORATE OF PUBLIC BANKING HAS ORDERED EACH OF ITS MEMBER BANKS TO DISCOUNT BY VARYING PERCENTAGES DEPOSITS MADE WITH INSTRUMENTS ISSUED BY THE DIRECTORATE OF PUBLIC BANKING OF ANY OTHER PARTY. PLEASE BE AWARE OF THIS. WHEN NEXT YOU DEBIT YOUR ACCOUNT, YOU WOULD BE WELL-ADVISED TO DOUBLE-CHECK ITS BALANCE. THANK YOU.

THE MANAGEMENT

Ale groaned. Turning in the chair, he looked at Emdy. Her eyes had narrowed. They focused on infinity as she wrestled with something in her mind. He coughed; she did not respond. "Hey—Doc."

She blinked, seeming in that instant almost to wake up. "Yes?"

"Who chartered your bank?"

"Social-Tech, why?"

"Then we both have trouble. Read this." He stepped away from the screen and settled into the sofa. While she crossed the room, he reached for interface. *Hey, Oracle.*

#Yes, sir?#

I never bothered to check this before—but who chartered your bank?

#The Muslim-Republican Directorate of Public Banking.# It paused, then: #I presume you have just heard from a Social-Tech chartered bank. You will be interested to know that Muslim-Republican debt instruments will be discounted at twelve point seven percent. This compares favorably with the average discount of thirteen point twenty-four, and—#

Enough.

#Yes, sir.#

He broke interface. Twelve point seven percent! It was not like he made a fortune to begin with—his average earnings, prior to his best-seller, barely covered his half of the expenses. He felt sick. A twelve percent cut in pay would leave him in the hole. The difference would have to come out of the royalties, which he had intended to save—or devote to luxuries. "Oh, shit," he muttered.

"My sentiments exactly," said Emdy from the screen.

"You, too?"

"I'm selling that phosphate to a Hanoi fertilizer factory—their bank's charted by MaoCom—and the discount on *that* is twenty-three point four. The Moroccans want their money in Inshallah-chartered credit instruments—and those have a three point eight percent *surcharge.*" Her face went blank for a moment. She shuddered, then spun back to the keyboard. Her fingers flew across it; numbers danced on the screen. Then she gasped. Her shoulders sagged. "Ale, I'm ruined!"

"What?" Rising, he bent over her shoulder. "How could you, you—"

She pointed to the screen. "I was taking a fifteen percent markup—but with these discounts. . . . Ale, I'm going to lose twenty cents on the dollar, and I'm committed to buying ten million dollars worth of phosphate! Not only am I ruined, I'm bankrupt. We're bankrupt. Everything. Gone."

The doorbell chimed. "There must be something you can do." He went for it. "Video."

"Broken."

"Nuts . . . all right, open up."

The big man in black denim who had earlier saved Ale from the police ducked his head under the doorframe and stalked into the vestibule. He held out his hand. "Ap Emfordee. And I know your name, Ale. How you doing?"

"Just fine." Though he took the proffered hand warily, he still almost lost his own to the other's crushing grip. "On second thought, I *was* just fine. . . ."

"That little bitty squeeze? That was nothing. You need a home gym, Ale—you need to realize the potential of your own body! The gym needs less than one square meter of open floor—But shucks, I shouldn't give you my sales pitch now, I'm not here on business."

That did not relieve Ale. "Oh? Ah. . . ." But he had to be polite. "Come on in."

"Well thank you, thank you." Stepping carefully over the components of the grow-wall-to-be, he followed Ale into the living room. As Emdy arose, he smiled. "Well, good evening, good evening."

With a somber nod, she said "Excuse me," and went to her office.

"I'm not interrupting something, am I? Your wife looks upset."

"Ah. . . ." He waved his hands vaguely. "Business problems, you know how they are. Have a seat. What can I do for you?"

"Well, I'll tell you." He grunted comfortably as he arranged himself on the sofa. "I'm here as this building's representative of the American Revival Party, and frankly, I'm taking up a collection. You pull a party lever?"

"No, I split my votes." He left unsaid the fact that he had never once cast a vote for an AmRev candidate. "To be equally frank, I'm not interested in going all the way with any one party."

"Well, that's just fine, I respect that position. It's what our democracy's all about. But I'll tell you, Ale, I think there is a position on which you would probably want to support our party, and that's our platform in regards to the Dac menace."

"I'm certainly willing to listen." With an inaudible sigh, he braced himself for fifteen or twenty minutes of boredom.

"As I said, I'm sort of taking up a collection today—but really, I'm collecting two things. First, members for the party, of course, but second, and probably more importantly, I'm looking for cash contributions to advance one of our party's most cherished aims: driving off the Dacs. Think you could support that, Ale?"

He spread his hands. "Who couldn't? But I do like to know what my money's buying in specific rather than in general."

The big man laid his palms on his thighs. "Weapons."

Ale blinked. "Weapons?"

"Yup. Now that the Coalition's not around to interfere, we're gonna get ourselves some anti-aircraft guns and blow those damn Dacs out of the sky."

Ale said, "Geez, Ap, I don't know—"

"Ale!" It was Emdy, calling from her office. "Come here, please."

"Excuse me, Ap. I'll be right back."

Emfordee said, "Take your time."

As he entered her office, she motioned him to close the door. "What's the matter, Doc?"

She kept her voice low, and glanced frequently out to the living room. "I just got off the pholo with that Ombudsman? The one who—"

"I know who you mean." He perched on the edge of her desk. "Go on."

She ran her fingers through her hair, then chewed on the edge of her thumb. "I wanted him to call it off—we've got to get Wef out, but I can't afford— We haven't got the money now, not with all this, and. . . ." Shivering, she trailed off.

"So what's the problem?"

"He won't give back what I paid him—"

"Did you expect him to? Bail's not refundable. He's not going to—"

"—and he wants the rest of it." She looked ready to cry.

"So tell him to take a walk." He shrugged. "If you haven't got it, you can't pay him, and that's that."

"I *told* him I haven't got it." She buried her face in her hands. She mumbled something.

"Sorry, I didn't hear that." He stroked her hair. "What'd you say?"

She lifted her face. Her eyes were red, hollow, imploring.

"He told me I should remember who he is. And that not all the cops have quit. And if I don't credit his party's account by tomorrow night, I might as well write Wef's epitaph."

TOP TEN NEWS STORIES OF THE HOUR

19 June 2188 0900 EDT
New England Region

<u>RANK HEADLINE   price LEAD SENTENCE</u>

SERVICE TEMPORARILY SUSPENDED

This update has been provided as a public service by all data management corporations participating in NEWSBANK/ , a news data base organized and supervised by the Directorate of Public Information.

To read any of the above news stories in full, simply highlight the title and press ACCEPT. The article will be transmatted to your unit's memory. Your bank balance will be debited by the sum in the column headed "price."

To see the headlines of the day's other news stories, simply scroll your screen up.

Thank you, and do be careful.

XVIII

One wary eye on the sky, Ale slipped outdoors to water his bonsai. The weather itself was against him. As if to provide cover for swooping Dacs, rainclouds lay low and heavy over New Haven. Panting, he scanned their swollen grey underbellies and kept his back to the wall. The day's CO_2 had to be higher than its humidity. The air tasted like leftovers.

Emdy's troubles blanketed Ale's mind as thoroughly as the stormclouds the city. He did not believe the Ombudsman would—or could—hurt Wef if she refused to pay, but what he believed was not the point. *She* was terrified. Emdy Ofivo thought the man would have Wef killed. She had kept Ale awake all night with her restlessness, her sudden clutchings of his arm at every pang of remorse. By morning blood stained the sheets in half a dozen spots, while tiny scabs formed on his wrists.

Clearly, he would have to convince her she had no cause for alarm.

Or else buy her a pair of gloves.

Actually, he faced two problems. First, the threat: Even though it had to be idle, the instinctive sounding-off of a disappointed criminal, and repeated in hopes of a windfall, to dismiss it Ale would have to prove a negative. It was so much harder to prove that something was *not* true than to prove it was. . . .

Second, Emdy was in rotten psychological shape. Too much evil had fallen on her in the last four days. She had already snapped once, she was in constant, if diminishing pain, she stood eyeball-to-eyeball with bankruptcy . . . she stood on the brink of madness, and life was trying to push her over. What she needed was a few weeks of peace and quiet in which to recuperate. He hoped she could get them. Any increase in pressure would destroy her.

Thunder crackled in the south; lightning spent itself on the choppy waters of Long Island Sound. It would rain, soon. Already the wind was strengthening, pushing cool hints of freshness past his face. He gave the pots a quarter-turn each and headed back inside.

The hovee shifted from ornament to utility just as he locked the sliding glass doors. A professionally calm voice said, "And now, an important announcement from London."

Colors vibrated into the shape of the Englishman who had emerged as the *primus inter pares* of the Seeleys. Once again, he sat in a plush office behind a wide, bare desk agleam with the holovision cameras' lights.

He nodded to his assumed audience. "My friends, we face a crisis, a crisis precipitated by the abrupt abdication of the previous regime. For the first time in living memory, we lack a true global currency. Word from around the world bespeaks financial emergency for millions of citizens. Further, in certain remote, rural areas, streeters have taken advantage of our temporary plight and are launching bandit raids on the automated convoys that transport agricultural products to processing plants. Needless to say, this threat to our security, even to our survival, can not be permitted to continue.

"But the real problem—" His index finger jabbed the air. "—is that, in order to control the world more efficiently, the Coalition installed hundreds of computer programs that are still running, still dictating nearly every facet of our daily lives. For these reasons and for others, the Association of Computer-Linked Experts has volunteered to serve as interim replacement for the previous regime while the various democratically elected parties investigate the best possible means of fulfilling the goals, the desires, and the will of the people."

A bead of sweat trickled down the side of his jaw. He ignored it; he clasped his hands on his blotter and looked directly into the cameras. "I wish I could bring you good news. I wish I could offer optimism. I wish I could say, 'Relax, fellow citizens, because all our problems have been solved.' I cannot. Inevitably, some disruption must accompany the correction of the Coalition's mistakes. We will do our very best to minimize that disruption. None will work harder than we in laboring to restore a democratically selected body that will perform the crucial task of providing our society with a driving force, a central philosophy.

"One thing of which I do assure you: We will be very

competent. Unlike the previous regime, whose leaders were capable primarily of attracting the votes of other individuals capable of attracting the popular vote, the Association of Computer-Linked Experts is composed entirely of incisive, informed, independent men and women who have demonstrated greater comprehension of their fields than almost anyone else alive. You may rest assured that our stewardship will not debase your inheritance. We will surrender, at the appropriate time, a central administration that pursues its democratically assigned tasks with diligence, honesty, and compassion.

"Thank you, and do be careful today."

The sphere dwindled to nothingness. Gradually it reformed into a spinning milky globe shot with fiery rifts that opened into a blinding white core. It cast a band of light that chased shadows across the walls.

Sprawled on the couch, Ale mulled over the speech. It sounded like a pure power grab, a bloodless coup in an empty palace. And yet there were things that needed to be done— urgent decisions which could not be delayed. And who better to administer the vital operations of the Coalition than scholars who wanted nothing more than to return to academia as soon as possible?

A sudden glare of lightning bleached the room; thunder burst just outside. The building shuddered. In the bedroom, Emdy yelped.

He got up and walked across the room. Storms always made him restless. When their wild energy charged the air, it soaked into him, provoking uncontrollable fidgets. He never felt more alive than when rain lashed the windows with fat, heavy drops that spattered like a million tiny fists knocking to come in.

He dropped into a dining room chair, looked around, screwed up his face as he considered working on the grow-wall, then bounced back to his feet and headed for the bedroom. Might as well see if Emdy was all right. Poor woman never could tolerate nature's pyrotechnics. Then he remembered the state of her eardrums, and felt like a cad.

He stuck his head inside. She had polarized the windows and doused all the lights but the one on the nighttable. She sat up in bed with a book in her lap. She held it upside down.

"Hi, Doc, you okay?"

"Why shouldn't I be?"

"Hey, sorry, I just— I mean, you yelled when the lightning hit, and I thought—"

"It was a little too loud for my ears, that's all." She slammed the book shut. "Is there a law against that? Did somebody make it illegal to be in pain?" She hit the switch on the bedlamp and plunged the room into darkness. "If you don't mind, I'd like to get on with my nap."

For an instant he hated her. For an instant he dreamed of snarling, "All right, if that's the way you want it," of kicking the door shut and stalking away asimmer with righteous indignation. . . .

But no, that was silly. What would it help? The digestion of his stomach by its own acids, that's all. That and bitterness, loneliness. No, when someone you loved got crazy mad with tension and fear you had to make allowances, had to shrug off their storms like the building did the thunder. Part of loving was not hating, and you had to make the effort.

So he took a breath, then let it out slowly, silently. "Sure, Doc. Get yourself some rest. I'll be in the living room."

"You're not working today?" Her voice sounded high and uncertain, as if unnerved by a darkness which she could not dispel without losing face.

"I'm on call." He leaned against the doorframe, not wanting to seal her into the room, alone with the gloom. "But the query volume's way down today, and we're on holiday status."

"Uh." She rolled over. "If anybody calls, I'm asleep. Close the door on your way out."

"Right. I'll see you later." He pulled the door shut and sighed, pausing for a moment in the hall, wondering what he could say or do to make her feel better. Then he shook his head. He could not help someone who was not ready to help herself.

In the living room again, he sat at the computer and ran his fingers idly across the sculptured keys. The time, the day, and the date stared out of the CRT monitor. Perhaps a game?

He called instead for the Top Ten News Stories of the Hour, and blinked when the cover screen came up blank, except for the line "Service Temporarily Suspended."

All right, sometimes—especially in an electrical storm—it happened that the program that measured the popularity of news articles began to yield gibberish, and the systems maintenance people had to abort it. It was rare, though; the day's weather did not seem violent enough to provoke it.

He keyed the ap-comp to search the news banks for lengthy articles on ACLE's accession to power, and leaned back, waiting for the first piece to scroll up on the display.

A moment passed, and another.

He frowned.

The video flickered, then glowed NO FILE.

"Impossible," he muttered. Hunching over the keyboard, he called up the Index to NEWSBANK/MR and jumped through the listings for the letter 'A.'

Ambidextrous Tele-factors, Ancient Grandeur on Display, Aomori Tides, Appalachian Harvests Up, Aquariums Hot Sellers, Argentinian Cattle Die-Off, Astrophysics Department Closes, Atlantic Claims Container Ship—

He jabbed the stop button. The "Association of Computer-Linked Experts" should have appeared before "Astrophysics." He retraced his steps, looking more carefully at the entry titles.

Four minutes passed before he noticed that no article had a dateline later than 0900 EDT the previous morning.

"Now, wait a minute. Nobody filed *anything* yesterday? Can't be...."

"What can't be?" said Emdy.

He spun around in the chair. "Doc! I thought you—"

"I'm too wide awake. And I heard you grunting out here, so I came out to see what the problem was. Having trouble?"

"No, I was just looking for news stories on ACLE and the Coalition, and I couldn't find any."

"Of course you couldn't. ACLE's squelching them."

"Come on, you don't really believe that."

She pointed to the ap-comp. "You're the one who says there's nothing on file."

"Yes, but—" He floundered as he sought for the words that would explain without giving offense. She was leaping to irrational conclusions, succumbing to paranoia because an avaricious bureaucrat had threatened her.

Scholars would never censor the news. Perhaps the news was less than the whole truth, but it was certainly a first approximation thereof, and scholars so loved the truth that in times past some had given their lives for it.

A gust of wind rattled the sliding glass doors; he jerked his head toward the terrace. "It's probably the storm."

She swiveled her head and glanced outdoors. "Now, that is lame, Ale, that is really lame."

"No, it—" He snapped his fingers. "Wait a minute. I know how to settle this. Maybe not to your satisfaction, but at least to mine."

She raised an eyebrow. "How?"

"I'll ask 'em—I mean, I am, in theory, a member of ACLE, yes?"

Her eyes widened. "Don't you dare!"

"But—"

"I will *not* have you getting people mad at you again, I will not!" Her voice cracked, and her forehead creased with pain, but she went on.

He had not meant to put more stress on her. She could not withstand it. He held up his hands. "I'll go through The Oracle. Nobody'll know who I am."

"If you believe that—"

"Emdy, you know how good its anonymity program is." He caught a softening around her eyes and pressed on. "And it's one sure way of finding out the truth, yes?"

"Well—"

"I'll be back in a minute." He closed his eyes, looked inwards, and skidded directly into interface. Achieving it that easily surprised him.

#Hello, sir. We are on holiday status today; no need to spend your time here, you know.#

Uh, that's not why I'm here—is some member of ACLE responsible for the newsbanks?

#Certainly. Shall I patch you through?#

It bothered him that someone had taken charge of the newsbanks. Few people assume power without intending to use it. Could Emdy be right? *Wait!*

#Yes?#

Uh. . . . No offense, but before you do that, do "Safeguard Verify with odd parity and check digits." He disliked making The Oracle prove that it would maintain his anonymity—the command smacked too strongly of accusation—but then he also needed continual reminders that The Oracle was just a switchboard program to which any skilled person could issue all sorts of instructions.

#Very well, sir.# It sounded frosty, but that was probably his own imagination.

His implant came awake. Numbers streamed past his eyes: The Oracle's execution of the proof package. Another list of numbers glowed inside his head: the predetermined "correct" answers to the package. His focus switched from stream to list to stream again, making sure that each line on the outside corresponded with the next line on the inside.

They did. All was well. The Oracle would keep his name a secret from anyone, no matter whom. *Thank you.*

#You're quite welcome. Should I patch you through now?#
Yes.

In the distance, conversations murmured like wind-tossed leaves.

#Yes?# It was The Oracle's voice, but another's intonation.

He took a deep breath, briefly considered the tactful approach, then thought to hell with it. *Why are you censoring the newsbanks?*

#What?#

Your spokesrep claimed ACLE was going to do such good things for the human race, so how come you're censoring the newsbanks?

#Good God! I haven't— One moment, please.#

The line went suddenly dead. He sat motionless, annoyed at the other's rudeness. He could have at least warned him—

#Terribly sorry to keep you waiting.# The man sounded flustered. #This is embarrassing. I— We— None of us had any idea that there was anything wrong. I must confess, I've had no time for scrolling through the banks since last night; it's been a most hectic fourteen hours, I can assure you. Apparently, the situation is this: in its last few hours, the Coalition brought a news blackout program on line. The little bugger is still running. We've been keeping a rather close eye on the pholo, though, and it doesn't seem to have affected that, thank God.#

The other sounded awfully sincere. Perhaps now was the time for diplomacy? *I see,* said Ale ruminatively.

#We are, of course, most grateful to you for bringing it to our attention, and I assure you that we'll have it taken care of at the first available opportunity.#

Well . . .

#And I am in a rush, so if there's nothing else—?#

No, no, nothing else. Much appreciated.

#Do be careful, now.#

Sure, sure, you too.

He opened his eyes. Emdy sat across from him, watching him intently. He stretched and yawned. "All set."

"What's that supposed to mean?"

He gave her the gist of his conversation with the ACLE member.

"And you swallowed it?"

"Emdy—"

"God, you're gullible. These people steal all our tax money, overthrow the Coalition, drive you and me into irrevocable bankruptcy—and you really believe that they're going to reinstate freedom of the press? Hah!" She jerked to her feet and headed for the kitchen.

He followed. "Emdy, they stole the Coalition's Treasury, not our bank accounts—and they had to steal it to get rid of the Coalition. Maybe you don't remember, but those were the people who were trying to kill me? You're not saying you'd rather have them still in charge, are you?"

Lips trembling, she finished filling her coffee cup, then set the pot down quietly. "At least I wouldn't be *ruined!* I've spent my whole life building up my business, and they come along and *poof*! Down the tubes. Everything we have is frozen, you know that? They've already slapped liens and attachments on everything." Desperate tears welled up in her eyes. "And there's a man in Hartford who's going to murder Wef because I don't have the money to pay him. And it's all because you goddam Seeleys think you're better than everybody else!" Her hand shook so violently that hot coffee sloshed onto the back of her wrist. "Ow!" She stared at it in helpless dismay.

He felt like saying, *I suppose that's my fault, too,* but was smarter than that. With two swift strides he was at her side. Relieving her of the cup, he took her hand and led her to the sink. "Cold water'll help."

"Thank you," she said numbly.

He turned the faucet on, held her hand beneath it, and slipped his arm around her shoulders. She stiffened, but did not pull away. "Emdy, listen, I understand what the last four days have been like for you. I know your ears hurt like hell, and what your business means to you, and that the Ombudsman terrifies you. But don't worry, okay? Your ears are already healing, and somehow the rest of it'll work out."

Face blank, voice dull, she shook her head slowly. "They destroyed me."

"Not on purpose, though, don't you see? It just happened. They're not out to get you. Not like the Coalition was out to get me. And they're going to do something about this exchange rate problem, they said so. Come on, it'll be all right. Don't brood on it. It only makes you feel worse."

She turned her face to his. Pain swam in her eyes, pain and

bitterness and desolation. Then she broke away and ran on silent tip-toe to the bedroom. He knew better than to pursue her.

—2—

They were each eating lunch alone, even while they shared the dining room table. He had tried to start a conversation, but she had ignored him—though she had accepted the proferred ham and swiss on rye readily enough. Glumly, he swept crumbs onto his plate.

The locks on the front door clicked. He snatched up a butter knife, and instantly felt silly. The hinges creaked. Emdy's eyes widened in horror; she stifled a scream.

"Hi, y'all!"

Ale let out his breath with a relieved whoosh. "Jesus, Wef, you could have knocked! You almost gave Emdy a heart attack."

The old man dropped a brown paper bag in the vestibule, eyed the pieces of the grow-wall with distaste, and stepped over them to Emdy's chair. He bent and kissed her cheek. "I'm real sorry about that, honey," he said softly. "Last thing I want's to scare the best cook in town to death."

She clutched his hand. "How are you? Did they hurt you? Are you hungry?"

"Fine. Nope. Yep." He grinned. "Stay put, I know where everything is." He slipped into the kitchen.

Ale called, "Did they drop the charges?"

"Never filed any in the first place." The refrigerator door chunked shut; wrapping paper rustled. As a beer can popped open, Wef gave a sigh of contentment. "Seems they grabbed me on orders from somebody in the Coalition, and when that dissolved there, well, they sort of hemmed and hawed and allowed as how they'd let me go if I promised to go home. Speaking of which, I leave here day after tomorrow." He came back into the dining room bearing a plate piled high with sandwiches, pretzels, and pickles. "Pickup's oh-nine-hundred on the roof."

Ale leaned back in his chair. "Well, it's good to see you again safe and sound, Wef." He nodded to Emdy. "This one was ready to buy you out of jail."

"That's cute." Wef winked at her.

"It's also true," said Ale. "And it's snowballed into—"

"Hush, Ale." Emdy waved her hands. "Wef doesn't want to hear—"

"I sure do, honey. If I caused you some trouble, I want to hear all about it."

She shot Ale an uncertain glance.

"Tell him, Emdy—maybe he can give you some ideas."

She dropped her eyes. Folding her napkin into ever-smaller squares, then opening it out again so she could refold it, she explained about the corrupt Ombudsman.

He listened intently, keeping his peace until she had finished. Then he reached behind his shoulder to take a braid between his fingers and bring its tip to his mouth. He chewed on it for a moment before spitting it out. "Why, that no-good sonuvabitch! I've heard about him—aren't many officials around on the take like that. Now, I can tell you right now that he would never of carried through on that silly threat of his, but—" He cocked his head and studied her pallor, her haunted eyes. "But I don't figure that changes the way he made you feel, does it?"

She shook her head.

"Well, then, we're just gonna have to teach him a lesson." He carried his beer over to the apartment computer. "Give me a couple minutes to myself here, let me see what I can come up with."

"Right." Ale started clearing the table and carrying the dishes to the sink. Emdy stayed at the table, chin propped up on her hands. She seemed not to notice him as he went back and forth.

"Ah-hah!" said Wef suddenly.

Wiping his hands on a dishtowel, Ale leaned over the counter and looked toward the living room. "What's up, Wef?"

The old man grinned wolfishly. "I think we've got it solved."

"Yeah? What have you got in mind?"

"Come watch—but stay off camera."

As Ale and Emdy walked over, Wef turned on the pholo and tapped out a number. In a moment a woman answered. Voice and face professionally bland, she said, "Hello, and thank you for calling."

Wef quirked his eyebrows. "Thank you for answering, honey. B. G. in?"

"Whom shall I say is calling?" Her fingers rested on the keyboard of her computer, and when Wef gave his name they typed it in. "May I ask what this is in reference to?"

"No."

Her poise faltered briefly. "Pardon?"

"No, you may not ask what this is in reference to." He flashed her a dazzling smile. "Just put me through to him."

"I'm sorry, sir, but my instructions are—"

"I understand perfectly, young lady, but the matter is confidential. Urgent, too. And I reckon you could even go so far as to say it's potentially remunerative. So what say you pass all that on to him, and let him make up his own mind whether he wants to talk to me or not?" He winked at her. "That way you're not disobeying orders, and he's not missing out."

She wavered visibly, once glancing over her right shoulder but finding no answer there. "Yes, sir. Let me put you on hold, though."

"Honey, you can hold me any time you want."

The sphere blanked, but not before she smiled. The words "Please Wait" formed in red in the middle of the sphere. Silvery harpsichord music welled softly from the speakers.

Wef touched the hold button on his own pholo, then turned to Emdy and Ale. "It's smooth sailing as soon as he gets on the line."

"But will he?" she asked.

"Sixty-forty." Holding out one spread-fingered hand, he waggled it from side to side. "Let's just sit back and see, why don't we?"

Ninety seconds later the red words faded off the sphere, which sparkled once then focused into the flattened nose and broad cheekbones of a black man in his thirties. His brown eyes, wide and astonishingly soft, took Wef's measure in a glance. "A rather tantalizing message, Mr. Wef DiNaini."

"Seemed about the only way to get through, Mr. Beegy N'foti. Forgive my breaking in on you like this, but good ol' Emdy Ofivo asked me to see if I couldn't dicker with you some about this arrangement the two of you had."

Beegy blinked. "Emdy Ofivo? I'm afraid I don't recognize the name."

"That's as good a place to start as any. I suppose it would surprise you to hear that there was some money in your party's account that should actually have been in Ms. Emdy Ofivo's."

"Any money in that account, my friend, belongs entirely to the party."

"You know, somehow I thought you might say that, so I took a little liberty and did some checking up on you."

Smiling, the man said, "Oh?" and raised a polite eyebrow.

"Uh-huh. Must say, I was impressed. That's quite a criminal record you have there."

The Ombudsman frowned. "I'm sorry, there must be some mistake."

"Well, now, that's just exactly what I thought, seeing as how you're a high party official and all, but I quick-checked the CrimeBanks anyway. Seven arrests. Your party really needs you, don't it? What I'm curious, though, I'd love to find out how you beat that child-rape case. On paper it looked open and shut."

The doe soft eyes hardened, flashed, and narrowed. "What is this? I've never been arrested in my life."

Wef shrugged eloquently. "That's not what the computers say. Man, you must get microscoped every time some other pervert feels up a little boy. Being able to stay in politics with the cops practically living with you is something else, I swear, my hat's off to you. How do you do it?"

"You're crazy, old man! What's your game?"

A slight smile crossed the refugee's seamed face. "No game at all—but just so you know I'm on the level, why don't you pull your file from the CrimeBanks yourself? I'll wait."

Now the man looked wary. "Okay. Hold."

The sphere snapped to black. Wef stretched and yawned and wriggled around on the sofa until he had settled himself properly.

Ale said, "Wef—"

"Hush. Ten, nine, eight, seven—"

The sphere blinked white then sharpened into focus. The man had aged five years. "What the hell is this? They've got me listed for—" His eyes flicked away from the camera. "For child molestation, manufacture and distribution of unlicensed pharmaceuticals, assault with intent to maim—" He slapped his desktop. "What is going on?"

Wef said, "Bet that computer spits your name out every time anything like any of your crimes happens in Hartford. You must get questioned twice a day. How do you put up with it?"

"Did you say 'Wef DiNaini'?"

"Uh-huh."

"Of Florida?"

"One and the same."

"Oh, Jesus. . . . Is that— Is Ms. Emdy Ofivo a friend of yours?"

"Uh-huh."

He passed a weary hand across his face. "Jesus Mary and Joseph. . . . Mr. Wef DiNaini, I'm sorry, I didn't kn—" He stopped abruptly, and drew himself up straight. "No. I won't cringe. But I'm not stupid. Nobody in its right mind would go for one of your friends. I regret the inconvenience to all concerned. Her first payment on your bail will be credited back to her account immediately. Good enough?"

"I think a personal apology might be in order."

Beegy N'foti looked sour, but after a moment's consideration said, "I suppose it would be. Is she there?"

"Uh-huh." He waved her into camera range. "Speak your piece."

The Ombudsman inclined his head in a slight bow. "Ms. Emdy Ofivo, I would like to apologize to you for any anxiety I may have caused you. I believe the, uh, paperwork problem has been cleared up at this end, which means your account should even now be reflecting the appropriate credits. I do not believe we'll need to get in touch with one another again, but should the need arise, you have my number. Please feel free to call. Good day, and take care." He leaned forward and reached for something out of view.

The sphere vanished.

Wef clapped his hands. "All right! *That's* taken care of. But lemme tell you, Emdy, that was a damfool thing you did. Don't *ever* get mixed up with his type again. Not that he'll hurt any of you but your pocketbook, but that his kind draws wiretaps like shit draws flies. And sometimes the prosecutors like to take a good long time while their cases develop. Knew a guy in Arkansas, when they finally hauled him off they had four years of pholo calls on tape. Took a hundred and sixty-eight people with him when he went down." He shook a finger at her. "You hear me?"

"Yes." She closed her eyes and bowed her head. For a moment her lips moved soundlessly. Then she lifted her chin. "But for you, Wef, I'd do it again in a minute."

—3—

Later that day, while Ale was bolting the grow-wall's uprights to their bases, Emdy said, "I told you they wouldn't stop censoring the newsbanks."

He looked up. "They said they would."

"They haven't. And they never will."

"C'mon, Emdy, they—"

"If they were going to, they would have. It's not like they have to *do* anything—they just have to *stop* what they're doing."

He put down his tools. "I'll find out what's going on." Going to the couch, he sat, slipped into interface, and once more made sure the anonymity program was working correctly. Then he had The Oracle patch him through to the ACLE person handling the newsbanks.

#Yes?#

I thought you were going to stop censoring the newsbanks.

The other's chagrin was nearly tangible. #Yes, I know, and we *are* going to do it, but we haven't had time to get around to it.#

Why is it so difficult? Just lay off the censors and—

#No, you don't understand, it's a program.#

So?

#Clearly, I'll have to explain.# The Oracle even transmatted his sigh. #The Coalition always used "guardian at the gate" censorship programs—the kind that verify news *before* it goes into the banks. But then we came up with a way to get around them.#

The sun-sea report.

#Exactly. What we *think* they did was to whip up a program that would erase items *after* they'd been banked. Now normally that's as vulnerable as a guardian program—but if you set it loose in the system, and have it replicate itself at locations it chooses itself, randomly—that makes it vastly harder to delete. You've got to track it down as though it were an infected rat. Unfortunately, they rushed it. The program has a bug in it that erases everything filed after its activation moment. Everything.#

I still don't see what the problem is. Granted, said Ale, *that makes it more difficult, but you should still be able to bag it.*

#Sure, but none of us has time to take it on. We're looking for somebody to do it, but haven't come up with anybody yet.#

Well, how long is it going to take? I mean, it is tarnishing your image pretty badly.

After a moment's silence, the ACLE rep said, #If it's so important to you, why don't *you* do it?#

What?

#You do it. There's no question it should be done, and you're right that it hurts our credibility to have it running.# He gave a small, happy snort. #Sometimes I'm such a genius I astonish even myself.#

Oh, I can't—

#Of course you can. Naturally, I'm not saying you need to do it yourself—you can hire someone to do that—but you're certainly capable of making sure the job gets done.#

But I—

#Listen, if it would make you happy, we'll name you Acting Director of Public Information. We hadn't intended to fill the position—we thought we hadn't any business directing information—but clearly there's a need for someone to take the responsibility, and to take it right now.#

Knowing just how displeased Emdy would be if he had anything to do with ACLE or government or politics, he looked for a way to avoid accepting the job. *But I've never had any experience.*

Impatience crept into the other's voice. #You're not going to be administering an empire, here—you'd just be hiring people to clean out the censorship programs. Come to think of it, you might as well get the monitor programs at the same time. And once you have, you've effectively abolished your post, and can resign. What could be simpler?#

But I have a full-time job already. The excuse sounded weak, even to him, but he could hardly give the real reason.

#Ah, but you're a Seeley. We'll borrow you from ORA:CLE—# The voice went away for a few seconds, then returned. #Yes, it's all confirmed right now, you're on loan to us for the duration.#

He checked with The Oracle himself.

#Yes, sir,# said the switchboard program, #it is true. You are on the ACLE administration's payroll as of this moment.#

To the ACLE rep he said, *Look, I'd really rather be a Seeley.*

#Well for God's sake, man, so would I! But at the moment I haven't the luxury of being able to choose—I have a responsibility that I must fulfill. As do you, whether you know it or not. You call, carping and grumbling about a problem I didn't cause—a problem that doesn't bother me quite as much as some of my other problems—and then you won't lift a finger to help out.#

He did feel guilty about that. But Emdy—

#Besides which,# said the ACLE rep, #have you noticed

you haven't done much consulting lately? There's a reason for that—the censorship program seems to be teaming up with the ORA:CLE Monitor Program and knocking out questions before they get through. So it's not as though turning down the DPI post would let you be a Seeley again—rather, you'll twiddle your thumbs until we find someone else to be DPI and that person clears out the censor. How's that?#

Oh, Jesus. . . . Look. Tell you what. Emdy was going to kill him. *I'll do it on one condition.*

#Hmm?#

No interference. No bureaucracy, no harassment , no time-wasting committee meetings—just let me do the job straight and quick, all right?

#Fine. Since you can interface, just have The Oracle pay any expenses you run up. It knows how.#

All right. I'll get on it right away.

Emdy was going to scream—but it was, after all, his duty as a scholar. Whether ACLE paid him or ORA:CLE did, he was employed to know the truth and to tell it. It was his life. And finally he could live it to its fullest. Once he got through the next few minutes.

Emerging from interface, he rubbed his palms, already sweaty, on the sofa cushion. Emdy leaned against the doorway to the kitchen with her eyebrows raised, her lips pressed together. He forced a smile and told her what he had just agreed to do.

For what seemed a full minute and might have been longer, she stood motionless, soundless, staring at him through gradually narrowing eyes. He groaned inwardly and got to his feet. He knew that routine. She was not by any means at a loss for words—she was forcing herself to hold back the words that wanted to spill out, words that could hurt, maim, possibly kill.

He had to cool her fury before it came to a full boil. He spread his hands. "Emdy."

No response.

"Please, love, don't glare at me like that."

She did not answer.

He was getting angry himself, but he tried to keep his tone reasonable. "Look, you fix it so I can't win! You get mad at me for me annoying the government, you get mad at me for helping it. You're not going to get hurt by this, honest. They're going to be grateful. Come on, Emdy."

She folded her arms; her jaw muscles tautened.

"You're mad at me because the exchange rate thing cost us so much money—then you're mad when I get a full-time job with a steady credit." He paused for a calming breath. "Emdy, I know you're frightened. I understand. I sympathize. But c'mon, this isn't cause for fear. This is going to help us, not hurt us." He held out his arms to hug her.

"No!" She backed out of the dining room. "And you call yourself a scholar! For the first time in a century there's been a revolution. Do you shut up? Do you lie low for a while? No, you forget everything you ever learned about revolutionary regimes, and you accept an appointment with one."

He regarded her in puzzlement. "I don't understand."

She slapped the countertop. "They eat their own, don't you know that? What you did, it's like a blind man trying to find safety on a laser range. You walked right into the field of fire. You're practically dead already."

"Now, honey," said Wef, coming through the kitchen toward them, "you're landing a little hard on Ale here." He stopped at the refrigerator and pulled out a beer. "It's not like he's setting himself up as Commissar High Muckety-Muck, with a big fancy office and his face on the hovee all the time. He's just doing a simple job that's going to make life a little some better for all of us." Popping the can open, he took a swig and wiped his mouth with his fingers. "You ought to encourage him."

"Crap!"

Ale wanted to speak, but Wef got there first. "Emdy honey, they could have given this job to somebody like that actor fellow, somebody who'd do a half-assed job at it while making sure he looked good on camera. They did that, the banks'd be empty for years." He burped, and patted his chest. "But they gave it to Ale, here, and you know he's gonna do it right, get it done with, and get himself out. Now what's so awful about that?"

She fixed him with a long, unwavering gaze. Then she tossed her head dismissively and turned to Ale. "Ale, I refuse to discuss this any further. I will not live with a man who willfully jeopardizes our lives. I cannot live in constant fear. You have to choose: the job or me."

He resented that. A person must be free to make its own choices; it was immoral of her to try to blackmail him into doing her bidding. Perhaps it was a symptom of her psychological state—yet if that were the case, it gave him all the more reason to resist. Gently, affectionately, but firmly.

"Emdy, I don't want to choose. I want you to stay. I love you with all my heart and soul. But I'm taking the job. If I want to live with myself, I have to take the job."

"That's what I thought." She nodded once, turned, and walked out the door.

TOP TEN NEWS STORIES OF THE HOUR

21 June 2188 0900 EDT
New England Region

<u>RANK HEADLINE   price LEAD SENTENCE</u>

SERVICE TEMPORARILY SUSPENDED

XIX

—1—

While the Apparent Stress Analyzer ran its self-diagnostics test, Ale pushed back in his recliner and rubbed his eyes. The Analyzer's software had to be glitched. In the last forty-eight hours he had pholoed one hundred eighty-three former supervisors of the Coalition's Directorate of Public Networks. He had questioned each about the censorship and monitor programs. Each had denied all knowledge of the programs. According to the Analyzer, each had told the truth.

Not that Wef was having any better luck fishing for the programs. In fact, to judge by the steady mutter of curses rumbling out of the living room, the old man kept running into brick walls.

For that matter, the electronic query Ale had sent to all seventeen thousand ex-CDPN employees had generated no response, either.

The Analyzer whirred softly, then beeped.

He cracked an eyelid. The diagnosis code on the LED self-test panel read "000." The machine claimed to be working perfectly.

With a sigh, wishing he could instead groom his surviving bromeliads, he levered his chair upright. "Next."

The computer activated the pholo and called the next name on the list Ale had compiled. CDPN ex-employee number one hundred eighty-four. He crossed his fingers. If this went on much longer, his voice would give out.

The sphere pulsed as it rang. On the fourth ring it sparkled and coalesced into the image of a middle-aged woman with coffee-colored skin and a tentative smile. "Hello," she said.

He smiled back, introduced himself, and explained why he was calling.

She seemed astonished. "I didn't even know they existed! You know how many teams CodePun had—we didn't know what other teams there were, much less what they were working on. I was on BACKGROUND, and—"

"BACKGROUND?" He glanced at the Apparent Stress Analyzer. No warning lights. "What's that?"

"A program we wanted to bring on-line next year. Would have been an option to basic service, expensive but good. The introductory version would basically search all public banks for all references to a given person, and organize the facts into a brief biography, as well as provide one bibliography of all that person's own writings, and another that listed author, title, and retrieval number of all public comment on that person. Later versions would have expanded the scope to cover just about any topic you wanted. I guess it'll never go through, now—but just think what a research tool it would have been!" Her brown eyes shone with enthusiasm. "You could get a complete report on anything or anyone with just a couple buttons." Now her eyes dulled. "Six more months, that's all we needed. After four years. . . ."

The machine insisted she was telling the truth. He tried not to scowl. "Did they ever warn you, in any way, that the censorship programs loose in the system might muck up your program?"

"No." She frowned, and chewed on her upper lip while she thought. "You know, I'm not sure it would glitch it out. No. BACKGROUND would run just fine—the problem would show in the compiled report—you'd get an incomplete one. What you *saw* would be accurate. You just wouldn't see everything there was in the banks. . . ." She gave a rueful laugh. "And that would pretty much defeat the whole purpose of BACKGROUND, so they really should have warned us."

Unless, he thought to himself, *the real purpose of BACKGROUND was not to work, but to* seem *to work.* . . . Aloud, he said, "Well, thank you. I appreciate your time and assistance. If you do happen to think of anything, please give me a call right away. We really need to know."

"Sure." She switched off with a wave.

His computer buzzed once; in the upper right hand corner of its screen glowed the words "Incoming Message."

Hoping the mass query had finally provoked a response, he touched ACCEPT. A brief memo filled the screen. He scanned it. It bore his landlady's ID/dress. She was raising the rent by $50.00 a month.

"Dammit!" He punched his open left palm. Slapping the

arm of the chair, he shouted, "Hey, Emdy—"

His cheeks went hot. He gritted his teeth. Eyes squeezed shut, he muttered, "Dumb, dumb. . . ."

"D'jou call?" shouted Wef.

Wearily, he got up and headed for the living room. He needed a break. He needed to talk, and not about elusive programs darting through an electronic sea. Wef would understand. For all his garrulousness, the old man made a good listener.

Why was it so hard for him to remember that his wife was gone? It should have sunk in by now, but he kept turning to emptiness, expecting to find Emdy Ofivo. Maybe Wef could explain it.

As he reached the living room, the doorbell rang. "Video."

The screen crackled, then showed an overhead shot of Ap Emfordee, still dressed in black denim.

"Open."

"Hi, Ale." He smelled like he had worked out heavily— the night before.

Ale did not really want to invite him in, but could not bring himself to be that rude. He stepped back and held the door wide.

"Thanks." He ducked his head as he came inside. Pure vanity. He would have had to jump to hit his head on that lintel. "Listen, sorry to bother you, but those AySeeleys put the chop on our cloudraker, and we were hoping you'd talk to them for us."

Ale closed the door, but did not lead the way to the sofa. He leaned his shoulder against the wall. "Your cloudraker?"

"The anti-aircraft emplacement we were ordering. God only knows why, but the factory told the AySeeleys what we wanted, and they cancelled the order. We got our money back right away, but that's not the point—we don't want the cash, we want the guns."

From the ap-comp, Wef said, "You all aren't thinking of shooting Dacs, are you?"

Ap turned. "Well, yeah, but primarily we'd go for the motherships. They're bigger targets, and losing 'em'd hurt the Dacs more—but yeah, we'd use the guns on individual Dacs, too."

While Ap's back was to him, Ale rolled his eyes. Wef glimpsed it, and buried a laugh with a cough. Ale said, "The ACLE heard about this, and cancelled your order?"

"That's right."

He was tempted to say *Thank God,* but suspected the big man might take it wrong. "So what is it you want me to do?"

"Well, you're a Seeley, right?"

"Uh-huh."

"We want you to call 'em up and talk some sense to 'em. Make 'em understand that we've got to have those guns."

Very nearly the last thing Ale wanted was for the AmRev Party to have an anti-aircraft battery at its disposal—but for the life of him he could not think of a graceful way to say that. "Uh, you've already told them all that yourselves, right?"

"You betcha—but d'you think they listened? Nah." His angry, swiping motion spread the stink of stale sweat. "Nah, they just got on their high horse and told us to bugger off."

"But that's exactly what they'll say to me!"

The big man narrowed his eyes. "You're one of them."

"No, I'm just. . . ." He shrugged his way through the partial deceit. "I'm a Seeley, yes, but I'm not one of the people in charge. It's not like they consult me before they make a decision. They don't even know who I am." But then, neither he nor anyone else knew who *they* were—the leaders of the ACLE stayed as anonymous in politics as they had in academia. "What I'm trying to say is, I can't help you."

Ap tensed. The slight bend at the knees and waist made him a figure of menace. "You *can't* help us—or you *won't* help us?"

Ale backed up. "If I spoke for you," he said rapidly, "it wouldn't do you any good. Your top people would have a lot more influence than I would—and if the, uh, AySeeleys are ignoring your top people—"

"Dammit, Ale! Is this the thanks I get?" His huge hands curled into fists, then opened back up like claws, as if unsure whether to strike first or to seize.

"Now wait a minute." He strove for a placating, reasonable tone of voice. Absurdly, he found himself wondering why no one had told the man he needed a shower. "I—"

Ap grabbed Ale by the shirtfront and jerked upward, lifting the Seeley to his tip-toes. "Listen, you are going to call them—" A knifeblade touched Ap's throat.

Wef and the knife had simply materialized behind the big man. "Let go."

Sweat glistened on Ap's face. "You're being real stupid, old man."

"The man with the knife is never the stupid one."

He drew his lips back. "I'll make you eat that damn blade."

"Let go of him."

Slowly, the massive fingers opened. Ale's shirt slipped free of their grip. He sank back to his heels and gave a sigh of relief.

"Ale," said Wef, "wanna make sure the front door's open so our guest can take his leave without anything holding him up?"

"Right." He swung it wide, then stepped aside so Wef could herd the man in black denim out, and kick it shut behind him. "Thanks."

A thud came from the hall.

"Nothing to it." The refugee ran his finger along the dull edge of the butter knife, and shook his head. "Absolutely *nothing* to it." He leaned into the kitchen; the knife clattered into the sink. "I better get back to work."

"Me, t—"

The doorbell rang.

"Oh, shit." Ale's heart beat faster. He wondered if the locks would hold against a determined assault by the big man. Probably not. "Video."

Through the fuzz on the screen showed white hair, an upturned face, and sharp pink eyes.

Wef opened the drawer where the carving knives were kept. "Trouble?"

"No, it's L'ai Aichtueni." It astonished him that his voice could stay steady while his knees could not. "Open."

She swept inside. "Good morning, Ale. Whatever did you say to get that man—" She pointed back to the corridor. "—so upset? He punched the wall so hard I thought his fist would go right through it."

"Ah . . . it's a long story, Doctor— L'ai."

"Water."

"Right. Sorry. Water." Again he planted himself in the vestibule, determined not to invite anyone into the living room. "Anyway. I hope you'll excuse me, but I am working, so, uh, what can I do for you?"

"We've been having some problems with censorship, and we were told you were the person to come to."

"We?" he said blankly.

"The Social-Tech Party. There's something in the system that deletes our press releases every time we enter them into the banks—and we just okayed an important new invention that's not getting us any press at all!"

"It's happening to everybody," he said soothingly. "We're working on it, but those Coalition people just set it loose. There's no documentation, no program directory listing for it anywhere—nothing. As soon as we find it, we'll be able to get rid of it, but—"

She pursed her lips. "Ale, I never thought *you* would adopt the party line."

"What?"

She made a gesture of impatience. "It's not happening to everybody—every time I turn on the hovee the letters ACLE slap me in the face—it's only the competition it's happening to."

"Now the hovee I don't know about." He scratched his head. "I just don't know. Wef and I are only dealing with the data banks."

"Sure you are."

"Honest, we're really looking. Wef is spending eighteen hours a day trolling for it. I've gone through all the records I could find, talked to nearly two hundred people—nothing."

"Crap."

"Water, I— You want a short-term solution?"

She frowned. "What?"

"Forget the data banks for the next few weeks. Buy hovee time. There's no censorship there."

"Ale, we spend millions maintaining and promoting the data banks. We're not geared up for straight hovee. And we can't afford it, either. We have to have the banks back."

"Okay, fine, it won't work. I'm sorry. We're doing the best we can; as soon as it's finished, the problem'll disappear."

"God, I've heard that so often." She shook her head in disgust. "You just better do something quickly, that's all I can say." Turning, she stalked toward the door.

"Open," he called. "G-bye."

The door slammed behind her.

For a few seconds he stared blindly at the wall, frustrated beyond measure that she had doubted his integrity. Him, Ale Elatcy—as good as accused of dishonesty and corruption! Never in his entire life— Abruptly he shook himself, like a dog coming in from the rain. "How you doing, Wef?"

The old man looked up from the keyboard. "Well, I'll tell you, Ale, I'm having one bitch of a time trying to get aholt of this censor program. Wasn't for the fact that news items kept disappearing, I'd be inclined to say the sucker was a figment of somebody's imagination." He chewed on the split ends of his right braid, then spat them out. "I'm going nuts, is how I'm doing."

"Yeah, me too. . . ." He sank onto the couch and stretched out, hands clasped behind his head and feet up on the far arm. "I can't believe Emdy's really gone."

"She ain't."

Ale jerked into a sitting position. "What?"

"Think on it some. 'Less she planned this about six months ago, she has got to be somewhere in Haven Manor 'cause she couldn't have arranged for transport out in only two days. The directorates don't give priority status just for marriage problems. Since she has probably redirected her mail, about two seconds with your ibn Daoud should tell you where she's staying."

Ale grunted, and lay back down.

"Want me to do it for you?" said Wef.

"Uh-uh." He closed his eyes. They were smarting.

"Thought you missed her."

He took a deep breath. "I do."

"Then—?"

"I don't know." He made a face. "Yes, I do. I'm not going to quit this DPI thing until the job is done."

"Figure that's what it'd take, huh?"

"Yeah, I'm afraid so. . . . Shit, Wef, if I could get her back by saying, 'Come back, I love you, I miss you,' I would—but there's no way that's going to be enough. She didn't walk because I didn't love her. She walked because she's half-snapped and has this paranoia about the governments." Rolling onto his elbow, he picked moodily at a loose thread on the sofa cushion. "In a way it's my fault. I knew how she felt and went ahead and took the job anyway."

"Could be," said the old man. "Could also be that—"

But he never got to finish his sentence, for the hovee cleared and a smooth, well-bred English voice said, "Please forgive me for interrupting your regularly scheduled programming. I promise to be brief."

Ale sat up. "What's going on?"

Wef said, "Shh."

The familiar face in the cube smiled sadly. "Quite frankly, we of ACLE had expected the individual parties harmoniously to compete for the privilege of serving the people. Instead, we find them engaged in acrimony, strife, and mutual recrimination. The political situation is in utter disarray. Why, one party was even attempting to purchase weapons!"

"Your buddy in the dirty pants," said Wef.

"He's not my buddy."

"That's right, disavow all knowledge."

"In consequence, we of ACLE have decided to sacrifice our aspirations for the near term in order to ensure that your next central government has your best interests in mind. We will conduct extensive investigations of all individual party leaders, and will rule as to each person's fitness to serve. Those deemed ineligible will either retire from public life, or have their parties barred from the elections, which are presently scheduled for early January 2196. Thank you for your attention, and please be careful today."

The cube flickered for an instant, then the face disappeared.

Ale became aware that his mouth was open. He closed it. "Twenty-one ninety-*six!* That's eight years. I don't believe this."

Wef cocked his head and regarded him calmly. "You're not believing much of anything these days, are you?"

"This is absolutely crazy—they can't take an eight-year sabbatical. I mean, they promised that—"

"Welcome to the wonderful world of power," said Wef.

—2—

Moving with exaggerated caution, Ale dropped three ice cubes into the water glass. He gripped the green bottle firmly, and filled the glass to the halfway mark with twelve-year-old Scotch. He let the faucet run a moment, then topped the glass off with cold water. It was his fifth Scotch-and-water of the evening. He figured he could finish that and one more just like it before he passed out on the sofa.

He could sleep in the bed, of course; oh, yes, he had it all to himself and could crawl between the covers any time at all without disturbing or offending anyone. But what was the point? A bed was for sharing, not just for sleeping. You could sleep anywhere—on the floor, in the bathtub, standing up. . . . Cows slept standing up, didn't they? Or was that only horses? Not that he had ever seen either except in holos, but that was irrelevant, that was confusing the issue, that was immaterial to his situation, which was that it did not matter where he slept, for he would sleep alone. All alone. For the rest of his life.

With a snuffle of self-pity he took a healthy swallow from the glass. So good, so smooth . . . he hated being alone. He had so much inside he wanted to get out, and no one to spill it to. Wef was gone for the evening, Emdy was— He would not think about where Emdy was.

Straightening up, holding the glass tightly, he began to navigate to the living room sofa. It seemed a terribly long way to travel, a route fraught with perilous carpets and dangerous doorframes, but he would manage. Somehow.

He had just emerged from the kitchen when the doorbell rang. He looked toward the vestibule in surprise. It was early yet. Wef would not return for hours. "Video."

L'ai Aichtueni's face smiled sheepishly out of the monitor. He set his glass down on the counter and tucked his shirt in. "Open."

She came inside with a shy, "Is it too late for apologies?"

He blinked, and tried to steady himself. "Why, no, it iz— isn't. No such thing as too late. Can I get you something to drink? Or eat? Or whatever?"

Smiling, she touched his arm. "No, thank you, Ale, I'm fine." With a gentle pressure on his left bicep, she guided him toward the couch. "I just stopped by to tell you how sorry I am for having behaved so abominably earlier today. I've not had a chance to relax for days, now, and I'm afraid I let the pressure get to me." She sat, patted the cushion beside her, and looked up into his eyes. "Will you accept my sincerest apologies—please?"

"Oh, sure, sure." He plopped down next to her. Her perfume filled his nostrils. It was a fresh scent, like a pine forest after a rain, but so delicate that he had to concentrate to enjoy it. He closed his eyes and breathed deeply. His head spun a little, but after a moment's thought, he attributed that to the Scotch. Then he realized the impression he had to be making. "I'm just sorry we haven't been able to find that program, you know? It's in there, that's for sure, but I'll tell you—"

"Oh, I know." She said it on the exhale, and leaned toward him. "I consulted one of our technical experts after I left here, and when I heard what he had to say, Ale, I was so ashamed of myself that my first thought was that I had to avoid you until you'd forgotten all about the incident. Then I realized that was the coward's way out. You deserve my humblest apologies."

Her eyes were the most fascinating shade of pink. . . . "I, uh— Thank you. Apology accepted, water under the bridge, and all that. All right?"

"Oh, yes!" She smiled up at him. Then her expression softened into sympathy. "I heard about Emdy, and wanted to say how sorry I am. I know what you must be going through, and if you need a friendly ear— or a shoulder   do remember that I'm here." She patted his knee lightly. "All right?"

"Thanks." Her warmth and evident concern touched him deeply. His eyes misted; he had to turn his face.

"You must be very lonely," she said. "To lose the source of your moral support just when you've taken on a tremendous civic responsibility must be devastating. Are you holding up all right?"

He shrugged, sniffed, and cleared his throat. "I— Well. . . ."

"I understand perfectly." She squeezed his forearm. "I think you need a hug, Ale Elatey."

He looked at her in surprise that stemmed equally from her offer and from his quick hot hunger to accept it. He did not speak, though. Her eyes loomed wise and pink in his as she put her arms around him. Their lips met gently, lingered, and parted.

Burying her face in his shoulder, she hugged him hard. Despite his awkward, half-sideways position, it felt good. Her slim arms had a fierce strength that offered refuge, security. Her soft white hair lay on his throat like silk. She made a sound.

"Hmm?"

Kneeling up on the sofa, she put her hands on his shoulders and pushed him back. "Like that." She stretched out alongside him.

Arm around her back, he drew her close. He breathed her perfume, stroked her hair with a clumsy, tentative hand, and kissed her again.

After a long minute she broke the kiss and leaned away from him. She stared straight into his eyes, and he felt as though her somber gaze burned through to his soul. She ran her hand down his side to his hip, and caressed him. "Will we be disturbed here?"

"Not for a while yet." He had difficulty speaking. His throat did not want to work. "A couple of hours."

"Much, much too soon." With a lithe motion, she swung off the couch and stood up. She held out her hands. "Come on."

He took her strong, cool grip and let her pull him to his feet. "Where?"

"This way." She slipped an arm around his waist, and led him directly to his bedroom.

She locked the door from the inside.

TOP TEN NEWS STORIES OF THE HOUR

22 June 2188 0530 EDT
New England Region

RANK HEADLINE   price   LEAD SENTENCE

SERVICE TEMPORARILY SUSPENDED

   To read any of the above news stories in full, simply highlight the title and press ACCEPT. The article will be transmatted to your unit's memory. Your bank balance will be debited by the sum in the column headed "price."
   To see the headlines of the day's other news stories, simply scroll your screen up.
   Thank you, and do be careful.

XX

—1—

Ale trudged into the living room, into the cold, grey light of dawn. A Dac flew by the window but did not stop. Rubbing the small of his back, Ale picked his way through an obstacle course of discarded beer cans. "Wef, the Australian says you might look at position sixty-four on the three-second interrupt tables on any newsbank program."

The old man turned bloodshot eyes to the Seeley. "Did he say why?"

"He said there was an unwritten office policy that you couldn't put a jump code there." Ale rolled his shoulders to work the kinks out. Of the last forty-eight hours, he had slept perhaps six. "He said any program that called for that got sent back for rewrite."

"Hmm." Wef chewed absently on a braid while he thought. "Sounds like somebody had that reserved. . . . I'd better take a look-see." He yawned hugely. Turning back to his console, he tapped out a series of commands and peered intently at the screen. "There's a jump code there, all right. Now leeme just—" His voice trailed off as he worked the keyboard. Then he straightened, and clapped his hands. "Hot damn! There it is."

Ale mustered the energy for a loud whoop. "Go to it, Wef! Erase away!"

"Not so fast, okay?" He mumbled to himself as he read the program. "Why does it do this, that's totally— Oh, shit. My goodness. No wonder it worked so well. Ale, look at this."

He leaned over the old man's shoulder. The symbols on the CRT made no sense to him. "Can you read that stuff?"

Wef looked momentarily startled, then said, "That's right, I forgot—" He tapped the screen. "Look, this stuff here, and this over there, it doesn't censor anything—it copies this program."

"Why would they—?"

"Into other computers."

He spread his hands in confusion. "So?"

"You know how the system's set up—thousands of computers linked into a data bank network—well, this section of the program here has it call up another computer at random, stash a duplicate of this program in its free memory, and put the proper jump code into position sixty-four of the three-second interrupt tables."

Ale blinked. Though numbed by fatigue, he thought he understood the enormity of the situation. "It replicates itself every three seconds?"

"You got it."

"Jesus Christ!" He collapsed onto the sofa. "It's alive. Every three seconds it infects another computer. . . . Wef, can you kill it?"

"I think so." The old man sagged in his chair. "But it means setting another self-replicating program loose. And God, I hate to do that."

"Afraid something'll go wrong?"

"I ain't afraid, Ale—I'm *certain*."

"Now, Wef—"

"No, you just hold on there. Look at this here." He pressed his index finger against a line of code. "I was thinking on it, and it occurred to me that even for the Coalition, shutting the newsbanks down completely was pretty heavy-handed, but that wasn't what they tried to do. What I think this here was supposed to say was, 'Erase anything entered into the system after 15 June having to do with the topics on Table A.' But what it really says is, 'Erase anything entered into the system after 15 June *and* anything having to do with the topics on Table A.' Which is a helluva difference. Now, you know whoever wrote this didn't intend to have that happen. But its fingers slipped, or its mind wandered, and we've gotten stuck with a self-replicating program with a big-ass glitch in it."

He put his hand on the tired old man's shoulder. "You're better than the Coalition guy, Wef. You wouldn't mess up like that."

The refugee snorted. "Don't count on it. I set something loose, it just might crash the whole system—and remember what happened when that Wichita net went down."

Exhausted, Ale nevertheless grinned. "I remember a newsbank article on that; the lead was something like, 'Twelve lives, forty million, and an elephant were lost as a result of' blah-blah-blah."

"That could happen here if I screw up." He reached back for his right-hand braid, brought it over his shoulder, and nibbled on its tip. "Jesus, I'm gonna have to think on this."

"If you don't want a self-replicating one, could I make a suggestion?"

"If it's any good."

"Uh—" He did not know quite how to take that. After a moment's hesitation, he shrugged. "I was just thinking, if you could write something that would call up, say, ten computers a second and erase the jump code at position sixty-four in each of them, well, then. . . ." He trailed off.

"Shit, Ale, I bought you an ibn Daoud, not an abacus. Ten a second! At a hundred megaherz it'll run a 10K program—" He sat up in his chair, his eyes wide and staring at a point above Ale's head. His lips moved soundlessly. He let out his breath. "Thousands of times a second. . . ." The chair squeaked as he swiveled back to the console. Keys clicked furiously.

Ale gave Wef's back a drowsy smile. Maybe the suggestion had revealed his ignorance of the finer technical details of the ibn Daoud, but it sure had galvanized the old man. And that was all that really mattered. He closed his eyes. Just for a minute. In a minute he would get up and water the bonsai. In a minute. . . .

"—do it?" asked Wef. "Hey, Ale!"

With a startled "Hmph?" he snapped his eyes open. His neck hurt. He wondered how long he had slept. And if he had snored. He could tell he had drooled. . . . Blushing, he shook his head. "I'm sorry, Wef, what'd you say?"

"I said, the program's written. Just to be on the safe side, it'll run for sixty seconds. Files claim we got seven thousand six hunnerd forty-three public data banks; this'll sweep all of 'em better'n once a second. You're looking at about a thirty-five thousand dollar comm bill, here."

"The DPI'll cover that." His vision was still fuzzy. Carefully, he scraped sleep crumbs from the corner of his right eye. "But will it work?"

"Hell, yes."

"Good." He smiled—knew it to be a sappy smile but was too tired to be able to do anything about it—nodded, and waited.

Wef drummed his fingers on the desk. "Well?"

"'Well' what?"

"You're the boss. You take the responsibility if it crashes a network. Do I do it?"

Ale stopped, his sleepiness gone, shredded like smoke in the wind. What had Wichita cost? Twelve lives, forty million dollars, and an elephant? All because something, somewhere, had gone wrong. Now Wef was inviting him to risk a similar avalanche. Twelve lives. That bothered him. As did the elephant. Increasingly rare, elephants. It was his decision. "Do it."

"Okay." He spun his chair about. "Keep your fingers crossed."

"You got it. Coffee?"

"Intravenously, if possible."

"Right." As he headed for the kitchen, the hovee shifted into the smooth-cheeked features of a morning newscaster. "—from London is that the ACLE will impose a two percent surcharge on withholding taxes to make up for the deficit inherited from the ousted regime. The tax is to go into effect immediately; it will be applied on taxes withheld from all income paid after 22 June 2188 0001 Greenwich Mean Time. Schedules released by the ACLE show the surcharge raising four hundred billion ST Dollars per year, and eliminating the deficits entirely by the year 2193. In other news—" His voice trailed off; his face blurred into a brown globe randomly dotted with amoeboid patches of blue; the patches swelled and shrank as the globe spun.

Wef made a noise.

Ale turned back to him. "What's the matter?"

The old man looked at the ceiling for a long moment. "You want the good news first or last?"

"Cheer me up first, then break my heart."

"All right. The good news is, the censor's dead."

"Congratulations."

"The bad news is, there's another censor still alive."

—2—

At a little after ten o'clock, as Ale was pouring his seventh cup of coffee of the day, L'ai Aichtueni breezed into the kitchen. He almost dropped his mug. How the devil had she gotten inside? Then a hazy recollection came to him, a vague memory of teaching the ibn Daoud to recognize and to respond to her voice. He made a mental note to reprogram the computer later.

"Hi, Ale." Hugging him, she pressed her firm body against his and kissed him on the cheek. "You need a shave."

"And twelve hours sleep." Until the hug he had been ready to ask her to leave, so that he could get on with his work, but she felt good in his arms, and he liked her. It was important to Ale that somebody like him. Somebody besides Wef DiNaini, somebody who would be staying around. "What's up?"

She squeezed him, and winked. "You mean, what else is up?"

A laugh escaped him; he nodded.

"This censorship stuff." Turning somber, she released him. "Our releases are getting into the banks now, but there's still something in the system that deletes our name every time it's entered—and nobody's even *noticing* our offer to evacuate Sydney."

"Speaking of that," called Wef from the living room, "when are you sending the Florida refugees back home? I was supposed to be outta here two days ago."

"That, too," she told Ale. "Soon, Wef." She lowered her voice. "We're not getting any publicity at all!"

"It's the same as before, Water. This is another program loose in the system. It's happening to everybody."

"But it's still not happening to ACLE, dammit!"

"I know." He groaned. "I know. But Wef has a theory about that. He figures it's a short, simple program with a list. Any word on the list gets erased—anything not on it, stays. And the ACLE wasn't around when the Coalition drew up the list, that's all."

"Crap." She folded her arms and fixed him with a belligerent stare.

"Aw, come on. I— All right. Look. I have another idea for you. It'll keep you listed until we get the program fixed."

She cocked her head. "What's that?"

"Change the party's name—you'll have to tinker till you find one that's not on the list—but maybe SoTe would work, or Ocial Ech, or—but you get the idea."

"Ale, we've put years into promoting that name! We're not going to abandon all the emotional associations people have with it. And besides, even if we did, what good would it do? We post a notice that says 'The (deleted) Party hereby announces that it is now known as the 'Never-Heard-of-Them,

Martha' Party? I mean, really, of all the ridiculous ideas—"

She broke off at a wordless bellow from the hall. Metal and plastic clattered. Something thudded against a wall. An angry male voice said, "Leggo, that's me!"

Ale shot the front door an anxious glance. Good. It was closed.

L'ai said, "What is that commotion?"

"Sounds like a fight."

"I know *that*." She walked to the vestibule. "But who? And why?"

He pointed to the screen above the lintel. "Let's find out. Video."

"Broken."

"Oh, you can't see anything through that, anyway," she said scornfully. "Open!"

"Hey—" But it was too late. The door had already popped its locks. He hurried to her side. Apprehension turned his stomach hollow and uneasy.

"Ale—it's Ap!"

She blocked the doorway; he had to lean over her shoulder. At the far end of the hall, Ap Emfordee was hurling one burly policeman into another. Three other cops were lunging at him. Embattled though he was, the big man lifted his head and shouted, "Ale! Help!"

He did not want to go out there. He certainly did not want to lend Emfordee a hand. But the man had saved him from the police once, and Ale figured he owed him something. Under his breath, he told L'ai, "Thanks a lot, pal," and stepped into the corridor.

One of the downed cops scrambled across the floor to an electric outlet. He plugged his stun club into it. Rising to his knees, he shouted "Clear for zap!" and aimed the club at Emfordee.

The other four policemen leaped back; one tripped and landed hard on his butt.

The club spat a loud, bright spark.

Emfordee's hair haloed out from his head; his eyes widened, rolled, went blank. He slumped to the floor.

Ale took a deep breath. Hands in the air at about shoulder height, both of them open and plainly empty, he walked down the hall. "Uh, Officer?"

The nearest cop stopped dusting his pantsleg long enough to glance up. "Yeah?"

"Uh. . . . I know this man here, and, uh, what seems to be the problem?"

"No problem. We got a warrant for his arrest. He didn't want to go." The cop examined Ale closely. *"You* got a problem?"

As Ale opened his mouth, L'ai strode up behind him. "Not if you show us the warrant," she said.

The cop raised his eyebrows and looked at her with interest. "You a lawyer, lady?"

"I'm Ap Emfordee's neighbor! As you seem to have rendered him unconscious, you have to show the warrant to his *ad hoc* representative. You know that."

"All right, all right." He called over one of the others. "Show 'em the warrant."

The second cop reached inside his torn jacket and brought out a sheet of stiff paper. "Who sees it?"

L'ai stretched out her hand.

"Okay." He slapped it into her palm.

She unfolded it, and held it at such an angle that Ale could read it, too. "They got the name and address right," she said.

"Uh-huh." He ran his gaze down the legalese until he came to the charges: *possession of projectile weapons; advocacy of violence; recruitment of members for an illegal political association.* He read the third charge out loud. "Since when is it illegal—"

"Since nine p.m. last night, buddy." He retrieved the warrant, and returned it to the cop in the torn jacket. "They outlawed the AmRev Party, and enticing people to join it can cost you five years."

—3—

"The Australian doesn't know anything about it, but the Korean said to look at slot eighteen on the ninety-second interrupt tables." Ale sank limply onto the couch. He was so tired that his joints ached; his bones seemed to throb. Light from the setting sun slanted across the terrace, reminding him that he never had gotten around to watering the bonsai. They could probably go a day without it. He hoped. It was too late for today, though. Watering a plant just before dark invites fungus attacks.

"Slot eighteen, eh?" said the old man.

"Yeah." It occurred to him that there was nothing in the refrigerator. They would have to pholo out for dinner. Chinese? Brazilian?

"Got it, Ale." He hummed to himself, hoarse and off-key. "It looks pretty similar to the other one."

"Then—"

BEEEP

He winced. "Wait a minute, Wef. The Oracle's calling."

Wef noddcd. "I'll get me a beer."   .

BEEEP

Hold on, hold on, I'm coming. . . . He slipped into interface easily, numbly. Fatigue might impair concentration, but it certainly diminished distractions. *Yes?*

#A call from the ACLE, sir.#

Put it through.

#Congratulations,# said the familiar intonation. #You've done a superb job so far, and I wished to compliment you personally.#

Thank you.

#Have you made any progress in eliminating the Oracle Monitor program?#

No, but we just found another censorship program.

#Have you erased it, then?#

Not yet.

#Good, good—perhaps you can modify it, then.#

Huh?

#As you know, the American Revival Party has been outlawed, and it is now a felony to advocate membership in it. It's been decided that it would be wise if the party's name never appeared in the data banks again.#

Wait a minute—

The other plunged on. #Since you've located the censorship program, it would be best if you allowed it to keep operating, with a patch at the appropriate locations to delete from the banks any reference to the American Revival Party. All other parties, of course, should be permitted full and free access. For the time being.#

Surprise stole his tongue.

#When you finish modifying this one, do write thorough documentation, please. We shall need it in future, should we have to delete other parties.#

Hot anger surged in Ale, startling in its intensity. What kind of nonsense was this? The other Seeley had to know—and know damn well!—that Ale would never go along with his suggestion. It was ludicrous. Insulting.

But he kept cool. A fiery argument would win him nothing besides the other's enmity. Carefully, with conscious restraint, he said, *I see*.

#We rather thought you would.#

He did not like that word "we." It created too strongly the impression of a powerful, efficient, and above all, well-informed organization. He said, *If there's nothing else, then—*

#We'll talk later. Be careful.#

He left interface for darkness. The sun had finished setting; the photocells had failed again. From the soft, regular breathing that came from the direction of the ap-comp, he deduced that Wef was catnapping. He snapped his fingers loudly to switch on the lamps.

They showered him with brilliance, and glinted off the scattered beer cans. He blinked. God, he was tired. Also hungry, and thirsty, and he needed to go to the bathroom. He did not get up. He sat still and turned things over in his mind.

His immediate superior had just given him a direct order—phrased as a strong suggestion, to be sure, but an order for all that—to maintain censorship. The question at hand was whether to obey.

His instincts urged him not to. A more recently-developed sense of self-preservation reminded him that disobedience had put Ap Emfordee in jail.

And yet how could he support censorship? How could they expect him to?

But did they? He wished he knew more. Perhaps his boss was acting on his own; perhaps someone higher up might overrule him on appeal—but. . . .

It was beginning to look as though Emdy Ofivo had been right. He never should have gotten involved. He should have kept his mouth shut and pretended everything was fine by him.

Slumping, he stretched his arms along the top of the sofa and gave a soft groan. Twenty-twenty hindsight was such wonderful stuff. So useful. . . .

What-he-should-have-done no longer mattered. He was in it now, in it up to his neck—figuratively, he hoped—and what mattered was his next step. Did he do what he was told? Or did he do what was right?

Wait, though. No one knew his name. So if he did what was right, the ACLE could not touch him. *If* the anonymity program had held. He closed his eyes and slipped back into interface.

#Yes, sir?#

Does ACLE know my name?

#Of course not.#

And you won't ever tell them?

#Never.#

Thanks.

Back in the real world, he relaxed. And smiled. Whether his boss was acting on his own or not, the censorship program was as good as gone.

He woke Wef up and told him to zap it.

Ninety seconds later the old man turned. "You ain't gonna like this."

He winced. "Don't tell me you couldn't erase it, Wef. Please?"

"Oh, hell, that sucker's gone, no problem there. But somebody sure as hell believed in fail-safes: there's a third censor still out there, and it's awful damn hungry."

—4—

It was nearly dawn: the third in a row that they would watch spill over the horizon. Ale's eyes felt like sandbags. He had knocked his coffee cup over twice in the last half hour, and his unshaven cheeks itched like hell. He bent over the desk and said, "Well?"

Wef typed now with one finger, and still hit the wrong key a third of the time. "I think so, but Jesus, Ale, lemme tell ya—"

A hand touched Ale's shoulder. Straightening up with a snap, he yelped.

"I'm sorry, Ale," said L'ai Aichtueni.

A blast of adrenalin hit too late. He panted. "Water. Didn't hear you come in." He took a deep breath. "Whooh, you startled me."

"I just came down to thank you both." Kissing him lightly on the lips, she slipped her right arm around his back and gave him a half-hug.

"My turn," said Wef.

She said, "Sorry, Wef, but that'd be hazardous to your health."

"I'm not *that* old!" He reached for her playfully.

With a laugh, she slapped his hand. "Why don't you check on your flight home? It should be listed by now."

His eyes widened, and gleamed with joy. "Really? It's finally set?"

"Uh-huh. You leave—"

BEEEEEPEEP

L'ai's good news sank to a background whisper as Ale slipped into interface. *What?*

#ACLE on the line, sir.#

Inwardly he winced. *Put him through.*

The familiar voice exploded in his mind. #Just what in the name of God do you think you're doing? I specifically told you to leave the censorship program running so the AmRev Party couldn't get any publicity. So what's taking up half the bankspace? Articles on our outlawing the AmRevs. Are you incompetent, man? Or insubordinate?#

Astonished by the other's ferocity, Ale recoiled. And decided not to declare his rebellion, even at the risk of seeming a fool. *Well, no, see, what it was, we couldn't write a program that would modify the censor without erasing it—only we didn't know that until it was too late. We tried, but gee, it just didn't work.*

#You don't expect me to believe that nonsense, do you?#

What nonsense? He may have kept the sudden anxious jump out of his tone, but not out of his heart. As though from a distance, he felt nervous sweat dampen the back of his shirt.

#My God, man, I haven't the foggiest idea of *your* ID/dress or talents, but I *do* know that your consultant on the job is Wef DiNaini.#

He went cold all over. Anybody who knew that much—and who had the other's access to the information networks—could dig a little, put two and two together, and come up with the name Ale Elatey. He caught his breath, and tried hard to keep his voice level. *Uh. . . . All right, I'll admit—*

#A wise idea.#

Now he strove for annoyed embarrassment. *I—all right, look, I thought I was pretty good, and it turned out I wasn't, okay? I'm sorry. Next time, I'll let Wef write it.*

Shock reverberated in the ensuing silence. #Do you seriously mean to say that you attempted a crucially important program by yourself, even though you have Wef DiNaini working for you?#

Not all by myself. Relief shot through him. Was the other really going to buy his story? *He did the preliminaries.*

#How in the world did you convince ORA:CLE Inc. to hire you?# Utter bewilderment slowed his tone.

I'm not a computer *expert,* he said. *My field—* Caution stopped him. No need to give any clues to his true ID/dress. *I thought I had it. I didn't. I'm sorry.*

#Yes. Well.# The other seemed at a loss for words. #You said "next time." Is there yet another censor in the banks?#

Yes. It seems to be called Ponzer. We think for Political News Zapper.

#Let Wef DiNaini handle it. Do you understand?#

He put all the sheepishness he could muster into: *Uh-huh.*

#And make *certain* that it deletes all references to the American Revival Party, do you hear me?#

Yes, sir.

#And be aware of this: if you fail, you will pay. Heavily.#
He cut out of interface.

Ale made his way back to reality, shaky at his near escape— and worried about what could happen later that day.

Because he would be damned if he let Ponzer stay operational in any way, shape, or form.

L'ai had gone. Wef sat in the swivel chair before the ibn Daoud, his fingers motionless on the keys. From the faraway look in his eyes, he had already returned to Florida. Probably plotting his next coup.

With a small smile, Ale touched the old man on the shoulder. Wef came to with a jerk. "Huh?"

"Let's get that Ponzer thing out of there, all right?"

"Ah...." The refugee shuffled his feet. "Listen, Ale, if it's all the same to you, I would surely appreciate it if you'd wait till I was home before you ran this erasure program. Nothing personal or anything, but t' tell the truth, I'd rather not be around when the shit hits the fan."

That scared him. Did *everybody* know more of what was going on than he thought? He forced a laugh. "Why do you think it will?"

"Come on, Ale, this is Wef DiNaini here." He tapped his breastbone. "Don't bull me. I've been looking at the private bulletin boards. Some of your colleagues figure freedom of information should be limited to folks with the right sort of academic breeding. That folks without the fancy degrees haven't got the equipment to tell a good idea from a bad one. Now, if they're saying this in public, what the hell do you think they're saying in private?"

Ale made a face. "Yeah. You're right." He sighed. "They want to keep the censors going."

The old man studied him thoughtfully. "The chopper picks me up in half an hour. My flight leaves Kennedy in two hours. If you'd wait till it lands—about six hours from now?—to run this program, I'd be real grateful."

He nodded. "Okay. It's a deal."

—5—

The pholo rang; the operator said, "Collect call for Mr. Wef DiNaini from Mr. Ale Elatey."

"Gee, I'm sorry," said Ale, "but he's not in. Please tell him to try again later."

"Than-kew," he said, and rang off.

So Wef had reached Miami airport safely. That was the signal. Ale turned to the keyboard and typed the commands to run the program that would wipe Ponzer out of the banks.

—6—

He dreamed of RAM and addresses and swift silent death by erasure. The day's last sun lay warm on his cheek but he did not care. He had completed his task. He would not let himself wake up—not even to stumble from the couch to the bedroom—until his body had recovered from its ordeal.

BEEPEEPEEP

He groaned, and rolled over.

BEEPEEPEEPEEP

He tried to cling to sleep, but it fled like fog in the wind. His eyelids rolled back of their own accord.

BEEPEEPEEPEEPEEP

"Dammit!" Slapping the cushions, he closed his eyes. *What was it?*

#A call from ACLE, sir.#

Oh, geez....Go ahead.

The voice was quiet, and even, and more menacing than a blood-curdling scream. #I warned you. But you wouldn't listen. You are going to be very, very sorry—Ale Elatey.#

TOP TEN NEWS STORIES OF THE HOUR

RANK HEADLINE	price	LEAD SENTENCE
#1 ACLE DENIES CENSORSHIP ROLE	.25	Pointing to its role as the eliminator of the censorship programs released in virtually all public data banks by the former regime, the ACLE today denied, through a spokesrep, charges that it has attempted to maintain the operational life span of those programs.
#2 * * * * * * AMREVS, FIDELISTAS ORDERED TO DISBAND	.20	#2 * * * * * * In a move criticized by the leaders of almost every party worldwide, the ACLE yesterday ruled that the platforms and by-laws of both the American Revival Party and the Fidelista Sempre Party *ipso facto* disqualified both parties from further participation in public life; both parties have threatened to appeal the ruling.
#3 * * * * * * TELEBETTER DRAWING SCIENTIFIC FIRE	.15	#3 * * * * * * Studies conducted by the research facilities at the University of Sydney suggest that TeleBetter, the over-the-counter aid to telesensoring, does indeed promote identity

crises in heavy users, a
university spokesrep
announced this afternoon.

#4 * * * * * *

**DAC SHIP NUMBER .15
SIX CLOSING IN
FAST**

#4 * * * * * *

Lunar observatory officials
reported this evening that
the most recent addition to
the Dac fleet garrisoning
the planet Earth is within
fifty million kilometers of
the L5 position; it is expected
to park in forty-five hours.

#5 * * * * * *

**FIRE SWATCH TO .10
BECOME PARK**

#5 * * * * * *

Officials of all of New York's
major parties have agreed
in principle that the
portions of 8th Avenue
damaged by a massive fire
on 15 June will not be
rebuilt, but will instead
become an addition to
Central Park.

#6 * * * * * *

**EARTHQUAKE .10
LEVELS QUITO**

#6 * * * * * *

A massive earthquake
registering 8.9 on the
Richter scale smashed this
equatorial South American
city at 2047 (EDT) this
evening, causing damages
estimated in the tens of
billions of dollars and taking
untold lives.

#7 * * * * * *

**PSYCHIC PREDICTS .10
DAC DEPARTURE**

#7 * * * * * *

In a copyrighted article
banked in the Marian-
Vegetarian Data Retrieval
Service this morning,
twelve-year-old psychic
FYG10 ACVYYG B4VU
predicted that all Dacs will
have left the Solar System
by the end of next year.

RANK HEADLINE price LEAD SENTENCE

#8 * * * * * *

**EMSISICKS
RUNNING FOR
SURVIVAL**

.10

#8 * * * * * * *

Former ho-soap star and
one-time political
wunderkind Aid Emsisicks
is battling for his political
life in a CCU election today;
polls give him less than a
forty percent chance of
holding onto his position.

#9 * * * * * *

**DACS GET LA
STREETER**

.10

#9 * * * * * * *

While thousands of Wilshire
Boulevard residents watched
from their windows, three
Dacs dropped from the skies
at 1045 EDT and slew an
elderly streeter; police are
withholding identification
pending notification of next
of kin.

#10 * * * * *

**LOUVRE OPENS
DOORS TO HOVEE**

.10

#10 * * * * * * *

In a move aimed at making
the Louvre, one of France's
most famed museums, more
accessible to the public, the
Social Gaullist Directorate of
Public Culture is entering
into a joint venture with
Cable Arts, Inc., the
company that made
broadcasting history last
year by holovising tours of
the Prado and the
Hermitage.

This update has been provided as a public service by all data management corporations participating in NEWSBANK/MV, a news data
base organized and supervised by the Marian-Vegetarian Directorate
of Public Information.

To read any of the above news stories in full, simply highlight the
title and press ACCEPT. The article will be transmatted to your unit's
memory. Your bank balance will be debited by the sum in the column
headed "price."

To see the headlines of the day's other news stories, simply scroll
your screen up.

Thank you, and do be careful.

XXI

—1—

It took Ale Elatey close to two hours to calm down.

He had not known fear could inundate him, could creep up past his heart and his throat until it submerged his very brain. The Dac attack had had nothing on this, nor had the gas explosion and its aftermath. Those had flashed like lasers, short and incredibly sharp, but through all their intensity he had known their possible resolutions, and known that one of those resolutions would come quickly. Now, though....

Now he swam in a fear so deep, so broad that the fear itself terrified him. The air, fouled by his own acrid sweat, clogged his lungs like a smotherer's pillow; the dusk world beyond the ruby DacWatch seemed wavery and insubstantial. Every noise came loud and brittle to his ears: his pulse raced when the refrigerator's compressor kicked in.

A better word for it was dread.

What was ACLE going to do to him? They had so many options—so many ways in which to attack, so many degrees to which they could harm him.

They could arrest him. He doubted they would do it surreptitiously—their regime was too new; the data banks, thanks to him, too free—but they could arrest him openly, try him, sentence him, and in the process make a fearful example of him.

Or was that too blatant an act of oppression for "liberators" fresh from a successful revolution?

Would they resort to the Coalition's methods? A bomb here, a laser there? The entire world a potential booby-trap for one Ale Elatey?

"No," he said to himself. Not only had he interfered with ACLE's policies, he had injured its pride. ACLE might murder him, but it would not permit death to surprise him. It would ensure that he knew exactly what would happen to him, and why.

They could cause him to disappear. And after that, to die. Quickly and painlessly, or slowly and not.

He thought, but was not convinced, that torture might be too crude for insecure rulers steeped in academia.

Academia. He gave a great groan. Sure. They could—they would!—ruin his career, have him fired and blackballed, watch him sink into the despair of enduring as someone he was not permitted to be, of clinging to skills he was not allowed to use.

And he groaned again as he remembered that at the moment, he had no academic career at all: officially, he was on loan to ACLE.

He had to resign from ACLE before he could go back to being a scholar.

Oh, good....

He did not want to close his eyes, slip into interface, and ask for a patch—his anxiety had reached such a level that it seemed to take hours to get inside—but he did it because he had to.

Oddly, the great chamber enveloped him in warmth and comfort. It was like coming from a winter wind into a room made snug by a woodfire crackling on the hearth. His tensions fell away, replaced by a delicious drowsiness.

#Yes?#

Let me talk to my boss at ACLE, please.

#Are you certain, sir? From what I understand, you are hardly likely to be welcomed.#

Just patch me through, will you? The murmur of distant Seeleys rose around him like the shields of a defending army. Here he could relax in safety and in peace.

#One moment.#

It ran closer to five minutes, five minutes during which he would have fallen asleep, so tired was he, had the door to his apartment not opened. That woke him. It disrupted interface, and pushed his heart rate over a hundred fifty beats a minute, but it banished fatigue marvelously well.

It was L'ai Aichtueni who entered. She smiled, dropped onto the couch beside him, and kissed his cheek. Her eyes did not quite focus. "Hi, Ale. I'm glad to see you're not busy. We have so much to talk about—"

He held up a hand. "Sssh, I'm trying to get through to ACLE."

She grimaced, but fell silent. As interface steadied around him, she began to draw interesting patterns on his thigh with the nail of her right index finger. At one point, the pattern became so interesting that he almost lost interface completely....

#Second thoughts, Ale?# said the familiar intonation pattern.

Not really. He tousled L'ai's white hair, but pushed her head away from his lap. The feel of interface intensified. *It occurred to me that, since my job is done, I have an obligation to resign my position for the record before I return to civilian life.*

#Ale, you also have an obligation to society.#

And I've filled it. Every censorship program has been deleted.

#Ale, we're not about to permit drooling idiots who think with their hormones to pour garbage into the nets. You know how dangerous that nonsense is; you must have read some of it. Unless checked, those Neanderthals will provoke the Dacs into slagging some buildings. Reactivate Ponzer immediately; list the AmRevs and the Fidelistas for total exclusion. No other parameters.#

Uh-uh.

#What do you mean, "uh-uh"?#

I mean I'm not going to do it—my job was to eliminate censorship, not maintain it.

#Consider this a direct order from the highest levels—get Ponzer fully operational right damn now, do you hear?#

Hey, I don't take orders from you.

#Are you mad? I'm your immediate superior. You—#

I resigned, formally and officially, a few minutes ago. I am no longer your immediate subordinate. I am a simple taxpayer, now. Which means, in theory, that you are my immediate subordinate. So get off my back.

#You are mad. We're in charge here, Ale, and we're telling you—#

He made a rude mental noise and broke interface.

"What's the matter, lover?" Her hand massaged the nape of his neck. Her glazed pink eyes came close to his. "You're so tense."

"Ah, it's that paranoid fool at ACLE—" He patted her knee and got to his feet. "He thinks the world needs a censorship program to keep people from shooting at Dacs."

"He might have a point." She sounded thoughtful.

"What?"

She lifted her chin. "I've been in politics for years, Ale, and people are—" She shrugged. "Don't ever quote me, but they're dumb is what they are. They believe anything you tell them, if you say it right and if you say it often enough. ACLE seems to think two parties—the Fidelistas and the AmRevs—are capable of saying it right, and saying it often enough. After all, that impossible man upstairs was seriously hunting for a factory to cast anti-aircraft guns for him. I think ACLE has legitimate grounds for concern."

He spun a dining room chair around and straddled it. "I just don't believe censorship's ever appropriate."

"Believe what you like—but neither is it ever appropriate unnecessarily to anger powerful individuals."

"How can you say that?"

She looked at him in wonderment. "Ale, how do you think you get to the top? Certainly not by alienating influential people."

"I don't know how *you* get to the top, but I get there by being good—no, great—at what I do. By being the best there is."

She nodded. "But in government, what you do is what you're told to do."

"I'm not *in* government any more!"

"I know." Her voice was flat. "But you should be."

"Look." He held up his hands. "I don't want to argue about this, okay?"

She gave a slight shrug. "Fine by me." Settling back on the sofa, she said, "Hovee—on."

—2—

He awoke the next morning to warm, blinding sunlight. Beside him, L'ai breathed lightly and regularly, releasing, in the last split-second of each inhalation, just the faintest hint of a snore. He thought he heard something in the closet. Or was that the tail of a dream?

Yawning, he tried to orient himself. His place or hers? He squinted against the glare of morning. By the window, lush yellow roses opened their petals to the day. His place.

But why so bright? He distinctly remembered setting the

window controls to full polarization and telling L'ai, "I am going to sleep in tomorrow."

And she had said she would join him, and while they played, they planned a brunch of Eggs Benedict and sausage and coffee served in the heavy silver pot that stayed warm for hours.

So why had the windows failed them?

Unless it was after noon, already. The apartment computer had standing orders to make certain the house plants got at least six hours of natural light a day. Less than that, and most wilted quickly.

A creak came from the closet. Not a dream. The building was settling. Or Mrs. M'ti Emtenne, whose closets backed up to his, was looking for a pair of shoes.

He rolled onto his back. "Time," he whispered to the ceiling.

The clock did not light up.

Oh, geez. He slipped out of bed, careful not to awaken L'ai, and padded into the living room. He snapped his fingers. None of the lamps came on.

Just to make sure he went into the kitchen and opened the refrigerator door. The silent shadows within confirmed it: the power was out.

As he trudged disconsolately to the bathroom, he wondered if it was the building that was blacked out, the city, or the region. The last regional power failure had lasted what, almost two days? Everything in the freezer had melted, and some of what they could not eat had spoiled.

When the fault lay at the building level, the power usually came back on within an hour or two. Even so, it made using the darkened bathroom a hit-or-miss proposition. . . .

He flushed, and then clucked at himself in exasperation. With the power out, the building's water pumps shut off, and he had just emptied the toilet tank. Which would give him the option of waiting till power was restored to flush it again, or carrying water up thirty-eight flights of stairs. . . . *Dumb, Ale, real dumb.*

The tank burbled as it began to refill. He heaved a sigh of relief. Apparently the power had failed only a few minutes ago, and the water tanks on the roof still held something. Good, good. He had better find and fill a jug or two, just in case.

He returned to the kitchen, and rooted around in the cupboard under the counter. Way at the back were four plastic four-liter bottles. He set them on the counter and pulled himself to his feet.

Then stopped at a distant whine. *Isn't that the elevator?*

He opened the front door a crack. Light streamed in. Puzzled, he undid the chain and looked out.

The hall lights glowed brilliantly.

"Wait a minute," he mumbled.

Something was wrong. Closing the door, he turned and leaned against it, glad for its firmness behind his shoulder blades. He needed the support.

His lights were off, but the building's were on. Impossible. How he could have blown all eight fuses simultaneously?

Even so, he checked. The fuses were fine. Nor had any of the circuit breakers been tripped.

Time to call the power company and find out what was going on.

He started for the pholo, only to stop with a curse. If he had no power, he had no pholo. He would have to use the booth in the shopping mall. Or no—Mrs. M'ti Emtenne would surely let him borrow hers. She would probably nosy all over him about Emdy's whereabouts and the state of their marriage, but even that beat a trip to the mall. He thought.

In any event, he would need clothes.

Stepping as softly as he could, he eased into the bedroom and began to pull on his pants.

L'ai opened her eyes—and shut them again immediately. "Darken the windows, huh Ale?"

"Can't." He fumbled with his shirt. "Power's out."

"Oh, no!" It came out a wail. She sat up. "Am I going to have to *walk* upstairs?"

"No, I think the elevator's working."

"But your power's out?"

"Uh-huh."

She collapsed back onto the mattress and pulled a pillow over her head. "Check your fuses."

"They're fine. I'm going next door to call the electric company."

"Wait a minute." She lifted a corner of the pillow and peeked out at him. "Your fuses are fine, your circuit breakers are fine, the rest of the building has power, but you don't?"

"Uh-huh." He glanced in the mirror. A little scruffy, but no more so than usual. Not enough to make Mrs. M'ti Emtenne shriek in horror. Or get motherly.

"I told you so."

"Told me what?"

"Not to anger influential people unnecessarily. Just wait, Ale Elatey. They're going to make your life miserable."

He shrugged with unfeigned weariness. *"Alea jacta est,* to borrow a phrase. Not much I can do about it now."

She made a disgruntled sound. Stacking the pillows up, she burrowed her face into the mound. "See you later, Ale."

"Yeah." He left.

When Mrs. M'ti Emtenne opened her door for him, a stethoscope hung about her neck. It looked remarkably out of place until she said, "You could wait for the bed to cool off before you let somebody else hop into it." She snorted. "I'll bet you didn't even change the sheets."

He blushed. She was right. "May I borrow your pholo? My power's out."

"Of course." She waved him inside. "Dreadful circuits in this building, you'd think after all the complaining we've done they'd have done something to fix them, but no, they expect us to live with them."

Her apartment was the mirror image of his: kitchen, bedroom, and bath to the left of the living room, instead of the right; windowless wall on the right dividing her apartment from the next over. Windowless, but not featureless: three lucite shelves running all seven meters from hall to terrace supported a score of glowing, bubbling fish tanks. Even with the air conditioning going the room was uncomfortably humid. In the winter, as he had seen, her windows fogged up permanently.

She gestured to the pholo, beyond the huge round fish tank in the middle of the living room. "So why did Emdy walk out on you?"

He raised an eyebrow. "You mean you didn't hear it through the closets?"

She was not to be shaken by a line like that. "I was probably sunbathing when it happened." She sat on a high-backed armchair and fixed him with a glare. "You shouldn't have let her get away from you, Ale. You'll never find her like again."

"Since the alternative seemed to involve locking her in her office, a course of conduct that the courts disapprove of—" His call went through.

A bright-eyed old man with impossibly bushy black eyebrows appeared in the sphere. "Customer service, may I help you?"

After Ale explained the problem, the old man glanced down

at his keyboard. When he looked up again, his face was wary. "Service was discontinued for lack of payment, sir. Didn't you read our notices?"

He leaned forward, as if into a stiff wind. This could get inordinately difficult. "My files should show that I'm on the automatic payment plan. Which means routine daily debits on my account in exchange for your discount. Since I know there was money in there yesterday, I know you got paid. If you'll consult my bank—"

Bending over his keyboard, the customer service rep jiggled in his chair. A frown tugged his lined cheeks. "Yes, the authorization's here in your file, as is the account number, let me just call your bank— Well, well, well." He lifted his eyes. "Your account activity statement shows credits to our account, sir. I don't understand this. I'll have to look into it, but in the meantime, we'll get your power turned back on right away. Do be careful."

"But—" He wanted to question the man.

The sphere vanished.

"Well, isn't that odd," said Mrs. M'ti Emtenne. "And I thought they said it was infallible."

"Nothing's infallible, I'm afraid." He rose to leave.

"You're making a terrible mistake with Emdy, you know." She got up, too, and blocked his path. "She's a fine woman, Ale Elatey, and with a little effort on your part—"

He escaped ten minutes later, just in time to see L'ai Aichtueni step onto the upbound elevator.

He should have gone to the mall, after all.

—3—

With the power off, there was not much he could do except water his plants, sit for a while in a chair pulled over to the terrace doors, and spend a few hours in interface waiting for a query on East Asia.

It was an unexpectedly pleasant way to pass a warm June afternoon.

Having the apartment to himself made quite a difference. It was, for one thing, much quieter. Surprising, how much ruckus even a beloved roommate raises in an average day: running sinks, rattling kitchen utensils, thunking closets and cupboards shut . . . noises which make no sound when they occur in the pursuit of one's own activities, but which thunder when caused by another.

Of course, the silence also meant that there was no one Ale Elatey could call out to with news or a question or affection. . . .

The sun was fifteen minutes set when the refrigerator kicked in and the living room lamps lit up. Rising from his chair, Ale told the sliding glass doors to polarize, and pholoed up to L'ai. "Power's back on—would you like to come down for the evening?"

She glanced down and to her left, then shrugged. "I suppose so. Give me five minutes."

He gave her more like fifteen, and she did not apologize for her lateness when she finally did arrive. "I can't stay the night," she said by way of greeting. "I go on duty at 4:00 a.m."

"That's a godawful hour." He moved over to the bar. "I thought you had enough seniority to pick your own shifts."

"I do. I did. But this way I get off at ten, and have the rest of the day to work on the campaign. How about a nice brandy?"

The cupboard yielded up bottles of everything but. "We seem to be out."

"Of the only thing I'll drink? Some host."

"I'll order some, hold on." He stepped to the pholo. "This time of day, they'll transmit it here in about thirty seconds."

He called in the order, but when the liquor store went to debit his account, the message NO SUCH ID/DRESS flared to life on both their screens. The shopkeeper said, "Real funny, Mac," and cut the connection. Shocked, Ale stared at where the sphere had been and did not move.

"Are they sending it?" asked L'ai.

"Uh. . . . No, no, they're not. . . ." The import of what had just happened finally sank in. He spun. "I think I've been erased."

She did not seem surprised. "You'll have to call the Directorate of Public Statistics."

"Do you know their number?"

She rose lazily from the couch. "They're in the banks. But I do know they close at five and don't open again till nine."

"Oh, damn."

She drifted toward the door. "I told you so."

"What? Where are you going?"

She turned, her expression bored. "I'm leaving. You're a loser, Ale. You could have had it made, but you had to offend those people at ACLE. Very dumb. I don't have time for dumb. It hurts the campaign."

"But—" He stepped toward her, his arms outstretched.

"Don't call me: I won't call you." She closed the door behind herself.

—4—

He awoke gripped by the fear that his power might have been shut off again. With no pholo it would be much more difficult to reestablish his identity. Remembering what Wef DiNaini had done to Emdy convinced him that he did not want, while drugged, to be subjected to Mrs. M'ti Emtenne's nosy solicitousness—or to the whimsies of the crowds in the mall.

But the ceiling clock flashed 0807 in cool green numbers; the bathroom lights came on at his cough.

And the refrigerator hummed steadily, cooling the emptiness within. He had to make do with a breakfast of crackers and suspect tuna spread.

Finished, he threw his plate in the sink and called Wef DiNaini. If anybody could advise him, it would be the old computer thief.

After listening to what had happened, Wef nodded. "Ain't much you have to know, Ale—give DPStat a call and they'll walk you through it. You're, uh, home alone today?"

"Yeah. Very much so."

Wef's eyebrows lifted, but he said nothing, for which Ale was grateful. "Make sure you got your doors locked and bolted before you take the drugs. Other'n that, don't worry about it. You'll be back in line in no time."

"Thanks, Wef. Take care, huh?" He pressed the disconnect button.

The sphere had hardly dwindled before he had punched out the number of the Directorate of Public Statistics, ID/dress Department, Erasures Division.

A middle-aged man with a round face and a somewhat harried expression answered. "Hi. Can I help you?"

"I hope so," he said. "I, um, I seem to have been erased. Is this the right number for that?"

"Yes, it is. Now. I need your full ID/dress. Not just the first five but the whole thing. Okay?"

"Sure. It's—"

"Go slow, okay?" He held up his right hand to display the bandage wrapped around his index finger. "I burned myself last night, so I can't type fast today."

"Uh . . . sorry to hear that. It's—"

"I was making cocoa, and I touched the pot."

"Well, that'll do it, won't it?" He did not know what to say in a conversation as bizarre as that. "Got to be careful with those cocoa pots, they'll get you every time. My ID/dress is—"

"Wait a minute." He bent over his keyboard. "Okay, go ahead."

"A. L. L. 8. O. A. F. A. H. S. C. N. F. F. 6."

"Right. It doesn't show." Beaming, the man looked up. His head bobbed up and down.

"Uh . . . yeah, that's the problem. Can we fix it?"

"Oh, sure! That's what I do. Now." He looked down. "Are you at 38-Q Haven Manor, New Haven, Connecticut, right now?"

"Yes, I am."

"Good." He smiled vaguely. "I'm going to send your massie a bottle. Do not open the bottle right away. Bring it back to the pholo and show it to me first. Okay? Do you understand?"

The problem with bureaucrats, Ale thought as he headed for the massie chamber, was that when they used simple words, he could never tell if it was for his benefit or for their own. Either way, it made him uneasy.

The chamber went *ding* as he reached the kitchen. *Well, at least he's quick. . . .*

He waited for the light to go out, then opened the door and picked the garish yellow bottle off the floor. About the size of a beer can, it weighed perhaps two ounces. A plastic ring was attached to its wide neck. The label, in thick letters of fire-engine red, announced it to be PROPERTY OF DIRECTORATE OF PUBLIC STATISTICS—UNAUTHORIZED POSSESSION PROHIBITED.

He carried it back to the pholo. "This is what you sent, isn't it?"

"That's the one. Now. This is important. Hold it so I can see it and take the top off."

Keeping it in camera range, he twisted off the top.

A beep sounded at the other end. "Empty it out. I have to see it, now."

He shook the huge capsule onto his left palm.

"Don't drop the bottle. Hold it by the ring so I can see it."

The container chilled the fingers of his right hand as it began to sublimate. He juggled it around until he could grasp it by its ring.

"Now the pill's going to leak out. Don't drop it, okay?"

Sure enough, the capsule had oxidized to the point where its contents spilled onto Ale's palm and began to evaporate. Purple, it was cold on his hand; cool and minty in his nose. The container had already boiled away.

"Now, your skin's going to drink up the drug. We have to wait until it does. You can let go of the ring. We don't need that any more. Remember, don't move the hand with the drug."

Cupping the splash of purple, he shook his right hand; the ring fell to the carpet.

"It'll take about fifteen seconds for the drug to soak in all the way. It's sort of boring, isn't it?" He stared at Ale's palm. As the seconds ticked by, his lips moved slightly. At last he nodded. "That should to it. How do you feel?"

"Wooden." The answer surprised him by popping out on its own—but it was accurate.

"Don't worry. You're supposed to feel that way. Now. What is your name? The whole thing, please."

His voice responded before he told it to. "A. L. L. 8. O. A. F. A. H. S. C. N. F. F. 6."

The bureaucrat's gaze flickered to a spot off-camera, presumably to a row of readouts. He nodded. "Please hold up both hands and spread the fingers out—not so high, about shoulder level will do it nicely."

Ale's hands moved immediately to the requisite position.

"Turn slowly— Stop. Hold it right there, please." He scowled. To himself he muttered, "Damn magnification always breaking down—hey, Jake! Troubles with the printreader on console sixty-three."

The other said something inaudible to Ale.

"I did too set it right. You want to see for yourself? Come here, just—" Exasperation washed over his face. "78FC, just like it says—" He slapped the top of his console. "Dammit, why the hell don't you tell a guy, huh? Is it so much trouble to update the damn manuals? All right, all right, what's the new setting? 6AF8. Got it." He reached for something out of pholo range. His upper arm moved. "Yeah, all right, that works now. Next time tell me, okay?"

In the meantime Ale waited patient as a tree, wondering idly what the fuss was about but not caring enough to ask. At the bureaucrat's next command, his body resumed its slow pirouette until it had twirled through a full circle.

"All right, sir, your fingerprints check out just fine. We're done here. It'll take us a while to get you back on-line, but everything ought to be up and running in about an hour. Okay? Do you understand me?"

"Yesss." His lips, stiff and rubbery, answered without consulting him.

"Great." He visibly caught himself. "Are you alone?"

"Yesss."

"Okay. When I say, 'Take care,' turn off your pholo, sit down in the chair you like best, and stay there for two hours. Don't go outside. Don't let anybody inside. Do you understand me?"

"Yesss."

"Okay." He smiled. "Glad we could clear this up so quickly, sir. Take care." He waved goodbye.

The pholo image dwindled. Ale's sluggish fingers reached for the controls. Before they made contact, a new picture appeared; a new voice said, "Freeze."

Ale's hand stopped; his arm hung in mid-air.

"Look at me."

His head swiveled back to the pholo sphere. A different face stared out at him. This one was long-jawed and narrow; it wore a malevolent grin. "Do not turn off your pholo."

Ale's mouth said, "Yesss."

"You will do exactly as I say, do you understand?"

"Yesss."

The stranger leaned back in his chair. "Let me confirm your identity: you are A. L. L. 8. O. A. F. A. H. S. C. N. F. F. 6?"

"Yesss."

"Fine. Let's not waste time, then. The ACLE bids you farewell: remove all your clothes, go out on your terrace, climb over the railing, and jump into the street. Do you understand?"

"Yesss."

"Then do it."

Zombie-like, Ale's body rose. His feet pivoted, then carried him to the sliding glass doors. His right hand slid the doors apart.

The wind whipped his face. The morning sun dazzled his

eyes. While his legs took one measured step forward, his fingers unbuttoned his shirt.

Across the street a teenage boy waved at him.

His fingers unbuckled his belt, let his pants fall; his legs pulled free of them.

A wolf whistle floated out over the abyss.

One foot kicked the slipper off the other, then waited to be unshod in its turn. His thumbs hooked under the waistband of his shorts and slid them down. His index fingers tugged off his socks.

The teenager shouted, "Hey! Hey!" then spun about and ran inside his own apartment.

Both of Ale's hands gripped the wroughtiron railing. The metal was cooler than the air. His right leg threw itself over the bar and straddled it. The toes of his right foot found the gritty concrete of the edge. Now his left leg would lift to pluck that foot off the flagstones to swing it up and over so it could join its twin on the outside, at which point his hands would release their hold and his knees would flex to hurl him backwards into the air.

He did wonder why.

TOP TEN NEWS STORIES OF THE HOUR

25 June 3188 0900 EDT
New England Region

RANK HEADLINE	price	LEAD SENTENCE
#1 FIDELISTAS THREATEN REBELLION	.25	In a speech immediately denounced by the ACLE as "mindless macho rhetoric," a leader of the Fidelista Sempre Party known by the *nom de guerre* of "Commandante Quatros" vowed that the ACLE's prohibition of the FSP would lead to civil war.
#2 * * * * * * **MAO/COM DISMISSES ATTACKS ON TELEBETTER**	.10	**#2 * * * * * *** A spokesrep for the Maoist/ Communist Directorate of Public Health alleged today that Australian and Zimbabwean scientists investigating the interface enhancement drug TeleBetter were "biased— they didn't develop it themselves."
#3 * * * * * * **NO MOVEMENT AT L5 AS SIXTH DAC STARSHIP ARRIVES**	.15	**#3 * * * * * *** Lunar and terrestrial observatories monitoring the Dac fleet as a sixth interstellar vessel looms up only ten million kilometers from L5 report that no member of the present armada seems to be making preparations for departure.

RANK	HEADLINE	price	LEAD SENTENCE

#4 * * * * * * *

**QUITO DAMAGE NOT .15
AS BAD AS
THOUGHT**

#4 * * * * * * *

Estimates of damage caused
by the major earthquake
that struck this Ecuadorian
city at 2047 (EDT) on 23
June have been revised
sharply downward following
on-the-scene inspections by
assessment teams from the
Muslim-Republican Party.

#5 * * * * * * *

**DAC KILLER JUMPS .10
TO HIS DEATH**

#5 * * * * * * *

A spokesrep for the ACLE
confirmed rumors that
ALL80 AFAHSC NFF6, the
New Haven Seeley who ten
days ago killed a Dac with
his bare hands, has
committed suicide; the
spokesrep said recent
marital troubles had left
ALL80 despondent.

#6 * * * * * * *

**HOLLYWOOD TO .10
MAKE HOLO OF
PSYCHIC'S
PREDICTION**

#6 * * * * * * *

A spokesrep for Universal-
Paramount confirmed this
afternoon that UP has
bought, for a sum "in the
seven-digit range," holo
rights to psychic FYG10
ACVYYG B4VU's prediction
that the Dac invaders will
abandon our system by late
2189

#7 * * * * * * *

**NYC FIRE COULD .10
HAVE BEEN
PREVENTED**

#7 * * * * * * *

Adjusters from insurance
companies liable for
$60,000,000 in casualty
losses suffered in the 15
June 8th Avenue fire say
that enforcement of any of
the parties' fire codes would
have ensured control of the
blaze within minutes.

RANK	HEADLINE	price	LEAD SENTENCE

#8 * * * * * * *

COPS CITE CLUE TO .10
LM2 SLAYINGS

#8 * * * * * * *

Lunar police have initiated a new round of interviews in their quest for the murderers of BHK30 BHXNDP JUH2, late President of Lunar Mining and Manufacturing Corp; a spokesrep for the department refused to go into detail, but did admit that new leads provoked the interviews.

#9 * * * * * * *

PORNO CHANNEL TO .10
LENGTHEN HOURS

#9 * * * * * * *

WSKIN, the blue-holo cable network, will begin providing twenty-four hour service, at no extra charge, said a spokesrep for the network this morning.

#10 * * * * * * *

EMSISO VOTED OUT .10
OF OFFICE

#10 * * * * * * *

Aid Emsiso, the former actor who attained brief prominence as a politician by relaxing privacy regulations governing the media's right to report on bureaucratic officials, was today voted out of office by disenchanted members of the CCU.

This update has been provided as a public service by all data management corporations participating in NEWSBANK/UE, a news data base organized and supervised by the Uhuru-Episcopal Directorate of Public Information.

To read any of the above news stories in full, simply highlight the title and press ACCEPT. The article will be transmitted to your unit's memory. Your bank balance will be debited by the sum in the column headed "price."

To see the headlines of the day's other news stories, simply scroll your screen up.

Thank you, and do be careful.

XXII

—1—

"Ale Elatey, you stop right where you are!"

High in the air, just about to clear the railing, his left foot froze. The muscles of his right calf immediately began to cramp. His ears ignored the whispering off-shore breeze to listen for the next command.

Not that his ears had been told to listen, of course, but implicit in any stop order is the corollary to wait. His body would obey all instructions, even if fully to understand them it had to awaken its slumbering brain.

And now his mind idled, abstractly relieved that Mrs. M'ti Emtenne had canceled the jump order. Even in standby mode his mind had wondered why his superior had issued a command that, within 4.77 seconds, would have left Ale in no condition to follow any more orders. His was not to reason why, of course, but it had seemed pointless.

"Get back on your terrace right now!"

Slowly, he lowered his foot to the sun-warmed flagstones, then returned his right leg to safety. It occurred to him that his hands hurt. He looked at them. Tendons stood up across their backs like cables; their knuckles were white. Ah. That explained it: he was squeezing the rail too hard. He reviewed the situation quickly. There seemed to be no orders to the contrary in effect, so he relaxed his grip. His hands stopped hurting.

From the next terrace over, Mrs. M'ti Emtenne said, "What in God's name is wrong with you?"

He considered her inquiry with the thoroughness it deserved. All was in order, even his hands. "Nothing."

Her jaw flapped soundlessly once, twice. She ran a hand through her unruly hair, and wrapped her terrycloth robe tighter around her. "You were getting ready to jump!"

"Yes."

She stared at him with what he recognized as exasperation.

That bothered him. He was obeying her express wishes. With what could she find fault?

A possibility suggested itself: His nudity might bother her. After all, she had not ordered it. The last boss had.

Then it occurred to him that he might be embarrassing himself, as well. It had never been his custom to stand naked before elderly women. He was not a semanticist, but it seemed to him that the syntax of "take off all your clothes and jump" did not even implicitly bid him deliberately to expose his genitals to single ladies twice his age. Therefore this was both accidental and undesired, which meant it was embarrassing. As there were no orders to the contrary in effect, he supposed it would be all right to blush.

He did.

Squinting into the morning light, Mrs. M'ti Emtenne studied his face. "You look so strange." For once he had trouble hearing her. "Your expression's so . . . so . . . I better call the cops." She snapped her fingers twice, and over her shoulder said. "Blue!" Then she looked back to Ale. "Don't you move, now."

He almost sighed with relief. That solved *that* problem. Since she had told him not to move, she clearly did not object to his nudity. Further, since she had not told him to put his clothes back on, his nakedness was now deliberate on her part, and therefore, not embarrassing to him. What wonderful news. To maintain the blush had already become a strain.

In the distance roared the engines of a blue.

—2—

He awoke in his own bed, in a cold sweat. His mind was crystal clear; his memories, sharp and humiliating. He could not believe that he had stood naked on his balcony in full view of Mrs. M'ti Emtenne. He almost wished he had jumped, after all.

It was no longer difficult to blush. Writhing, he groaned, and covered his hot cheeks with his hands.

Beside him, something squeaked.

He turned his head. The dark blue frog sharing his pillow regarded him through bright, unblinking eyes. It squeaked again.

He squinted hard, sure it would metamorphose into a twist of blanket, a crumpled shirt.

It did not.

Nor did it breathe, he noticed, and it kept its mouth shut when it squeaked. He started to sit up when it hit him: *Christ, a peeper!* Somebody had sent the mobile remote monitor into his bedroom. Somebody was watching him that very instant.

Its tiny, unwebbed fingers held an earphone, which it extended to him. The squeak came from the earphone.

He jerked away as though from a scorpion.

The earpiece squeaked again; the mobile mini hopped toward him.

He hurled himself out of bed, and landed on all fours beside it. Scrambling to his feet, he grabbed a slipper and waved it like a club.

The monitor dropped the earphone and raised its front legs into the air.

Ale panted. He had the thing at his mercy now. One quick swipe would knock its microcameras out of alignment, and probably destroy the fine tuning on its coordination. He inched forward.

The thing crossed its hands over its head and cowered.

"Oh, Christ." He tapped the slipper into the palm of his left hand, wondering if he should go ahead and smash the device or not.

Moving slowly and purposefully, the mobile twisted a little back and to the left. It extended its right hind leg. It nudged the earphone across the rumpled sheets toward Ale.

"No way. You think I'm going to stick that in my ear, you are crazy." He could imagine too many ways to booby-trap such a thing: it could utter a post-hypnotic trigger—or explode. Or an imbedded nano-laser could perform a crude pre-frontal lobotomy. Or something could set up a destructive resonance with his implant and cut him off from The Oracle. Or—but the list ran on.

The monitor knelt, and clasped its hands imploringly.

Ale stopped, then, and thought about it in a different light. The monitor had been on his pillow when he had awakened. Had it been there for a while, or had it just landed there? He thought back.

He had not come to fuzzily, ignorant of his surroundings—he had awakened with a sudden spurt of shame, a burst of self-consciousness so acute that any movement, any hint of a witness would have curled him into a ball and made him die of humiliation.

So the monitor had been squatting there for some time, waiting.

An assassination tool would have inserted the earphone by itself, while he was unconscious.

The odds were, the monitor's teller meant him no harm.

That heightened his curiosity to the point that he sighed, set down the slipper, and sat on the edge of the bed. "Okay. I'll do it." He picked up the earphone and plugged it in.

The squeak modulated down into a thin, strong voice. "Well, Jesus Christ, boy, you sure do take a lot of convincing!"

"Wef?"

"No, it's your great grandaddy, come back from the dead." He recoiled. "What?"

"Of *course* it's Wef, you idiot!"

"Hey!" He winced. "Not so loud, huh?"

"It'd serve you right if I busted out your eardrum completely."

"Wef, what's going on?" He looked around the room. The roses in the window had passed their prime; their petals were browning around the edges. All seemed real enough, but he could not shake the feeling of being in a dream. "Why are you talking to me through a monitor?"

"Without going into all the picky details, let's just say that when your name pops up on any net, anywhere, I hear about it. Speaking of which, you might consider backing up my press release stating that you're not dead yet."

He rubbed his temple. "Why would I want to do that?"

"So your friends and relatives don't send flowers."

"Huh?"

"Just take a looksee at the latest batch of newsbriefs. Seems somebody at ACLE got a bit too anxious to whitewash your cause of death."

"Oh, Jesus. . . ."

"Yeah. Well, anyway, while I was digging around trying to find out the truth, I ran into the blue's report on your little skywalk. Figured anybody could use a guardian angel, it was you. So I transmatted ol' Froggy on up to your massie, and for the next some while, you got yourself an android pet. Anything goes wrong, just shout my name real loud, I'll see what I can do."

Ale was touched. "Wef, I don't know why you're doing this—"

"Somebody's got to. You're out of your league, Ale, and somebody don't watch over you, you're a dead man."

"Thank you."

"My pleasure." The frog waved a hand negligently. A chuckle came through the earphones. "Besides, this sucker's fun to run."

Ale smiled. "Speaking of that—why don't you use the throat speaker?"

"It's broke—and to fix an unregistered remote, you have to find an unregistered repair cart. Didn't have time for all that." A note of concern crept into his voice. "This works okay, doesn't it? Guy I rented it from swore it did, and it tested out okay."

"Yeah, it works fine, Wef." He got up from the bed and started looking for his pants. They were in none of the usual places: over the chair, on the doorknob, flipped over the top of the closet door. . . . as he took another pair from the bureau, he wondered if the first pair still lay on the terrace. He would hate for a Dac to make off with his ID/dress card.

"Suggestion, Ale: Froggy ought to be right with you at all times. Whyn't you let him ride on your shoulder?"

He could almost see the picture he would present with a blue frog apparently whispering in his ear. "Are you kidding?"

"Hell, no—he won't fall off. And he's not slimy, either, if that's what you're afraid of."

"I *know* he's not slimy—androids never are. But just— I mean, can you see me opening the front door with that perched right there at eye level? Some of my neighbors'd have a heart attack on the spot."

"It's for your own protection."

"Even around the house?"

"*Especially* around the house."

"Oh, all right." He shook out a fresh shirt and slipped it on. Then he held out his hand. "Come on."

The monitor hopped for his palm. It missed—

"Oh, Jesus—"

—but caught his shirttail on the fall and hung on grimly. Wef sounded sheepish. "I, um, haven't had much time to practice."

"Don't do that again, Wef. Please?"

"I won't miss next time."

"I don't believe *any* of this." Ale headed for the kitchen for some food.

— 3 —

After lunch, he went to his study, set Froggy on the desktop, and pholoed Mrs. M'ti Emtenne. When her face appeared, he said, "I callcd to thank you."

She snorted. "Don't be silly. Anybody would have done it in my place. I just happened to be out on my lounge chair, that's all." Shc eyed his image carefully. "I read what they did to you—has it worn off now?"

"Yes," he said automatically, then stopped. "You *read* it?"

She smiled, then. "So you didn't know you were on the news again, eh? Newsbank/SD, Number Nine. You're getting to be a real celebrity, Ale."

"I'm not sure I want to be—not for that, anyway. But thank you for telling me. If you'll excuse me, I want to check out that article."

"Sure you don't want to be a celebrity." She winked. And abruptly grew serious. "I'm very glad I was there, Ale. And I hope they catch whoever did that to you. People like that shouldn't be allowed to run loose."

He nodded. "Thanks. Take care."

"You, too."

The sphere darkened when he hit the disconnect button. He reached out to flick on his computer.

BEEPEEPEEP

The OraCall triggered fear. It came out of nowhere, caught him totally by surprise. It set off a shudder so strong that for a good ten seconds he could do nothing but shake, helpless in its grip. Then he caught his breath; he set his jaw. And slipped into interface.

#Good afternoon, sir.#

ACLE hasn't threatened me enough?

#This is non-ACLE calling, Mr. Ale. To be precise, you are invited to a meeting of all Seeleys who are not part of the prcsent government.#

Oh?

#Yes.#

When does it start?

#Right now.#

Psychic presences coalesced all around him, but no voices arose. Apparently The Oracle was muting the cavern. He sat in silence, wondering what the purpose of the meeting was, hoping it would be revealed soon. It now made him nervous to be in interface. Even with Wef's monitor standing guard, his body felt incredibly vulnerable.

One person spoke. #This session is hereby called to order. I'd appreciate it if we kept things simple. We haven't got time for slavish obedience to Robert's Rules of Order and other parliamentary rigamarole. Now, I don't want to ride roughshod over anybody's rights as a CLE, but as long as I'm chairing this meeting, I'm not going to put up with any nonsense. Is that clear? Would anybody like to move that I be replaced as chairman?#

The Oracle polled the Seeleys swiftly: #Motion, sir?#

No.

#Okay. The Oracle says no motion for replacement has been made. Fine. The reason we got together is to vote on the question of whether we should strip the ACLE-government people of their tenure as Seeleys, and deny them access to The Oracle. Yes, what's the question?#

As another speaker came on-line, the internal voice became fast-paced, breathless. #That is pretty severe. What are the grounds for justifying it?#

#Conflict of interest!#

#A nice catch-phrase, but I'd prefer to hear how it applies to this specific case.#

#Oh, for God's sake, we're supposed to be in the business of finding and disseminating the truth.#

#For a fee,# said the second.

#So? Nobody works for free.#

#What, precisely, *is* the conflict of interest here?#

Impatience infused the chairman's intonation. #ACLE seems to be in the business of ruling the world. As you may have noticed, that already involves some manipulation of truth. I've got no objection to ACLE as *customers*—I mean, we'll sell knowledge to anybody—but I really don't think propagandizing politicians should have full and free access to ORA:CLE's facilities.#

A new set of speech patterns came on. #We've been monitoring this discussion, and we do rather resent your insinuations.#

#Of course you do,# said the chairman. #Your power's based on continued, uninterrupted access to The Oracle and all the data bases it links to. No wonder you're opposed to this.#

#As you said, time is too short to waste on niceties. I would only remind you that we have inherited the mechanisms forged by the Coalition—which include the ability to ah, silence? each of you.#

Ale had intended to keep quiet, but the threat changed his mind. *You have the mechanisms* only *because you have popular support—but how long will you last if the people get the proof that you lied about the Coalition and the Dacs?*

Silence hung sullen and heavy for a good forty-five seconds. Then the ACLE spokesrep came back with: #Ale Elatey, you're a dead man.#

TOP TEN NEWS STORIES OF THE HOUR

25 June 2188 1600 EDT
New England Region

RANK HEADLINE	price	LEAD SENTENCE
#1 QUITO LOOTERS AMBUSH RED CROSS	.25	Ducking Dac attacks and police fire in this quake rent, three-kilometer high Andean city, hundreds of looters jammed telemetry to a Red Cross relief convoy at 1124 (EDT) this morning, and stripped the vehicles down to their chassis.
#2 * * * * * * SIXTH DAC STARSHIP DUE IN THREE HOURS	.20	#2 * * * * * * Astronomers at lunar observatories are still predicting that the sixth Dac Starship to invade the solar system will decelerate to a halt in the L5 position seconds after 1800 (EDT) this evening.
#3 * * * * * * AMREVS SCREAM FOR ALIEN BLOOD	.15	#3 * * * * * * The leadership council of the American Revival Party today endorsed a document charging the ACLE with being the "ideological clone of the Coalition," citing in particular the ACLE's

avowed refusal to attempt to intercept the Dac ship now enroute to L5.

#4 * * * * * *   **#4** * * * * * *

ACLE URGES CALM   .10

Expressing blunt distaste for the "suicidal pseudo-heroics espoused by the Am Rev Party," a spokesrep for the ACLE today restated her party's policy of not provoking "aliens who can melt the continents and boil away the seas."

#5 * * * * * *   **#5** * * * * * *

DAC KILLS   .10
JOHANNESBURG
TRADER

A fifty-nine-year-old businessman became the Johannesburg area's fourth Dac victim this year, as a result of an 1145 EDT attack.

#6 * * * * * *   **#6** * * * * * *

AUSSIE OUTBACK UP   .10
IN SMOKE

Brush fires fanned by gale-force winds have consumed close to a thousand square miles of arid outback; the first CD/DPS fire-fighting team has yet to arrive on the scene.

#7 * * * * * *   **#7** * * * * * *

LUNAR COPS SEIZE   .10
LM2 VP AS
MURDERESS

Lunar police confirmed this afternoon that they are holding PKU40 AINQYK RAXO, Vice-President of the Lunar Mining & Manufacturing Corp. and heir-apparent to the slain BHK30 BHXNDP JUH2; unnamed sources within the department are quoted as saying, "We've got everything but the motive."

#8 * * * * * *		#8 * * * * * *

#8 * * * * * *

THOUSANDS STARVE ON MAUI   .10

#8 * * * * * *

Social-Tech relief teams have arrived on this picturesque Pacific island too late to save thousands of Hawaiians from the effects of a program glitch that temporarily re-routed all supply ships away from Maui.

#9 * * * * * *

DAC KILLER ALIVE   .10

#9 * * * * * *

With a quotation from Mark Twain, New Havener ALL80 AFAHSC NFF6 denied today reports that he had committed suicide; ALL80 was not available for further comment.

#10 * * * * * *

AID EMSISO TO STAR IN HOLO OF PSYCHIC'S PREDICTION   .10

#10 * * * * * *

A spokesrep for Universal-Paramount confirmed this afternoon that Aid Emsiso, former ho-soap star recently trounced in a CCU election, has agreed to play the lead in UP's production of FYG10 ACVYYG B4VU's prediction that the Dacs will flee the solar system by the end of 2189.

This update has been provided as a public service by all data management corporations participating in NEWSBANK/SD, a news data base organized and supervised by the Social-Democratic Directorate of Public Information.

To read any of the above news stories in full, simply highlight the title and press ACCEPT. The article will be transmatted to your unit's memory. Your bank balance will be debited by the sum in the column headed "price."

To see the headlines of the day's other news stories, simply scroll your screen up.

Thank you, and do be careful.

XXIII

Dac in hot pursuit, a blue thundered down the street, streaking past Ale's apartment at terrace level, its jets roaring. Startled, he dropped a screw, and had to dismount the stepladder to hunt for it. With his luck, it had probably rolled under the half-finished grow-wall, and would have to be teased out with a pair of chopsticks.

He knew he should have attached the base trim first.

A second blue whipped by his window, traveling in the same direction as the first, moving so quickly that he saw it as a blur. The doors to the terrace rattled in their frames.

He went to look out; something hard and small crunched underfoot. The screw. He bent to pick it up.

By the time he straightened again, a newscaster stared out of the hovee cube. Her lips moved, but the blue's fading rumble drowned out her words.

"Volume up one," he called sharply.

"—orders to arrest on sight all policymakers of the present regime. The three parties urged civil service employees to stay on the job, pending next week's constitutional convention, which will determine the shape of the next world government. In that regard, the parties have agreed that delegate slots will be apportioned to all extant parties on the basis of membership, with individual delegates to be elected by popular vote of the members."

Her gaze flicked from the prompter back to the cameras; a smile spread across her face. "The three parties have also issued an urgent public appeal for information pertaining to the ID/dresses of the ACLE policymakers. Apparently no one is sure who they are. In other news—"

The hovee marbled black and green.

His earphone *click*ed.

He turned. The mechanical frog hopped across the floor,

intent on keeping him in sight. At every hop the earphone *click*ed. Probably a very subtle short in there. Probably drive him crazy before the day ended. . . .

He scooped it off the carpet, stared into its impassive face, then gave a sigh and put it on his shoulder. Its cold feet groped for purchase.

"Ale."

"Yes, Wef?"

"I thought you ought to know—ACLE's on the warpath."

"That's not surprising." He started to recount the news brief he had just seen.

"Yeah, I caught it. But what she didn't say was that ACLE's got hold of some blues—and the AySeeley's are telling them themselves. They're going after all the Seeleys who voted them out of ORA:CLE, and after damn near every political figure who's said anything against them. What I hear is, they've got about a hundred thousand ID's on a bust-list. Yours is one of 'em."

"Oh, thanks." He sat on the arm of the sofa. "That's not surprising, either, but it's not very encouraging. . . ."

The old man laughed.

"For a guardian angel you're real short on sympathy, Wef."

"No, no, see, that's the bad news. The good news is these AySeeleys don't know jackshit about telling a blue, and they have apparently wrecked something like fifty of them already. In three hours."

Ale frowned. It was, of course, good to hear that ACLE's vaunted efficiency did not extend to manipulating the police vehicles, but . . . but few tele-factors who wrecked devices while interfaced with them emerged wholly sane. He could take no pleasure from the thought of brain-burned scholars.

"Wef, how many arrests have they actually made?"

The other's voice sobered abruptly. "A couple hundred, at least. And more every minute."

"Seeleys?"

"Mostly politicians. I have to confess that don't bother me too much."

"Those politicians are the only ones willing to go after ACLE, Wef."

"Just a bunch of good ole boys dying to help mankind, huh, Ale?"

"No!" It came out sharper than he meant. "Just a bunch of

self-serving types who might, if I'm lucky, put ACLE behind bars before it can kill me."

Wef said, "That, too," and fell silent.

Ale felt restless. Surely he had something more momentous to do than construct a grow-wall. The century's greatest power struggle was raging all around him; surely he should be in there fighting for truth and justice and everything else he professed to believe in. But how? He paced the length of the living room, stopped at the front door, about-faced, did it again.

Wait. He had the Dac gun. With that in his hand, he could hold any AySeeley until the law arrived. So he would take it, track down....

Ah, yes, he thought, *there's the rub.*

Unless.... Dropping into a chair, he closed his eyes and found interface. *Hey, Oracle.*

#Good afternoon, sir. Let me advise you in advance that ACLE is trying to jam my transmissions. Their efforts result in static surges—not harmful, but apparently alarming to those who experience them. Was there something you wanted?#

The AySeeleys who just got expelled—are they covered by your anonymity program?

#Yes.#

So you won't release their ID/dresses?

#Nor will I release yours, as they have been demanding for hours, now.#

They know mine, already.

#I used "yours" to denote the plural.#

For a moment he wondered if he could do anything. But no, The Oracle-in-the-middle's programming was as close to being tamperproof as anything could get. *Yeah.* He prepared to release his grip on interface. *Thanks anyway.*

#You're welcome.#

As he reentered reality, another idea occurred to him— something along the lines of the BACKGROUND program the Coalition's Directorate of Public Data Banks had been working on.

"Hey, Wef!"

Almost immediately, the earphone said, "Trouble?" The frog on Ale's shoulder swiveled its head from side to side.

"No, just—" His hovee went dark. "Damn."

Wef's voice rose an octave. "Ale, what's wrong, I don't see any danger—"

The old man's panic embarrassed him. He wondered if the

monitor's cameras could pick up his blush. "Easy, Wef. Everything's okay. I was calling 'cause I had an idea, but then the hovee blew a laser or something—"

"That's not your set, it's ACLE. That list I told you 'bout, with a hundred thousand ID/dresses? They got a program running to crash the systems of everybody on that list."

Startled, he hurried to his ibn Daoud. "Trash my system?" He ran his hand over the keyboard. "Did they burn it out, what did they do to it?"

"I said 'crash'! It's going to cold-boot itself every two minutes unless you erase the program—look for it in your directory under the filename STATE. Once you delete it, you're safe—as long as you're not linked to any major network."

"But I am!" His fingers flew over the smooth plastic keys.

"That's what I thought. You're going to have to disconnect. STATE is loose on all the networks now. ACLE's trying to keep the opposition from getting organized."

Once he had deleted the program, he unplugged the ibn Daoud's jack to the gateway device that had made his machine one node in the ST Network. It was, he realized, the first time in nearly ten years he had been so isolated.

Suddenly he shivered. He grew more isolated by the day. Emdy was gone, Wef had returned home, L'ai avoided him—ACLE had threatened to kill him!—and now he had cut himself off from the public data banks, the emergency warning system, everything. His only link to the outside world lay imbedded in his skull, a little behind his right temple: his ORA:CLE implant.

He rubbed it thoughtfully. Then snapped his fingers. "Wef, I almost forgot the reason I called."

"What's that?"

"Well, the first problem in dealing with the AySeeleys is finding them, right? Remember that BACKGROUND program the Coalition was writing?"

"Sure. What about it?"

"Well, I was thinking you could adapt it to identify the ACLE people."

The old man's voice sounded skeptical. "How?"

"Simple." He found himself craning his neck awkwardly to look into the monitor's glass eyes. He picked it up, set it on top of the ibn Daoud's case, and talked directly to it. "Well, not really simple. But I just remembered that when Yuai Bethresicks came here—" God, it seemed a century ago that the Coalition Agent had been there. Maybe longer. "—when he came, he knew I was a Seeley. Said it was in my ID/dress file."

"Maybe it was, but so what?" Wef made the monitor shrug.

"If you get a program that pulls Seeleys out of the ID/dress banks—"

"Ale, I'm a Ninety, not a Ninety-nine. I don't have that kind of access."

"Yuai was only a Thirty-six—and you've got to be able to get that high."

A sigh whistled through the earphones. "Yeah, I can. . . . But do you know how long'll it'll take to search even one billion records?"

"Start with the Nineties and work your way down—most Seeleys are pretty high up in public grant time."

A snort, as if in self-reproach. "Uh-huh. But that still doesn't give us AySeeleys."

"Here's where BACKGROUND comes in. Use it to compile bios and bibliographies of every Seeley the first program finds. Oh, make sure the first one kicks the ID/dresses out as it selects them—we can't afford to wait, and the rest of it goes easier if we work with them one by one, anyway."

"The rest of it?" Wef said warily.

"Listen. Next comes a semantic analysis of every Seeley's publications, to set up a linguistic profile for each one. At the same time it's doing the same thing for the public pronouncements of the top dogs in ACLE. Link the profiles with the known physical facts on each side—age, sex, race, the like— then cross-analyze the two lists. Bingo! You've got them identified."

"Ale," said Wef in disbelieving tones, "you got any idea how long this is going to take to write, not even mentioning how long it'd take to run?"

"Wef, I know it's going to take forever for the whole thing to run, but it should turn up some ID's, at least, almost immediately."

"You're crazy, boy! Absolutely crazy!"

"Would it be easier—or quicker—to try to crack The Oracle?"

The frog stayed immobile, but the earphones groaned. "You got a point there, Ale, you got a definite point . . . all right, I'll give it a try."

"Thanks, Wef." He let out his breath with a whoosh, and

only then realized he had been holding it. "If there's anything I can do to help—"

"It'll surprise hell out of both of us." The old man muttered to himself a bit. "Look, you've got two machines up there, so I'll be sending you up some stuff and you can run it for me."

"No problem. Any time you're ready."

"Yeah, right. Later."

—2—

The announcer looked worried. A glistening thread of sweat threatened the integrity of his makeup. His voice had faint ragged edges. "Six major American public networks have crashed since 1:00 p.m. this afternoon. The Marian-Vegetarian Southeast Regional Network has been brought back on line, but the other five remain out of operation. Social-Tech party leaders have already accused the Association of Computer-Linked Experts of sabotaging their San Diego Network in an attempt to disrupt communications between the party and its faithful. The Greater Houston heat wave has claimed fourteen lives since the Muslim-Republican Texas Network went down at 2:57 p.m."

Deeply troubled, Ale waved the set off. It was monstrous that a power struggle could deprive people trapped in a Texas heat wave of air-conditioning. The builders of a lot of those skyrises had permanently sealed the windows. Did no one care that old women were baking to death?

The earphone said, "You awake there, boy?"

"Yeah, Wef, wide awake and waiting."

"Good. Hook the little guy—the ibn Daoud in your office?—to the pholo. *Not* to the network outlet—jack it into the pholo. I'll comm some stuff on up to you."

For the cables to reach, he had to move the pholo controls to the middle of his office floor, but in five minutes he stood up and dusted his hands off. "All set, Wef."

"Observant, aren't you?"

"What do you mean?"

"Look at your screen."

He walked over to the ibn Daoud. The status line said RECEIVING CROSSMATCH. "How'd you know I was ready?"

The monitor waved a froggy hand.

"Ah. Of course." He shrugged. "So what have I got here?"

"You can't get onto the network 'cause STATE's still loose. We're gonna use this little guy as a receiving station; it'll comm stuff over to the big guy in the living room, which'll run CROSSMATCH."

"And CROSSMATCH is—?"

"The one that compares a single identified Seeley's linguistic profile with the linguistic profiles of all known Ay-Seeleys. Got me two machines down here compiling the profiles right now. CROSSMATCH is one bitch of a program, though; haven't got room to run that one, too. Your ibn Daoud'll do it nice. Oh, yeah, something else: I got to thinking about holograms."

Ale frowned. "Holograms?"

"Far as Seeleys go, you're a little some strange—most of 'em have a real thing about anonymity. Struck me that some of those public addresses on the hovee mighta featured holographic facades, if you know what I mean."

"Yes." He chewed thoughtfully on a thumbnail. "Yes, I know exactly what you mean. Synthesized voices, too, probably.... Will that screw us up?"

"Heh-heh-heh." Through the earphone came a sound that could only be Wef puffing happily on a fat cigar. "It could have, if ole Wef hadn't been on the job. But I figured that these folks might use electronic stand-ins, and they might use synvoice, but they are probably going to stick to their own words. Doubt if they'd go as far as hiring speech writers. That comes later."

"Okay, Wef, I give up. What'd you do?"

"The profiles come in two parts—call 'em 'A' and 'B'. 'A' is physical characteristics, 'B' is lingo. The program's set up so that the better the match between the linguistic traits, the more it ignores the physical. Get over a seventy-five percent linguistic profile match here, and it's gonna kick that ID/dress out as a probable AySeeley even if the ID belongs to a black Australian male and the hovee speech was supposedly given by a blonde female from Helsinki."

"Okay, good, so what do I do at this end?"

"Cable your two machines together, comm CROSSMATCH over to the one in the living room, delete it from the one in the den, which you should then set up to receive from me, then just sit back. CROSSMATCH is going to look for its raw data on the little guy. Oh, yeah—you want a record of these

ID/dresses you can use before the program's finished, get your printer set to run. CROSSMATCH'll write them to bubble, of course, but you won't be able to get at that file till it's all over. Got it?"

"Got it." He set about doing it. It took less than fifteen minutes. Then he stepped back and told the watching frog, "Hey, Wef! It's all set at this end."

"High time," said the grumbly voice. "The first batch of Seeleys is on its way."

The ibn Daoud operated in absolute silence. He stood before it, staring at its blank CRT screen, willing it to yield results right then. It gave him no hint at all, not even a click, before the first letters burned across its top line. He leaned forward, heart racing.

"BCM99 SSQABP RADO. Best match on A: eighteen percent. Best match on B: eleven percent. Composite best match: twelve percent. Rating: No."

"Damn," he said softly, "Hey, Wef!"

Perhaps fifteen seconds later, the old man said, sleepily, "Now what?"

"It just processed—and rejected—an ID/dress, but it didn't print it."

"For folks in Category No, all you'll get is a screenprint. You're going to get hardcopy on all Category Maybes and all Category Yesses."

He nodded. "Sophisticated nomenclature, Wef."

"Hey, nothing but the best, Ale, and don't you forget it. Now let me get back to my nap. Call me, you got a problem."

"Will do. Take care."

"You, too."

He stared at the screen a little longer. Another rejected possibility stretched out along the second line. He yawned. And went back to work on the grow-wall.

An hour passed in a stillness broken only by his occasional grunts, and the soft chime of metal tools on tubing. Then the printer clicked.

Dropping his wrench, he scrambled to his feet.
BEEPEEPEEPEEP
What rotten timing. He closed his eyes. *Yes?*
#Yes, sir?#
What is it?
#What is what, sir?#
You called.

#No, sir.#

He rejected the notion that he could have imagined the OraCall—it was more than a sound, it was a physical sensation. Sudden fear washed over him. *Run diagnostics on my implant, please.*

#Certainly.#

In his mind's eye, two columns of numerals scrolled past. The paired entries matched each other perfectly from top to bottom.

#I read it as one hundred percent, sir.#

Yeah, he said glumly, *me, too.*

#Will there be anything else?#

No, not right now, thank you.

#Very good, sir. Do be careful.#

He broke interface and shook his head. Strange. Worrisome. But uninitiated OraCalls did occur—random noise plagued every electronic system, even the best. As a Seeley, he had to live with it.

He headed for the printer, once more eager to find out whether CROSSMATCH had kicked out a probable or a definite AySeeley.

BEEPEEPEEPEEPEEP

Hey!

#Sir?#

What's going on?

#Did I call you again?#

Yes, dammit, you did.

#I regret to say it's not me, sir. Shall we run diagnostics again?#

Ah—

BEEPEEPEEPEEPEEP—

This time, it did not stop.

—3—

BEEPEEPEEPEEPEEP

The noise was driving him crazy. An unbroken, unvarying sound, no matter how loud, will eventually fade into the background, even if it continues to drown out other noises, and even if it begins to cause physical damage.

The OraCall would not fade.

BEEPEEPEEPEEPEEP

ORA:CLE, Inc. had hired some of the cleverest audiologists in the world to design a sound that one could not ignore, no matter what.

BEEPEEPEEPEEPEEP

Forty-five minutes of an unignorable sound is far, far worse than bamboo shoots under the fingernails, to pick an example at random.

BEEPEEPEEPEEPEEP

For one thing, bamboo shoots under the fingernails do not totally mute the rest of the world.

BEEPEEPEEPEEPEEP

The damn OraCall submerged even The Oracle.

BEEPEEPEEPEEPEEP

He sat at Emdy Ofivo's desk. Through waves of physi-physical pain, he punched out the emergency services pholo number. Only when he had tapped the last digit did he realize that the system did not work.

Mind dulled, he stared blankly at the wall. The New Haven area pholo nets had to be down. He could wait for them to come back up—but that might take hours. Days, even. Bringing a network up was a complicated business.

BEEPEEPEEPEEPEEP

Oh God it hurt!

BEEPEEPEEPEEPEEP

He could barely think.

The monitor hopped onto the desktop, turned about to face him, and waved its tiny arms wildly.

BEEPEEPEEPEEPEEP

Ale said, "What?"

It touched the tip of one finger to the side of its flat head.

BEEPEEPEEPEEPEEP

He did not understand what it meant. "Wef." God it was hard to talk. The damn OraCall blew the words out of his head before his tongue could get a grip on them. It made holding a thought like flying a kite without a string.

BEEPEEPEEPEEPEEP

The monitor leaped for his shoulder, tugged his earlobe, and gently tapped the earphone.

BEEPEEPEEPEEPEEP

But he understood. Apparently Wef was trying to talk to him. The OraCall masked him, though. Ale could not hear a word the old man was saying.

BEEPEEPEEPEEPEEP

In short, broken sentences punctuated by gasps and sobs, he tried to explain what was happening. The agony was breaking him. Tears streamed down his face. He squeezed the edge of the desktop with both hands. They wanted so badly to scrape at the implant, to rake, to dig until they had torn it out, that it took all his strength to keep them away.

BEEPEEPEEPEEPEEP

His vision was fading, now, blurred by tears, constricted by pain. He sat in the deskchair and rocked back and forth. He had to do something, and quickly, or the OraCall would kill him.

BEEPEEPEEPEEPEEP

He knew, then, with a sudden sick certainty, that he would survive only if the implant were removed.

BEEPEEPEEPEEPEEP

And then it came to him: salvation lay three floors up, in L'ai Aichtueni's skilled hands. She was a doctor. She had a medi-kit. She should be able to perform an emergency operation.

He shoved himself to his feet. Beyond the pain—between the pain—the promise of relief ebbed and surged across his mind, soothing, then laying bare. The promise, like the pain itself, was so overpowering that when it came, he could do nothing but experience it; its intensity washed away everything but the—

BEEPEEPEEPEEPEEP

Racked by waves of paralysis, he made his halting way into the hall. He stumbled to the elevator, and pressed his cheek against the smooth cool metal of the doors while he waited for them to open. He staggered inside it, and the OraCall blared so loud that he could barely remember what button to push.

BEEPEEPEEPEEPEEP

On the forty-first floor, a stranger held the door for him while he shuffled out of the elevator. L'ai's apartment was to his right, twenty or thirty meters down. He walked with one hand on the wall for support, and peered blindly at the numbers as he passed them.

BEEPEEPEEPEEPEEP

He rang the bell.

BEEPEEPEEPEEPEEP

She opened the door with a puzzled frown. "I thought I told you—"

He could not hear her; he could only watch her lips and

hope to understand. "Help." Oh God it was killing him! He made feeble noises, and for a moment could not quite remember why he was there.

"I'm busy." She made to close the door.

He held up a hand. "No. I need— Please, for God's sake help—"

She cut him off with a curt, "You're a drunken loser and I don't help either of that kind." She slammed the door in his face.

The return trip seemed to take hours. His door did not recognize his voice, so distorted was it by pain. He had to punch the code, and it had been so long that he could not remember, he could only pound helplessly on the paneling until Wef's monitor somehow convinced the system to let him in.

He fell inside, onto the parquet floor of the vestibule. Pushing himself onto hands and knees, he lifted his head. A breeze from the open sliding glass doors laved his face, but did not heal him. Dimly, he wondered why they were open. He should close them. His head hurt too badly.

Sobbing, he hauled himself into the kitchen. He reached up and yanked open a drawer. Silverware showered on his head, clattered to the floor. He selected from the glittering array the shortest, sharpest knife of all. If L'ai would not cut the implant out, he would.

His hand shook as he lifted the blade to his temple.

The massie chamber door swung open.

Through it stepped a Dac—holding a gun.

TOP TEN NEWS STORIES OF THE HOUR

25 June 2188 1200 EDT
New England Region

RANK HEADLINE	price	LEAD SENTENCE
#1 DAC ARRIVES ON SCHEDULE; REINFORCEMENTS, NOT REPLACEMENTS	.25	The sixth Dac ship to in the system in the last si years pulled into its L5 s within seconds of the ET predicted by astronomer initial reports indicate n of its predecessors maki ready to leave.
#2 * * * * * * *		#2 * * * * * *

This update has been provided as a public service by all data agement corporations particpating in NEWSBANK/MC, a news base organized and supervised by the Maoist-Communist Direct of Public Information.

To read any of the above news stories in full, simply highlig title and press ACCEPT. The article will be transmatted to your memory. Your bank balance will be debited by the sum in the co headed "price."

To see the headlines of the day's other news stories, simply your screen up.

Thank you, and do be careful.

XXIV

—1—

The Dac leveled its gun at Ale's chest. He shrank back. Instinct surviving even agony, he raised his hands.

The OraCall cut off. Abrupt silence hit like a sledge. His knees buckled, but held. A last shred of pride forbade genuflection to his executioner.

Wef's voice in his hear said, "Holy Sweet Jesus!"

The Dac squawked once, and waved the gun.

He could not tear his gaze from its eyes. A thought came to him, slowly, rising to his consciousness like a bubble through molasses: *I should do something.* . . . But he was too tired; his head, too sore. He waited for the Dac to act, and he watched in numb fascination.

It tapped something on its torso. A metal something clipped to its harness.

Ale squinted, unintentionally leaning forward and provoking the Dac into brandishing its weapon more fiercely.

But it had tapped a second, holstered gun. How odd. In every picture he had ever seen, the alien carried only one gun. Why did this one have two? Especially when it had but one holster.

With its free hand, it fumbled in a cloth pouch hanging from its harness. A moment later the hand emerged holding a dull, translucent—

Ale's stomach turned.

—beak.

"What's going on?" It came out hoarse and whispery.

The Dac laid the beak on the counter. It nodded. It touched a red oval button on its belt. Something in its assortment of gear went *click*.

It's taking my picture?

It pressed the button again, then edged past him. Turning as it moved, it kept him covered the entire time. He did not breathe.

It slipped around the corner and disappeared.

Trembling, he lowered his hands. The breath whooshed out of him. Sweat glued his shirt to his back; his pulse roared in his ears. Silence rang in his skull like a bell.

From the living room came the rumblehissclick of closing terrace doors.

Only then did he realize that the Dac had reclaimed the gun he had taken for his own.

"Holy Sweet Jesus," said Wef. "You are a lucky sumbitch, you know that?"

"Lucky?" One semi-hysterical laugh flew out of his mouth— one laugh only, because it would hurt too much to repeat it. "Lucky?"

"Yeah. All that and you're still alive."

He sagged against the sink. Slowly, he said, "You do have a point. . . ."

"Message for you from The Oracle."

He frowned; at the flash of pain he hurriedly smoothed out his forehead. "The Oracle is contacting me through you now?"

"It didn't want to use the OraCall."

"That was thoughtful."

"Yeah. To paraphrase: Somebody slipped in the program that made it call you like that. It located the program and deleted it. It apologizes."

"Oh, yeah, right."

"Well, it does."

"Big deal, an apology from a switchboard." Ale snapped his fingers. "The printout!" He started for the living room.

The monitor followed in small hops. "What printout?"

Over his shoulder he said, "The implant started beeping just when CROSSMATCH was printing out the first ID/dress." Standing by the printer, he tore off the top sheet of fanfold paper and raised it high so he could read—

He gasped. "Ohe Ainainine is the number one AySeeley?"

"WHAT?"

At Wef's bellow, his head twinged. His knees weakened; he moved to the couch and collapsed. The last Director of the Coalition was now head of the ACLE? Had led a revolution against herself? He held the paper in shaking hands. "That's what it says, Wef."

"Ain't no way!" The monitor hopped onto the sofa cushion beside him. "Some kind of bug—"

That was deflating, but more likely. After all, Ale himself

had feared that the program would not work—until it began running. At that point he had just leaped to the conclusion that what worked at all, worked perfectly. With a sigh, he said, "Yeah, I suppose you're right . . . damn, all that sweat for nothing!" He shook his head. "But why would it kick out her ID/dress?"

"Uh. . . ." The earphone pulsed gentle static. "Well, she's got a string of publications, right? It must have compared them— No, 'cause first it searched the Nineties for ID/dresses of Seeleys. It only did profiles on those people. And CROSSMATCH wouldn't run without a profile. . . ." The old man sounded genuinely puzzled. "Ale, I'm afraid she *has* to be a Seeley."

"But that's crazy! I mean, if this is right—" He waved the paper, now wrinkled from his clutch, at the monitor. "If this is right, she threw herself out of office!"

The monitor lifted its small blue shoulders in a shrug. The earphone said, "Why don't you pholo her up and ask her?"

"Hah!" But then he blinked. "Hold on. I can call her—but I need more than this. You can get into her files. Check. See if she is really listed as a Seeley."

"And if she is?"

He relaxed on the couch and smiled. "If she is—" Picking up the monitor, he put it on his lap and stroked its back. "If she is, you can pop that news item into the data banks. It'd probably be enough to close ACLE down completely. And you'd make about a billion dollars, I'd guess. . . ."

—2—

He must have fallen asleep, because he came to with a start at the voice in the earphone: "She is a Seeley, Ale! I have all the proof we need." The old man chuckled. "And the royalties are already rolling in. ACLE's gonna be on the street by nightfall—the ones who aren't in jail, that is."

"Huh?" Blinking, he stretched out his arms and arched his spine. It sounded like he was cracking his knuckles. "Jail?"

"Yeah, somebody from the Social-Tech party's going to get in touch with you; you'll give it the names and addresses on your printer. They'll take it from there. So, you going to talk to her?"

"I suppose." He rubbed his eyes, and yawned. "At this stage, though, is it for anything more than historical interest?"

"Um. . . ." Wef sounded embarrassed. "Well, there is still one censorship program—thought I had 'em all, but I just tripped over this—and it's absolutely buried where no one can find it, and—"

"And you want some clues as to how to get rid of it, right?"

"Sure. The only other option is to set loose some sort of virus program that'll not only delete any censorship program it runs into, but will reproduce itself so you can't erase *it*, and that ain't very elegant."

"All right, I'll talk to her." He punched her number into his pholo.

Her familiar features filled the pholo sphere within seconds. "Oh," she said dully. "Ale Elatey."

"Yes. Look. You're losing your power now, right?" He leaned forward. "But this Chinese puzzle of censorship programs you set up to stay in power is still running. Or at least one of them is. It's not going to help you any more, and you might as well tell me how to get at it."

Her eyes widened. "Not a chance."

He sighed. "Come on. I'm going to put Wef DiNaini on it, and he'll get rid of it eventually—you know he will."

She paled, but said nothing.

"Why make him work harder? What's it to you?"

Apparently about to speak, she clenched her teeth together. Her jaw muscles stood out.

"Please. Be reasonable. If anything, the program's going to protect the people who are on their way to arrest you. Why do you want to help them?"

"You're a madman," she said quietly, though not calmly. "You are a miserable little Eighty and you will not listen to your betters. I will tell you once, and only once: Do not put Wef DiNaini on this. Let it go. Leave it alone."

He shook his head. "I'm sorry. I can't."

"Very well," she said, bringing the antique pistol into view for the first time and raising it to her temple, "let it be on your head."

She pulled the trigger.

—3—

Five minutes passed, at least, before Wef's whisper came into his ear: "Holy Sweet Jesus!"

Ale's own voice shook. "Wef, I never—"

"It's not your fault. I don't know what the hell she was covering up, but it had to be something pretty awful." He paused, cleared his throat, then said, "Wanna find out what it was?"

"How?"

"I have that virus program ready to run."

He rolled his head back and stared at the ceiling. Ainainine was dead. ACLE was being overthrown even as he sat there. Finding whatever secret she had killed herself to protect would neither help the revolution nor harm anything but her reputation. Whether she had looted the Coalition treasury, or had had a kinky fondness for horses, was now a matter of historical interest. So why should he bother?

Because he was a historian, of course.

And because she had tried to kill him too many times.

He sat up. "Do it, Wef."

"Okay. Program's reading in, now. It'll be a while before—"

BEEPEEPEEP

Reflexively he jumped, and touched his hands to his temples.

"Ale! What is it?"

The OraCall did not repeat, and he relaxed. "The Oracle's calling. Hold on." Sitting back down, he closed his eyes. *Yes?*

#Hello, sir. I now have the answer to your question of 16 June 2188. Would you prefer it verbally, or shall I hold it in storage for you?#

Question? He frowned. *What question?*

#You asked me why the Coalition was trying to kill you. At the time, I could not access certain facts that are now available to me. I have the answer. Would you like to hear it?#

Hell, yes!

#Put briefly, you knew that Tan Wang Ch'i's great-great-grandson developed, in the early twenty-first century, the theoretical mathematics necessary to build a device capable of causing even a relatively small star to go nova.#

So? That's common knowledge—in my field, at least.

#Not any more, sir.#

Don't be— He caught himself. He swallowed hard. *Are you saying that I'm the only person alive who knows that?*

#Until someone else conducts extensive research on Tan

Wang Chi, or on early twenty-first century astro-mathe-physicists, yes, sir.#

He shook his head, stunned. There must have been hundreds, maybe thousands of people who had known....*But I don't understand. Why was it so important?*

#Because the Coalition had found a way of using Tan Liu Lan's theories to help destroy the Dacs.#

He sat up straight. *You're kidding!* A monstrous thought occurred to him. A ridiculous question, but it had to be asked. *They weren't planning to blow up the sun, were they?*

#Oh, no, sir.#

He let out a sigh of relief.

#It was Jupiter they had in mind.#

—4—

The Special Assistant to the Director of the Coalition of Public Directorates had written the Project JoveStar Prospectus six years previously, just after the announcement of the Unilateral Cease Fire. For nearly that long it had lain undisturbed, known to three individuals at most. Thousands had died so that it could lie undisturbed. Now it scrolled by on his screen.

"Human-piloted bubble ships have proven themselves capable of penetrating the electronic defensive perimeter around the Dac craft. Their disadvantage is that one bubble ship cannot carry ordnance sufficient to cripple a Dac vessel. Successful strikes on the Dac starships have, to date and on average, provoked, in retaliation, the complete and total destruction of one medium-sized city and 10^6 km^2 of farmland per successful strike—*not* per ship struck. Computer simulations indicate that twelve successful strikes are required completely to destroy one Dac starship. Computer simulations further indicate that to overwhelm the Dac defenses and permit us to destroy both of their starships in one swift engagement would require the simultaneous launch of 500 bubble ships, $+/-$ 27. The simulations conclude that despite the simultaneity of the attack, better than fifty percent of the world's farmland would be reduced to slag before the attack succeeded."

A cold, dead feeling ran up Ale's spine. Half the farmland gone? How many would starve? Two billion? Five billion?

The report continued. "The simulations suggest that the only possibility of a victory other than Pyrrhic exists at a moment of maximum confusion for the invaders. *Nothing we have tried has induced confusion within the enemy ranks.* The Astrophysics Department, however, insists that such a moment can be created by using the Tan equations on the planet Jupiter, causing it, in effect, artificially to go nova. *As long as the initial shock wave takes the Dac fleet by surprise,* a massive bubble ship attack, coordinated with the arrival of that shock wave, will produce the desired results without provoking intolerable retaliation."

Ale leaned back and closed his eyes. Yes, he could visualize the electro-magnetic pulse of the shock wave obliterating the instruments on the Dac starships, leaving them vulnerable to an onslaught of thousands of bubble ships. And he thought he began to see the reason for all the censorship.

"There are certain problems," said the report, "in implementing the strategy outlined above. (1) The Astrophysics Department estimates that even using mass transmitters to get Lunar-built equipment out to the Jovian moons, the project will take eight years. (2) Eight years hence, the Space Force must be ready (a) to mobilize 1500 bubble ship pilots on two weeks notice, and (b) to put 500 of them into the air within seconds of the shock wave's arrival. (3) The attack will fail in its ultimate objective if the Dacs hide from the shock wave in the shadow of the moon. *Our only hope of success lies in this taking the Dacs by surprise.* While their onboard instruments may be sophisticated enough to detect the changes that AD maintains will precede Jupiter's ignition, it is reasonable to assume that they have not come to Earth in order to undertake astrophysical research. They might well be looking elsewhere at the crucial moment. (4) We must assume the Dacs are monitoring as many of our broadcasts as is within their technical capability. (5) It is, therefore, imperative that the Coalition and the public give the Dacs no warning of the imminence of their destruction. Complete censorship must be maintained, no matter what the cost."

Suddenly Ale groaned. *This* was why the Coalition had tried to kill him. Why ACLE had ordered him to maintain the censorship programs.

Because if news of Project JoveStar got into the data banks— as it would if any gambler with an eye for a few million dollars learned of it—and if the Dacs were, indeed, monitoring—then much of the planet's surface would be baked to a crisp. And at least half the race would die of famine.

And Wef DiNaini had just eliminated the last censorship program.

He turned to the monitor. "Hey, Wef!"

The earphone said, "What now, Ale? I'm busy."

"Can you call off that virus program? And get the censors back on line?"

"No, and no, and what the hell's the matter with you anyway?"

"You can't stop it? C'mon, Wef, you can think of a way."

"Uh-uh. Nope. I'd have to crash the entire system to purge this sucker. And even then it's probably bubbled itself somewhere, so it'd show up again as soon as that memory came back on-line." His voice changed, then. "Just why is it you want the censor-eater out of the way, boy?"

"Oh, Christ, Ale.... Look. I'm going to send you a document. If it goes public, you can figure most of the human race is dead in a couple hours. After reading it, maybe you'll think of something. I'll get back to you. I've got to talk to The Oracle."

"Sure, Ale." Puzzlement infused the other's voice. "I'll let you know what I think."

He slipped into interface immediately after transmatting a copy of the document to Wef. *Hey, Oracle!*

#Yes?#

Project JoveStar—will it work?

#It should, yes.#

When will it be ready to go?

#Four years from today, plus or minus eighteen days, twelve hours.#

He grimaced. *Can we keep it a secret that long?*

#Not one chance in a billion, sir.#

How long do we have?

#Five days, plus or minus six.#

He froze. *You mean somebody might already have it?*

#Precisely.#

Does someone have it?

#I don't know, sir. And I am not programmed to find out.#

Christ . . . is there any way to keep it out of the data banks?

#Now there is only one way, sir. Shut down the networks completely.#

—5—

He needed help on this one, lots of help, and Wef could give him none. "Sure I can crash the nets, but what *good* will it do?"

"It'll keep the planet from getting slagged, that's what it'll do."

"Uh-huh. 'Course, it don't get rid of the Dacs for four years. And by then the whole system's gonna have collapsed—you do remember Wichita?"

He winced. Yes, he remembered that. And for that to happen on a world-wide scale and last for four years . . . it did not bear thinking about.

But what else could he do?

Christ, was he stuck. He had traveled a long and torturous road, only to find its end at a high blank wall that offered neither meaning nor escape. It was more than he could do alone. And it had to be done. Soon. Before the news got out. Before a seventh Dac ship swam into the parking lot at the L5 position. Before . . .

To whom could he turn? Who did he know with the talent, the insight. . . . *No,* he thought, as the answer came and he chased it away, *No, I'm not going to call in the Seeleys. Too many people involved. Too much chance one of'em'll let something slip.*

But what else could he do?

Five days plus or minus six, The Oracle had said, before someone stumbled over something that led it to Project JoveStar.

Perhaps if he, like Ohe Ainainine, had a censorship program up and running, he could sit back and wait for the 25nstruction crews to complete the project. Meanwhile protecting its existence. Zealously.

But he had neither the program nor the time.

He would have to roll the dice, no way around it.

Hey, Oracle!

#Yes, sir?#

I want a Seeley conference immediately.

#And the topic, sir?#

Ah. . . . How about, The Imminent Extinction of the Human Race?

TPTNNW TRE FTEHU

5Jn 18 60ET
e nln ein

AK EDIE   rc   LA ETNE
1   nomdsucsrvae oa olto
JPTRGIGNV

XXV

—1—

Ale calmed himself with three deep breaths, then spoke through The Oracle: *Thank you for attending. I'm sorry if I've interrupted anyone's plans, but we have a problem. I know why the Coalition was killing us.*

A storm of applause caught him by surprise.

Thank you. I'm afraid, however, that we're in even worse trouble now.

Curiosity coalesced out of the stillness.

The Coalition long ago launched a delicate, long-term plan that would almost certainly enable us to defeat the Dacs. The plan depends entirely on the element of surprise. Should news of this leak out, the Dacs would take evasive action, and would probably destroy half the planet in retaliation. Again that vision of slagged-over wheatlands rose before his eyes, and he had to pause before he could continue. *The Coalition established an intricate array of censors and detectors to keep the plan a secret. At some point in time, they went over the edge and began to assassinate anyone whose researches might lead it to details of the plan. I, for example, was researching the great-great grandfather of the mathematician/astrophysicist who first developed the mathematics upon which the plan depended.*

The Oracle interrupted with a relayed question: #Aye, so that's the Coalition's motive, but the Coalition's gone, and I dinna understand why you say we remain in trouble.#

Because Wef DiNaini has eliminated the last of the censorship programs, and at any moment someone could find this project filed in the archives, and release it to the data banks. We have to assume that the Dacs are monitoring our mass media constantly. Once they learn of the plan. ...

#Och, then put the censors back on-line, and we have nothing at all to fret about.#

I'm afraid it's not that simple. He explained about Wef's

virus program and its invulnerability. *The Oracle estimates that we have less than five days before Project JoveStar becomes a household phrase. We must do something. We are the experts. We must find a solution. And we must find it now.* He gave that a moment to sink in. *I will not transmat it to you, but the Project JoveStar Prospectus is on file with The Oracle. Please read it now.* Then he waited.

Panic swept the massive chamber before half the Sceleys had finished perusing the report. #It'll never work, but they'll retaliate anyway.#

#Nein! It will work, but too well! From such a mini-nova radiation enough intense to sterilize the planet comes.#

#Don't forget the other orbital bodies. My word, the sudden dispersal of so significant a fraction of the system's total mass is guaranteed to disrupt all the planets' orbits—why, Earth could wind up in a long ellipse that would render the planet utterly uninhabitable.#

#Is so, but what matter? Have preliminary figures accurate to within one order magnitude say shock wave strip atmosphere completely off planet. First we burn, then we choke. No good.#

#*Alors, mes amis, alors!* The events of the far future are irrelevant to us, are they not? We have the five days of life remaining, that is all. Radiation, orbits, collision—they do not matter to us.#

#What the man is trying to say, folks, is we're going to die!#

#He's right! We're all dead, right now, and it's Ale Elatey's fault!#

Now wait a minute, he said angrily, *I*— But if he had not convinced Wef to tamper with the censorship programs, none of this would have happened, so.... *You're right. And that's why I'm trying to do something about it.*

#You bloody barstid! You've done bleeding well enough, I should think!#

#Hai! Hai#

Hold on, please.

#Ale, baby, Amo send you something make you regret you ever opened you damn mouth in the first place!#

Jesus Christ, would you listen to me!

The chamber plunged into silence as The Oracle hit the mute switch. #Go ahead, sir—they may shout all they like, but no one will hear. Those who wish to listen to you are now free to do so unhindered.#

Thanks.

#You're welcome.#

Please hear me out. I'm not a scientist, but I don't think I have to be to make a suggestion that real scientists can work into some sort of physical device. The problem is that their communications and detection equipment are too good for us to take them by surprise. The Coalition figured that the electromagnetic pulse generated by Jupiter's going nova would blind and deafen them long enough for us to hit them. But any nuclear device that explodes reasonably close to the L5 position is going to have the same effect.

#Oh, I say, Ale, we have tried sneaking nuclear weapons into the launch lanes dozens of times, and failed each time. If the ships pause in near-Earth orbit for "customs"—#The other's intonation actually supplied the quotation marks. #—they are vaporized when the inspectors find the bombs. If they attempt to evade "customs," they are vaporized as soon as they leave NEO. We haven't the ghost of a chance of placing weapons in the L5 slot.#

I was thinking more along the lines of launching an empty ship, and then sending the bombs up via massie.

That brought a moment of pensive silence, until a voice said, #But you know, the problem with Señor Ale's solution is that to manufacture the bombs will perhaps take more time than we have. And I am not certain that it lies within our power to make a bomb small enough to fit within the confines of a cargo ship, yet powerful enough to wreak the necessary havoc.#

Well, I was thinking that if the ship were full of warm air, and we filled it with high-pressure gas from Jupiter— He knew from bitter experience how explosive a match that could be. *Wouldn't that do it?*

#Puh-leeze! Don't you know the difference between oxidation and a nuclear reaction? You need fusion, not expansion.#

#I'm afraid whoever that was is right,# said another. #At a quick calc, you'd need twelve massies transmatting Jovian gas to one chamber to get the gas dense enough to fuse spontaneously.#

#Um. . . . This used to be classified information, but we do have fifteen ultra-large mass-transceivers out at the Jupiter System Labs right now.#

That brought on a very long silence. A silence disturbed

only by the faint crackle of thousands of the world's best minds running frantic calculations. And then:

#Holy holy holy.# Awe filled that voice, and triumph edged it. #We can do it. We can!#

—2—

By the time Ale returned to interface from his dinner break, the scientists, engineers, and technicians had worked everything out. In theory, at least.

#It's really very simple.# said their spokesrep. #You make the entire cargo bay of the ship a massie chamber, have all fifteen JSL massies transmat maximum loads of gas into it simultaneously, and hey presto! A micro-nova, right there in the space lane.#

#Quite, quite,# said another. #But don't you think we should point out that—#

#No!#

#My good man, we have an obligation!#

What is it? Ale asked warily.

The answer came back as though through gritted teeth. #The problem is really very simple, too. When we light this off, it's going to be somewhat closer to us than to L5. It's going to do a lot of damage.#

How much?

#Our figures show severe disruption to the entire atmosphere—total depletion of the ozone layer, unacceptable warming at virtually all altitudes, creation of dozens of rather unpleasant chemicals. . . . To tell you the truth, probably twenty percent of the population's going to die within five years of the explosion. After that . . . well, we think things will revert to normal. We think. We hope.#

Can't you set it off farther away?

#The Dacs only give us one lane to the Moon. The closest point on that lane to L5 is midway between the Earth and the Moon.#

Another voice burst out: #Stand back for genius, boys and girls! The Dacs give us a near-Lunar orbit, right? Let's take advantage of it!#

What do you mean? asked Ale, who really wanted to ask what they were talking about in the first place.

#Slingshot it behind the Moon, so that it comes out headed straight for L5. They'll zap it soon as it leaves NEO, so we won't get quite as close as if we blew it halfway between here and the Moon, but it'll be one helluva lot farther away from us!#

#The timing on that will have to be perfect.#

#But we'll get only a quarter of the rads we would have otherwise.#

Huh?

#Inverse square law,# said someone impatiently. #Twice as far, a quarter as much.#

#Hot damn! That will absolutively do it!!!#

How long will it take?

The mood fell like a poor souffle. After a moment someone said, #To get everything set . . . sixteen days, give or take six hours.#

By which time everyone will know all about it, and the Dac fleet will be ready for us.

No one mentioned that the fleet would also have crisped the planet by then.

It seems, said Ale cautiously, *our only choice is to keep this a secret.*

#And just how the hell are we supposed to do that?#

He knew how. Grimly, sadly, he started to tell them—then stopped. No sense in putting that on their consciences, too. *I'll take care of it. But let's get the project organized first. The team modifying the cargo ship is going to have to operate on its own, completely independent of the networks. No broadcasts, nothing. It's going to be a bitch, but you'll only be able to contact the Jupiter System Labs twice: once to tell them what it is they're going to have to do, and the second time to give them the exact moment that they should do it. We can't risk the Dacs finding out any of this.*

It took close to an hour before all roles were assigned, and transportation arranged for everyone who needed to be at the modification site. They argued about that, but Ale insisted—and won.

Then he broke interface and used the monitor to call Wef DiNaini.

The old man sounded apprehensive. "What is it, Ale?"

"I need a program, Wef."

"And why else would you call?"

He bent forward in his chair and rubbed his temples. "Wef,

we're going to have to crash the entire system—the whole damn thing, every bit of it—and keep it crashed for sixteen days."

Wef's voice trembled. "Everything?"

"All of it. The works."

"You can't do that without warning them, Ale! People gonna starve—freeze—hell, when the nets go down, so does the electricity that drives the pumps that put water into people's houses. Holy Sweet Jesus, Ale, people are gonna die by the millions."

He knew that. He knew it so completely that what he most wanted to do was vomit. He clutched his stomach. And said quietly, "Better that than by the billions."

—3—

He stared at his screen, still lit by its faithful batteries. It displayed, as it had for the last ten days, the single message he had permitted Wef to insert:

DRAW WATER. ORDER FOOD. THE GLOBAL NETWORK WILL CRASH AT 0900 GMT, OR 0 HOURS AND 0 MINUTES FROM NOW. YOUR ELECTRICITY WILL FAIL. IT WILL NOT COME BACK ON FOR FIFTEEN DAYS AND EIGHTEEN HOURS. EMDY OFIVO, ALE ELATEY NEEDS YOU, GO HOME.

Except for the CRT, the apartment was dark. The world was dark. He knew ten days had passed only because he was keeping a journal. On paper, with a pencil, primitive as that struck him, because the batteries would fail if the system accessed the bubble memory more than a few times.

The days had not gone quickly. With almost nothing to do but keep his bonsai in the shade, out of the wind, and just damp enough to survive, he had watched minutes stretch into hours, and hours into months.

Time had gone slowly, but once passed, had vanished: pile one completed empty day on top of another and the hours collapse into each other, because there is nothing to keep them distinct. The stack is no higher; the eventful, memorable past, no further away.

So little had happened to distinguish one day from another:

The building at the corner of Park and Chapel Streets had caught fire on Tuesday. The Dacs got those who reached the roof; the ones who made it out the ground floor exit fought a pitched battle with the streeters before overwhelming them. Thursday a boy in a red T-shirt had jumped from a balcony across the way. Saturday a woman in the room below his living room had screamed—once. Sunday—it was Sunday, wasn't it?—he had helped Mrs. M'ti Emtenne throw dead tropical fish over the railing, into the silent forest below.

So little had happened. So much of it was awful. And the world had five more days to endure.

—4—

Thirsty, unshaven, his stomach rumbling, he stood in his darkened living room and leaned against the terrace doors. He stared at the crescent moon. They had timed the micro-nova to flare above the Earth's night side, because fewer people would be outdoors, and fewer people would be blinded by the glare. He would know not to look. He wondered what the streeters would do.

Die, probably, as so many millions must have in the last two weeks.

The door rattled under someone's fist.

Reluctantly, Ale pulled himself away from the terrace. Holding the candle high, he walked to the door and opened it: ready to jab flame into the eyes of a looter.

The yellow light flickered on the pale, worried face of Emdy Ofivo.

"Ale—"

"Emdy." He wrapped her in his arms and held her tight. "Emdy, oh God, thank God you're all right." Then he released her, took her hand, and led her to the sliding glass doors. "Up there—"

"I tried to stay away, but if— if something's about to happen. . . . I wanted to say what I should have said before."

"I want to, too." His watch said ninety seconds to go. "But we don't have time to say it all. Or else we'll have all the time we need to say everything we never did and then some. We'll know soon." He slid the doors open for the breeze, but kept her from going outside. "If there's a very bright light—don't look up till it fades."

"What's going on?"

Before he could answer, dawn struck bright and furious. A bubble ship bursting from its silo broke the surface of the harbor and climbed toward the new sudden star. Its roar slapped them five seconds later, four seconds after the ship had vanished in the glare.

He put his arm around her shoulders and drew her deeper into the living room. Where he kissed her. While lights flashed on in the building across the street, the hovee clicked. A normally steady voice shook as it read, "1500 bubble ships of the United Space Force, acting in conjunction with a fusion explosion arranged by a team of Seeleys, have launched an all-out attack on the six Dac ships parked at the L5 slot. The latest computer projections give the attackers a seventy-four percent chance—make that a seventy-six percent chance—of victory. Seventy-eight percent. With casualties approaching 1300 pilots. Well. Eighty percent. The projections keep changing. Eighty—"

The rest of the night was very long, but quick, and not at all dark.